"There's something you should know, Will."

Will stiffened, the angry panic shooting through him. What could Taylor possibly say to make things right? Here they were, stranded in the middle of nowhere, with no chance of reaching his daughter, Andi—and Taylor somehow managed to find humor in the situation?

"That mudslide did the trick. It threw us to the other side of the river, where Andi is."

Face burning, Will ducked his head. "I'm sorry. I don't usually lose my cool like that. I never intended to scare you."

"It's okay," Taylor said softly. "You're worried for her. I understand." A look of surprise moved through her expression. "And you didn't scare me." Her blue eyes met his. "I'm not afraid when I'm with you."

The weight of Taylor's admission hung in the air between them. Something in her tone—awe or wonder, maybe?—unsettled Will. He watched her face, an ache spreading through him at the wounded vulnerability in her eyes...

SMOKY MOUNTAIN DANGER

April Arrington

April Arrington grew up in a small town and developed a love for books at an early age. Emotionally moving stories have always held a special place in her heart. April enjoys collecting pottery and soaking up the Georgia sun on her front porch.

CONTENTS

LOVE INSPIRED® SUSPENSE
INSPIRATIONAL ROMANCE

ISBN-13: 978-1-335-49854-0

Peril in the Smoky Mountains

Copyright © 2023 by Harlequin Enterprises ULC

Smoky Mountain Danger
First published in 2021. This edition published in 2023.
Copyright © 2021 by April Standard

Targeted for Revenge
First published in 2021. This edition published in 2023.
Copyright © 2021 by Karen Vyskocil

Recycling programs
for this product may
not exist in your area.

For questions and comments about the quality of this book, please contact us at CustomerService@Harlequin.com.

Love Inspired
22 Adelaide St. West, 41st Floor
Toronto, Ontario M5H 4E3, Canada
www.LoveInspired.com

Printed in U.S.A.

PERIL IN THE SMOKY MOUNTAINS

APRIL ARRINGTON

&

KAREN KIRST

2 Thrilling Stories

Smoky Mountain Danger and *Targeted for Revenge*

LOVE INSPIRED SUSPENSE

INSPIRATIONAL ROMANCE

Be strong and of a good courage...
for the Lord thy God, he it is that doth go with thee;
he will not fail thee, nor forsake thee.

—*Deuteronomy* 31:6

For Billie Ann.

ONE

William Morgan, wrapped around his daughter's finger from the day she'd been born, had caved in to her requests often over the years…but he'd never agreed to anything as unpredictable or potentially dangerous as a weeklong journey down Tennessee's wild and scenic Bear's Tooth River.

"It's not too late to turn around, you know?" Will palmed the steering wheel of his truck and eased around a steep curve, the engine rumbling louder as the truck ascended the steep mountain. "We could drive back down the mountain, call Jax and tell him we changed our minds. Spend the week at one of the campgrounds we used to go to." He glanced at his daughter in the passenger's seat. "You used to love fishing at Badger's Crossing. We could be there within the hour, if you'd like?"

Andi, staring ahead silently at the bluet wildflowers lining the curving road in front of them, turned her head and locked her brown eyes with his. "I knew you'd try to back out."

Will flexed his jaw and returned his attention to the road. Drumming his fingers against the steering wheel, he sifted carefully through his thoughts for the right words. "I'm not backing out. I'm merely suggesting—"

"That we back out."

He stifled a sigh. Since Andi had hit her teens, every conversation with her had become a potential land mine, and when she'd turned seventeen two months ago, prying more than five words from her at a time had become almost impossible. Until Jax Turner, a sixty-year-old river guide and family friend, had mentioned he planned to lead a new tour of the Smokies down the rarely traveled white water of Bear's Tooth River.

Andi had latched on to the idea and had pleaded with Will for over a month to reserve the two seats still available on the one raft Jax, who ran a small business of river tours, had advertised. Jax's river trip had been the one and only topic she'd allowed him to broach with her without stoic resistance.

"The last thing I want to do is back out, Andi," Will said quietly. "I'm just concerned about the river. Jax has only run it a couple times and I've never run it at all. It's risky, and I don't like the idea of not knowing what lies ahead."

She continued staring at the road, her mouth barely moving as she spoke. "Then I don't understand why you agreed to it in the first place."

That was easy, Will thought, slowing the truck as they reached the mountain's summit. "Time." He eased the truck over to a small graveled clearing, parked between a large SUV and a small sedan and cut the engine. A broad river flowed several feet in front of a large boulder that served as a drop-off point. "I wanted to spend time with you—to talk, to laugh, to just enjoy each other's company again for once."

Andi's mouth tightened. "You could have that anytime, if you didn't work every single day."

"Someone's got to pay the bills," he said quietly. Pay for construction jobs wasn't steep nowadays, but the gigs were easy to come by and he needed every one he could get to put Andi through college in another year.

"I know. But what good's a house if no one's ever in it when you come home?"

Will closed his eyes, a fresh surge of guilt moving through him. "Andi—"

"Besides," she said, "you don't always know what lies ahead, anyway." She looked at him then, her eyes meeting his, then roving over his expression. "You didn't know Mom would walk out on us, did you? And even when you did, you couldn't stop her."

Will drew his head back at the anger flashing in her wounded eyes. It'd been sixteen years since his wife, Heather, had left him and abandoned Andi, and he'd hoped the passage of time would help ease Andi's pain. Instead, Andi's anger had only increased—as had her resentment for him, it seemed.

He moved to speak, but there was nothing he could say, so he remained silent and returned her stare.

Andi unsnapped her seat belt, opened her door and got out of the truck. Moments later, the truck's tailgate lowered with a squeak and bags rustled as Andi lugged them across the bed of the truck.

Will got out of the truck and dragged a hand over the tight knot at the back of his neck. The sound of rushing water filled the rocky clearing and expanse of open sky on either side of the river. It was a surprisingly cool morning for summer in Tennessee, but the fragrant scents of pine, wildflowers and fresh earth filled his lungs and lifted his spirits a bit. Will had grown up in this neck of the woods, so the Smoky Mountains had always felt like home to him.

"'Bout time y'all made it." Jax, standing by a large raft anchored by the boulder, sauntered over and thrust out his hand. "I was beginning to think you'd changed your mind."

"He tried to," Andi bit out. She strolled by, a bag slung over her shoulder as she headed for the raft.

Jax winced and one corner of his mouth tipped up in a slight smile. "She giving you trouble already?"

Will pinned a smile in place—one he'd had to dredge up more often than not lately—and shook Jax's hand. "Seems that way." He strolled to the truck bed and retrieved a couple of bags of supplies. "Thanks for saving the last two seats on the raft for us. If nothing else, I hope a week trapped together on a raft will give me some time with her."

Time to try to get Andi to understand how much he loved her and, hopefully, bridge the distance between them. A distance that grew wider and more impassable each day.

Jax grabbed a bag, too. "Come on. I'll introduce you to the rest of the group."

Will followed Jax over to the smooth boulder where a young man and woman stood, shrugging on life jackets.

"Meet Beth and Martin Hill," Jax said, sweeping his arm toward the couple. "Recently married. Came up from Florida for their first family vacation this year."

Will smiled, a sincere one this time, and held out his hand. "Congratulations."

Martin shook his hand firmly, a wide grin appearing as he glanced at his wife. "Thanks. Couldn't be happier, or more eager to hit the river, huh, honey?"

Beth nodded. "I've been looking forward to this for weeks. We've been on a few rafting trips before but never one as exciting as this one promises to be." She fastened the last buckle on her life jacket and raised her brows at Jax. "Are the views along this stretch as impressive as they say?"

Jax laughed. "Oh, don't nothing compare to the sunsets out here, and after we camp the first night and run the second set of rapids, there's a waterfall that'll take your breath away." He glanced at Will. "Course, we'll need to put the raft to shore at Hawk's Landing so we don't head over the falls downriver."

Will nodded, his smile dimming. "That's a definite."

"Speaking of the falls," Jax said, motioning toward a woman who stood several feet away, her back to them as she studied the landscape ahead. "We got a guest who's looking especially forward to those. Taylor? Come on over and meet your rowing partner." Jax glanced at Will and grinned, speaking in low tones. "Andi told me on the phone when y'all booked the trip that she preferred a seat up front, so I figured you needed a partner, and I think Taylor will be a good one."

Will frowned, squinting against the sharp rays of the morning sun as the woman strolled across the rocks toward him, stopping when she reached his side. Blond hair, dark blue eyes and a wary expression met his.

"Taylor's a photographer," Jax said. "She's eager to get the perfect picture of the Smokies."

She smiled slightly. "I don't think there's such a thing as perfect, but something close to it would do."

Will studied the camera she held with both hands, her graceful fingers curled tightly around the edges. "I'm Will—" he motioned toward Andi, who eyed them closely "—and that's my daughter, Andi. You and I are rowing partners, it seems." He lifted his hand in invitation. "It's nice to meet you."

Taylor studied his hand, her eyes moving from his palm and up his arm to his face. Her gaze—strangely vulnerable and apprehensive—darted away from his as she lifted the camera with a rueful smile, seeming to motion that her hands were full. "It's nice to meet you, too."

"Well." Jax rubbed his hands together briskly. "Let's get this show on the road."

Will lowered his hand and watched as Taylor joined Beth and Martin as they secured bags into the raft. Andi eyed Will from the other side of the boulder, then walked to the raft, hopped in and took her seat at the helm.

Will shook his head and trudged toward the raft, the uncomfortable churn in his gut reminding him the opportunity to back out had passed.

Taylor Holt had braved dangerous paths before, but the fierce churn of white water below the bank of Tennessee's Bear's Tooth River shot ice through her veins—especially since the first day of rafting had been relatively calm and uneventful.

"Glad you don't run 'em blind."

She tore her attention from the violent currents and focused on the man towering by her side on the rough-hewn overlook. "What?"

"The rapids." He dragged a broad hand through his dark hair, his toned biceps flexing below the short sleeves of his damp T-shirt with the movement, and pinned his dark gaze to hers. "Some people don't scout. They dive headfirst down these waters and don't give a thought to what lies ahead. Good to see you're not one of them."

Taylor tried to smile, but her mouth tightened into a thin line instead. She studied the kindness in his brown eyes, the soft contours of his lips and relaxed posture. During the initial twelve miles of their rafting journey and one peaceful night of camping by the river with the rest of the group, she'd picked up additional bits of comforting information about Will Morgan. The single father approached rapids with caution, admired peaks of the Smoky Mountains along calm stretches of water and patiently tried to engage his teenage daughter in conversation despite her uninterested glances and monotone responses. All of this should've eased the tension tightening Taylor's grip on her camera.

But the hardest lesson Taylor had learned in her thirty-five years of life was that a handsome face and welcoming expression could mask an insatiable desire to inflict pain, and not only had this led her to refuse Will's polite handshake yesterday, but it'd also led her to keep a healthy distance between them at all times.

She lifted her camera, adjusted the aperture for a greater depth of field and snapped pictures of white water boiling around bone-splintering boulders. "I like to see what I'm getting into."

Especially since she hadn't seen the danger coming with her late husband. On the surface, Preston Holt had been a successful real-estate agent, selling beautiful homes to hopeful families while seeking to establish one of his own. But beneath his calm exterior, he'd hidden a resentful nature and violent temper. Both had become increasingly evident after he and Taylor had married. Until the morning she...

Hands shaking, Taylor lowered the camera and pointed toward one side of the rapids. "There's a hole on the right. And we'll need to steer clear of—"

"You're joking, right?" Will tipped his head back and narrowed his eyes at the gray clouds hovering low among the mountain range. "It rained five out of seven days last week and showered for an hour after our raft hit the river this morning. That water's gotta be hitting three by now."

"What's hitting three?" Andi, Will's daughter, climbed the slippery overlook in their direction, her rafting helmet in one hand.

"The water," Will said absently, cupping Andi's elbow and steadying her. "It's running three thousand cubic feet per second. Maybe more."

"All the better for an exciting ride." She shrugged off his touch, walked past him and stood beside Taylor. "Whatcha think, Taylor? It's at least a Class IV, ain't it?"

Taylor nodded. "At least."

"It's pushing Class V." Will's tone hardened. "The water's fast and high. Too high."

"Not for you." Andi peered up at Taylor, excitement in her brown eyes, and smiled. "Or Taylor. You've run Class V rapids before, haven't you?"

Taylor studied the teen's hopeful expression. Andi's smile, the first Taylor had seen her flash on the trip, was sincere and brightened her expression. The defiant look she'd given Will yesterday had vanished a bit more with each mile they'd traveled downriver. Andi was much more approachable when she let down her guard.

Taylor smiled back. "Yeah. A few."

"You're not afraid," Andi announced, facing the rapids. The humid summer breeze tugged a long strand of brown hair free of her braid as she studied the river. "You're itching to run 'em."

Taylor tensed, realizing Andi was half-right. She did long to run the rapids—but not because she wasn't afraid. The swift currents crushing against carved earth terrified her, but feeling anything other than the numb despair she'd carried for five years would be a welcome relief. And navigating the roaring waters would drown out the thoughts needling the back of her mind…at least for a while.

"I'd like to take on the challenge," Taylor said. "But not just for the action. I'm a travel photographer, and *Wild Journey* magazine only buys photos of the most impressive, rarely traveled trails. From what I've heard, they're after shots of this river in particular." She pointed downriver at a bend where steep green mountains converged, swallowing the rapids and obscuring the view. "According to Jax, the best falls are miles ahead and I need the shots." She wagged her camera in the air. "Otherwise, I can't make a sale."

"And if we don't hightail it over these rapids soon, we won't make it to the next campsite by nightfall. We just got to be sure to shore up at Hawk's Landing before we hit the falls." Jax, their gray-bearded river guide, ambled up onto the overlook, propped his hands on his lean hips and grinned. "Ain't nothing like pushing through one last set of chaos before resting peaceful under the stars."

Taylor smiled. Jax's easygoing nature and good sense of humor made it hard not to like him. He looked to be in his early sixties, had a deep appreciation for nature and reminded her a lot of her first foster father, Kyle. She'd lived for three months with Kyle and his wife as a teen during a time when she used to dream of finding a family of her own. Years before she met Preston and years before his death, after which she spent each passing year alone.

"It's the chaos part that bothers me," Will said, a half-hearted smile appearing. "This is the roughest stretch of water I've seen in a while. We'd do better to hike back upriver and call it a d—"

"No way." Andi huffed and glared at Will. "Why'd you go through with this if all you planned to do was drag me back home the second day?"

Will frowned. "Watch your tone, please. I agreed to this trip to spend time with you, but this—" he swept a muscular arm toward the rough rapids "—was not part of the agenda."

"We've run tough rapids before—plenty of times."

"None like these," Will said, lowering his voice on his next words. "I'm just watching out for you."

"You're saying you don't think I can pull it off. Finding an excuse to go home and get back to work. That's what you're doing." Andi glanced at Taylor, her cheeks turning red as she whispered, "I can't wait till I turn eighteen next year. I'm leaving the second I do, no matter what he says." Eyes glistening, she started walking back down the overlook. "I should never have come out here with you."

"Andi!" A muscle ticked in Will's jaw as he called after his daughter, then smiled tightly at Taylor. "Sorry about that. She's…"

Hurt. Afraid. Aching for attention. Taylor recognized the signs. She shook her head. "It's okay. I didn't mean to encourage her."

But you did. Will didn't say the words, but the accusation in his dark gaze screamed the sentiment. He shoved his hands in his pockets, staring as Andi rejoined Beth and Martin at the raft. The lines of pain creasing Will's forehead made Taylor long to reach out and offer comfort. Cup her hand around the stiff set of his broad shoulders and squeeze.

Instead, she gripped her camera tighter, lifted it and snapped another photo of the rapids.

"You brought her to the right place, Will." Jax eased past Taylor and clamped his hand on Will's shoulder. "Those rough waters are good at pushing people closer together. Closer to God, too."

Taylor followed Jax's line of sight as his gaze moved across the river, up the lushly forested mountain peaks, and lingered on the low-hanging fog and clouds.

"Those are His waters." A note of pride entered Jax's tone. "His smoke. Know what my ol' pops used to say?" At Will's silence, he continued. "Used to say, when the world broke a man, all he had to do was come to God's land and let Him know he's here. Peace is in this place—all around. You just got to look for it."

Taylor's throat tightened. She swallowed hard, blinked past the wet blur along her lower lashes and listened to the rhythmic crash of free-flowing water against rugged stone. From where she stood, she saw nothing but violent rapids, the threat of rain and a less-than-welcoming rowing partner.

Will moved out of Jax's comforting grip and faced them. "In the past, I always ran a river first before bringing Andi with me. That way I'd know what I was getting her into." His dark eyes met Taylor's briefly. Then he cast Jax a questioning look. "Can you guarantee that we'll get my daughter safely over those rapids?"

Taylor looked down and dragged the toe of her waterproof sneaker across the dry rock.

Jax's brow furrowed as he shook his head. "You've lived in these mountains long enough to know that I can't guarantee you anything. No one can. I'm leading this tour, but we decide as a group whether or not to turn back." He rocked back on his heels and drew in a heavy breath. "But what I can tell you is that I don't think you're gonna gain any ground with Andi if you turn back now. That sun'll set and the rain'll roll in before we'd be able to hike back more than a mile and who knows where we'd end up spending the night then. We'd be at the mercy of whatever's roaming around us, and they don't call this river Bear's Tooth for nothing." He shook his head. "There's no way to portage past these rapids. Only way through is on the water. We either take a chance on running 'em, shore up at Hawk's Landing and camp safely for the night, or we hike back and chance getting lost in the dark."

Will stared at the rapids, remaining silent, then headed back down the steep, rocky bank. "I'll check with Beth and Martin," he said over his shoulder. "See what they want to do. If they're gung ho on tackling the rapids, I'll agree to it—but only if the majority of the group votes to proceed."

Taylor watched him take long strides down the bank to the raft, which was tied off at a calm section of the river. She studied his handsome features as he spoke to Beth and Martin and glanced at Andi, who stood, arms crossed, several feet away.

"Why'd he bring her here?" Taylor asked softly. Face heating, she apologized to Jax. "It's none of my business and I don't mean to pry. But if Will lives here and knows how dangerous this river is, why'd he bring her?"

Jax grunted, the sound half regretful and half frustrated. "She's restless. Angsty like a lot of teens, you know? But she's angrier than most. Been pushing Will away, threatening to leave. Took off on him for a week two months ago. Gave him a good scare."

"And her mom?"

"Ain't in the picture. Never has been, really." Jax rolled his shoulders and sighed. "I've known Andi since she was small enough to cradle on one arm. Back in the day, she and Will used to rock climb and run rapids all the time, but Will works long hours now. Andi's good at it. Loves the water. When I told her I was setting up another run down these rapids, she begged to come and talked Will into it. He's so desperate to hold on to her he'd agree to just about anything right now."

Taylor watched Will move to Andi's side by the water, her grip easing on her camera.

"And you?" Jax asked.

She bit her lip as he peered into her eyes. "What about me?"

"You booked a ticket for this ride, too. Why'd you come out here?"

Her breath quickened and she moved to speak twice before finally saying, "To take photos. I came for the falls."

Jax smirked. "Yeah. You keep telling yourself that."

Taylor stiffened as he turned and walked away.

"And while you're at it," Jax added, working his way down the steep rocks, "pray we make it through those rapids in one piece. If anything happens to Andi, Will's gonna come after us both."

This trip had been a mistake, and every mile they traveled added another.

Will narrowed his eyes against the spray of cool water and firmed his grip on the paddle as the raft bounced along choppy water downriver. His gut sank further each time Andi's long braid, lifting and lowering with the jerky movements of the raft, slapped against her back in front of him.

"How's the view from up there?" Jax shouted from his position in the back of the raft.

Andi laughed. The sound echoed off the rocky banks that pinned them in on both sides. "It's gorgeous!"

Will's skin prickled when the first set of rapids emerged into view. He should never have agreed to bring Andi down this river without running it first— no matter how badly she'd wanted to come. "Sit lower, Andi, and use the foot cups. We're about to hit the rough stretch."

"I'm fine." Andi glanced over her shoulder, her eyes bright with excitement below her helmet, and grinned at Taylor, who was seated beside Will. "The rapids are a thousand times bigger down here than they were from the bank."

Taylor nodded. She maintained her focus on the rapids ahead, but her knuckles turned white around her paddle. "They always are."

"Second thoughts?" Will asked.

She met him head-on, determination flashing in her blue eyes and a blank expression on her face. "No. Just excited."

She was lying. The tight set of her pink mouth and the flush along her smooth freckled cheeks gave her away. Another time, another place, he'd be tempted to pursue the truth. Maybe even attempt to delve deeper into her past and discover the source of the shadows lurking in those beautiful blue eyes. Something— or someone—had put those shadows there, and he couldn't help but wonder what secrets she was hiding.

But that had always been his biggest flaw, hadn't it? Falling hard for a troubled woman. Wanting to protect and heal. No matter how hard he'd tried, he'd failed with Heather. And she had not only divorced him, she'd abandoned Andi, too.

Clenching his jaw, Will faced forward, ignoring the pretty ripple of Taylor's blond hair below her helmet and the brush of her warm forearm against his as she paddled. Andi came first. Always. There was no room in his life for a woman, especially one whose hardened demeanor reminded him more of Heather than he felt comfortable admitting.

"They do look a lot faster up close," Beth said, her voice shaking slightly behind Will. He couldn't tell if it was from excitement or fear.

"No bigger than Old Bend." Her husband, Martin, seated beside her, laughed. "And we tamed that beast the second we hit water, didn't we, baby?"

Despite his anxiety, Will grinned. Martin and Beth, young and in love, were eager for adventure, and the white water swirling and crashing along bends and drops offered excitement the vacationing couple couldn't resist. They'd enjoyed traveling the river yesterday and had looked even more forward to today's rougher journey.

"Adrenaline pumping back there yet?" Will asked. He knew the feeling well. Missed it from his early days of braving rapids and hiking rough terrain.

"You know it," the couple called out in tandem.

Their energy was contagious. Taylor laughed with them, the brief expression of delight on her face catching Will's eye despite his best intentions to keep his focus elsewhere.

The splash of waves grew louder, and the raft, positioned sideways, drifted toward the mouth of the rapids.

"We're up," Jax shouted. "Paddle forward!"

Five paddles hit the water. Jax, Martin, Beth, Taylor and Will paddled together, pointing the nose of the raft into the rapids that carried them over the first thrash of white water.

"Stop and hold!"

At Jax's command, Will lifted his paddle and held on to the raft, his heart hammering against his ribs as Andi hunkered down. Swift currents lifted the raft, yanked it over a smooth underwater boulder, then plunged it, nose-first, into turbulent waters below.

Andi flopped forward against the raft's nose, as did the rest of them, pressing together in a heap as the raft dropped into lower rapids, then reared back up, slinging them all backward in a tangle of paddles and limbs.

Cold water splashed high in the air, slapping their cheeks and pouring into the bottom of the raft. The raft rocked, tilted, rose and lowered. Dodged sharp rocks and smooth boulders. Over and over, until the current shot it free of the first set of rapids and lowered it onto a brief stretch of smooth water, tugging them farther downriver.

Andi sprang up, tilted her head back and released a triumphant yell. Her energetic cry, heavy with excitement, echoed along the banks of the river and reverberated against the rugged mountain range. She looked back at Will, the sheer joy on her face making his breath catch.

"That was amazing, Dad!" Water droplets fell from her helmet, coursed down her cheeks and pooled at the corners of her bright smile. "Absolutely amazing!"

And just like that, it was worth it. The grave misgivings he'd experienced when he finally gave in to Andi and booked the trip, the uncomfortable argument in the truck's cab yesterday morning, her monotone responses upriver and angry outburst on the overlook. All of it. Just for the sight of that one smile. A glimpse of the bighearted, joyful girl he'd known Andi to be years ago.

"Yeah," Will rasped, his throat closing as he smiled. "Amazing."

"Paddles up, you heroes!" Martin lifted his paddle, urging everyone to high-five paddles above the raft.

Laughing, they slapped their paddles together.

Taylor tapped Will's paddle with hers a second time, her grin relieved. "No need for second thoughts, huh?"

Captivated by the healthy pink in her cheeks and excited light in her eyes, he grinned back. "Guess n—"

"Steady." Jax's command rose over the increasing roar of water. "Second set's coming."

The raft rocked, then rotated on swift currents that spun the nose back around.

"Forward!" Jax yelled.

Will dug his paddle into the water, flinching as a wave slammed into the raft, lifting one side of it out of the water. Andi tumbled sideways along the raft's floor, her hands scrambling for a renewed hold.

The rapids turned violent, forcing the raft toward a hole on the right.

The roar of water almost drowned out Jax's shout. "To the left! Hard!"

Will dug his paddle back into the current, pushing strongly with the others, trying to correct the raft's course, but the rapids sucked them farther to the right. They raced along the outskirts of the hole, dipped down, then lifted high on a wave, the bottom of the raft aimed straight for a mammoth pile of rocks jutting out from the center of the river.

"Brace!" Jax shouted.

Will's muscles seized as his attention fixated on the back of Andi's helmet, a thin protection against the rocks. "Andi, hold o—"

The raft slammed into hard stone and a wave flipped, then pinned, it against the rocks, dumping everyone into the river.

Rapid currents pulled Will under. Green mountains and gray sky disappeared and water filled his ears, nose and mouth. He spun uncontrollably to the left. Then a wave swelled and threw him to the right. Lungs burning, he kicked until his feet hit the rocky riverbed. Then he shoved off and swam upward, his head finally breaking the surface.

He spit out a mouthful of water and dragged in a ragged breath. Disoriented, he bobbed along the rising swell of a wave, blinking hard against the spray of water, focusing on clouds, rocks, then water until he spotted the flash of Andi's red helmet several feet downriver.

"Dad!" Her arm flailed in the air before she was sucked underwater.

Will kicked with the roiling rapids, pivoting his body toward Andi as he floated over rough waters downriver. She reappeared on the swell of a wave, stopped near a boulder at a bend in the river, then went back under.

"Swim, An—"

Waves rolled over Will, spun him, then slammed him into the hard boulder. He gripped a rough edge with both hands, heaved his upper body out of the water and glanced over his left shoulder, where Andi struggled two feet away.

Her arms thrashed above the water and the red helmet emerged again. Will reached out with one hand, gripped Andi's forearm and pulled her to the surface, where she gasped for breath.

"Swim to me, Andi," Will shouted, his throat raw. She was a great swimmer, and so close. If he could just pull her closer and get her safely to the boulder— Why couldn't he pull her closer? "Andi, swi—"

"I—I can't!" A series of waves beat at Andi, washing over her face, stealing her breath. Will pulled harder until she reached the surface again, gasping, "My foot's caught. I—"

The current sucked Andi back under, ripping her arm from his grip. He tightened his hold on the rough edge of the boulder and lunged deeper into the water, his hand plunging low, fingers slipping under the shoulder of Andi's life jacket and yanking her back up.

She barely broke the surface this time, coughing and sputtering, still trapped by an undercut rock, now at least three feet away from the boulder. Away from him.

Her eyes, wide and panicked, clung to his face. "Don't let go, Daddy." Blue tinged her trembling lips. "Please don't let me g—"

White water engulfed her again, obscuring the red helmet.

"No!" Will yanked hard, straining to maintain his grip on the boulder as the current dragged Andi farther away, stretching his arm to the point of pain. "Someone help m—"

Waves slapped his face, stinging his eyes. He curled his hand tighter around Andi's life jacket and scanned the raging waters for help. No one was nearby and he couldn't see the raft. He and Andi had drifted downriver, away from the group. There was nothing but white water breaking against thick stone.

"Andi!" Will's arm shook as he struggled to pull Andi back to the surface. How long had she been under this time? Three seconds? Four? Dread seeped into his veins, flooded his chest and spilled onto his cheeks. If he let go of the boulder now, tried to free her and failed, he might lose his hold on her completely and be swept downriver while she'd be left alone to dr—

Please, God, help me. He couldn't let Andi drown.

Couldn't watch his baby girl flail beneath the water until…

"Please, God, don't take her from me."

TWO

In the end, there's only us.

Lungs burning, Taylor kicked against the river's current and strained to reach air. Her foot struck a stone on the riverbed, a sharp edge cutting the sole of her waterproof sneaker, digging into her heel.

Do you see this now?

Preston's face appeared behind her tightly closed eyelids: his brown eyes wide and urgent, lean cheeks slicked with sweat and voice oddly calm as it passed sneering lips. Even now, she could feel his blunt thumbnails digging into the base of her throat. For some reason, he'd always attacked her neck first.

"In the end, Taylor," he'd say, staring down, squeezing tighter, "there's only us. Do you see this now?" Tighter. "Do you see?"

Taylor kicked harder, stroked her arms vigorously through the churning water and finally broke the surface. She opened her eyes and dragged in air, her chest swelling in tandem with the wave that moved beneath her, shoving her toward the left side of the river.

Gray sky, white froth and sharp mountain peaks flashed by as waves rolled her supine, jerked her upright and yanked at her limbs. Water burned her nostrils, flooded her ears, filled her mouth. She spit it out and kept her eyes on the sky, focusing on the thunderhead directly above her. The misshapen charcoal-colored mass watched, mute and detached, as the rapids flung her onto her back and thrust her farther downriver.

Maybe... she thought. Maybe Preston had—

Taylor slammed to a stop, her left rib cage hitting a solid wall.

The swirling clouds slowed and the mountains stilled. Her legs stretched out in front of her, the relentless current pulling her feet around a boulder. Taylor rolled over, threw her arms out and scrambled to take hold of the massive rock. She curled her palms around a jagged edge and dug her nails in.

Breath rasping from her shaky lips, she blinked away a fresh spray of water and peered upriver. The raft, pinned upside down against a rock when she'd last seen it, was no longer visible. Jax, who'd been clinging to the raft, reaching for Beth and Martin as they'd struggled in the water, had disappeared from view behind a long, unfamiliar stretch of rough rapids and rocky bends in the river. There didn't seem to be a soul around.

How far had she drifted?

"Andi!"

Taylor started at the desperate cry, recognizing the deep tone of Will's voice. It rose above the crash of water and echoed against the steep, rocky banks surrounding them, seeming to originate from the other side of the boulder where she'd found refuge.

Carefully, she pulled hard on the boulder, lifted her

upper body out of the water and plastered her hips and legs against the rock. Waves beat at her back, but she dragged her knees up, tucked the soles of her feet against the boulder and scaled its face, edging around its rough-hewn corner through the water until the fingers of her right hand bumped Will's.

At her touch, his broad-knuckled grip tightened on the boulder and he looked up. His eyes, intense below the rim of his helmet, locked with hers over the muscles straining in his outstretched arm.

"She can't breathe." His other arm flexed, yanking harder at a life jacket submerged in the roiling white water. A red helmet rose toward the surface, then sank farther below. "Her foot's caught." His lips trembled. "Please help her."

Taylor tentatively gripped his white-knuckled fist on the boulder, testing the solidness of his hold, then inched one hand over his thick wrist and down his flexed forearm. Her stomach dipped at the uneasy feel of heavy male muscle beneath her shaky fingertips, but she inhaled sharply and forced her body closer, following the curve of his upper arm, shoulder, then chest.

Level with him now, she wrapped her palm around the strong dip between his neck and shoulder and called out above the roar of the rapids, "Can you take my weight and still hold on?"

He nodded, the rough stubble lining his clenched jaw brushing her wet cheek.

A heavy wave slammed into her back and she bobbed between the boulder and Will. Clenching her teeth, she let go of the boulder and shifted her weight onto him.

He grunted as she carefully climbed across his

body against the fierce barrage of water. The color in his cheeks deepened to a fierce red and tremors ran through his outstretched arms.

Taylor tucked one hand beneath the lower edge of his life jacket, secured her grip, then dropped below the water's tumultuous surface. Cold water engulfed her and the fierce current tangled her long hair over her face and obscured her vision.

She reached out, her fingers groping blindly down Will's submerged arm until a hard, round surface hit her palm. Almost instantly, a hand latched on to her wrist and pulled.

Andi's brown eyes, wild as she thrashed underwater, widened up at Taylor. She stabbed one hand toward the riverbed, pointing at an undercut rock that trapped her foot.

Taylor released Will's life jacket and grabbed Andi's instead. She dived deeper through the raging current until she reached the undercut rock. Probing past the rock's jagged edge with one hand, she grabbed Andi's ankle and pulled. It didn't budge.

Above her, a muted sound escaped Andi as she continued kicking with her free leg. The motion, once fast and frenzied, had weakened, and Andi's eyes began to close.

Taylor released Andi's life jacket, grabbed Andi's ankle with both hands and braced her feet on the riverbed. She pulled Andi's foot to the right, then left, tugging hard, her hopes fading as her lungs screamed for oxygen until—*finally*—it popped free!

Relieved, Taylor shoved off the riverbed and swam up. Her arms strained for the water's surface, but Andi, her energy spurred on by the release, kicked frantically, striking her temple.

Tumultuous water, like vicious hands, snatched her limbs and dragged Taylor away, churning her body through rough waves and slamming her against rocks. She fought her way back to the surface and stole one deep breath before the rapids sucked her under again. Dim, murky light from an unreachable sky melted away and dark depths rolled over her, smothering her burning lungs, clogging her throat. The loud rush of water receded, silence descended and a heavy sensation settled over her weak limbs.

Maybe... Taylor closed her eyes and unfurled her fists. Maybe Preston had been right.

The sharp pull on Will's arm released. He fell back against the boulder, his biceps stinging and his heart faltering painfully until a red helmet burst through the surface of the water.

Andi, openmouthed, sucked in a strong breath.

Will fisted his hand around her life jacket and dragged her in, hauling her onto the rough edge of the boulder. Fingers trembling, he touched her cheeks, shoulders and hands—all blue-tinged and cold, but otherwise sound. "Thank God." He spun back to the river and reached down, but his hand only met the spray of icy water through empty air. "Where's Taylor?"

Andi coughed, her rapid breaths slowing to long drags of air. "I... I kicked her." She stared up at him and her expression crumpled. "She got my foot free. Then I—" A sob escaped her. "I didn't mean to."

Will scanned the river, hoping for a glimpse of her. Maybe she swam to another boulder and managed to pull herself to safety? Or found refuge on the other side of the bank?

Whitecapped waves broke against rocks on the right side of the river, deep water poured over steep inclines on the left and thick trees lining both banks of the river bent with the wind above empty ground. Taylor was nowhere in sight.

"There." Andi's wet arm brushed his jaw as she pointed to the left, her fingertip aligning with the flash of a blue helmet in the distance that floated along a bend in the river. Taylor lifted an arm in the air briefly before she disappeared beneath the surface. "She had nothing to hold on to when I—" Andi's voice broke. She moved toward the water but doubled over, a cry of pain escaping her as she cradled her ankle with both hands. "We can't just leave her."

"I know." Instinctively, Will covered Andi's hands with his own and moved them aside. Deep abrasions and slight swelling marred her smooth skin. Gritting his teeth, he shoved painful thoughts of what might've happened to the back of his mind and focused on Taylor, who reemerged and floated on her back, limbs barely moving, near the bend in the river. She had to be exhausted, and now her safety depended on the mercy of the rapids.

Water moved high and fast, the few rocks leading toward the river's bank were too far apart to be quickly traversed and no one else was nearby. The only chance of reaching Taylor quickly—or at all—was through the water. But plunging back into the rapids would be risky and meant leaving Andi behind...

Will lowered his legs back into the river. No way

would he abandon Taylor—especially not when she'd risked her own life to save Andi's. "Stay here."

"I can cross the rocks and make it to the bank, then—"

"You'll stay here." He cupped Andi's chin, tugged her face toward him and met her eyes. "Your ankle the way it is, you got a better chance of falling back in than making it to the bank." His breath caught at the thought, but urgency surged through his veins, pushing him farther into the water. "Wait here. I'll get Taylor, then come back for you."

"But I can help. Let me go with y—"

"*Please*, Andi!" Every second carried Taylor farther away. He dropped lower, cold water rising over his chest. "Just this once, do what I say."

She stared down at him, trepidation flooding her expression. "You'll come back?" Her voice shook. "Promise you'll come back."

Will studied her face, the dimple in her chin, high cheekbones and wounded expression. All were so reminiscent of Heather at the same age. Chest aching, he forced himself to release her and eased fully into the water. "I promise."

Swift currents yanked him away and he stretched his arms out, leveraging himself against passing rocks to control his direction. Water, whirling violently along a slight drop, sucked him under, then thrust him back to the surface. He inhaled, rubbed his wet eyes and glanced over his shoulder.

Andi stared back at him. Expression worried, she shifted to her hands and knees and crawled across the boulder toward the string of large rocks leading to the left bank of the river.

"Don't, Andi!"

Roaring rapids drowned out Will's shout, and her small figure, crouched on the boulder, right arm stretching out, hand touching a neighboring rock, disappeared around the bend in the river.

Nice. He grimaced, though he had to admit Andi's actions were unsurprising. For the past two years, she hadn't listened to a word he'd said. Why should now be any different?

Biting back his fear, he peered up at a small sliver of sunlight that barely cut through the gray storm clouds gathering overhead. *You wanna help me out, God?* His chin trembled. *Maybe get Andi safely across the rocks to the bank? Please?*

A soft drizzle began, rain coating his cheeks, mingling with the rapids' misty spray. Mountains, on both sides of him, loomed taller, impeding his view of the sky, as the river shoved him over a long succession of rocky drops. Rocks, trees and increasingly dark clouds swept past, each stretch of rapids dragging him farther away from Andi, seeming to go on forever.

Will forced his tight muscles to relax and surrendered his body, feetfirst, to the current, following its swift pull, gaining ground. Water sprayed his face, stinging his eyes, but he managed to keep his head up, eyes focused ahead.

And there—several feet ahead to the right—floated Taylor, her body traveling along a smooth stretch of water that flowed toward a thick log protruding from the bank. Beyond this, the rapids converged and disappeared over a steep waterfall, a merciless crash of water echoing in the distance.

His muscles seized. "Taylor!"

She gave no response, and the slow tread of her arms and legs had stopped. The current continued to carry her.

Will shifted his weight to the side, pushed off a passing rock with his feet and swam along a swelling wave in Taylor's direction. He kicked hard with the current and grabbed at her hand, floating limply on the water's surface, but missed.

The log—his only chance of anchoring himself and Taylor to the bank before reaching the falls—drew closer. Lunging, he made one last, desperate grab and latched on to her wrist.

Will drew her in, tucked his hand beneath the shoulder of her life jacket and flung his free arm toward the log…only to watch in dismay as the current spun him away, forcing him and Taylor to the edge of the waterfall.

He wrapped his arms around Taylor's limp, unconscious form. Pictured Andi, stranded miles away. "Please, God—"

For a moment, the river's bank tilted, laid on its side, then fell away. Will's gut hollowed as they plunged over the steep falls.

A swift burst of racing water and wind mixed, slicing over and around them, diving between his and Taylor's tangled limbs, then spit them out, tumbling them into a new set of raging rapids at the base of the waterfall.

Will broke the water's surface, inhaled deeply and threw his free arm out. His hand hit a large rock, gripped a jagged edge, then pulled. Holding Taylor tight to his side, he dragged them both out of the sucking current, then carried Taylor across two large rocks until he hit hard ground.

Falling to his knees, he focused on an exposed root of a cedar tree until his dizziness subsided, then gently laid her down. He removed Taylor's helmet and eased her head to the side.

Water drained from her parted lips. He brought her face back to his, covered her mouth with his own and delivered five strong breaths. Compressions were next.

Hands fumbling, he removed her life jacket, pressed his palms to the center of her chest and pumped firmly. The feel of soft flesh and fragile bone beneath the frantic press of his hands froze his movements.

Too much pressure or not enough? What if he did more damage than good? And if this didn't work, was there anything else that would?

"Taylor?" He leaned close, brought his ear level with her mouth, but couldn't hear or feel her pull in a breath.

Tilting her head back, he provided more oxygen. "Come on, Taylor. Help me out. Breathe."

He pressed his fingertips to the delicate skin below her jaw, feeling for a pulse.

A ragged sound left her lips. Her chest lifted on a strong inhalation and her eyes opened.

Will sagged with relief. "'Bout time." He forced a shaky smile. "For a second, I thought—"

Her hand struck his wrist, dislodging his touch from her neck. She scrambled backward, but barely moved, her weakened legs struggling to push against the sandy bank beneath her and her shaky arms failing to drag her exhausted body away. Ragged coughs racked her frame, but her eyes remained pinned to his face. Terror darkened the blue depths.

"Easy..." He looked down at her and held his hand up slowly, palm out. "You were in the water a long time. Almost drowned."

She clutched her neck, her fingers covering the small area he'd touched below her jaw. "Ba—" Voice breaking, she dragged air in between shaky, blue-tinged lips, then tried again. "Back off."

"I didn't mean to scare you. I was just—"

"I said, back off."

He studied the fear and accusation moving through her expression, noted the shade of bright pink that bloomed across her pale cheeks, then slowly rose and walked to the river's edge.

Will tried to shove his hands in his pockets, but the soggy cloth clung to his palms. He'd never revived someone before. Hadn't been sure what to expect. But it certainly hadn't been this. He understood her fear: she'd almost drowned, he was little more than a stranger to her and the rapids had put them both through the wringer. But still...

"I wasn't trying to hurt you," he said softly. "You saved my daughter's life. I wasn't going to stand by while you struggled."

He glanced back at her. Taylor still cradled her neck with one hand and the other lifted to her face, her fingertips trembling as they touched her lips. She looked so vulnerable, so lost.

Will jerked back around and eyed the steep waterfall several feet upriver. Violent water poured in erratic patterns over rough rocks and knotty roots. The falls had plunged them into a gorge, and there was no way out but up the one-hundred-foot wall beside the falls.

He peered beyond the sharp incline toward the dark

clouds. Light rain still fell and he blinked against it, flinching as a low rumble of thunder rolled in the distance. It originated upriver, where Andi—injured and alone—still waited for him. Only now, she may be tumbling down the same watery path he and Taylor had traveled, or she could still be dragging herself across the rocks, trying to reach the bank—the bank opposite the one on which he stood.

Either way, more than a raging river separated them. A storm brewed, daylight faded and miles of unfamiliar terrain lay ahead. And who knew what dangers would creep through the darkness to where Andi sought refuge for the night? That was if she made it out of the river and could find decent shelter from the storm.

He should never have brought Andi out here.

"We're even."

The steel in Taylor's tone surprised Will. She stared back at him, eyes wary.

"Like you said." Taylor sat upright, pulled her knees to her chest and wrapped her arms around her shins. "I helped Andi, and now you've helped me. I can take care of myself from here on out. So that makes us even."

"No," he bit out. "It doesn't." His throat tightened, making it difficult to speak, but a dark restless hollow inside him kept spewing words. "My daughter's hurt. Stranded miles upriver on the other side of the waterfall, waiting on me to make good on my promise and come back for her. A storm's moving in, the rapids are impassable here and it'll take me an hour—or more— to scale that wall without equipment. There's no way I can make that climb tonight."

Will stifled a groan and closed his eyes. What if Andi hadn't made it to the bank? What if she'd given

up and sat exposed, right now, on the boulder where
he'd left her, shivering as the storm approached?

No. Whatever might've happened, Andi would've
kept going. Matter of fact, if he was a betting man,
he'd wager his last dime that was exactly what she
was doing right now. Soon as the rain started sprin-
kling down on her, as headstrong as she was, Andi
would've moved even faster across those rocks, dragging her injured ankle behind her. And she'd be at the
mercy of whatever lay beyond the thick trees lining
the riverbank.

They don't call this river Bear's Tooth for nothing...

Will's throat closed as he recalled Jax's words.
The waterfall blurred, melting into the rain-drenched
wooded terrain surrounding it.

"I'm sorry," Taylor said quietly. Her face flushed a
deep shade of red. "I didn't mean to—"

"To what?" He clenched his fists. "If not for you
and Jax—" *and me* "—agreeing to continue, Andi
would—"

Lightning shot above them, streaking over the waterfall like a dozen spindly legs, and a vicious crack of
thunder rattled the ground beneath his feet.

Will grabbed both life jackets and helmets. "Can
you walk?"

Taylor pried her attention away from the waterfall
and blinked up at him. "What?"

"Are you able to stand—" he stabbed a hand toward
the rocky base of the waterfall "—and hike back that
way? There might be a dry place below one of those
outcrops where we can wait out the storm."

Taylor nodded jerkily. "Yes." She stood slowly, her
legs visibly trembling. The movements cost her. Pain

showed in the tight press of her lips and flinch of her shoulders, but she straightened and met his eyes. "I'm sorry. I never meant to put Andi in danger."

She meant every word. Regret was right there in her voice, in her eyes, in the slight quiver of her dimpled chin. And it wasn't her fault. The decision to bring Andi to the river this morning had been his alone, and nothing could undo that now.

Will caught himself reaching for Taylor, the urge to console her and seek reassurance for his own misguided intentions almost overwhelming. But neither of those actions would erase the guilt gnawing at his gut or lead him to Andi any faster. Instead, he walked away.

THREE

She should've thanked him. Should've realized Will was trying to help her, rather than have mistaken his pain for anger.

Taylor frowned and forced one heavy foot in front of the other, her lungs aching and muscles shaking as she hiked toward the waterfall. Shoulda, coulda, woulda, right? Too late to fix it now. Or was it?

Will, leading the way to the falls, paused a few steps ahead and glanced back at her. "You good?"

She squinted against the fat raindrops hitting her cheeks, but couldn't make out his expression. Night had fallen, rain had intensified and the blinding pulse of light preceding each roll of thunder proved the storm had settled right on top of them for the foreseeable future.

"Yeah," she called out. "I'm okay."

Though she was certain he already knew that. He'd maintained his stiff posture and heavy tread over the half mile they'd hiked so far, but every six feet, he'd slowed his pace and glanced over his shoulder to make sure she still followed. The slight downward tilt of his head hinted he was giving her a once-over, and satis-

fied she still stood upright, he'd faced forward and resumed hiking.

"We're almost there." Lightning poured over the
sky and flooded the riverbank, briefly bringing his
sculpted cheekbones and chiseled jawline into sharp
relief. "There's an opening to the right of the falls just
ahead. Might be a decent place to get out of this."

Even now, after Will had selflessly dragged her
from the river and breathed air into her lungs, Taylor
stiffened in his presence. Stranded alone in this rough
backcountry, being pummeled by the violent throb of
the storm surrounding them, would've been enough to
raise her guard. But each blinding flash of lightning
illuminated his impressive height and muscular girth,
heightening her apprehension. It was clear he blamed
her for their current predicament and for endangering
his daughter.

Though she should be used to shouldering blame.
Her marriage to Preston had been filled with accusa-
tions and recriminations. But she used to believe that
no matter how strong Preston had been, if she kept her
spirit stronger, he couldn't break her. No matter how
much he'd blamed her for his attacks, no matter how
tightly he'd clenched his hands around her throat or
how sharply his heel had hammered her ribs, if she'd
just held on to that sliver of hope that still pulsed inside
her and prayed, something would change. God would
deliver some form of relief, and eventually she'd escape whole. When she'd finally found the courage to
pick herself up, leave him and find a place of her own,
she thought she had.

But Preston had proved her wrong.

"Taylor?" Will, now still, studied her closely. His

eyes narrowed beneath the steady rivulets of water streaming over his brow and his expression softened as he lowered their life jackets and helmets toward the ground. "Do you need me to help y—?"

"No." The word left her lips sharper than she'd intended. She squeezed her eyes shut, then focused on the steep waterfall ahead. "Keep going. Sooner we get there, sooner we're out of this."

Heavy wind tore through the tree line and shoved at their backs, driving her point home. Will nodded, hitched the life jackets and helmets back into his arms and pressed on.

She followed, stumbling twice over piles of sharp rocks, until the waterfall's steady roar cut through the chaotic thunder booming above them.

Will pointed to a stretch of dry rock wall below an outcrop. "Wait here. I'm gonna slip inside that opening and take a look."

Taylor ducked beneath the outcrop and pressed against the wall. Sharp rocky edges dug into her back, but they were solid and supportive, prompting her to sag against them. Every muscle in her body screamed beneath her skin and she rolled her head to the right, peering into the space Will had entered.

Inside, the small cave was black and shapeless, but each flash of lightning lit up the space, revealing a smooth, rocky floor, uneven walls and a high interior ceiling. Will's large frame moved slowly and carefully. His long legs took small steps and his strong arms reached out, palms testing the sturdiness of each wall.

"It's safe." His deep voice drew closer as he approached her. His brown eyes, intense, skimmed her trembling length. "Can you make it in on your own?"

Her limbs balked at the thought of moving, but she nodded, slowly pushed off the wall and trudged inside. The sound of the pounding rain receded as dry walls enveloped them in a stone cocoon.

"We passed some deadfall outside," Will said.

It was dark for a moment, the relentless lightning having briefly stilled. The disembodied timbre of his voice sounded strangely comforting.

"Some of the wood is sheltered by the outcrop," he continued. "It should be dry enough to burn with a bit of elbow grease. It won't take me long to round it up."

Shivering, Taylor sat on the dry stone floor and drew her knees to her chest. "Okay."

Lightning relit the cave on Will's departure and she was alone. Minutes—which felt more like hours— passed, her raspy breaths echoing against the walls, hitching each time blustery wind cracked tree limbs and the shallow walls of the cave groaned. She lifted her hand to her chest, touching her tender sternum where she assumed Will's hands had forced water from her lungs. Her clothes were wet and the swimsuit she wore beneath them clung to her clammy skin, sending a chill through her.

Will returned, his arms filled with thin twigs, sturdy sticks and a handful of dry moss. His heavy footsteps echoed in the small space as he drew near her side, dumped the stack of wood on the stone floor and knelt beside her.

"Hopefully, there's enough dry wood here to build a fire and get us through the next few hours. From what I could tell, none of our supplies floated downriver with us." There were scuffling noises as he shifted his weight and dug around for something in his pockets.

"No telling where our dry bags are by now—we can look for those in the morning—but luckily, one tool traveled with us."

He held up a small item and lightning flashed, reflecting off the sharp edge of a knife before darkness settled over them again. Taylor stiffened.

"This is one time I'm glad I forgot to pack something," Will continued. "Jax borrowed my knife this morning to cut a throw line, and I never got around to putting it back in the dry bag."

He put the knife down, stood, then walked around the cave. Stones clinked in different directions. Then he returned and dumped several large rocks onto the floor beside the knife.

The storm raged on, rain pummeling their crude shelter, as Will worked to build a fire. He broke a thick branch in half with his foot, carved a groove down the center of one half and shaped a point at the end of a smaller stick.

He stopped abruptly, dragged a broad palm over his face and kneaded the back of his neck, his huddled form a dark outline against the backdrop of lightning.

"Here," Taylor said, reaching out. "I'll get the fire started while you catch your breath."

He stilled. Then his hand fumbled over hers, tucking the pointed stick into her grasp.

She felt her way around the pile of dry wood, using the rhythmic bursts of lightning to guide her movements as she strategically stacked the dry wood, used the rocks Will had gathered to form a fire ring, then built a fire. It'd been a while and she struggled, but finally found success, then sagged back onto her knees and watched the flames grow.

One corner of Will's mouth lifted in a wry grin. "Thanks for that. Hate to admit when I'm beat, but that river stole the last of my reserves for the day."

She nodded. "From all of us, I think. Everyone is probably exhausted by now." A spider escaped the woodpile and scurried away from the hot flames. "Wherever they are."

Will's grin faded and his gaze drifted toward the rain whipping sideways outside the cave's entrance. Jaw clenching, he stared at it silently.

"Was Andi okay?" Taylor asked. "When she came out of the water?"

"Her ankle was sprained, but not broken, as far as I could tell. Other than that, she was as hardheaded as she's ever been." Will closed his eyes and rubbed his thumb and forefinger against his eyelids. "Even if she—or the others—made it to the bank, they won't be able to make any calls. There's no cell service out here. It'll take at least two days or more for them to hike back to the drop point and send help."

Firelight danced over his lean cheeks. Taylor studied the tight press of his mouth. "Do you know if anyone else is planning to run the river this week?"

"No." He opened his eyes and stared at the fire. "There's always a chance, but..." He shoved to his feet, jerked the hem of his wet T-shirt up to his midriff, then froze, his dark eyes meeting hers. "I'm soaked. My shirt'll dry faster if I spread it by the fire. Do you mind if I take it off?"

She looked away from his toned abs and focused on her hands. "No."

Thick smoke filled her nostrils and the fire's flickering flames cast an eerie red glow, almost like blood, across her exposed palms. Her fingers shook and a tight knot formed in her chest as memories assailed her, dragging her back to a moment five years ago that she'd never been able to fully leave behind.

"What have you done?" Preston hadn't moved at all that morning when she'd dropped the gun, covered the gaping wound in his gut with her hands and pressed hard. Blood had seeped between her spread fingers while she'd pleaded with him to hang on. He'd stared up at her from his supine position on the kitchen floor of the small house she'd rented, shock and anger in his dilating eyes, his voice fading as he'd continued. *"You can't fix it now."*

Shivering, Taylor twisted her hands together and rubbed her wet palms hard.

Will cleared his throat, his voice hesitant. "I don't mean to make you uncomfortable, but Andi wears a suit under her clothes when we hit the river. She's probably cold to the bone right now." His words weakened on a saddened tone. "Anyway, I've got my back turned. If you've got a suit on and want to dry it out, you have the privacy to do it. You've got my word."

Taylor touched her wet T-shirt absently, then glanced at Will, whose back was—true to his word—facing her. Firelight and shadow played over his muscular stature.

"I—I'll take you up on that," she said. "Thank you."

His dark head dipped and he maintained his position.

Quickly, she slipped her hands under her T-shirt, peeled her swimsuit off her shoulders, arms and down her waist, then stood and tugged off her shorts long enough to remove the suit. She redonned her shorts and shirt, spread her suit out by the fire and crossed her arms over her chest.

"Okay," she said. "I'm done now."

Will returned to his seat beside the fire. He kept his eyes averted as he held his hands out, warming them by the flames. "You built a good fire. We'll be dry soon." He glanced at her, then quickly looked away. "I imagine you're exhausted. I promise you're safe with me. I'll keep an eye on things if you want to lie down and get some sleep."

She scanned the floor. "I'm not too keen on that, but it's not so much you I'm worried about right now. I've seen at least three spiders crawling around. I'm not anxious to stretch out beside them or lean against a wall they may be nesting on."

A low laugh escaped him. "After all we've been up against today, spiders are what's worrying you?"

His smile, for a brief moment, brightened his expression and obscured the shadows in his eyes.

She managed to smile back. "Guess so."

He glanced around, rolled his lips together as he thought, then slid closer and presented his back to her again. "Lean back against me. If we do this right, you can sleep sitting up."

Taylor hesitated as she studied the strong curves of his exposed back. His bare upper body, relaxed by the fire, seemed much less intimidating. Which was worse? Taking a chance on a half-naked stranger, or risk being bitten by a black widow?

"Taylor?" His voice, softening, barely rose above a roll of thunder. He eyed her over his shoulder. "I know it's easy for me to say and much harder for you to believe, but I promise you, you got nothing to fear from me."

She waited, weighing her options, but fatigue won out. Sighing, she slid around and scooted closer until her back met his. Immediately, his dry solid warmth cut through her soggy T-shirt and heat bloomed across her chilled skin. Her muscles relaxed, her body sagged against his supportive weight and, soon, the sporadic crackle of the fire made her eyes heavy.

"Do you pray?" Will's deep tone filled the empty cave.

Blinking slowly, Taylor turned her head to stare at the fire. "I used to." Still did, at times.

"Will you pray for my daughter?" Will asked. The deep, worried throb of his voice vibrated against her back, beckoning her to press closer, to plant her hands on the floor, her elbows touching his. "That she stays safe until I find her?"

Words formed in Taylor's mind, her lips moving silently in prayer out of habit before stilling. For a moment, she watched flames lick the dark walls surrounding them, then asked, "Does He answer you?"

Will's back flexed as he turned his head, his soft breath brushing her left ear. "Sometimes."

"But not every time?"

He shook his head. "No. Well…maybe. Sometimes I think He answers, just not in the way I expect. Not in a way I'm looking for. So maybe those times, I'm not able to hear Him."

"Maybe," she repeated. But maybe those times, He didn't answer at all.

"I've lived without Him," Will continued quietly. "And I've lived with Him. The latter is by far the better.

At least for me. I keep talking to Him, and He comes through one way or another. Whether I hear Him or not, I believe He always pulls me through the rough times." His tone firmed. "Always."

Taylor closed her eyes, watched the muted orange glow of the fire behind her eyelids and whispered, "Then why let it happen at all?"

"What?"

"The rough times. Andi, stranded on her own." The center of her chest throbbed. "The awful things we do to each other." She pressed her hands together, the memory of blood on her palms almost tangible. "Why does He let it happen at all?"

Will tensed, and she could feel him searching for words.

Taylor pressed closer to him, tilted her head and waited. Strained to hear his voice, a reassurance of some kind. But smoke continued to fill the dark cave. Outside, the storm raged on. And an answer never came.

Birds chattered, water rushed in the distance and something firm and slightly uncomfortable poked Will's temple. He opened his eyes and gradually focused on a thin ray of light inching across the rocky ceiling above him.

Andi.

He sat upright, his quads and abs smarting at the abrupt movement, and looked around. A life jacket lay on the floor behind him, the small impression where his head had rested still visible. The fire had died, leaving only black ash and charred wood behind, and Taylor—along with her swimsuit—was gone.

Will stood, grabbed his dry T-shirt and tugged it on as he walked out of the cave. Fresh, clean air rushed into his lungs and cool mist eased over his bare skin. The storm had moved on, leaving wispy clouds scattered across a slowly brightening sky. Sunlight pooled behind a dense cloak of fog, the sun struggling to burn through as it rose between two mountain peaks.

Taylor stood on the bank of the river, her shapely silhouette, in its stillness, a stark contrast to the violent river, smoky fog and faint streaks of lavender and pink above the mountain peaks. Her head was tilted back, her face lifted toward the high, rocky bank that walled in the waterfall. White water roared over the waterfall and plunged into swollen rapids below, crashing against sharp rocks.

An uneasy ache spread through Will as his gaze followed hers, studying the tangle of green rocks, small bushes and winding vines. Somewhere on the other side of that imposing wall, miles away, Andi, injured and afraid, had spent hours alone in the dark wilderness.

Why does He let it happen at all?

Taylor's question had stayed with Will last night long after she'd fallen asleep, and it had tugged at his subconscious even as he'd slept—rising to the forefront of his mind and tangling with his fitful dreams. It had only receded when he'd opened his eyes, focused on the pulse of lightning outside the cave and forced himself to recall the few things that had gone right that day: Andi, from what he'd been able to gauge, hadn't broken a bone during the overturning of the raft, Taylor had managed to save Andi from drowning when it had seemed there was nothing more that could be done and, even after plunging back into the water and leaving himself at the mercy of the river—a reckless choice but the only viable one available at the time—he'd pulled Taylor to the bank and they'd managed to find shelter from the storm.

He could've easily overlooked all of those blessings—very easily. Still could, if he didn't keep his eyes and heart open.

Taylor's heart seemed firmly closed. The terror in her eyes yesterday on the riverbank as he'd looked down at her had to be a result of more than the day's events, and the despair underlying her question last night in the cave hadn't escaped his notice. But what had caused it? And why, with Andi stranded alone miles away, did he feel a longing to stay close to Taylor's side? To find a crack in her armor and reach the softer, wounded side she'd offered a glimpse of last night when she'd asked her quiet question?

Will left the mouth of the cave and made his way down the soggy bank, his shoes surprisingly sturdy across the muddy ground. A soft breeze rattled the tall trees, shook the branches above him and dropped residual raindrops onto his bare arms. Despite the growl of his empty gut and cotton-like feel of his tongue, the high mountain peaks and steady flow of the river sparked a renewed sense of energy in his muscles and quickened his step.

He lifted a silent prayer of thanks for waking refreshed despite his disturbed sleep. But even though his body physically seemed ready to tackle the formidable barrier of rock, a sense of uncertainty roiled within him. Andi, wherever she was, had probably not had the benefit of a sheltering cave last night, and she definitely hadn't had someone with her to share the fear and shock of the day's painful events during the stormy hours until sunrise. Every bit of his focus should be on reaching Andi as soon as possible and nothing— or no one—else.

Will reached Taylor's side, studied her profile, then spoke. "It won't be easy, but it's doable."

A blond curl lifted in the morning breeze, danced across her freckled cheek, then rested on her lips. She tucked it behind her ear and nodded. "It's steep, mostly limestone with several big holds. But there's a lot of vegetation and probably loose rocks hidden along the crevices." Sunlight glowed behind the fog hovering above them and cast a golden hue over her face and neck. She turned her head, her blue eyes locking with his. "What's your guess on the height?"

Will shoved his hands in his pockets as he focused on the rock wall. "Hundred, hundred and ten feet. A bit more, maybe? But at those numbers, the exact measurement doesn't really matter, does it?"

"No." Her confident tone faded. "Halfway up, one slip, one fall, it's over." She drew in a strong breath and pointed at the river. "I searched every inch of the bank I could reach this morning, and none of our dry bags made it over the falls. All our equipment is either pinned beneath the raft or hung up on rocks upriver. We've got no harnesses, rope or chalk. And so far as I know, no one's ever scaled this wall. We won't have any anchors to use as a guide."

Will narrowed his eyes. "We?"

A determined expression crossed her face. "Yes."

"Look—" he held up a hand "—I know I put a lot of the blame for what happened on you, and I'm sorry for that. Last night, I was angry and afraid for Andi. But you're no more responsible for our predicament than me." He swallowed hard, choking back a surge of guilt and fear. "I'm the one who brought Andi out here, and as her dad, I'm responsible for finding her. You're under no obligation to climb those rocks or scour these mountains for her. There's no reason you can't stay here, safe on the ground."

"There's one reason," Taylor said softly. She studied his face. "I like Andi. She's got spirit and drive. And you saved my life yesterday. Something I don't think I properly thanked you for." Her gaze shifted. Drifted to a point over his left shoulder. "You seem like a good man, and considering the circumstances, you could probably use some help. I'm not offering because I feel like I have to. I'm offering because I want to."

He shouldn't accept. Climbing that wall would be dangerous, and there was no telling what threats lurked beyond it. He should turn her down gently, embark on the journey alone and find a modicum of comfort in the fact that she remained somewhere relatively safe.

But the supportive feel of her leaning into him last night in the cave still lingered with him this morning, and the thought of scaling the wall and hiking terrain with someone by his side rather than on his own was too tempting to refuse. Her willingness to risk her life again—in spite of the doubts she'd expressed hours earlier in the cave—for Andi…well, he couldn't help but admire the strength in that choice.

"Have you climbed walls like this before?" he asked.

"Yeah. Routinely." She faced the waterfall again, her eyes tracing the water's path as it poured over the rock wall, plunged into the rapids and broke among submerged rocks. "But I've never free soloed before. It's a whole nother game climbing an unfamiliar route alone without equipment."

"We've got one thing in our favor." Will tilted his head back and watched as a ray of sunlight pierced the fog above them. "If we climb together, neither one of us will be alone."

FOUR

Taylor leaned forward on the riverbank, dug her heel into the mud and straightened her back leg, stretching her right calf muscle. The tight pull in her leg gradually subsided, giving way to warm flexible strength, but that small release did nothing to still the unsettling fear roiling within her, and the roar of the waterfall to the left of her only enhanced her anxiety. She'd barely been able to take her eyes off the massive falls during the ten minutes she and Will stretched on the riverbank in preparation for the impending climb.

"Trust," Will said, holding out a helmet.

Straightening, she raised her eyebrows and searched his expression.

"Free-climbing that wall isn't just about physical strength." He lifted the helmet higher and gestured toward her head with his free hand. "May I?"

She eyed the relaxed position of his muscular arm and long fingers, then slowly nodded. "Please."

He moved closer and eased the helmet onto her head. "A lot of what's needed during the climb is here." His thumb touched the center of her forehead gently before his big hands lowered and fastened the helmet's strap beneath her chin. "The rest—" he pressed his wide palm to the left side of his chest "—is here."

The warmth of his touch lingered on her forehead and bloomed over her cheeks. Fingers trembling, she reached up and checked the chin strap.

"Does it feel secure?" he asked.

"Yes."

She glanced at the waterfall, its majestic height, powerful water and rugged strength almost mesmerizing. The sun had fully risen over the mountain peaks and burned off most of the thick fog above them, flooding the waterfall and narrow gorge with golden hues of light. Water sparkled in every direction.

"Despite the dangers," she said softly, "it is a beautiful sight."

"Shame your camera didn't make it down the river with us." Will put on his helmet and secured his chin strap. "Like you said yesterday, one decent pic of these falls would make the cover of any magazine. Probably fetch a pretty payday, too."

"Probably." Taylor stretched her arms overhead, her muscles trembling. "I just hate that we found it the way we did."

The hesitant look of admiration forming on Will's face melted away as he examined the steep wall in front of them. "It's no wonder why no one's ventured this far downriver before. The only way out of here is up. There are plenty of ledges, so it won't be all wall, but the parts that are just rock will be challenging." He faced her unexpectedly, his somber gaze searching her expression. "Are you afraid?"

A lie hovered on the tip of her tongue. It was so tempting to return his stare, lift her chin and shrug off his concern for the sake of holding this charismatic stranger at a distance. She'd made the mistake of blindly trusting a man once before and it wasn't wise to do it again—especially in these remote, treacherous surroundings. The safer bet would be to put on a brave face and hope he didn't see beyond it. But something in his direct scrutiny hinted he already knew she was second-guessing herself, and the patient kindness he'd shown her over the past hours made her long to lean on him more than she should.

"Yes," she admitted quietly, lowering her arms to her sides. "I'm afraid of just about everything lately."

His expression gentled as he scanned her trembling frame. "If you'd like to lead, I'll climb close behind and promise to do everything I can to support you. Do you trust me enough to try that?"

Trust. One small word rife with so much risk. Taylor fiddled with the hem of her shorts, then forced herself to nod despite the painful kick of her heart against her ribs.

Will smiled. A warm gleam of affection entered his brown eyes, enhancing his handsome features. He held out his hand, palm tilted up in invitation. "Ready?"

Hesitating, she slid her hand in his. The warm strength of his fingers curled around hers and eased some of the nervous tension clamoring through her. "Ready."

They walked to the wall together, hands clasped, until they reached the base of the waterfall. A misty spray of water wet Taylor's cheek and she wiped it away with her free hand.

"Here." Will tugged her farther to the right, away from the spray of the waterfall to a sunlit stretch of rugged wall. "Dry hands make for a better grip." He cradled both of her hands in one of his and proceeded to rub her palms dry with the hem of his T-shirt. "Remember to feel your way up as much as see it. These falls are like a living entity—they move, breathe. And there'll still be damp places from the rain on the fragile parts of the outer walls. Those spots can crack or break if you're not careful." Pausing, he drifted his thumb gently over the tender skin of her wrist. "You don't have to do this, you know? It's not too late to change your mind and keep your feet on the ground."

"No." Taylor squeezed his hands and smiled tightly. "Andi's waiting, and the more help you have, the faster you'll find her." She slipped past him and eyed the rocky ledges, dense vegetation and smooth stones stretching up toward the sky. "We could follow the largest ledges up the right side, then pivot to the outcrop on the left. What do you think?"

Will nodded slowly, his eyes tracing the path she'd pointed out. "Looks like the safest and straightest line to me. You still want to lead?"

"Yes."

He motioned toward the base of the wall. "Take your time. I'll be right behind you."

Taylor inhaled, grabbed on to a low ledge with both hands and hauled her lower body onto the wall. The rough feel of rock beneath her fingers and press of uneven stone into her heels made her pause.

Oh, boy. What had she gotten herself into? It was one thing to imagine scaling over a hundred feet of slippery mountain wall, but it was quite another to leave the ground and cling to rocks in midair.

"Breathe," Will said softly from below. "Keep your eyes up and focus on one hold at a time."

In spite of it all, Taylor grinned. Though his words were kind and patient, he wasn't quite as confident as he seemed. There was a slight hitch in his voice. Not much, but just enough to let her know she wasn't the only one harboring fears of missing a hold, losing her footing, plummeting a hundred feet and breaking against the rocks below.

"You lilted." Still grinning, she reached up, grabbed a smooth edge and hauled her body two feet higher up the wall.

"I what?"

"Lilted." She lifted her left foot to a higher ledge, tested its stability, then, satisfied with its support, climbed higher. "Your tone pitched on your last syllable. I noticed you did it twice last night, too. Once on the riverbank and once in the cave." Another ledge, another three feet higher. "I'm guessing you're as nervous about this climb as I am and don't want to tell me."

A breeze rustled the lush green vegetation that grew at awkward angles from cracks in the wall. Taylor carefully plucked a damp clump of moss out of a large crevice and probed with her fingers for a safe hold.

"I didn't lilt."

Taylor grinned wider. If she wasn't mistaken, Will's voice had deepened at least an octave. And anything that released a bit of the tension was welcome right now—even a good-natured argument.

"Yeah, you did," she said. "There's no shame in it. I just thought you should know I'd picked up on it and it's kind of comforting." She rested for a moment, breathing deeply as she pressed against the wall. "Not that I'm glad you're uncomfortable. I suppose it's just nice to know I'm not alone in being concerned about making it to the top of this wall." She slowly glanced over her shoulder and peered down at him. "Are you coming or are you just gonna leave me hanging here?"

A slow smile spread across his handsome face. "Glad I could entertain." He grabbed the lowest ledge, hefted himself onto the wall and traced the path she'd traveled, ascending with grace and purpose. When he drew within arm's length, he tapped her ankle gently. "Let's take our time with the next hold," he said in a more relaxed tone. "We can't risk taking a route we can't reverse out of, if needed."

"Okay." Taylor faced the wall again, her stomach dipping.

She didn't know what unsettled her more: the fact that she clung to a hundred-foot wall without rope or a harness, or the knowledge that the only person standing between her and a potentially deadly fall was a charismatic man she'd only known for forty-eight hours and had agreed to trust just minutes ago.

Her attention drifted toward the water cascading over the rock wall several feet away, her eyes clinging to the repeated crash of white water against the boulders below.

"Taylor." Will's calm, focused gaze connected with hers. "Look up. That's where we're headed."

Maybe it was the confident tone of his voice. Or maybe it was the sight of him, strong and capable, planted firmly on the stone ledge below her. Either way, she did as he directed—tore her eyes away from the boulders below and pinned her gaze on the rock wall above her.

For over an hour, they moved slowly and methodically, right arm lifting first, left leg following, then left arm and right leg. Up and up they climbed, the distance between their feet and the bank below lengthening with nerve-racking intensity on each successful series of ascensions. The sun rose higher and blazed hotter, drying limestone and rock and warming stones beneath their fingertips until they almost burned to the touch.

Taylor ran her left hand over a smooth ledge above her, cringing as the scraped skin of her fingertips snagged on the rough rock. Heat from the sun-warmed stone intensified the painful pulse in her hand and blood oozed from a cut on her thumb.

She renewed her grip and pulled, lifting her sweat-slicked brow just above the ledge, and an exhausted laugh burst from her dry lips. "We're almost there! I can see the top. It's only four feet away." Tilting her head to the side, she stared at the summit, too afraid to glance over her shoulder and look down at Will. "Once we make it past this ledge, we're there."

Wind whistled, the chirps of birds peppered the air and Taylor stiffened against the rocks, straining to hear Will's voice.

"That makes you my new best friend." His warm, lighthearted tone and soothing voice was a balm to her trembling muscles. "Ain't gonna lie—" two heavy exhalations sounded below her "—I've been hoping to hear that for a while now."

Taylor smiled but halted the movement, flinching as her chapped lips cracked and a stinging sensation burrowed deep into her gums. She licked her lower lip carefully, then said, "I'm with you. Let's get this over with."

One strong inhalation and one heavy tug and her upper body cleared the ledge. She bent at the waist, lowered her cheek to the smooth stone and rested her arms for a moment, flexing her fingers against the heated rock.

Her tender biceps almost sighed with relief. Only one more heave and haul and she'd reach the summit. She closed her eyes and breathed deeply. Dry dust billowed up, coating her face. Something rustled to her left and a soft rattling sound filled the air.

Taylor froze and opened her eyes slowly.

Three feet away, level with her face, two black eyes glared back at her from a triangular head. The coiled brown body expanded, the black markings along its five-foot length swelled to twice their size and the tip of its tail lifted in the air, a sharp rattle assaulting her ears.

"Taylor?" Will placed his left foot on a narrow jut of rock, gingerly pressed down to test its stability, then, confident it would hold, planted his foot and lifted himself a foot closer to her. "I know you're tired, but this isn't the best place to rest." He dredged up the little bit of humor he had left and tried for a lighthearted tone. "The only thing standing between us and a nice, sturdy place to collapse is one more four-foot climb."

No response.

He studied the stiff set of her legs, noted the tight clench of her calf muscles and frozen position of her feet on the rocks supporting her. The upper half of her body, bent over onto the ledge above him, wasn't visible. "Taylor?" He frowned. "What's going on up there?"

For a moment, the rush of water over the falls and

the steady breeze swirling between them and flapping their shorts against their bare thighs were the only sounds. Then Taylor's voice, a mere thread of a whisper that barely carried across the distance between them, emerged.

"Snake."

A bead of sweat stung Will's eye and he winced, blinking it away. "What'd you say?"

"Th-there's a snake." Her voice shook, panic lacing her tone. "About three feet to my left. Coiled on the ledge."

His chest tightened. "All right. Don't pani—"

"Will?"

"Yeah?"

"It's looking at me." Her voice pitched higher. "And it's angry."

He blew out a slow breath. "Okay. Don't panic. Just stay still."

"I am," she whispered loudly. "But I can't stay like this forever."

"I know. What color is it?"

"B-brown. With black markings." Her left leg shifted and pebbles rained down, pelting his head and shoulders. "It has a rattle."

He focused on her elbow, propped on the edge of the stone the upper half of her body rested upon, and racked his brain, struggling to form a mental picture, to focus. "Probably a timber rattlesnake."

"Is it venomous?"

Will dragged his teeth over his bottom lip. "Yeah." A gasp escaped her and he tacked on, "But in all the time I've lived here, I've never heard of a fatality occurring from a timber bite. Or any snakebite, for that matter."

"And how long is that?"

"That I've lived here?" At her confirmation, he continued. "All my life. Thirty-six years." He swallowed past the tight knot forming in his throat. "Chances are, he's more scared of you than you are of him. That's why he's throwing his back up. He's just telling you to keep your distance. To go your way and let him go his. Just breathe and stay calm."

She was quiet for a minute, then said, "Easy for you to say. He's not flicking his creepy tongue three feet from your nose."

A half-hearted smile crossed his face. "Yep. I got you, and I can't say I'd rather be the one up there."

Though he'd trade places with her in a heartbeat if he had the opportunity.

Her calf muscles flexed and a heavy, somewhat exasperated breath left her. Good. Better she get mad at him than freak out and risk a snakebite. Or worse... risk knocking them both back down the rocky bank they'd spent over an hour scaling to a fate of either broken bones or death.

"Keep talking to me, Taylor," he said calmly. "Tell me what you need."

"I need to be away from this thing." Her voice cracked. "What do I do?"

The helpless plea made him long to reach up and console her. To touch her leg and reassure her that he had her back. But given the circumstances, it was best not to do anything that might startle her.

"Take a few deep breaths, look around and get your bearings," he said. "Then move slowly and carefully along the route that's the straightest line to the summit and the farthest away from him."

"Okay," she whispered.

"He's not mad at you," Will consoled. "He's just doing his morning bout of sunbathing. Go your way, and he'll go his."

"You promise?"

He tilted his head back and looked up. Mouthed silent words as a wispy cloud drifted across the blue sky above them. *Lord, please protect her. Lift her up.* "I promise."

Taylor remained frozen in place for a couple of minutes. Then her feet shifted to the right, moving slowly across the rocks she stood on, and after another minute or two, her upper body rose from its prone position on the ledge. She pulled her legs to the ledge, too, shuffled on her knees a few feet to the right, then reached up, grabbed the top ledge and hauled herself onto the summit, her long blond hair, shapely legs and colorful shoes disappearing out of sight.

"Thank You," Will whispered, glancing at the sky. Now it was time for him to ante up, too.

Steeling himself, he focused on the footholds and ledge a few feet above him and followed the same path Taylor had climbed. He reached the ledge, lifted his lower body onto it, and sure enough, there sat the timber rattlesnake, coiled like a thick inner tube, dark eyes pinned to his and rattler waving high in the air.

"What's up, buddy?" he asked softly. "You trying to give us a hard time today?"

The snake raised its head a bit higher and flicked its tongue out, the forked tip aimed directly at his forehead.

"Yeah." Will moved with slow, measured steps to the right. "You're as pretty as Taylor described."

"You two having a private moment, or you want to come up here and join me?" Taylor's blue eyes, wide and anxious between the long curtain of her hair, stared down at him from the summit and she held out her hand.

Will grinned up at her, the worried expression suffusing her pretty features as she studied him sending a wave of warmth through him. "Oh, I'm coming up."

Sucking in a strong breath, he sprang up, grabbed the top ledge and hauled himself to the top. A soft hiss and rattle faded behind him.

Taylor grabbed his arms and pulled, and they fell back onto the flat slab of stone in a tangle of limbs. His chest hit hers and her breath left her in a whoosh as he fell on top of her.

He tucked his arms around her and, cradling the back of her helmet, rolled them over several times until they were a safe distance from the ledge. Rising up on his elbows, he looked down at her and grinned slowly. "Just for the record, you lilted twice during your episode with our little timber friend. And I guarantee your voice pitched higher than mine ever has."

The tension in her eyes receded and she tilted her head back and laughed, the sound exhausted but infectious. "You're probably right about that."

Sweat sheened her brow, the cute freckles sprinkled across her nose had increased and a hefty dose of sunburn reddened her smooth cheeks.

Will lifted his free hand slowly and smoothed a wet strand of blond hair from her forehead. "You did good back there," he said softly. "Real good. Thanks for trusting me."

Her laughter faded and her gaze traveled over his face, a look of warmth entering her blue eyes that moved him more than he'd expected. "Thank you for keeping me going."

FIVE

Normally, Taylor would've panicked by now. Pinned flat on her back to hard stone beneath a muscular, six-foot-two man had a tendency to provoke her defenses—as it had last night by the riverbank when Will had revived her. But at the moment, the firm weight of Will's thighs resting on hers and the gentle support of his warm palm cupping the back of her neck felt comforting. Almost…safe?

Will looked down at her, the amusement sparkling in his brown eyes dimming and a rueful expression crossing his face. "Sorry. Didn't mean to crush you."

He lifted his large frame off her and sat upright, tugging her with him. Seemingly assured she'd regained her balance and was comfortably seated, he released the back of her neck and backed a few feet away.

Immediately, Taylor missed the secure press of his touch and the warmth of his palm against her hair. Which was ridiculous, really. She barely knew him, had only just met him yesterday, and had no intention of lowering her guard with him now. But still…

She touched her nape and her fingers sifted through

the strands of her hair, smoothing over her skin where a faint trace of his touch still lingered.

"Did I hurt you?"

Taylor glanced at him. The worried tone in his voice stirred a pleasant sense of affection within her. One she hadn't felt in years. "No."

"I was rough last night when I helped you by the bank." He frowned, his lean cheeks flushing. "I panicked, so I wasn't as gentle as I should've been when I gave you compressions. And just now, I didn't mean to drag you across the ground or make you feel—"

"You didn't hurt me," she said softly.

"Not at all?"

She smiled. "No."

His shoulders sagged and a low breath escaped his parted lips, his relief almost palpable. "That's good, then."

He removed his helmet and rubbed the dark stubble on his jaw with a shaky hand. His dark hair, sticking up in adorable tufts, ruffled in the breeze.

Taylor had the surprising urge to scoot closer to his side and smooth the wavy strands back into place. Instead, she bent her upper body over her legs, stretching her thighs, calves and arms for a few minutes, and watched as Will did the same. Her hands shook as she stretched farther and touched her toes, her thumbs and forefingers stained with dried blood.

Will stood, glanced around and pointed at a large rock near the rapids. "There's a low boulder over there, where we can dip our feet in the river safely. Maybe wash our faces and cool off before we hike upriver. There's no way we can cross the rapids here. We'll have to hike back up into the mountains until we find a safe place to cross the river to reach the other side of the bank. It's best we rest a few minutes before we tackle that."

Nodding, Taylor removed her helmet, then joined Will by the rapids.

He placed one foot in the center of the low boulder, kept his other leg planted on the bank and held out his hand. "May I?"

"Please." She slipped her hand in his, the supportive feel of his touch moving up her arm and relaxing her muscles as she stepped onto the boulder.

Once she was safely seated, he settled beside her, leaned down and scooped up handfuls of white water, splashing it on his face, over his head and down the back of his neck. She did the same, relishing the feel of cold mountain water pouring over her hot cheeks, neck and chest.

Taylor watched the powerful surge of water rushing toward the falls, then tipped her face up, taking in the wide blue sky and high green mountain peaks. A warm summer wind whispered through the tops of cypress trees lining the riverbank and two hawks circled high above them, coasting on the swift current.

The Smokies transformed up here. From this height, the massive bone-crushing boulders downriver looked harmless. The raging white water seemed rhythmic and soothing as it swept along carved earth, and the rugged mountain walls rising high behind them seemed powerful and majestic.

She eased back on her hands and admired the view. "Jax may have been right about one thing yesterday."

Will, splashing water on his jaw and rubbing his chin, paused and raised his brows.

"When he said there's peace here," she clarified. "That you've just got to look for it… I couldn't see that yesterday, but sitting here now, by the river instead of in it, and on top of the falls instead of stranded on the bank below, it does feel like a different place."

Sighing, Will leaned back on his hands, too, and surveyed their surroundings. "Yeah. It does."

Taylor lowered her legs closer to the spray of white water, savoring the cool mist against her sore calves and ankles. "Maybe this is the kind of view Andi had last night and this morning," she added gently. "At least, I hope so."

Will's mouth tightened and the rush of water filled the brief silence between them. "It's what I prayed for," he said. "And I'm hoping He came through on that because He's answered us at least once already."

She frowned. "What do you mean?"

The corner of his mouth lifted in a half-hearted smile. "He got us up the falls, didn't He?"

Taylor glanced at the rocky wall several feet behind them and suppressed a shiver at the thought of the snake beyond their sight, basking on a ledge in the hot sun. "I have to admit, us making it up that wall on our own did seem impossible."

Will smiled wider, flashing straight white teeth. "Crazy."

She grinned. "Stupid."

He laughed. "You got that right." His dark gaze held hers, then roved slowly over her face, the appreciative gleam in his eyes making her breath catch. He moved to speak, but seemed to think better of it, ducked his head and looked away.

"Go ahead." She tilted her head as he glanced back

at her, confusion in his eyes. "Just now, what were you thinking?"

He ran a hand through his dark hair and studied the impressive landscape before them. "What we just did—" he made a sweeping motion toward the falls "—being here, sitting with you like this. It takes me back. Rolls back the years and makes me feel younger."

"Jax mentioned that you and Andi used to run rapids and rock climb all the time together. Did you do the same when you were a teen?"

A nostalgic expression crossed his face. "Yeah. These mountains have always been home for me. I was born and raised about forty miles from this spot in Stone Creek. Not a single weekend during my childhood went by without me and some friends packing a bag and hitting a trail or river. There's not a place in the world as precious to me as this backcountry, and I miss those carefree days of exploring these mountains." He met her eyes again, a soft smile appearing. "Makes me wonder what it would've been like if you and I had met back then as kids, instead of now, under different circumstances. How easily I might've taken to you."

Cheeks heating, she bit back a grin and squirmed on the rock. "You barely know me."

He nodded slowly, amusement lacing his tone. "I know enough to know I'd have been interested."

Well. She cleared her throat awkwardly, pleasure fluttering in her belly as she admitted silently to feeling the same way about him. Only, she wasn't quite ready to share that. "But we didn't meet then."

"Nope." He looked away, a heavy sigh escaping him. "I met Heather."

"Andi's mother?"

"Yeah. I fell in love with her spirit, her energy. She was a bit reckless, but she loved life and the outdoors. Enjoyed everything both had to offer. In some ways, she was a lot like you." He glanced at her beneath his thick lashes, an apologetic look in his eyes as he said, "She was strong, independent. Kept her guard up almost all the time and had a tendency to push people away—especially me."

Taylor stared down at her shoes. Swung her legs slowly back and forth between the boulder and spray of white water.

"But she's very different from you in the way that she regards others," he continued. "Last night, I was wrong to blame you for everything that's happened and you had every right to hang back on the bank and sit this climb out. You could've left me to find Andi on my own, but you chose to come with me instead." His tone hardened. "Heather would never have done that. It took me a long time to realize that she has little empathy for others, and she's already abandoned Andi once. I have no doubt she'd do it again, given the chance."

Taylor looked up, her heart clenching at the thought of Andi watching her mother leave. "How old was Andi when Heather left?"

"Eight months."

Oh, no. Andi hadn't had to watch her mother walk away. She'd never actually had the chance to get to know her mother at all. Or what it was like to have one. "And you've raised Andi on your own since then?"

Will gave a jerky nod. "Though I haven't done a good job of it. Heather and I married at eighteen. We had Andi one year later. Then Heather divorced me and was gone eight months after that. I was twenty—still a kid in a lot of ways myself—and I've spent the majority of my time since then working. I started entry-level in construction, then went to school nights and weekends over the years until I worked my way up to project manager. I've worked overtime more than not and had to pinch every penny I earned to support us both. But that's no excuse. Andi deserves better than a part-time dad. She deserves a better life than the one I've given her, and she knows it. That's why she's so desperate to get out of here and away from me as soon as she graduates from high school next summer."

Taylor picked at the dirt under her nails, hesitating. This wasn't any of her business, and she wasn't exactly sure he'd welcome her two cents, but Will vastly underestimated himself as a father.

"I'm not so sure I'd bet on that being why Andi's so anxious to leave." The expression of helplessness, pain and regret on Will's face made her ache. "Sometimes, it's not a person that's causing the hurt—" she clenched her fists "—but the place. These mountains may feel like home to you, but for Andi, maybe the place you love just brings back painful memories of a mother who didn't stay and love her back. Maybe she thinks if she leaves these mountains, she'll leave that pain behind, too."

Taylor closed her eyes briefly, recalling the anguished days, weeks, months and years that followed the morning she'd shot and killed Preston. No matter how hard she'd tried, she'd never been able to shake the pain of that day…or the years of pain before it when God had abandoned her to Preston's cruel hands, refusing to answer her prayers.

"Thing is," Taylor whispered, "the kind of pain Andi

carries is impossible to shake no matter how far someone runs, and when you're alone, that's when it hurts the most."

She opened her eyes and looked at Will. Her heart warmed at the concerned look in his eyes and she allowed herself to wonder, just for a moment, how different her own life might have been if she'd met Will instead of Preston all those years ago. If she'd been blessed with the caring protection and safety Will provided, rather than the violent pain and fear Preston had brought into her life.

"Just from the short time I've spent with you," she said, holding Will's gaze, "I can see you're a great dad, who's doing the best you can. Andi is lucky to have you. And she needs you—no matter how much she may be pushing you away. Don't give up on her, because when she spends enough time alone and finally realizes she needs you, it'll be harder than ever for her to find her way back to you on her own."

Despair. Will had never felt the full impact of that emotion up close, but there was no mistaking it in Taylor's eyes an hour ago. And it wasn't just her tone. It was in the dark shadows lurking deep in her eyes, the slumping curves of her usually strong-set shoulders and the dimming of her previously bright expression. Her cheery laugh had dissolved almost immediately when he'd shared his frustrations and fears regarding Andi.

Why had he done that, anyway? What had provoked him to spill his innermost worries about his relationship with his daughter to an almost-stranger?

Will frowned as he yanked his foot free of the suck of mud and hiked farther upriver, leading the way along the sunlit riverbank as Taylor followed closely by his side. He scanned the landscape for the thousandth time, searching—unsuccessfully—for any sign of Andi, and wondered absently if maybe he'd overshared with Taylor because of what they'd been through the past twenty-four hours. Or perhaps it was because he felt a connection with her. A kind of connection he had never felt before with a woman—including Heather.

That realization alone rattled him. The last thing he needed to do was take a chance on inviting another woman into his and Andi's lives, and he'd been very careful over the past sixteen years to avoid the flirtatious glances of pretty women who'd caught his eye and politely reject dinner invitations from women with whom he'd been tempted to explore a relationship. Because involving a woman in his and Andi's lives might allow her an opportunity to hurt him and, more important, Andi all over again—just like Heather had.

Only, Taylor wasn't Heather. And the more time he spent with Taylor, the more his admiration grew.

He sneaked a glance at her, his gaze lingering a bit longer on her flushed cheeks and parted lips than he'd intended.

The pink blooming in her cheeks traveled down her graceful neck and she looked up at him, those beautiful blue eyes of hers meeting his for a brief magnetic moment before she smiled softly and refocused on the trail. Her footfalls beside him were steady, but she'd said little since they'd left the summit by the waterfall.

Not that he'd spoken much, either. At first, he'd been so surprised by her compliment by the river that he'd latched on to her words and held them close—a bit too desperately, he mused wryly.

I can see you're a great dad, Will.

Man, how he'd needed to hear that, and to hear the sentiment slip from Taylor's lips so sincerely and so warmly, he'd been at a loss for a reply. It had not, however, escaped his notice that there had been an undercurrent of profound pain in her words.

Someone had hurt her—but who? And why?

His body stiffened at the thought of someone harming Taylor even as his mind balked at spending time on thinking about Taylor's past at all. Right now, Andi needed him. That was where his attention should be— on finding Andi. He shouldn't be focused on Taylor, no matter how attracted he may be to her or how vulnerable she seemed.

But something inside him longed to dig deeper. To try, however unsuccessfully, to coax Taylor into opening up and giving him a glimpse inside her heart so that he could offer to shoulder some of the painful burden she so obviously carried.

The kind of pain Andi carries is impossible to shake no matter how far someone runs, and when you're alone, that's when it hurts the most.

When you're alone...

"Do you have family here in Tennessee?" Will grimaced as his blunt question hovered on the summer air. Not exactly the smoothest approach to opening a personal conversation.

Taylor glanced up at him in surprise, the defensive glint he'd grown accustomed to seeing flashing in her eyes.

"Sorry." Regrouping, he spread his hands and smiled sheepishly. "I don't mean to overstep into your private life, but judging from the terrain—" he gestured toward the endless stretch of violent rapids, rugged mountain ranges and muddy bank before them "—and the distance we need to cover to reach a safe place to cross the river and find Andi, we'll be hiking for at least a day or two. I thought holding conversation might help pass the time. Guess I forgot how out of practice I am."

Her brows rose. "Out of practice?"

"Yeah. You know." He shrugged, his words catching in his throat. "Spending time with a woman."

Her mouth parted and she cast a slow look over him, her gaze sweeping over his face, chest, arms and legs. "You..." Disbelief crossed her face. "You mean you don't—?"

"Don't date?" His face flamed. "No. Not since before I was married eighteen years ago."

She tilted her head and stared up at him, a blank expression crossing her face. "You classify this as a date?"

Great. Just great. Now she probably thought he was an uncouth idiot, on top of being inept at conversation. How in the world had he managed to steer the conversation here?

"No." He dragged a hand over the increasingly painful knot forming between his shoulder blades. "I meant—"

"Because if this is a date," she said, her lips quirking, "I'd say it's a pretty lousy one, seeing as how you haven't even offered a girl a glass of clean water."

He halted midstep.

Taylor stopped two steps in front of him, faced him, then winked. "Of course, I'm not what one would label a good date, either, considering I had a hand in your daughter almost drowning, insulted you after you saved my life and almost let a snake scare me into knocking us both off a hundred-foot drop." She trailed a hand through her long hair and frowned down at the tangled strands wound between her fingers. "Not to mention, I'm not exactly at my prettiest. My hair is filthy, I'm sweating like a pig and, well, as much as I hate to admit it, I'm pretty sure I stink a little bit."

Will grinned. "Pigs don't sweat all that much. You don't stink that I can tell. And from where I'm standing—" he took her in, all five foot seven of her shapely length, then admired her charming smile that he hadn't witnessed in all its glory until this very moment "—you're plenty pretty to me, even if you do have mud on your chin."

Her cute smile widened. "Thank you. And I'd say the same about you." She dipped her head, her cheeks darkening to a deeper shade of red. "I mean, you're easy on the eyes, too."

That shy look almost did him in. Despite the fact that he'd failed to make her comfortable enough to offer an answer to his question while simultaneously embarrassing himself, he was glad he'd stumbled into the exchange if only for the chance of glimpsing her sense of humor…and discovering she might be as drawn to him as he was to her.

"Thanks," he said. "And though I can't offer you a glass of clean water, I think I might be able to find a handful of wild strawberries."

As if on cue, her stomach growled.

Chuckling, he walked over to the thick clump of lush green bushes lining the riverbank, his own gut rumbling at the thought of food. It'd been at least sixteen hours since they'd last eaten, and they'd burned off every bit of the light lunch they'd stopped the raft to eat yesterday during the early leg of their river journey.

"Think I saw a clearing through the tree line a few feet back," he continued. "Might take me a few minutes to dig up some berries but—"

"I'd like to come with you, please."

Will paused at the edge of the bushes, waiting as she joined him, then swept a thick clump of branches aside and gestured for her to precede him through the small clearing he'd made.

She thanked him, then paused as she passed, the soft skin of her bare arm brushing his. "Will?"

He remained still. Resisted the urge to press his thumb gently to her chin and rub away the small smudge of mud that had taken up residence there. "Yeah?"

"In answer to your question, I don't have any family," she said quietly. "Not in Tennessee or anywhere else. I married years ago and I..." Her voice faded so much her words were barely discernible. "I've been widowed for five years now."

Breath catching at her loss, he did reach out then, hesitating as her eyes met his. When she lifted her chin in silent invitation, he touched his thumb to the slight indentation and rubbed the mud away, revealing clean, soft skin.

"I'm sorry, Taylor," he whispered.

Her vulnerable gaze lowered to his mouth and lingered there a few moments before she ducked her head, dislodging his touch, and ducked past him into a small clearing peppered with thick swaths of trees and bushes.

Will followed, stopping as a breeze danced over

his sweaty forehead, and admired the play of sunlight over Taylor's blond hair as she bent and poked around a low-lying set of bushes.

"There's plenty of sunlight in this meadow," he said, glancing around the lush green clearing. "There's bound to be some wild strawberries."

"And blackberries." She straightened and held out her hand. Several plump berries filled her small palm. "How 'bout we split the first course?"

He smiled. "Sounds good."

She tipped her hand and spilled half of the blackberries into his palm. He popped a few in his mouth and closed his eyes, savoring the plump flesh and tangy juice on his parched tongue.

Taylor released a small moan of pleasure. "These are delicious."

"I second that." Will's stomach rumbled loud enough to elicit a laugh from Taylor. "Might need to find a few more, though."

Over the next half hour, they scoured a dozen more promising plants and bushes and were rewarded with several more handfuls of blackberries, wild strawberries and a few blueberries, which served as a makeshift breakfast.

"Not exactly bacon and eggs," Will said, rubbing his belly, "but that should get us by for a little while at least."

Taylor nodded and licked her lips, which were stained an adorable shade of red. "Most definitely." She smiled. "Must've been because I was starving, but those berries were the best meal I've had in a long time."

Will cocked an eyebrow. "Better than a rib-eye steak in a five-star restaurant on a first date?"

She grinned. "Mayb—"

A loud crash broke the peaceful stillness of the sunny meadow, birds scattered and two bulky figures barreled through a set of tall bushes fifty yards behind Taylor.

Will froze. "Taylor," he whispered quietly, holding out a shaky hand. "Turn around and walk back toward me very slowly."

SIX

Eyes wide, Taylor turned slowly. There, on the opposite side of the meadow, stood two black bears, head-to-head, eyes locked. The largest bear emitted a series of aggressive grunts, ducked low, then sprang up, swiping his massive paw across the smaller bear's nose.

Immediately, the smaller bear lunged, charged head-first and wrestled with its dominant counterpart. The two rose on their hind legs, locking teeth and claws as they flung each other to and fro. Their black hides rippled in the sunlight, thick clumps of fur flew in all directions and fragile branches broke under the animals' muscular bulk.

Taylor backed toward Will, her arms stiff by her sides. Her feet moved blindly behind her, stumbling over slippery mud and tangled twigs, and she reached back with one arm, her fingers searching for Will's hand.

His warm palm closed around hers and tugged, guiding her back a few feet until she reached his side. Edging in front of her, Will pressed one long leg against hers and nudged her into slow, measured steps in the direction of the riverbank.

The battle between the bears continued. Growls, cracks and crashes echoed around the tree-lined clearing.

Taylor glanced over her shoulder. The mud-slicked bank they'd traveled lay a mere five feet behind them now, each careful step they took bringing them closer to a safer distance from the angry bears.

She gripped Will's solid biceps with her free hand, drawing comfort from his solid strength, then whispered, "We're almost there. Five more feet to the tree line and one more foot after that to the bank."

His hand tightened around hers in response.

The chaos ceased. Having managed to writhe its way free from the clutch of the dominant bear, the smaller bear dived through crushed bushes and hustled out of sight.

Four feet. Taylor glanced behind her once more and bit her lip. Three, now.

Sharp popping sounds rang out across the clearing, echoing against the tree line. Ears back, the dominant bear, facing them, stood motionless and eyed them from afar. The popping noise continued as the bear clacked his molars together and pawed the ground.

Black eyes, angry and intent, pinned to Taylor's face, surveying, measuring…weighing whether or not to attack. His lips drew back, daggerlike teeth emerged and a deep growl rumbled in the animal's wide chest.

Strangely, Preston's angry hiss whispered through her mind, rolling through her on a familiar wave of debilitating fear.

Don't move. Stay right there, and I'll come to you.

Her legs froze, still three feet from the tree line and four from the riverbank. A sensation of terror snaked up her spine and wound about her like a massive fist, tightening around her throat, constricting her lungs and spurring goose bumps on her flesh. She could easily recall the feel of the hard kitchen tile beneath her back as he'd approached. Feel the desperate urge to flee at the same time her limbs refused to move.

"Taylor?"

When you make mistakes, Taylor, you have to pay for them. It's the only way to learn.

"Taylor." Will squeezed her hand hard and, gaze trained on the bear, spoke in low tones. "Keep walking to the side and back slowly. He's wound up and on the defensive. We're just in the wrong place at the wrong time." Will straightened and rolled his shoulders, the protective posture of his muscular back lifting, edging fully in front of her and obscuring her vision. "We're leaving now, buddy. We'll be out of your hair in just a sec."

Body trembling, she tried to focus on the baritone of Will's calm voice and forced her feet to move again. They resumed backing away, covering three more feet of muddy ground until they finally reached the tree line.

A branch poked sharply into Taylor's back and she rose to her toes and peered over Will's shoulder. The bear stood where it had moments before, hunched low to the ground, staring them down.

Slowly, Taylor reached back with her free hand, lifted the branch overhead and slipped underneath. Mud squelched beneath her shoes and her legs faltered, sliding unsteadily.

"Will," she urged softly, lifting the branch higher and tugging his elbow. "Come on."

He eased beneath the branch and joined her on the bank, then cupped her raised forearm with his palm and helped her lower the branch. Thick stems and wide leaves slowly curtained the bear's glare.

The urge to run shot through Taylor's veins, but she linked hands with Will instead and continued taking slow, measured steps sideways up the riverbank. Beyond the tree line, twigs snapped, leaves rustled and sporadic glimpses of the bear's dark fur appeared between gaps in the tree line.

"He's following us." Taylor's throat felt raw, her words leaving her in shaky bursts.

Will kept his gaze on the bear's movements behind the thick foliage and raised his voice over the roar of the rapids beside them. "What's behind us? Is the path clear?"

She gripped his hand with both of hers and looked over her shoulder. "No. There's a sharp incline filled with rocks and it merges with trees. There are low branches, thick brush."

Rustling continued behind the trees, drawing closer.

Will raised their entwined hands above their heads and spoke louder. "If he charges, don't run—that'll provoke him. Stand your ground, shout him down and fight. Throw your back up and try to look bigger than he is. It's the only way to scare him off."

The rhythmic crash of branches and leaves beyond the tree line slowed with each of Will's words. An eerie stillness settled over the bear's hulking form as he stopped moving and watched them retreat.

"There's something wrong with him," Taylor said, waving her arms alongside Will as they increased the distance between them and the bear. "He should've run from us by now, but he's not afraid of us. He's—"

"Predatory." Will's mouth tightened, his eyes sharpening on the tree line. "And the two of us would fill his gut a whole lot more than those berries he trampled." Releasing her hand, he reached back and pressed his palm to her middle, nudging her farther back. "Find a path through the brush behind us and get a head start, but don't turn your back."

"No. I won't leave you."

"You're not leaving me." He glanced over his shoulder, his warm gaze meeting hers. "You're helping me. Helping us." His big palm pushed her again as he turned his head and refocused on the dark hulking figure poised several feet away. "Go, Taylor. Keep your eyes this way and make a path for us."

She hesitated, her attention torn between Will's strong hand pressing against her belly and the imposing figure lurking among the trees.

"Please go," Will repeated, raising his arms back over his head in a warding-off motion.

Branches rustled along the tree line, and Taylor, galvanized by a surge of adrenaline, took one unsteady step backward, then another…and another, until her outstretched arm met the soft brush of leaves.

Feet stumbling over an uneven pile of rocks, she felt her way back through the thick underbrush. Thorns scraped her bare thighs and low-hanging branches ensnared her hair, yanking hard, delivering sharp stings to her scalp as she passed, but she forged on, breaking thin branches, stomping tangled shrubs and carving a path for Will, who fell farther and farther behind.

She reached the end of the thicket of trees, bushes

and rocks, and the familiar suck of mud returned as her thin water shoes settled into the wet riverbank. Grabbing a thick, low-hanging branch closest to her, she wedged her shoulder underneath it, forced it up, then waited, watching as Will crouched and traced her steps, easing his way back through gnarled branches and sharp stones.

"This way," she beckoned, her pulse pounding in her ears, melding with the roar of white water that surged along the rapids beside her. "There's an opening right behind you. About seven feet back."

Will, still crouching low, worked his way through the tangled brush, ducked beneath the branch she'd raised and stilled by her side.

They waited. Listened. Water splashed over boulders and crashed along the riverbank. Birds chirped overhead, and a squirrel wound its way up the thick trunk of a nearby birch tree. But the rhythmic rustle of the bear's movements had stopped and the sinister feel of its stalking presence receded.

"I think it's gone," Will said quietly. He eased back on his haunches and exhaled. Blood trickled over his left biceps and streamed in thin rivulets down his tanned forearm.

"You're hurt." Taylor lifted his arm and inspected the blood trail, seeking the source.

Will joined her, probing along the injury on his upper arm with his fingertips. "It's nothing—just a cut. A thorn caught me on the way through."

"It *is* something," she said. "Something bad enough to bleed at least." She grabbed the hem of her T-shirt, located the cleanest section of cloth and tore the fabric, ripping a long strip free. "Lift your arm out, please."

He did as she requested, his soft breaths whispering through her hair as she bent over his injury, wrapped the cloth around his biceps and tied a knot, securing it into a makeshift bandage.

"There," she said softly. "That'll at least help stop the bleeding."

His fingers brushed her temple, stroked her damp hair back over her shoulder. Then his warm palm cupped her cheek. "Are you all right?"

The gentle caress of his touch and low throb of his voice almost coaxed her into sagging against him, resting her head on his wide chest and sinking into his protective embrace.

Almost…

"I'm okay." Her voice, when it finally emerged from her constricted throat, sounded gravelly. She cleared her throat, gently removed his hand from her cheek and stood. "We better get going. Put some more distance between us and the bear."

She didn't wait for him to follow, but headed off instead, taking brisk—if slightly unsteady—steps across the muddy bank and up the increasing incline of the winding bank. So much for wanting to keep her distance from him. Every moment she spent with him in this wild backcountry revealed another layer of his caring nature, protective instincts and gruff tenderness she'd never found in a man before. Any one of those attributes would be enough to attract a woman's attention, much less all three at once.

After a few moments, his heavy tread fell in step beside her and she could feel his gaze on her. His careful inspection of her expression made her cheeks burn and her skin tingle where the gentle support of his palm still lingered.

They continued walking in silence, slipping over wet stretches of the bank where puddles of rain had accumulated overnight and climbing over tall piles of stones and boulders along bends in the river. Last night's storm had dumped so much rain into the river the white water swelled twice as high as it had the night before, each set of rapids barreling faster down the landscape and leaving no safe place to cross the river.

Three hours later, they'd covered almost two and a half miles, stopping every half mile to scan their surroundings and call out to Andi. They received no response, and each time silence greeted Will's calls for his daughter, his expression darkened, his hopes visibly dimming. Which was no wonder, considering what they'd just been up against. If they'd run into an aggressive black bear here, there was every chance Andi may have run into one wherever she was now.

Taylor stumbled midstep. That terrifying thought alone would be too much for any loving father to endure.

Soon, the sun rose high in the sky and heat beat down on their heads and shoulders. Taylor paused, wiped her sweaty forehead with the back of her hand and plucked her damp T-shirt from her midriff, fanning it away from her skin and creating a breeze against her sweat-slicked abs.

"We've covered a lot of ground." Will stopped beside her and dragged his hand through his wet hair. "Almost three miles, if I've calculated correctly. We can rest here for a while, if you'd like, then head farther upriver. See if there might be a safer place to cross?"

Taylor shook her head. "I'm good if you want to conti—"

Will lifted a hand, halting her speech, then looked away and tilted his head. "Do you hear that?"

In the distance, a soft beating sound emerged. The rhythmic whooshing grew more distinct as it drew closer, transforming into a strong pulse of power that rebounded crisply off nearby mountain peaks.

Taylor's pulse kicked up a notch and her eyes widened as she met Will's gaze, an equally excited hope returning to his expression.

He smiled. "Rescue chopper."

Will could barely suppress the renewed energy charging through his veins at the thought of a helicopter approaching. Automatically, his feet slipped and slid over the muddy riverbank as he lunged forward, running toward the sound of whirling blades.

"It's up ahead," he shouted over his shoulder. "Just around the bend, from the sounds of it."

Maybe Jax, Beth and Martin had fared better than he'd assumed. Maybe they'd made it out of the rapids and hiked far enough upriver to reach a cell signal, call for help and summon a rescue chopper in their direction. Maybe—his heart slammed against his ribs—Andi had already been rescued. Maybe it wasn't such a stretch of hope to imagine she sat in the chopper now, miles above him, looking safely down on the wilds of the Smokies.

Please let her be there, he prayed silently.

Taylor's voice, a mere wisp of a sound that faded even more with each of his pounding steps, barely broke through the wind whistling past his ears. "Wait!"

He kept running. Jumped over a scattering of sharp rocks lining the bank. Ducked beneath the low sprawling limb of a spruce tree. Something sharp jabbed his cheek. He swiped at it and pressed on.

The tree line fell back and a mud-slicked bank appeared again. He stomped through it, tilting his head back as he ran, and scanned the sky. There, about two hundred yards out, he spotted the barest outline of an approaching helicopter high above.

"There it is!" he shouted.

He glanced around wildly, registering a steep, densely foliaged embankment on the opposite side of the river and a less imposing bluff to his right. No way would the pilot catch a glimpse of him here, wedged between two high banks, hidden beneath dense vegetation and overshadowed by the roaring force of the river.

The bluff's sloping face—though mud-slicked—was scarcely populated with trees and bushes…but scalable. And the only other option was to stand here beside the rapids, stare helplessly at an unreachable sky and hope that the pilot passing above would glance his way.

Nope. This might be the best chance he had of reaching Andi today. He had no choice but to try.

Sprinting toward the base of the bluff, he waved an arm in Taylor's direction. "Stay here. I'm gonna try to get as close as I can."

"Please, Will. Don't g…"

Taylor's words faded away as he dug his hands into the muddy bluff, grabbed a handful of wet earth and hauled his body onto the sloping face. Keeping close to the ground, he yanked his hands and feet from the mud and climbed higher. Faster. Seeking out drier sections of earth as he ascended, straining to maintain his grip, reaching with his right arm, then left. Climbing higher and higher.

The whir of helicopter blades drew closer. Body jerking on a bolt of urgency, he sprang up, swiped at the trunk of a river birch—and missed!

Wet ground gave way beneath his feet and he slid haphazardly downward, gaining speed, his arms scrambling for a secure hold. Then, abruptly, he stopped.

He glanced down, his eyes meeting Taylor's.

She blinked up at him, pain flooding her pretty features as she stiffened her upper body and repositioned her foot against the trunk of a birch below her. Her left shoulder and back wedged tighter against his right hip and thigh, providing a stable support for the right half of his body.

He stared down at her, momentarily taken aback by her strength, relief and admiration surging through him.

"You wanna get your bearings back?" Her voice trembled and she grimaced under the increasing pressure of his weight as he slid farther down. "I can't brace you here forever."

Immediately, he renewed his hold on a somewhat dry section of ground and yanked, lifting part of his weight off Taylor and heaving himself upward.

The helicopter approached, its underside barely visible through a clump of branches above him in the distance.

Will stretched his arm out, reaching for a higher handhold, when a sharp crack rang out high above and an increasingly loud crash barreled down the sloping bluff.

"Oh, no," he whispered hoarsely, craning his head around to look down at Taylor. "Go back, Taylor!"

"What?" Frowning, she stopped midclimb, then froze as her gaze swept past him toward the top of the bluff.

"Go back," he shouted. "Mudslide!"

The word had barely escaped his lips when the earth shifted beneath his hands and a heavy tangle of slimy mud, uprooted trees and crushed deadfall waved down the slope, slamming into them.

Will shifted his weight, throwing himself onto his back, and did his best to control his descent toward Taylor, his body shifting and sliding rapidly along mud and loose soil. Debris swept past him and plunged over Taylor, sweeping her away from her safe perch against a tree trunk and tumbling her down the bluff.

Shoving off with his hands, Will maneuvered himself in Taylor's direction, reached her side and shot his hand out, grabbing her arm and hauling her to his side. He wrapped one arm around her waist, tucked her cheek to his chest and covered the back of her head with his hand, protecting her as best as he could against the onslaught of debris rolling over and under them.

A sharp cry escaped her, and she curled her fists into his T-shirt and wrapped one of her legs around one of his, holding on as they sped down the sloping embankment.

Wood cracked, leafy branches swept past them and stones of various sizes bounced in every direction, narrowly missing his head.

"Will!"

Frantic, Taylor clutched him closer as they tumbled, twisted and rolled at full speed. The roar of the rapids rushed closer and the hard mud-slicked bank and boulders flashed below.

Will's throat closed. This was it. They'd come as far as they'd ever get. At the speed they traveled and height they plummeted, their bodies would slam against the rocks, shattering their bones and cracking their skulls. And if they were lucky enough to be carried over the boulders by plunging earth, they'd be thrown into the river and tossed along the rapids, most likely drowning minutes after they hit the white water.

A panicked, humorless laugh burst from his lips. In moments, they'd be right back where they started, at the mercy of the water, gasping for breath as violent white water snatched their life by slow, cold degrees of suffocation.

Andi. Will tried to open his eyes, tried to focus on the blue sky swirling above, his view impeded by each rolling wave of thick mud and painful dig of tumbling debris. The whir of helicopter blades disappeared and the roar of sliding earth filled his ears, drowning out every ounce of hope that still whispered in his soul.

Andi. He'd failed her, and may never see her again.

SEVEN

Taylor flinched as a broken branch dug into her waist, tightened her fists on Will's shirt and pressed her cheek against the base of his throat.

"Andi…" His warm skin vibrated against her cheek on the hoarse whisper, his words laced with pain and desperation.

Mud shoved them farther down the embankment and coated their arms and legs. She squeezed her eyes shut and savored the protective strength of Will's arms around her and hand cradling the back of her head. Gratitude swept through her on an oddly comforting sensation.

Wherever they landed, whatever happened next… at least, this time, she wasn't alone.

The heavy crash of debris raining down around them was overcome with the roar of water.

The river. Taylor tensed. They were headed straight for the river.

Their descent continued, the muddy earth beneath their bodies slipping, sliding, then flinging them through the air. Memories of rocks and hard ground flashed through her mind, sending a fresh wave of panic through her. Her stomach dropped and her muscles tensed in preparation for impact.

Icy water smacked against her limbs and face, surged over her head and sucked her body farther downward until her feet hit hard earth—the riverbed, maybe?—and her legs buckled beneath her.

Weightless, her limbs jerked up, pulled along a swift current that lifted her body and rolled her to a supine position. Her face broke the water's surface and she dragged in a lungful of air, her throat burning. She reached out, grasping for a renewed hold on Will, but her hands only met water and rocks.

"W-Will!" Her lips, cold and wet, trembled. She licked away a fresh spray of white water and tried to regain her bearings.

Wispy clouds and blue sky flew past overhead. Green foliage, blurry, sped by in her peripheral vision. She kicked her legs and stroked her arms, just managing to lift her head and scan her surroundings.

Boulders, steep drops and the spray of white water filled her vision. Bracing, she lowered her head as the rapids plunged her over a series of drops that seemed to go on and on.

She cleared a drop and the rapids spit her out to a smoother stretch of water. Raising her head again, she immediately recognized the angry churn of the falls.

"No!" Taylor beat fiercely against the water with her legs and arms, straining to regain control.

They'd made it safely over the falls once; there were no guarantees they'd escape unscathed a second time. And Will…

Panic surged in her chest as she frantically looked around. Where was he?

Up ahead, to the right, a thick log protruded from the bank. Taylor kicked and swam against the fierce current, stretched out her arms and lunged, managing to grab the log. She dug her nails in and pulled her upper body onto it.

"Will," she shouted, scanning the area for any sign of him.

Water swept past, dipping over low falls and churning around boulders. A minute passed, then another and another, each second stretching into an eternity.

Where was he? Surely he'd traveled the same path she had. They'd been holding on to each other when they'd hit the water.

Her mouth ran dry as another thought occurred to her. What if he'd traveled ahead of her? What if he'd already plunged over the falls?

Mouth parting, she stared downriver at the point where white water converged, sped up and dropped over a steep edge, out of sight. If he'd plunged over the falls alone, he could be at the bottom of the gorge now—unconscious like she had been last night. At the mercy of the water. Stranded alone like his daughter.

Andi...

Taylor froze, the painful tone of Will's voice as he'd called for his daughter minutes earlier still fresh on her mind...and heart.

No. She shook her head, a sob rising in her throat, and lowered her chin to the log. Will loved Andi so much—Taylor had recognized that almost immediately after meeting the two of them. For Will and Andi to lose each other like this—

"Please, God..." Her voice surprised her, the hesitant words she whispered out loud, amid the vicious roar of white water, pouring from a deep-seated ache in her chest. "Please bring Will to safety. Please let him and Andi survive this and find each other."

She hadn't spoken to God directly in so long she wasn't sure if He heard her. And she had no idea if He would even answer someone like her. Why should He when she'd lived apart from Him for so long?

I've lived without Him...and I've lived with Him.

Taylor closed her eyes and breathed deep, drawing strength from the memory of Will's words.

I keep talking to Him and He comes through one way or another.

"Please," she pleaded again. "Will's a good, faithful man. He deserves all the help You're willing to give. Please help him. For his sake, if not for mine."

"Taylor!"

Her eyes sprang open. She bolted upright and swiveled her head in the direction of the shout. It originated upriver. Somewhere to the lef—

"Will," she shouted back, a wide smile fighting its way to her lips.

There he was, floating on his back, feetfirst, around a sharp bend, being swept swiftly along the current in her direction.

Taylor stretched over the log and reached out with one hand, her other arm wrapped snugly around the log beneath her. "Swim over as close as you can! I'll grab you and pull you in!"

Will rolled over and swam vigorously in Taylor's direction, his dark eyes darting between her and the rapidly approaching falls, then back again. A panicked urgency suffused his expression as his progress slowed, the powerful rapids yanking him in another direction.

He glanced at the falls again, his eyes moving over various paths along the water, a worried look appearing. The current moved fast, dragging him closer and closer to the impending drop.

"You trust me?" she shouted.

His dark gaze met hers and his mouth parted soundlessly.

"I won't leave you!" She stretched her arm out farther, her fingers grasping in his direction. "If you go over, I'll follow. We're in this together, I promise." A fierce energy swept over her and entered her voice. "Do you trust me?"

He drew closer, the window of opportunity narrowing. A look of resolution entered his eyes. "Yes."

"Then do it!"

He lunged out of the water toward her, but the rapids yanked him back, causing him to fall short half a foot.

She managed to snag his upper arm as he passed, her fingers curling tightly around his biceps. He latched on to her arm in return, his hand grasping her upper arm, as well.

His weight pulled her upper body down to the edge of the log. She wrapped her legs around it and hooked her feet at the ankles, straining to maintain her grip as he pulled toward her.

When he drew close, he grabbed the log with his free hand, yanked himself out of the swift-moving current and hauled his body along it and onto shore.

Taylor released his arm once he had his bearings, shoved herself upright and carefully crawled backward along the log.

"Taylor." A strong arm wrapped around her waist and lifted her from the log. "Hold on to me."

Moments later, she was pressed tight to Will's side and she curled her arms around his shoulders as he dragged them onto the riverbank. They lay still for a couple of minutes, their chests heaving with labored breaths, and raspy coughs escaped them sporadically.

Soon, Taylor's breathing calmed and the burning sensation in her lungs subsided. She stared up at the blue sky, the bright late-afternoon sun warm on her skin and a small, unfamiliar feeling unfurling within her.

"He answered me," she whispered.

It was silent for a moment, save for the rush of the river.

Will shifted beside her, his legs moving restlessly. She rolled her head to the side and met his eyes.

His brow furrowed. "What'd you say?"

"I said, He answered me." Smiling, she added softly, "When I made it out of the water, I couldn't see you. I didn't know where you were. If you'd gone over the falls or—" Her voice broke and a relieved laugh burst from her lips. "I was so scared and I had no idea what to do. So I did what you said. I kept talking to Him. I prayed and asked Him to help you. To help Andi." Her smile widened. "And there you were. You just came out of nowhere, calling my name."

She tipped her head back and looked up at the sky again, a silent prayer of gratitude moving through her mind. "I've never heard Him answer me before. But He answered this time."

Another breeze swept over the river, bending the trees that lined the bank and cooling her wet skin. The gentle feel of it strengthened that pleasant sensation blooming in her chest.

A growl of frustration erupted beside her and Will shot to his feet.

Startled by his abrupt movement, Taylor sat up as he paced quickly in front of her, stalking in one direction, then the other, narrowing his eyes at the mountain range in the distance.

"You call this an answer?" His hands balled into fists by his sides and an angry hiss escaped him. "This isn't an answer," he said through gritted teeth. "Don't you see where we are?" He waved an arm in the air, stabbing his hand at the falls. "We're right back where we started. We scaled a wall and spent the better part of the day hiking almost four miles just to end up right back where we were hours ago."

Taylor's smile slowly faded.

His expression contorted in anger and his voice hardened. "There's no way that pilot saw us—if it even was a rescue chopper. Andi's already spent one night alone in the middle of nowhere, injured. There's no way we can regain the ground we've lost just now. We've got no shelter, no supplies, no food or clean water. And you call this an answer?"

Heart breaking at the fear in his tone, she looked down and twisted the hem of her T-shirt. Water spilled from it and splashed against a rock beside her. "I only meant—"

"What?" Will bit out. "What did you mean? That He did us a favor? Andi is miles away, alone in backcountry. That bear you and I saw earlier today—" he swept his arm toward the sprawling landscape at his back "—that's only a peek of what's out there. The best estimate I've ever heard for this area suggests there's two bears roaming every couple of square miles surrounding us. There are at least three miles standing between me and my daughter right now."

Pain laced his tone and his chin trembled. He spun away and tilted his head back, the knuckles of his clenched fists turning white by his sides.

"You call this an answer?" he shouted to the sky. "How could You do it? Andi needed You and—" Voice cracking, he raked a hand through his thick hair, then bent, grabbed a loose stone from the bank and hurled it into the rapids.

Taylor watched as the stone smacked into a spray of white water, skipped over the swell of a wave, then bounced onto the opposite bank. It settled on a smooth stretch of rock—close to where she and Will had sat hours earlier, relishing their success of scaling the wall and evading a snake.

She stood, her smile slowly returning. "You done with that temper tantrum of yours? Because if you are, there's something you should know."

Will stiffened, the angry panic shooting through him intensifying at the sound of Taylor's chipper tone. When he faced her, the bright smile spreading across her face only made it worse.

"You good now?" she asked, grinning wider. "Because I want to make sure you hear what I'm about to tell you."

What could she possibly say right now to make this right? And what in the world did she have to smile about? Here they were, stranded in the middle of nowhere with next to no chance of reaching Andi before tomorrow, and she somehow managed to find humor in the situation?

He swallowed an angry retort—along with a good, healthy dose of pride—and nodded slowly. "Go ahead."

"We're not in exactly the same place we were hours ago," she explained calmly, motioning toward the river behind his back. "We're on the opposite side of the river than we were this morning. We're on the same side Andi is on now."

He glanced over his shoulder and stared across the rapids at the smooth stone he'd sat on with Taylor hours before, divulging his secrets and fears, drawing comfort from her consoling words. Then he spun around and studied the unfamiliar stretch of riverbank and thick forest that lay before them now—a completely different view than the one he and Taylor had faced this morning.

"We don't have to find a place to cross the river now," Taylor continued. "That mudslide..." She grimaced. "It wasn't my favorite part of the day so far, but it did the trick. It threw us to the other side of the river."

Will looked at the new terrain before them for a few more moments, then studied her face, a hesitant note entering his voice. "That's only a good thing if Andi made it across the rocks to the bank."

Her expression gentled, an understanding light entering her eyes. "Is Andi as stubborn as you?"

His lips twitched despite the residual fear and anger simmering inside him. "Yeah. She's twice as stubborn."

"Then she definitely made it. And I'd say that's a pretty good answer for the situation we're in right now."

Yep. She had a point. God had given them an answer—he'd just been too angry and stubborn to see it. Instead, he'd railed against God and Taylor, blaming them both for Andi's predicament. That alone was enough to shame him.

Face burning, he ducked his head and kneaded the back of his neck. "I..." He cleared his throat and tried again. "I'm sorry. I don't usually lose my cool like that. I never intended to offend you. Or scare you. Or—"

"It's okay," she said softly. "You don't have to apologize. You're a great dad and you're worried for your daughter. I understood." She tilted her head, her gaze drifting over him slowly, and a look of surprise moved through her expression. "And you didn't scare me." Her blue eyes met his and a blush bloomed along her freckled cheeks. "I'm not afraid when I'm with you."

The weight of her admission hung on the air between them. Something in her tone—awe or wonder, maybe?—unsettled him. He watched her face, an ache spreading through him at the wounded vulnerability in her eyes.

"Taylor. Has someone h—?"

"We better get moving." She looked away, that brief flash of vulnerability masked and set aside, almost as though it had never existed. "The sun'll set in a couple of hours, and we need to find a place to bed down for the night, don't you think?"

He moved to answer, but she turned away, stepped carefully over the rocks scattered along the riverbank and began hiking into the woods ahead.

Will rolled his shoulders and stretched the strained muscles in his arms and legs, then followed in her wake, contemplating all the while what—*or who*— had put that look in Taylor's eyes.

For over an hour, they hiked through thick forest, ducking beneath leafy branches, forcing their way through thorny underbrush and climbing over fallen trees. A sore, tender feeling began to spread through Will's arms and legs, weighing him down and slowing his steps. He couldn't help but notice that Taylor's previously energetic pace had waned, as well.

Will, breathing deeply, stopped as they reached a small clearing and took stock of their surroundings. "This might be a good place to set up camp for the night." He motioned at the woods surrounding them across the meadow. "There's plenty of deadfall and a sturdy oak over there where we can set up a lean-to for the night."

Taylor wiped her brow and sighed. "Sounds good to me. What would you like me to do?"

Her shoulders sagged and the color in her face had receded, her complexion having paled slightly. There was an almost imperceptible tremor running through her legs—not much, but enough that he noticed.

Will frowned. All of that was to be expected. She'd climbed two embankments, tumbled down a mudslide, dragged herself and him out of the river and had hiked at least five miles today with little food and no clean water. And yesterday's drama was in addition to today's challenges. It was a miracle they'd made it as far as they had.

He winced. "Look, you've got to be exhausted. Why don't you sit and rest while I take care of the lean-to?"

She closed her eyes and leaned her head back, her face tilted to catch the fading glow of the sun, which slowly lowered below the horizon in the distance. "Aren't you tired, too?"

The graceful curve of her neck caught his eye, and he watched as a bead of sweat trickled down from her nape, veered over her shoulder and settled in the gentle dip within her collarbone. An errant strand of her hair fluttered in the breeze and caught on her thick eyelashes. He admired her elegant profile for a moment, then tore his gaze away and looked down instead, kicking a large pine cone that rested beside his shoe.

"Yeah." His voice sounded husky. He cleared his throat, rubbed his palms over his thighs and smiled. "To be honest with you, if I stretched out on the ground right now, I wouldn't be able to move again for at least ten hours."

"Then we'll both build the lean-to." A twig snapped as she faced him, her clear blue eyes brightened by her grin, and her pretty features drew him in again. "Together," she added softly.

Together. His smile grew so much his sunburned cheeks smarted. He liked the sound of that word on Taylor's lips. A whole lot more than he'd expected.

"I'll take you up on that." His conscience told him to stop there, to resist voicing any more thoughts aloud and avoid hinting at any ounce of sentimentality. But the emotions welling within him tumbled off his own lips before he could halt them. "I won't say I'm glad we're stuck out here, but if I had to be in this position again, I can't say I'd want anyone else by my side other than you. You're an amazing woman, Taylor Holt. I hope you know that."

The bright spark in her blue eyes started to fade and her grin slipped.

What was wrong in what he'd said? Had he offended her? He hoped not. Despite not knowing which words had hurt her, his hands rose slightly as if to take them back. To gather them up and hide them away. If for no other reason than to see that relaxed look of happiness return to her expression.

"I used to think so," she whispered. "A long time ago."

She walked away, her long blond hair swinging gently across her back. She bent and picked up a sturdy dead branch off the forest bed. "Is this a good length for the support beam of the lean-to you're planning?"

He shrugged. "It'll do fine. Tayl—?"

"Can we just focus on the lean-to for now?" Her voice trembled and she dipped her head, avoiding his eyes. "Please?"

Will hesitated, wanting to continue the conversation. Wanting to ask more questions—any she'd allow him to—just so long as she opened up to him a bit more. But clearly, she wasn't ready for that.

"Of course," he said softly. "Whatever you want."

Collecting branches, snapping each to the right length and arranging them into the formation of a slanted roof between the trunks of two oak trees took over an hour and sapped the last bit of strength left in Will's body.

"Well," he said, inspecting the crude shelter, "it's definitely not a five-star hotel, but it'll get us through the night." Spotting a large gap in between two logs, he sighed and looked up. Dusk had fallen and there were no clouds in the slowly darkening sky, which eased his worries a bit. "There'll be a big gap over our heads, but there aren't any clouds, so no chance of rain tonight, that I can tell. We could pile some moss over the top if you'd like? Just to be safe?"

Taylor shook her head and smiled. "Nah. It's summer, so it won't get too chilly tonight, and besides, I kinda like the gap. It's like a moon roof. Or a little window to the stars."

Will laughed. "That's a nice way of looking at it." He waved a hand at the wide opening. "After you."

She slipped under the small roof and settled on the ground, a heavy sigh of exhaustion escaping her. Will followed suit and sat beside her.

"The house itself might not be worth market price," Taylor said, her gaze moving slowly over the scenery before them, "but the view is worth a mil."

He followed her gaze, his body relaxing as he took in the sights before them. The sun had dipped below the horizon and a glorious blaze of color spread across the night sky, then slowly receded, casting a pink and lavender glow over the misty meadow in front of them.

Trees rustled on the other side of the clearing. Will sat up straighter, his hands clenching against his thighs as the low rumble of the bear from hours earlier returned to his mind. But then two figures emerged, one large and one small, gracefully making their way into the center of the meadow, and emotion washed over him.

"Taylor," he whispered, touching her forearm. "Look."

There, just visible amid the light mist settling over the clearing, a mother elk and calf strolled across the damp ground, bent their heads and grazed soundlessly several feet away.

"Oh, how beautiful," Taylor whispered. Blue eyes on the elk, her hand sought his, her warm fingers slipping between his and her soft palm pressing snugly to his own. She watched quietly for a few minutes, then said softly, "Maybe it's another answer. One we haven't been looking for." Her tone was thin. Uncertain, but laced with a thread of hope he hadn't heard in her voice before. "Maybe this is His way of telling us there are more good things to come."

Under the increasing fall of darkness, she leaned more heavily against him. He lifted his arm carefully, slid it around her shoulders, and she drifted into sleep, her cheek resting against his chest. Her slow, steady pulse, beating rhythmically just beneath her skin, mingled with his own, their heartbeats a soothing sensation between their joined palms.

There were no more questions and no more answers. No more conversation of any kind for the rest of the night. But as sleep tugged heavily at Will, he couldn't help but smile, despite the fears he still harbored for Andi's safety. Just the feel of Taylor's even breaths whispering over his chest, the warm weight of her pressing against his side and the hint of hope in her words—the thought that God would help them make it out of this...and find Andi—was enough to calm his worries for the night.

EIGHT

Warmth bloomed over Taylor's skin and a soft orange glow seeped through her closed eyelids. She stirred slowly, breathing deeply, and opened her eyes.

A white T-shirt lay beneath her cheek and the muscular curve of Will's chest supported her head, lifting slightly with each of his slow breaths. Carefully, so as not to disturb him, she removed her palm from his shoulder and sat up.

His even breathing paused. Then his chest rose on a deep inhalation and he rolled his head to the side, settling when he found a more comfortable position against the logs forming the wall of the lean-to at his back.

Taylor smiled and watched him silently for a few moments, admiring the relaxed sprawl of his toned limbs and peaceful set of his handsome features.

She studied his tousled hair, defined cheekbones, stubbled jaw and wide chest. Last night, she'd been so exhausted that she'd fallen asleep moments after sitting beneath the lean-to. Her last memory before drifting off had been enjoying the sight of elk grazing in the meadow as the sun had slowly disappeared behind the mountain range in the distance. Soon after, she'd closed her eyes and the comforting weight of Will's strong arm had settled around her shoulders. Rather than unsettling her, the protective strength of his gentle hold had eased her fears and his supportive touch had stayed with her all night.

I'm not afraid when I'm with you.

Her heart skipped a beat as she recalled her words from yesterday. She couldn't believe she'd uttered them out loud, but they were just as true today.

Being around Will felt completely different than the time she'd spent with Preston.

With Preston, she'd tiptoed around him in person and in conversation, always afraid to do or say something that would ignite his temper. Each morning, she'd choked back her fear, poured his coffee and prepared his breakfast with a steady hand, her fingers cramping for an hour afterward from the strain of fighting off nervous tremors to avoid spilling anything and setting off his temper. And each night, she'd pulled back the top sheet—the clean white sateen set Preston liked—and lain stiffly in bed, waiting and wondering, always wondering through the long dark hours, if his attention would turn to her...and how badly his touch might hurt.

In all the years she'd lived with Preston, she couldn't recall a single night she'd slept peacefully. But last night, in Will's arms, on damp ground in the middle of backcountry, she'd slept more deeply and soundly than she ever had before.

Will's lips parted and a soft sound escaped him.

Taylor sat quietly for a minute, and when he didn't awaken, she eased out of the lean-to and moved away quietly, strolling across the meadow. Tall grass, beaded with dew, brushed her shins and tickled her knees. Disturbed by her steps, two butterflies fluttered up from the thick grass and flew away, their colorful wings silhouetted against the golden sun rising in the distance, peeking over the mountain range.

Stopping at the edge of the meadow, she hugged her arms across her chest and blinked away the last lingering dregs of sleep as she watched the sun's bright glow spread slowly across the sky. Her muscles ached, her throat was parched—all things considered, she should feel pretty ragged by now.

But she didn't.

She grinned, tipped her chin up and savored the gentle warmth of the sun's rays. The higher the sun rose, the more the sky lit up with color. Pink, lavender and purple streaked in all directions, creating a stark contrast with the white mist hovering low along the mountain range.

"You trying to tell me something?" she whispered softly, her gaze drifting over the spectacular sky above her. "Because I'm ready to listen now. I'm ready to do my part."

That small feeling that had stirred within her yesterday grew a little bit more. It streamed through her veins, warmed her skin the night air had cooled and lifted her chin higher.

You're an amazing woman, Taylor Holt. I hope you know that.

A twinge of regret returned, drawing her spirit down, and her vision blurred. A hot tear rolled over her cheek and settled in the corner of her mouth. She licked it away, the salty taste lingering on her tongue.

Preston had taken so much from her. She'd given

him so much. Much more than she'd realized. And somewhere along the line, sometime during the years she'd spent with him, she'd lost her strength and her faith. She'd lost the person God had meant her to be.

I can be a better person, she prayed silently. *I can be who You meant for me to be. Who Will thinks I am.*

Or, at least, she hoped so. She looked down and twisted the toe of her shoe in the grass, her shoulders sagging. It was an easy thought. An easy dream. But it was a much harder accomplishment to bring to fruition in reality…especially when she was on her own.

A high-pitched call rang out and a broad-winged hawk flew overhead, coasted on the morning breeze along the tree line and circled over the thick forest beyond the meadow.

Taylor wiped her face, studied the mesmerizing sunrise once more, then glanced back at Will. He still slept, propped upright against the wall of the lean-to, head to the side, his chin resting on his shoulder.

They'd both been exhausted last night, and if his muscles had been as overworked as hers yesterday, he'd wake up to a stiff back and sore arms and legs.

Her stomach growled and she rubbed her belly, smiling absently. He'd probably be starving, too. She looked around and her gaze settled on a thick swath of bushes near the edge of the meadow, butting up against the forest. Clumps of red were visible, low among the leaves. Wild strawberries, probably. Same as the ones they'd found yesterday morning and apparently plentiful in the immediate area.

She shivered slightly and hugged her arms tight across her chest. Bears were plentiful around this area, too, according to Will. Bears like the ones they'd encountered yesterday, ones that had stalked them like prey and seemed pretty agreeable to taking berries off the menu and putting her and Will on it instead.

Taylor glanced at Will, then the forest, and back again. Well, it couldn't be helped. She was hungry, Will would be hungry when he woke, and they both needed some form of energy to hike the miles they were bound to face on their journey upriver today.

She inhaled, rubbed her shaky palms together and set her shoulders. Berries it was, then. And the sooner she tackled that pile of bushes, the better. With any luck…and maybe a little of God's help, the bears would sleep in this morning and she'd finish picking what she needed before they started roaming.

Please, Lord, she prayed silently. *Keep the bears at bay.* A bear encounter certainly wasn't the best way she could think of to start the day.

Over the next half hour, she picked through the thick bushes, plucked wild strawberries from their stems and gently piled them in the pouch she'd created in her T-shirt by folding up the hem. Branches cracked and rustled several times in the distance, setting her nerves on edge and causing her to freeze in place, but luckily, in each instance, the culprit turned out to be a frisky squirrel or hungry chipmunk.

Still, she didn't care to take any chances, so she picked up the pace, collected another handful of berries in a hurry and kept scanning the forest in front of her, peering deep into the dark areas in the distance where dense trees choked out the light of the sun.

"Breakfast as usual?"

Taylor squealed and spun around, her hands lifting

in front of her and the hem of her shirt unrolling, the berries tumbling to the ground.

"Sorry." Will raised his hands, palms out, and grimaced. "Didn't mean to startle you."

Sighing, she pressed her hand to her chest, her heart pounding beneath her palm. "Well, you did. I thought you were a bear."

His lips twitched and one dark brow rose. "Bears talk?"

Oh, boy. No doubt he was handsome, but first thing in the morning—his thick hair tousled, strong jaw lined with dark stubble and a teasing grin on his face—he was downright irresistible.

Biting back a smile, she narrowed her eyes. "This thing you're doing right now—" she wagged her pointer finger at the soft curves of his mouth "—is it sarcasm? 'Cause it's kinda hard for me to appreciate it at the moment, seeing as how we were almost eaten yesterday doing exactly what I was doing when you snuck up on me."

He shook his head, his smile growing. "Oh, I didn't sneak."

She poked her finger at his chest. "You snuck."

"All right." He laughed and covered her hand at his chest with his own, his thumb stroking the back of her wrist softly. "Maybe I did sneak, but I didn't mean to, and I promise I won't do it again." His dark head lowered and his lips brushed her knuckles softly. Then his brown eyes met hers again as he teased, "And I promise to save the sarcasm for a more appropriate place and time."

She bit her lip, the gentle touch of his mouth against her skin dancing over her wrist, up her arm and slipping dangerously close to her heart. "A m-more appropriate place and time?"

"Yeah." The teasing light in his eyes faded and a warm, hopeful expression took its place. "After this is over. When we get out of here."

He wanted to see her again. Another time, another place. After all of this? Her mouth parted, but words wouldn't emerge. That sweet tingling he'd stirred within her settled deep in her chest, stealing her breath.

The hopeful look in his eyes receded and a rueful expression appeared. "I didn't mean to overstep just now or make you uncomfortable. I just—"

"No. I..." She took a deep breath. Savored the excitement running through her, the pleasant trembling in her limbs so different than the kind of feelings Preston had always evoked in her. "I'd like that." She smiled. "Very much."

He smiled back. "I was hoping you'd say that." Clearing his throat, he glanced down at their feet and a laugh escaped him. "Sorry about spilling breakfast." He squeezed her hand, then squatted, picked up a strawberry and dusted it off. "I'll round the berries back up if you'd like to rest in the lean-to again before we head upriver."

"No, thank you." Taylor knelt beside him, placed her hand on his warm forearm and met his eyes, her heart turning over in her chest. "We'll pick them up together, then eat while the sun finishes rising. By then it'll be time for us to head out."

That charming grin returned, and before they began gathering the strawberries, Will repeated softly in the same gentle tone from last night, "Together."

* * *

Will kept a steady pace up the winding riverbank, slowing his steps a bit to keep by Taylor's side and avoid overtaxing her slightly slower gait. After the sun had fully risen, they'd finished off the last few berries, then hiked back to the riverbank and renewed their journey upriver, scanning the thick woods around them for any sign of Andi.

"Andi!" He listened carefully, studied the woods, rocks and river surrounding them, but only the sporadic chirp of birds, rustle of small animals in the trees and steady rush of the rapids met his ears.

There was no answering call and no sign of Andi.

A slow burn of restless energy coiled in his middle and his legs strained to break into a sprint, wanting so badly to race up the steady incline of dirt and rocks, round each tree-lined curve and scream her name. But that wouldn't be wise.

For one, his mind was in better shape than his body. The little bit of juice he and Taylor had gleaned from their breakfast of wild strawberries hadn't gone very far in rehydrating them, and his gut still growled on an angry demand for food. His muscles were weak, there was no way of knowing how far they'd have to hike to reach Andi, and it wouldn't be long before the taxing demands of the past three days took their toll.

Better to conserve his energy…and help Taylor conserve hers.

He glanced to his right, his gaze trailing over her flushed cheeks, bright eyes and determined expression. Her pink lips parted on swift breaths as they approached a rocky incline and admiration flooded through him at the thought of all she'd sacrificed so far for Andi…and for him. For two people who were perfect strangers to her only four days ago.

Will lifted his hand, his fingers grazing the soft skin of her forearm before curling loosely around her elbow. "Careful here." He pointed to a trail of stones that glistened beneath the morning sunlight. "There's a wet stretch near the bend in the rapids. It'll be easy to fall. You can go first if you like, and I'll follow close behind. That way if one of us slips, maybe we can manage to hold each other up."

Those beautiful eyes of hers looked up at him, a warm look of gratitude momentarily breaking past the shadow of exhaustion lining her features. "Thank you."

It'd be so easy to dismiss his concern for her as residual appreciation for the way she'd saved Andi from drowning, her ceaseless determination to accompany him on his journey to find Andi despite the dangers they faced and, most especially, the quiet words of encouragement she'd shared with him last night, calming his tirade against the unfairness of their situation and reminding him of his own sentiments that God still answered prayers even in the most difficult of times.

But that wasn't the whole truth. The strong and unexpected connection he felt for Taylor ran deeper than that, and he couldn't help but feel a strong surge of guilt. His focus should be on Andi right now. Not on Taylor, and especially not on pursuing any form of future with her.

Only…after hearing the hopeful but uncertain note in her voice last night as she'd questioned if God might be helping them even now—well, maybe this was part of that answer, too. Maybe there was a reason God had dropped him in the middle of backcountry with Taylor and not someone else. Because he couldn't resist embracing this newfound sensation of support she provided him. The kind of gentle companionship she'd offered him last night that had eased his worries and lightened his burdens. And a small voice inside him kept urging him to stick by her side to see where these feelings would take him.

"How far have we come?"

Will blinked and gripped Taylor's elbow tighter as she carefully stepped onto another wet stone. "What?"

"Miles." She glanced back at him, a concerned look passing over her face. "How many do you think we've covered so far?"

He stilled on the slippery rocks and shook his head, then glanced back at the rough terrain and up at the position of the sun, mentally calculating their progress. "Two miles? Maybe two and a half?"

She nodded, a shadow of exhaustion entering her expression. "I can see a smooth boulder just up around the bend, past the trees. Do you mind if we rest there for a few minutes?"

Yes, he did. All he wanted right now was to press on. To keep pushing with all he had to scale the next mountain and cover another mile. Anything to increase his chances of reaching Andi sooner.

"Sure," he said softly anyway, noting the slight breathlessness in her voice and slump of her shoulders. "As long as you'd like."

They pushed on, slowly stepping over deep crevices between wet stones, rounded the river bend and made their way to a smooth boulder near a set of rapids. Taylor sought a sunny spot on the sloping rock and Will followed, sitting beside her with a heavy breath.

Sunlight cut through the high trees and poured over the riverbank, warming their overheated skin even more, but the light spray of water from the rapids kept them cool, the sheen of mist forming tiny droplets on their faces, necks and bare arms and legs.

"All this water," Will said, watching the sunlight sparkle over the beads of water coating the back of his hands. "And we can't drink it."

"I know." Taylor lifted her legs up a few inches and swept her hand over the sheen of moisture on her skin. A wry smile appeared. "It's so clear and looks so fresh, it's all I can do to keep from dunking my head in the river and gulping."

He studied her face, her pretty features that had grown so familiar in such a small amount of time, and he caught himself wanting to lean against her. He wanted to dip his head, bury his face in the graceful curve of her neck and release the tears that burned at the backs of his eyes against her sun-kissed skin. To feel her arms curl around his shoulders and hug him close. To draw strength from her comforting presence.

"We could," he said softly. "But then we might end up regretting it later." A renewed surge of guilt assailed him as he thought of Andi being alone, with no one to share her fears or comfort her. He faced the river again instead, blinked hard against hot moisture brimming along his lashes and clenched his jaw. "Andi probably feels the same way right now. She's probably dehydrated, exhausted and hurting, too."

He stared as white water crashed along the bank, spraying his legs.

Taylor's hand curled around his knee and squeezed gently. "Andi's strong. Very strong." Her shoulder nudged his. "If she takes after you as much as I think she does, she won't give up easily. She'll keep fighting."

Will dragged his hand through his hair and tried, unsuccessfully, to voice agreement. Thing was, Andi couldn't be more headstrong if she tried. There was no telling what chances she'd taken or what reckless choices she'd made. Like most young adults he knew, she thought she was invincible.

"We're going to find her," Taylor said. "We won't stop looking until we do. No matter what."

He looked up then, his eyes searching hers, and nodded.

She gave an encouraging smile, but it slowly faded as her gaze moved past him, focusing on something beyond him in the distance. "I was wrong," she whispered.

He frowned, his throat tightening. "What do you mean?"

Slowly, her smile reemerged—full-blown and relieved. "Look." She pointed at an area over his left shoulder. "She found us first."

He spun around on the boulder, his eyes scanning the thick woods behind him, and there was a small figure with an oversize dry bag slung over her shoulder, shoving through low-hanging branches and limping out onto the bank.

"Andi!" Will sprang to his feet.

She froze, her head swiveling in his direction and her eyes focusing on his face. The dry bag fell from her shoulder and her expression crumpled. "Dad!"

He slipped twice over the rocky bank, almost breaking his neck as he ran toward Andi, but it was worth it when he finally reached her, wrapped his arms around her and hugged her tight.

She sagged in his embrace, slumping heavily against him as sobs racked her small frame. "I th-thought I'd never find you. Didn't know if you had drow—" As her voice broke, her hands curled around his neck, then patted over his shoulders and chest before lifting to cup his face, her thumbs rubbing over the thick stubble lining his jaw. Her relief was almost palpable as she searched for words, a dazed look in her eyes. "You... you look different. You're getting a beard."

A chuckle rumbled deep in his chest, then burst from his lips. Tears spilled over his lashes and poured over his cheeks. He smiled. "If it'll make you happy, I'll shave it the second we get home."

Andi shook her head, her breath catching on another sob. "No. Finding you makes me happy. Just seeing you. I didn't know if..." She buried her face against his chest and wrapped her arms around his waist— the same way she used to when she was a little girl. "I love you, Daddy."

Immediately, he hugged her tight and kissed the top of her head. He breathed her in, the scent of rain, soil and pine lingering in her hair. "I love you, too," he whispered, his voice catching as he savored the moment.

It felt like a lifetime since he'd been able to hold her close, safe and protected, without her pulling away. For the first time in years, Andi had met him halfway.

NINE

How could Heather have left them?

Taylor ducked her head and wiped away a tear as she watched Will hug Andi close, tuck her head beneath his chin and kiss her hair. How could a mother ever abandon her daughter? And how could Will's wife leave and put him behind her for years with no regrets at all?

"Are you hurt?" Will's deep voice vibrated with emotion as he skimmed his hands over his daughter's shoulders and arms, then tipped her chin up and inspected her face.

Andi looked up at him, an expression of relief appearing. "Just my ankle. But it's not too bad."

Will knelt in front of her and tapped her left leg. "This one?"

"No. The other." As Will gently probed Andi's right ankle to ascertain the injury, she glanced across the riverbank at Taylor and a hopeful eagerness lit up her face. "You're okay?"

Taylor nodded. "Thanks to your dad. He pulled me out of the river. Basically saved my life."

"We saved each other," Will clarified, cradling Andi's ankle with both hands. "Taylor saved me as much as I saved her." He glanced at Taylor, his eyes roving slowly over her face. "Kept us going last night, too. I was losing hope, but she reminded me it was worth it to keep going."

Andi's smile trembled and her eyes filled with a fresh onslaught of tears. She reached down and squeezed Will's shoulder, then hobbled past him on her left leg, crossing the rocky bank until she reached Taylor. "Thank you."

Andi threw her arms around Taylor, making her catch her breath in surprise. The young girl pressed her cheek to Taylor's shoulder and cried softly.

"I'm so sorry," Andi whispered brokenly. "I didn't mean to hurt you when you helped me in the rapids. I didn't mean t—"

"Shh," Taylor soothed, her heart breaking at the desperation in Andi's voice. "You don't need to apologize." She smoothed her hand over Andi's back as it trembled and added, "You didn't do anything wrong. Not a thing."

Andi shook harder in her arms. "I should've listened to Dad when he said it was too dangerous to go downriver. I shouldn't have made everyone get back in the water. Jax, Ms. Beth and Mr. Martin fell in the river and I don't know if they made it out. I looked for them while I walked downriver, but I didn't see them. What if they didn't make it?"

"Hey, now." Will crossed the bank and reached their side. "There's every reason to hope they're safe and well right now." He drifted his hand over Andi's hair as she cried in Taylor's arms. "And you're not responsible for what happened. We all made a decision together as a group, and the majority of the group chose of their

own volition to proceed downriver. Myself included."
He glanced at Taylor, a tired but teasing grin on his
face, and winked. "Although I'll remind you both that
I was the only one wise enough to dissent."

Oh, boy. There was that charm again. It was more
than enough to make a woman weak in the knees where
he was concerned.

Taylor waited a moment for the pleasant flutter in
her chest to subside, then lowered her head until her
mouth was level with Andi's ear and whispered, "As
much as I hate to admit it, your dad is right."

Andi's sobs slowed and she lifted her head from
Taylor's shoulder, her wide brown eyes moving from
Taylor's grin to Will's. She bit her lip, then grinned,
as well, her tears ceasing and a laugh escaping her. "I
hate admitting it, too."

"Good," Taylor declared. "I'm glad I'm not the only
one. And from now on, we'll have to work extra hard
at keeping his ego in check."

She laughed harder, stepped back and wiped her
face with the back of her hand.

Will kissed Andi's cheek, then mouthed *Thank you*
at Taylor over Andi's head.

Cheeks heating, Taylor hid her blush of pleasure
and gestured toward the dry bag Andi had dropped
near the tree line. "That's a huge dry bag you hauled
downriver with you, Andi. Please tell me it's the one
Jax packed with bottled water."

Brown eyes sparkling with relief and excitement,
Andi grabbed the dry bag. "Yep. It is. And there are
iodine tablets, too, so when the bottled water runs out,
we'll have a way to sanitize the river water. I found it

stuck along the bank when I was walking downriver. Never found the rest of them, though."

"That's okay," Will said. "One dry bag's more than Taylor and I had a few minutes ago. And there are probably other things we can use in it."

For the next few minutes, Will dug through the dry bag and handed Taylor everything he found that might be of use. In addition to six bottles of filtered water and the iodine tablets Andi had mentioned, there were neutralizing tablets, as well, that would help provide cleaner, fresher-tasting river water after they'd purified it. All things considered, Taylor considered this a luxury.

A flashlight, blanket, cargo net, lighter, waterproof matches, two small towels and one plastic sandwich bag filled with six granola bars—one treat for each member of the group, courtesy of Jax, Will guessed—were also found.

Three bottled waters were guzzled down first. Taylor forced herself to slow down as she drank, sipping rather than gulping, and savoring the moist feel of the water in her mouth. The liquid provided relief for her dry, chapped lips, too, and she poured a little water in her cupped palm and splashed it on her sweaty face, almost sighing with pleasure.

"Oh, I'd kill for a bar of soap and bottle of shampoo right now," she groaned.

"Don't have any soap or shampoo," Andi said around a mouthful of granola bar. "But I found the campsite Jax talked about half a mile upriver—" she took another bite of granola and chewed "—and there's a cool swimming hole not far from it. A decent fishing hole, too."

"Andi." Will, grinning, eyed his daughter over the bottle of water he held near his lips. "Please chew and swallow first. Then talk. Being in backcountry is no excuse for neglecting your manners, especially when we're in the presence of a guest."

"Oh," she garbled. Face reddening, she chewed slowly, swallowed hard, then continued. "I know how to get back there if y'all want to go?"

Taylor glanced at Will, who raised a questioning eyebrow.

"What d'ya say, Taylor?" he asked. "You up for hiking another half mile today?"

She nodded eagerly. "If it involves a prepped campsite, a cool swim to wash the grime off and a chance at eating something other than berries and granola, I'm all for it."

Will drained the last drops of water from his bottle, then motioned toward the river. "Let's fill these empties, drop in a few iodine tablets and repack 'em. By the time we get ready to settle tonight, they should be purified."

They did as Will suggested, repacked the dry bag and headed through the tree line back upriver with Andi leading the way. It was slow going and Will insisted that they stop several times along the way so Andi could sit, prop her injured ankle up on a log or rock and rest. She argued good-naturedly with him each time, but the look of sheer relief that crossed her face when she sank onto the ground made it evident that she needed the rest breaks—probably more than she was taking, but Taylor could tell Will didn't want to push his luck and risk ruining the peaceful truce he and his daughter seemed to have reached.

Half a mile upriver, the thick tree line parted, a clearing emerged and a deep, cool mountain stream glistened in the late-afternoon sun. The roar of the rapids could still be heard over the trees, but an area of bare dirt near the stream remained relatively peaceful, and there was a perfect spot to build a fire.

Taylor sighed. If only the trip had gone as Jax had planned. She had no doubt the entire group would've spent the past two nights relaxing by the fire and enjoying each other's company. As it was, they were still stranded in the middle of nowhere without knowing if a rescue party would come or if they'd be able to hike their way out of backcountry. But then again, had the trip gone as planned…she never would've spent the past two nights with Will. And now that they'd found Andi safe and sound, she couldn't help but look back on the time they'd spent together with gratitude. Neither she nor Will had spent those nights alone. Instead, they'd had each other to lean on.

She dragged her foot across the ground, watching as blades of grass bent in passing, then slowly rose. Being able to trust and depend on a man was definitely a first. She was grateful she'd had the opportunity to experience that with Will. And…she found herself longing to hold on to that feeling. To hold on to Will.

"Taylor?"

She jerked around to find Will studying her closely. "I'm sorry—what did you say?"

"I asked if you wanted to take a dip in the stream, or if you'd rather rest first." He narrowed his eyes, concern crossing his face. "You okay?"

Andi squealed and a splash quickly followed. "It's

chilly!" she called from the water, laughing. "Come on in, Dad."

Taylor glanced at the stream and smiled as Andi beckoned Will with a wave of her hand, then floated on her back, her arms sweeping slowly by her sides against the gentle current.

"Oh, I'm fine," Taylor said, slipping her hand under her shirt and ensuring the straps of her swimsuit were secure on her shoulders. Satisfied, she grabbed the mud-stained hem of her T-shirt, whipped it over her head, then grinned. "And I bet you ten to one that I hit the water before you do."

Will's mouth twitched. "You're on."

She toed her shoes off while he kicked his own off, then tugged his shirt over his head and tossed it on the ground. Then he held out his hand.

"May the best man win," he teased.

"May the best woman win," she countered. Ignoring his hand, she shoved his bare chest with both hands, laughed as he stumbled back with a look of surprise, then raced toward the water.

His powerful steps followed quickly in pursuit, the feel of him at her back spurring her on. At the bank, she jumped and plunged feetfirst into the deepest stretch of the water, her head submerging just as he splashed in beside her.

Cool water washed over her skin, flowed with delicious ease through her grimy hair and provided a refreshing chill when she kicked to the surface and her head emerged again. After scaling a wall, being caked in mud and having tumbled through rapids twice, it was a gift straight from heaven. Ah, wonderful!

Water splashed in her face, stinging her nose.

"You cheated." The deep rumble of Will's soothing voice drew closer and moved around her in a slow circle, punctuated with splashes. "Your actions officially disqualify you from the race, and I win by default."

Taylor laughed and wiped her face, blinking water droplets from her lashes furiously until his handsome face came into focus in front of her. "Nope. That was a fair head start. You're at least a foot taller than me and that evened things up as they should be."

Will grinned, his muscular arms moving in circular motions as he treaded water next to her. "Hmm. I might give you a pass on that." He glanced at Andi, who no longer floated on her back but treaded water several feet away, watching them silently. "What's the verdict, Andi? Did Taylor win?"

Andi's brown eyes, a wounded light in them, left Will and she stared at Taylor. A pensive expression overcame the half smile that faded from her face. "No. I was here first."

Will waded farther out to the middle of a calm stretch of the stream near the campsite, grabbed a smooth stone from the riverbed and stacked it on top of the small pile he and Andi had created to form a small dam to trap fish. Three feet to his left, stones clinked, and he glanced over, watching as Andi hefted a large stone on top of the emerging wall. She knew the drill; they'd gone through these motions at least a dozen times during her childhood years when they'd camped frequently on the weekends.

At the time, he'd suggested they fish using the survival technique for fun—thinking it'd end up being a novelty of sorts—but now, considering their present circumstances, he was grateful he'd started the tradition.

"You wanna tell me about earlier?" he asked, retrieving two more stones. He carried them over and placed them on the pile.

Andi fished another rock out of the water, added it to the wall of the small dam and lifted a dark eyebrow. "What about earlier?" she asked blandly.

"You know what. That stunt you pulled with Taylor." He jerked his thumb at one fully formed wall of the low dam they'd built. "And sit down and elevate that ankle before you strain it so badly you can't hike tomorrow."

She released a long-suffering sigh, limped onto the grassy bank, plopped down and propped her right heel on a rock. "I don't know what you're talking about."

Stifling a groan of frustration, Will shook his head and tackled a new section of the stream, gathering up an armload of stones and carrying them over to the unfinished section of the dam.

An hour earlier, he could've sworn things were looking up. But less than two minutes after he and Taylor had plunged into the deep end of the stream, Andi's good mood had vanished. When he'd asked who'd won his and Taylor's race to the stream, Andi had shot him and Taylor both a dirty look, given a tight-lipped response, then limped back out of the stream, claiming she was too tired to swim.

Her supposed "rest" had lasted all of ten minutes, until the moment he and Taylor had finished their swim, dried off as much as possible with the small towels from the dry bag and redonned their clothing over their swimsuits. As soon as he'd invited Taylor to walk to the shallow end of the stream and help build a dam to catch fish, Andi had sprung up from her supine position on the grass, hitched her injured leg up and literally hopped on one foot to reach him faster, insisting she would be a better assistant.

Not willing to reject Andi's voluntary offer of help—something that hadn't occurred in over five years—he'd accepted. Taylor, fidgeting with her shorts and avoiding his eyes, had quickly agreed it was a good idea and announced she'd stay behind at camp and build a fire.

Having Andi by his side again lifted his spirits, no doubt. But walking away from Taylor, especially after glimpsing a look of awkward discomfort on her face, dragged his good mood right back down again.

"What's bugging you, Andi?" he asked, filling in the last opening of the small dam.

"Nothing's bugging me."

"Then why were you so rude to Taylor?"

"I wasn't rude."

"Yeah, you were."

"Is that how you interpreted it?"

"There was no need for either of us to interpret it." Will spread his hands and raised his shoulders. "Your tone tipped us off."

Her mouth tightened. "So there's an *us* now? As in you and Taylor?"

Will dropped his head back and heaved out a sigh. *Lord, this one's Yours. You made her.* "You gotta be kidding me..." He inhaled a slow breath and tried again. "You see anyone else out here, Andi? It's just you, me and her."

Her nose wrinkled. "I'm well aware of that."

"And your attitude." Will grimaced. "Believe me, that right there is a whole other entity."

Hurt flashed in her eyes and her chin trembled. She turned away, staring at the rugged mountain range to the left of them.

"Andi…" Will took one step toward her, but when she stiffened, he stepped over the dam and grabbed the cargo net he'd pulled from the dry bag. "I can't make things right if you don't tell me what's wrong." He unrolled the net, stretched it out, then grabbed one end and hung it on a stick he'd wedged between two rocks on one end of the dam. "I'm only trying to help, you know? I'm doing my best here."

He'd always done his best. Problem was, his best didn't seem to be good enough anymore. Hadn't been for at least a decade.

Flinching, he picked up the other end of the net and stretched it across the opening between the dam walls, then threaded a second stick through it on the other side. He pulled it tight, creating a snug dead end in the middle of the shallow stream, and secured it to the riverbed by placing several heavy stones on the lower edge. Water gurgled through the netting easily, and after a patient wait, he should be able to wade in and scoop out at least three bass if he kept his hands slow and controlled.

Satisfied with the trap, he joined Andi on the bank, sat beside her and propped his elbows on his bent knees. They sat silently for several minutes, the only sounds the gurgling water, whispering buzz of bugs as they flew over the stream and a steady chirp of crickets in the thick woods along the opposite side of the bank.

Soon, the sun dipped in the sky, its lower half obscured by a distant mountain range, and a sharp ray of sunlight cut across the stream and spilled over Andi's face. Suspicious moisture gleamed in her eyes.

"Help me out, please," he said softly. "I don't understand."

She continued staring straight ahead, then parted her lips and said in such low tones he had to lean closer to hear, "It's always been just us."

"Yeah." Of course. For more than a decade. Nothing new there. "I'm not following you."

"Just us." She faced him then, tears welling on her bottom lashes. "But now she's here."

"I thought you liked Taylor. Just a few days ago you were siding with her against me."

"That was before."

He huffed out an exasperated breath. "Before what?"

"Before you spent two days alone with her," she said slowly. "Then became an *us* with her. Without me."

Oh, man. She was jealous. This was definitely a new argument. How in the world had he not seen this one coming? And how should he navigate it?

"None of the three of us ended up where we were three days ago because we had a choice in the matter," he pointed out gently. "I didn't choose to be separated from you. I'd never choose that, Andi."

One fat tear spilled over her lashes and rolled down her left cheek. "You promise?"

"I promise." He lifted his hand and gently wiped the tear away with his thumb. "The only reason I came out here at all was to spend time with you. To take whatever time you'd give me. I miss you. I've been missing you for the past several years. More than you'll ever know."

Confusion suffused her features. "I've been right there at home all the time."

"No, you haven't."

Her shoulders sagged. "I only took off the once. And I didn't do it to hurt you or scare y—"

"I know." A breeze sifted through the trees and swept over them. He smoothed an errant hair from her forehead. "But it hurt me just the same. I was terrified."

She looked at him in surprise.

"Yep." Throat tightening, he turned his head and watched the water stream through the net. "Dads get scared, too, you know? Especially when it comes to their daughters." He swallowed the tight knot in his throat. "For almost a week, I worried myself sick imagining what might have happened to you out there on your own. You didn't call—not once. Wouldn't answer any of my calls or respond to my text messages, either." He hesitated, but considering this might be his only opportunity to make his point, he forced himself to forge ahead. "How did you feel when you couldn't find me two days ago?"

Her face paled. "Awful."

"You were afraid for me?"

She stared at the ground and nodded.

He drew in a deep breath. Steadied his voice. "Multiply that fear by ten and add five more days to the duration. That's how I felt when you ran away two months ago."

Her head dipped farther down and she bit her lip.

"Where did you go?" he asked. "I know you don't want to tell me, but I got no place to go right now and I'm sticking to your side till you give it up."

At first, he didn't think she'd speak. It occurred to

April Arrington 143

him that she might refuse to ever tell him, just like the dozens of times over the past two months when he'd asked the same question. And he might never find out what she did the week she disappeared. But then...

"I went to Nashville to see Mom."

His spine stiffened and he studied her face, looking for any twinge of pain, hoping not to find it. But it was there, flooding her eyes, and he didn't have to ask. He knew the answer. "You found her."

Another nod. Her voice shook. "I looked her up. Found her online. Did you know she sings in a club?"

"Yes."

"I wasn't old enough to get in," she continued. "So I followed her home."

He took a moment to collect himself. "What happened?"

"She recognized me. She knew who I was without me telling her." She faced him, her eyes clinging to his. "Did you send her pictures of me? You told her I wanted to see her?"

Reluctantly, he dipped his head. "I send her a photo every year on your birthday and I let her know you still ask about her. I told her I'd welcome her, if she ever wanted to stop by to visit you. That I wouldn't turn her away so long as she was willing to do right by you. I never told you because I didn't know how she'd react. And I didn't want you to get your hopes up, then get hurt if she didn't show."

Her voice faded to a pained whisper. "She doesn't want me. Never will."

Anger lanced through his heart so badly he clenched his teeth to resist shouting. Instead, he wrapped his arms around her and pulled her close, tucking her into his side and pressing his cheek to the top of her head. "You're wanted," he said fiercely. "Wanted and loved. I'll never be able to tell you how much. There aren't enough words for how much I love you. And it's her loss—*not* yours. I promise you that."

Andi curled her small fists in his shirt and buried her face in his chest, her next words breaking his heart into so many pieces he didn't think he'd ever be able to put them back together. "It doesn't feel that way."

She shook in his arms, her whole body trembling, and his shirt grew damp beneath her tears.

"I know, baby," he whispered painfully. "I know."

They sat by the stream for another hour and he held her while she cried, rocking her gently like he used to when she was a child, smoothing his hand over her hair and wishing he could lift the burden from her. Make it so she never hurt again.

His resentment for Heather intensified, and he tried his best to pray it away. Tried to appreciate the blessing God had given him recently in providing him an opportunity to get to know Taylor—a good, compassionate woman who he was sure would never knowingly hurt Andi or him the way Heather continued to do.

The thought of Taylor waiting for them back at the campsite, her warm smile and giving nature…the warm, supported way she made him feel—it brought him a great relief he'd never felt before. And his heart lightened a little at the prospect of what could potentially lie ahead. A second chance at a relationship, an opportunity for Andi to form a friendship with an honest woman who would respect her. And as for he and Taylor, maybe a friendship stronger than the one he'd only imagined he'd had with Heather. Something more. Maybe even in time…love?

Then Andi pleaded, "It's always been you and me, Dad. Promise it'll stay just us."

TEN

Taylor tossed another log onto the campfire she'd built and stepped back as it sparked and shot red-hot embers into the dusky sky. She looked up and smiled. The late-afternoon sun was only half an hour away from setting and splashed bold golden colors across the horizon. In the distance, along the darkest fringes of the sky in the opposite direction, two stars blinked down at her, and the surrounding trees, their tall tips cloaked in mist, pulsed with the rattle of cicadas.

She closed her eyes, swaying slightly to the chorus of the crackling fire, the whispering stream and throbbing sound of wildlife.

Those are His waters. His smoke.

And His mountains, Taylor added silently, recalling Jax's words. What was it Jax's pops used to say?

When the world broke a man, all he had to do was come to God's land and let Him know he's here. Peace is in this place—all around. You just got to look for it.

She hadn't believed it. Not then. But if she were honest with herself, she was beginning to. Having experienced such turmoil over the past few days, she'd never expected to find such a tranquil scene as this one and the elk from last night. But both moments had provided the same peaceful sense of security.

Twigs snapped several feet away and the low murmur of voices drifted in.

"Hey," Taylor called as Will's and Andi's figures emerged around the bend. "How'd it go? Are we having fish for supper?"

Andi didn't answer. She continued staring down at the ground as she walked, her shoulders stiff and hands shoved in the pockets of her shorts.

"Managed to snag five rock bass," Will answered, holding up a small pile of fish wrapped in the spare cargo net. "They're not the biggest in the world, but it's something other than granola and berries."

Taylor grinned. "That's enough to make me happy." She reached out and touched Andi's arm when she limped past. "Would you like to help me cook the fish? I rigged up a little grill of sorts. Piled some rocks right next to the fire, so we could spread them out and cook them faster."

Andi glanced up, her eyes red and slightly swollen. She opened her mouth to speak but stopped, glanced back at Will, then said, "Yes, please. Thank you."

Hesitating, Taylor met Will's eyes and raised a brow in question. He shook his head slightly, a sad smile emerging.

"Okay. Let's get supper started." Taylor gentled her tone and rubbed her hands together. "May I borrow your knife, Will? I thought we could clean 'em and gut 'em by the stream first."

He smiled—a real one this time. "You not afraid to get your nails dirty?"

She laughed and trailed a hand through the tangled

strands of her hair. "Considering I'm carrying about half the backcountry in my hair, I don't think it'll really make that big a difference."

Will chuckled and Taylor thought she caught a hint of a smile forming on Andi's face, but it disappeared just as quickly as it emerged. There was a cloud of sadness hanging over both of them, but she couldn't decipher what it was, and considering she was little more than a stranger to Andi, she didn't feel comfortable asking the young girl.

So, she chose to lead the way to the stream instead. They hauled the fish to the stretch of water closest to the campsite and Taylor started scaling the fish. Will cut off the heads and Andi washed the gutted fillets in the stream, then stacked them in a neat little pile, and they returned to the campsite.

Taylor spread the fillets out on stones next to the flames and they sat around the fire silently for a few minutes, their gazes lingering on the spectacular sunset over the western mountain range, then drifting over the bright pulse of stars as they emerged in the dark velvet background of the eastern sky.

"It's an odd feeling," Taylor said quietly.

Will shifted next to her and she could feel his eyes on her face. "What is?"

Taylor gestured toward the sky. "Being caught between day and night. Sun and stars. Feels like you're in a limbo of sorts. Like things could go either way." She studied the sunset as it slowly faded away. "Before you came back, I remembered what Jax told us the first day when we were scouting the rapids. I have to admit, I'm beginning to believe him."

"What did he say?" Andi asked softly. She sat, legs

crossed, on the opposite side of the fire, staring into the flames.

Taylor smiled. "That there's peace all around. You just have to look for it." The last of the sunlight receded and night fell, bringing the flames of the fire into stark relief against the darkened landscape, and more stars fought their way out of obscurity, shining brightly down at them. "He was right. It's beautiful."

A quiet sniffle emerged from Andi's direction.

Taylor frowned, her heart aching as the glow of the fire lit up the sad expression on Andi's face. "Andi, has your dad brought you out here before?"

She shook her head. "Not here. But we've been to plenty of places like it."

"When we used to camp, we stuck closer to home," Will added, easing closer to the fire. "There are several gorgeous campsites out our way, aren't there, Andi?"

She remained quiet for a moment, then smiled a little. "Yeah." She wiped her eyes with the back of her hand, then watched the flames of the fire flicker, a soft giggle escaping her. "I remember our trip to Badger's Crossing. We rode the rapids, then camped overnight." Her smile grew. "A skunk got in Dad's tent."

Will laughed and leaned back into his hands. "Took me a week to get the stink off me. No matter how many showers I took or how long I scrubbed, I couldn't get rid of it."

Andi perked up a bit. "He made this weird mixture with baby shampoo to kill the stink and bathed with it for a week, so he smelled like an infant for days."

He winced. "I think we're wandering into the territory of overshare, Andi."

"And then there was the time when we ran across

that wild boar on the trail," Andi continued. "It had its babies with it and went after Da—"

"I think the fish are ready." Will, his cheeks scarlet beneath two days' worth of dark stubble, dragged a hand over the back of his neck. "Who's ready to eat?"

Taylor grinned. "Don't change the subject. I was enjoying Andi's stories." She tipped her hand toward Andi. "Please continue."

Eyes brightening, she licked her lips, shot Will a look, then said, "One time, we went spelunking, and when a bat flapped around the cave, Dad ran so fast I almost couldn't keep u—"

"Okay," Will said, his whole face scarlet. "That's enough sharing for the night." He rubbed his hands together briskly and picked up one of three long sticks he'd placed by the fire. "Taylor, would you like the first fish?"

She bit back a laugh. "Wait a sec. You're afraid of bats?"

He cocked an eyebrow. "You telling me you aren't?"

"I didn't say that, but we're not talking about me right now." Taylor raised her eyebrows in return. "So you're really afraid of bats?"

He blew out an exasperated breath. "Yes. All right? I'm terrified of them." An expression of revulsion crossed his face. "They have pointy ears, a pig nose and creepy feet." He shuddered. "We're not on good terms."

Taylor laughed louder, the thought of his muscular bulk taking off in a sprint at the mere flap of wings almost impossible to believe. Only...

"But that first night," she said, her laughter fading. "When we were stranded in the storm, you went inside that cave and told me to wait outside while you checked it out." She tilted her head as he met and held her gaze. "There could've been bats in there."

He dipped his head. "I suppose."

"But you went in anyway."

"Yeah."

"Why?"

His dark eyes left hers and drifted over her face. "For you."

A wave of affection surged through her chest. "For me?" she whispered.

"Yeah," he said softly. "You were hurt and afraid. There was a storm brewing and you needed shelter."

Her breath caught, those delicious emotions within her intensifying. With Preston, she'd always been afraid and he would never have put her comfort before his own. But the first day she'd met Will, he'd been willing to face one of his fears just to make her—a stranger at the time—safe and comfortable. He was a true...

"Gentleman," she said out loud, admiring the play of shadow and light from the fire over his wide shoulders, strong jaw and mesmerizing brown eyes. "You're a good man, Will."

A tender smile crossed his face, and sincerity entered his tone. "I only did what any decent person would do."

Her smile returned. "Unless you'd been alone. If you'd been by yourself, would you have gone in that cave?"

He laughed. "Probably not. I'd have rather risked getting hit by lightning." His laughter died abruptly. "You saved my daughter's life, and she's the most precious person in the world to me. If Andi had been with me, I'd have done the same for her." He drew his head back and glanced at Andi, his tone sobering. "We've always been a team, haven't we?"

Nodding, Andi stared back at him, relief shining in her eyes. "Yes. You and I are the best team."

And no one else is a part of that. Andi hadn't said the words, but her tone was clear.

Taylor gripped the log she sat on with both hands and rubbed her thumbs over the smooth wood absently. That was why Andi had been so short with her earlier today when they'd swum in the stream. She'd shared a close moment with Will, much as she had just now, and Andi had been threatened by it.

Taylor glanced at Andi, who smiled up at Will as he handed her a fish skewered on a stick, and her chest tightened at the sadness still lingering in her eyes. She looked down at the fire, regret moving through her as she watched orange embers pop, then scatter, mingling with gray smoke and drifting on the night breeze toward the stars.

The last thing she'd ever want to do was make Andi feel as though she were trying to pull Will away from her, but it seemed as though that was what Andi thought she had done. But even worse, the thought of pulling away from Will for Andi's sake, of not exploring the bond they'd begun to form—one that was strong and good—was as equally disturbing to her.

She'd never known a good man like Will before. Had never dreamed she'd ever begin to feel the way she did for him—

Wait. How did she feel about Will? She was attracted to him, sure. He was a handsome man. But it had grown into more than that. The feelings she'd begun to experience for Will were warm and tender and tugged strongly at her chest. It almost felt like… like falling in love.

Her breath caught at the realization, and when she glanced at him, when she met his eyes and felt that tender tug in her chest again, she knew without a doubt. At some point during their short journey through the backcountry, this strong, kind and considerate man had quickly ducked beneath her guard and slipped right into her heart. So quietly. So unexpectedly. And she was falling in love with him.

"Aren't you going to sleep, too?"

Will smoothed a stray hair off Andi's cheek after she lay down by the campfire and shook his head. "Not yet." He spread one of the towels from the dry bag over her—not the best blanket, but it would do in a pinch. "As tired as I am, I'm still too keyed up to sleep."

He was also too full of past regrets. Too worried about the present. And too fearful of what the future may hold.

Andi lifted her head and peeked around him at the grassy bank near the stream. "How long do you think she'll stay out there?"

Will glanced over his shoulder and studied Taylor's silhouette beneath the moonlight. She stood near the stretch of stream where they'd swum earlier that afternoon, her head tipped back, attention on the bright full moon and impressive expanse of stars glittering above them. The glistening night sky was so wide and encompassing it seemed to take on a life of its own, drawing closer with each passing hour and lowering like a sparkling curtain around them, hugging the mountain peaks and moving with the breeze.

Two hours earlier, as they'd sat by the fire, Taylor had grown quiet after their lighthearted exchange over their first night in the cave and had become increasingly withdrawn as they'd eaten fish. He and Andi had continued sharing anecdotes of past camping trips and reminisced over the good times they'd shared together years ago as the moon had slowly emerged, but as relieved as he was to find Andi opening up to him again—actually sharing her pain rather than hiding it—he couldn't shake the feeling that the more Andi embraced him, the more Taylor seemed to pull away. And when they'd finished eating an hour ago, Taylor had thanked him for the meal, excused herself and slipped quietly away while he and Andi had continued chatting by the fire.

"She's been out there by herself for so long," Andi added quietly.

Reluctantly, Will pried his attention away from Taylor and faced Andi again. "I think she's used to being alone. She mentioned that she doesn't have any family. That she was married once but that her husband passed away."

Andi, eyes heavy with sleep, blinked slowly as she looked at Taylor again. "What happened to him?"

"I don't know. Didn't seem appropriate to ask at the time."

"Does she have any children?"

"No." Will managed a small smile and squeezed her shoulder. "And having you is one of the blessings I've always been most grateful to God for. When your mom left, I had you."

His mind wandered back then, mulling over memories of sleepless nights, mixing formula at two in the morning, soothing cries, leaving for work at 5:00 a.m., putting in overtime, picking Andi up from daycare, then…starting it all over again.

It had been grueling, exhausting work. But there had been so many rewards—like that brief window of time between eight and nine at night when he'd soothed and settled Andi for the night. The grin that had always lifted Andi's rosy cheeks during her bath when he'd trickled warm water over her shampooed hair. The giggle that would burst from her toothless gums when he'd tickle the bottoms of her tiny toes, and the most precious moment—the one where she'd drift off to sleep in his arms, curled into a ball, her light weight snuggled happily against his chest. Right over his heart. Those moments drew away all the day's pain and filled him with fresh energy to tackle the next one.

Nothing in the world had ever been more valuable to him than that time spent with her.

"We always had each other," he added softly. "Neither of us were ever alone. I don't think Taylor's ever had that."

Andi's brown eyes studied his face, then drifted over to Taylor. "So she doesn't have anyone?"

Will shook his head. "Not that I know of." He nudged her chin gently with his knuckle. "That's why I always try to remember that everyone struggles with something, and sometimes my burdens pale in comparison with others'. No matter how much I may hurt, it's important to save room in my heart to help others when I can."

"That's why you went in the cave," she whispered slowly, her lashes lowering. "So she wouldn't be alone."

He lifted his hand, smoothed his thumb over her flushed cheek and pondered that. Yeah. That had been part of it. But even then, as early as that after meeting Taylor, something else had driven him. That small voice inside him had slowed his steps during their walk from the riverbank to the cave, kept his gaze moving back over his shoulder to check on Taylor's progress, to make sure she still held her own despite her injury. A silent pull on his mind and heart had kept his attention and concern on Taylor—a feeling of kinship. Familiarity.

It was as though his heart had always known her. As though he may have been waiting for her all this time without even knowing it.

"Maybe I did it for more reasons than that." He tensed and glanced down at Andi, the thought having escaped his lips before he realized he'd uttered it.

But she was asleep now. Soft breaths moved past her parted lips and her body almost sagged with exhaustion against the hard earth beneath her.

"Sleep well, angel." He bent, kissed her temple, then stood.

Taylor was still standing by the stream, her head tilted back toward the sky.

Will walked in her direction, then hesitated briefly, his shoes shuffling over dirt and grass as he glanced back at Andi's sleeping form, highlighted by the fire. Then he resumed walking until he reached Taylor's side.

She continued studying the sky, but her blue eyes

darted his way once as he shoved his hands in his pockets, then shifted away and refocused on the stars.

"Find something interesting up there?" he asked softly.

A small smile tugged at the curves of her lips. "I hope so. That's where you told me to look."

His brow furrowed. "I did?"

She nodded and a light breeze whispered between them, ruffling her hair and trailing a blond strand over her graceful neck. His gaze lingered there.

"When we were scaling the wall," she said. "You told me to look up. You said, that's where we were headed."

He laughed. "Guess I was aiming too high, because we sure didn't reach the top of that bluff the next day."

She laughed, too, the gentle sound stirring a pleasurable sensation in his chest. "We tried at least. I think that's what matters."

"Yeah. I suppose you're right about that." He narrowed his eyes and peered in the distance, the bright, sprawling reach of moonlight and stars darkening the rugged landscape. "With any luck, that rescue chopper will swing back by either tomorrow or the next day. It'd help if we were on higher ground. Somewhere above all these woods and rocks." He gestured upriver, toward a high mountain peak. "If I remember right, about two miles that way, we passed an outcrop once we cleared that first set of rough rapids before the second set dumped us. It's a crag I'd guess to be about five thousand feet up or so. If there's someone out there looking for us, that'd be a good place to be seen. It's high and by the river, but we'd have to pass through a ravine to get there. We could head out first thing in the morning and should make it by midafternoon."

"And Andi?" she asked, glancing back at the fire. "Will she be able to hike that far and make the climb with her ankle the way it is?"

He looked at Andi, a sense of pride moving through him as he watched the firelight dance over her cheeks and arms. "She'll try. She made it all the way to us on her own. And if she gives out, I'll carry her the rest of the way."

"You never get tired, do you?" She looked at him then, admiration in her blue eyes as they roved over his face.

"I'm tired all the time," he admitted, his cheeks heating. "Some days I just go through the motions. Do whatever is needed to wrap things up at work, get home and check on Andi." He held her gaze, kept his voice soft. "I don't ever want her to feel like she's alone."

Taylor smiled up at him, a pained look of longing moving through her expression. "Andi's lucky to have you."

"Who did you have at her age?" He bit his lower lip, waiting for her answer, hoping he hadn't pushed too far.

"The staff at three children's shelters." She looked away, resumed staring at the stars. "Then two sets of foster parents. And two years after I aged out of the system, I had Preston."

"Your late husband?"

She nodded.

"Did you know your parents?"

"No. From what I was told, I was abandoned outside a hospital as an infant. There's no record of who my parents are."

"And Preston? How did you meet him?"

Her mouth tightened. "I found work as a secretary in a real-estate office in Nashville. I enjoyed it more than I expected. I think it was because I got to see so many newlyweds, families and retired couples find their dream homes. A place to love, laugh and rest. A haven." Despite her tense tone, she smiled. "That was the good part. The best part, actually. Getting to help people find that and seeing how wonderful it felt to have your dream fulfilled." Her smile faded. "I think that's why I was drawn to Preston. He was a real-estate agent—the best in the area—and he'd show me these beautiful homes, walk me through them, sell me the dream. He made me think I could have that. He made me believe that he and I could build that dream together."

"And did you?" Will asked quietly. "Build the dream?"

"No." Pain twisted her expression, her features highlighted by the moonlight. "He walled us inside a nightmare."

It hit him then. The panicked, fearful look in her eyes when he'd knelt over her by the riverbank two nights ago. The desperate way she'd scrambled back across the dirt away from his hands, his touch.

"He hurt you." Anger stiffened his tone and his hands clenched into fists inside his pockets.

"All he knew was pain," she whispered. "That's what his father taught him. What his grandmother taught his father. Pain and anger filled the house where he grew up, and he filled ours with it, too." Her chin trembled. "I thought maybe if I prayed hard enough… if I showed him a different way—a different kind of love—maybe he'd understand. Maybe he'd try to work through his past and embrace a better way of living. But he never did."

His throat tightened at the thought of what she'd endured. "I'm sorry, Taylor. I can't imagine what that must've been like."

"Can't you?" Her gaze sought his, her look of certainty catching him by surprise. "Heather did the same, didn't she?"

He shook his head. "She never—"

"Scarred you on the outside," Taylor agreed. "But she scarred you here." She touched her chest, her fingertips resting over her heart. "She hit you and Andi where it would hurt the most, didn't she? Then took off and left you with the pain? Left you to deal with it alone?"

His eyes burned. He looked away and focused on the moon that glowed in the distance, just as Taylor had for so long, and swallowed hard against the knot that formed in his throat. "Yeah."

"Sometimes…" Her voice faded as she stared at the moon, too. "Sometimes I can't understand why He doesn't answer. Why He doesn't help us when we need Him so badly."

Will's vision blurred and he blinked hard, choking back his anger and shoving away his doubts. He pulled his fist from his pocket, unfurled his hand and covered Taylor's with his own. "But He's helping us now, isn't He? Just like you said He was by using the mudslide to get us to the other side of the river." He looked down at her, the hint of relief beginning to shine in her eyes, giving him hope. "And at the moment, neither one of us are alone."

A tear rolled down her flushed cheek and pooled in the corner of her mouth. She turned her hand over, threaded her fingers through his and squeezed. "I'm trying to believe that."

ELEVEN

Taylor folded a small towel and put it back in the dry bag that lay by the charred remnants of the previous night's campfire. "Did you sleep well last night?"

Andi, who sat on a log on the other side of the campfire and sipped purified water from one of the plastic bottles they'd filled yesterday, nodded slowly. "Yes. Thank you." She glanced at the nearby stream, where Will squatted on the bank, dunked his hands into the stream, then splashed water on his face. "Did Dad?" She frowned up at Taylor, an accusatory note in her tone. "And did you?"

Taylor wiped her hands on her shorts, knocking off the dust and grime from smothering the last smoldering dregs of the fire and cleaning up their small campsite. "Yes, he did. After you fell asleep, he stayed up a little longer and we talked for a bit. Then he lay beside you and slept soundly. I tried to doze, but I couldn't, so I stayed up and kept an eye on things for a while."

Until sunrise, actually. After Will had taken her hand in his, they'd stood beneath the night sky together for almost an hour. They'd barely spoken after she'd shared a little of what she'd been through with Preston.

Instead, they'd continued staring up at the moon, thinking, and—surprisingly enough, Taylor reflected—she'd prayed silently.

For years, her relationship with God had faltered, then faded. Some of it had been due to the increasing pain and fear in her marriage and some of it had arisen from the flood of doubt and disappointment that had taken root in her heart for so long. And the guilt…that was always there. Probably always would be.

"You didn't sleep at all?" Andi asked.

"I couldn't." Taylor shrugged. "But in a way, it was a good thing, because I was able to stay up and keep a lookout. It gave me peace of mind to know that you and your dad were safe while you slept."

Andi's brow furrowed as she contemplated that. She took another swig of water, then tipped the bottle Taylor's way. "There's not much water left. Would you like some?"

Taylor smiled. "No, thanks. After I help your dad pack up supplies, I planned to take the empties downstream a bit. When we were swimming, I noticed a spring running nearby and thought I'd pull us some water from there. We'll still need to purify it, but it might have a cleaner taste."

"What will have a cleaner taste?" Will, rubbing his wet hair with one of the small towels, walked across the grass and joined them by the extinguished campfire.

"Water from the spring downstream," Taylor said.

"Oh." A mocking expression of disappointment crossed his face as he teased, "Thought y'all were rustling up a five-course breakfast."

Taylor grinned. "Thinking about that rib-eye steak again?"

He laughed. "Not gonna lie. I might've dreamed of one a time or two last night."

Taylor laughed with him, took a moment to admire his boyish grin and teasing tone, then glanced at Andi, whose eyes moved from her to Will and back slowly. "Well," she said, "think I'll gather up the empties and head to the spring." She bent, dug around in the dry bag and pulled out two empty bottles. "I'll fill these and drop in some iodine. I saw a strip of brush nearby that'll probably be full of wild strawberries, and we'll need fuel for today's hike, so I'll pick a few handfuls of those, too, while I'm there." She smiled at Will. "When I get back, I'll help you pack u—"

He held up a hand. "No. I can take care of this."

"Then I'll help Taylor." Andi stood, brushed off the back of her shorts with one hand and held up the empty water bottle she held in the other. "I drank more water than both of you put together, so the least I can do is help fill the bottles back up."

Will's brows rose. He studied Andi for a few moments, then looked at Taylor. "That okay with you?"

Taylor nodded, a strange mix of apprehension and hope moving through her. "Of course." She smiled. "I'd love the help."

After collecting the empty water bottles, she and Andi made their way upstream toward the spring. An early-morning mist still floated over the stream and riverbank, but a slight chill lingered in the air about them, cooling their skin and chasing away the last bit of sleep still clinging to them. Taylor glanced around, eyeing the stream and surrounding woods, but all seemed calm and peaceful.

Relaxing, she inhaled a strong lungful of sweet, clean mountain air. "It really is beautiful out here."

Andi murmured an assent, still limping slightly from her injury. "Me and Dad used to do this all the time." A blush snaked down her neck. "Well…not exactly this. I mean, we've run a ton of rapids before, but we've never gotten stuck out in the middle of nowhere like this before. Usually it's a lot more fun."

Taylor grinned. "I knew what you meant. And I enjoyed your stories last night. It sounded like you and your dad used to take a lot of wonderful trips together."

"Yeah." She glanced over her shoulder at Will, who moved around the campsite, packing up supplies and cleaning up any scraps they'd left behind from last night. "I'm hoping we'll go on more of them now." She shrugged and a small laugh escaped her. "Except maybe the end result will be better."

Taylor nodded. "Now, that's a hope we can all get behind."

Andi's smile slipped and her steps slowed. "Do you…?" She glanced at Taylor under her lashes. "Do you think we'll make it out of here?"

Taylor slowed her pace to match Andi's. "I think so." She smiled gently. "Your dad's like you—intuitive and strong—and I believe he'll find a way to get us out of here safely. Matter of fact, that's what we're going to tackle today by hiking to the outcrop."

Andi's downfallen expression lifted a bit. "How long will that take?"

"Oh, a few hours or so. But considering what all of us have already been through, that'll be a breeze." She looked up, studied the splash of color from the morning sunrise as it spread across the clear sky. "Did you hear the helicopter two days ago?"

"Yeah. It was so far away, though."

"It flew over me and your dad at one point." When they reached the spring, Taylor stopped and gave Andi what she hoped was a look of confident encouragement. "It was right there. Close enough to see us if we'd just been on higher ground. Away from the trees. That's why we're going to the outcrop. We're going to climb to the top and flag it down the next time it passes."

Shadows of doubt crept into Andi's eyes. "Are you sure it'll come back?"

Taylor's heart melted at the wounded look of uncertainty on Andi's face. Andi had lived her entire life without a mother, and the loss had left so many unanswered questions and distrust in her life. Something Taylor understood all too well.

"I don't know." She lifted her hand, then hesitated, her hand hovering near Andi's temple for a brief moment before she slipped her fingers under the fall of Andi's brown hair and smoothed it back gently. "We'll pray about it, okay? And if nothing else, I know your dad will take care of you."

Andi stiffened, her eyes trained on Taylor's face, then—in an almost unconscious gesture—leaned into her supportive touch. But it only lasted a second.

Abruptly, Andi pulled away and rubbed her temple, then limped toward a clump of bushes near the stream. "I'll get the berries," she said over her shoulder as she walked away.

Taylor sighed, watching as Andi bent and began poking through a thick bush in search of berries. Wouldn't do to push her too much or intrude on her space. And with the luck she'd had recently, Andi might interpret her offer of comfort as an opportunistic move to wedge herself between Andi and Will.

She proceeded to the spring, cleared several rocks out of the way, lined up the water bottles on the ground and began filling them one by one. Two bottles were filled, then a third, and she pulled a small pack of iodine pills from her pocket and added one into each bottle, then secured the top.

For a while, the steady snip of Andi picking berries, light gurgle of water into plastic bottles and chirp of birds filled the air. Then a soft rustling sounded nearby and a dark, familiar shape emerged from the tree line near the bushes where Andi stood.

Taylor froze, then straightened from the spring slowly and spoke softly. "Andi."

She didn't hear her. Instead, Andi bent lower, her brown hair swinging over her shoulder as she continued riffling through the bushes for more berries.

"Andi."

Finally, she looked up, confusion in her eyes as she surveyed Taylor. "What?"

"You need to stay calm and walk over here slowly." Taylor, eyes glued to the bear, watched as it roamed closer, nosing its way toward one of the bushes. "Drop the berries."

Frowning, Andi straightened and followed Taylor's gaze, her eyes widening as she noticed the black bear. "Taylor…"

Panic laced her voice.

"It's okay," Taylor soothed. "I'm right here. Just stay calm and walk toward me."

Body trembling, Taylor tried to slow the thoughts

jumbling together in her mind. What had Will said? The "stay calm" part she remembered, but what else?

The bear raised his head, his bulky form bobbing slightly as his nose worked, sniffing the air, searching for the source.

What else had Will said? Stay calm, and don't... Don't what?

The bear stopped bobbing, lowered his head and locked eyes with Andi.

Oh, no...

"Taylor?" Andi's voice pitched and her hands dropped, scattering berries at her feet.

The bear grunted. Took one step toward Andi, then another. And another.

"Taylor!" Andi spun and took off, stumbling as her injured ankle failed to support her weight.

Don't run, Taylor recalled Will saying. *Stand your ground, shout him down and fight.*

"Don't run, Andi," Taylor shouted. "Don't r—"

The bear charged, his muscular bulk barreling through the bushes, storming across the grass, chasing Andi as she fled.

Taylor snatched up two handfuls of rocks and ran toward them both, her shoes slipping and catching between stone crevices on the bank of the stream as she shouted, "No! Get out of here and leave her alone! Go!"

The bear continued its pursuit of Andi and gained ground, its heavy breaths rasping closer and closer.

Try to look bigger than he is. It's the only way to scare him off.

"Get out of here!" Taylor screamed and yelled, her voice choppy as she ran, gasping for air.

"Tayl—!"

The bear lunged, his paw swiping at Andi's back. Its claw caught her injured leg and jerked her off her feet. She hit the ground, her palms slamming onto the dirt to soften her fall, then scrambled wildly through the grass as the bear dragged her backward by her foot. A sharp scream burst from Andi, piercing the still morning air.

"Let her go!" Taylor ran faster, drew back her arm and slung a rock at the bear's head.

He flinched, growled deep in his chest, then rose up on his back legs and lunged over Andi toward her instead, his sharp claws extended.

She flung another rock, but it glanced off his broad shoulder and bounced harmlessly across the ground. His wet nose and massive head butted into Taylor's belly, knocking her off her feet. Her body slammed onto the ground, the impact stealing her breath.

There was a brief moment of stillness as a familiar terror took hold, snaking through her, paralyzing her muscles, and she blinked at the clear sky above. Disjointed thoughts rushed through her mind, her attention latching on to one coherent thought that hissed through her as she recalled Preston's voice.

Don't move. Stay right there, and I'll come to you.

A low growl resumed, black fur brushed her exposed legs and a sharp claw dug into her thigh.

Galvanized with pain, anger and years of pent-up terror, Taylor shot upright, kicking and punching. Her feet hit thick fur and muscle, and her fists pounded soft tissue. Angry growls erupted from the bear, but she pressed on, lashing out and striking him until everything around her became an agonizing blur of blood, pain and anger.

* * *

Will double-checked supplies, ensured everything had been accounted for and packed them back into the dry bag. He'd just secured the bag when an ear-splintering scream pierced the air.

Andi.

He shot to his feet and ran in the direction of the sound, his heart hammering against his ribs as he peered ahead. There, dozens of yards ahead, running toward him, was Andi.

"Dad!" She tripped and stumbled, almost falling to the ground. Blood trailed over her shin and coated her injured ankle.

He met her halfway, catching her as her leg finally gave out. "What happened? Where's Taylor?"

Chest rising and falling on heavy sporadic breaths, she motioned over her shoulder in the direction of the stream. "B-bear…has Taylor."

His hands clamped around her upper arms and he eased her to the ground. "Where?" She didn't answer. Her face paled and her teeth chattered. "Near the stream." She gulped in air. "By the bushes."

Will sprang up and ran again, forcing his legs to cover as much ground as possible while he scanned the area. And there, between the stream and a row of bushes, was Taylor, fighting off a black bear.

She was kneeling on the ground, legs and fists flailing, striking blow after blow on the bear's head and shoulders. Vicious growls and angry huffs echoed around the small clearing, just yards from where the stream peacefully flowed, creating a nightmarish contrast.

Throat closing, Will pumped his legs harder and waved his arms in the air. "Here! Over here!"

The bear jerked back, stepped away from Taylor and glared in his direction.

Will hustled faster, surging up the grassy slope in the bear's direction. "Get! Go on! Get out of here!"

Taylor was on her feet now, a large stick in her hands. She swung it at the bear and advanced toward the animal, hoarse shouts bursting from her lips. She swung a second time, then another. On the third swing, she landed a hard blow to the bear's eyes and nose.

Flinching, the bear reared backward, crashed through a line of bushes, then turned and ran, his black hide disappearing behind a thick swath of trees.

Taylor fell to her knees, heavy sobs escaping her as she crumpled to the ground and lowered her forehead to the grass.

"Taylor?" Will drew to a halt beside her and touched his hand gently to her heaving back. She didn't answer—just continued sobbing. "He's gone now. You're safe now."

She curled closer to the ground.

"Is she okay?"

Will glanced over his shoulder and found Andi standing behind him, tears streaming down her face, balancing on her good leg. "I don't know," he whispered. "Taylor? If you're hurt, I need to see so I can help. Can you stand?"

Again, no answer.

Will crouched down, eased his arms beneath her and gently rolled her into his arms. Apart from a wound on her thigh, she looked relatively unharmed, as far as he could tell—which was a miracle in and of itself.

He lifted her to his chest, then stood, the desperate cries racking her body, making his hands tremble. She buried her face against his neck, her hot tears rolling over his skin.

"Dad?" Andi dragged her forearm over her wet face, her tears drying but expression startled.

"It's all right," he said softly. "I think she's shook up, is all. Let's take her to the stream and help her rest a few minutes."

Andi shuffled around on her good leg and limped by Will's side as he carried Taylor over to the stream, eased her onto the bank and sat beside her.

Immediately, Taylor returned to his open arms, pressed her cheek to his chest and gripped his T-shirt. "I—I killed him."

A wry smile twisted his lips. He smoothed his hand over her back and hugged her close. "Nah. You just gave him a scare, is all. That bear got off easy, all things considered."

She shook her head, her hair tickling his chin. "Preston."

His smile faded. "What'd you say?"

"Preston," she repeated, her voice hitching. "I killed him."

Will froze. "Your husband?"

He met Andi's shocked gaze over Taylor's head, then refocused on Taylor as she shook in his arms.

She was in shock. Confused. That was all. "Taylor." He leaned back, gently cupped her jaw and lifted her tearstained face from his chest. "What are you saying?"

She looked up at him, fresh tears flooding her blue eyes and dimpled chin trembling. "Five years ago, I…" Her voice broke and, sobbing, she continued. "Things got really bad. He attacked me almost every day over the smallest things." She shook her head. "No matter what I did—or didn't do—it would set him off. I knew if I didn't leave him, he'd end up killing me. I didn't want to believe that—I'd prayed so hard for God to change him—but I knew it was the truth. So I left him. I got an apartment and told him I wouldn't come back. That it was over." Tremors racked her body. "Things went okay for a month or so. Then he started calling. Started stopping by, asking me to change my mind. He apologized, begged for forgiveness. You know…" She looked away, her hair falling over her cheek, and tried to smile, but her lips twisted, shame engulfing her face. "Did the usual things I used to fall for."

Will smoothed her hair back, tucked it gently behind her ear.

"But I wouldn't give in," she continued. "One morning, I got dressed for work, went to the kitchen, poured a cup of coffee, and when I turned around, he was standing right there, watching me." She stared at the ground, an empty look entering her eyes. "He said, 'Don't move. Stay right there and I'll come to you.'" Her voice shook. "That's what he always said before he…"

Chest aching, Will cupped her cheek. "Before he'd hurt you?"

Taylor nodded, then whispered, her voice breaking, "Except that time he had a gun. And we fought." Her blue eyes met his again, shame flooding her features. "After I shot him, I tried to help him. I tried to make it right. But he said, 'You can't fix it now.' And he was right." Her expression crumpled. "I can't ever make it right. I can't take it back."

"Tayl—"

"He won't ever forgive me."

"Preston?"

"No. God." She stared up at him, blue eyes wide and voice breaking. "He won't ever forgive me, will He? For giving up on Him, or for what I did to Preston?"

Will studied her face. Watched her lips tremble and the dark shadows of despair return to her eyes. Reaching out, he cradled her face in his hands and drifted his thumbs through the tears streaming down her face. "He always forgives. All you need to do is ask."

A ragged breath left her as she stilled. "You believe that?"

"Yes," he whispered. "I do. I believe there's nothing we could ever do or not do that would cause Him to abandon us."

She continued peering up at him, her cries slowly subsiding.

"You did what you had to," he said softly. "Preston gave you no choice but to fight back. You're not a victim—you're a survivor. A strong, caring, wonderful woman who saved my daughter's life twice. And mine at least once." Emotion swelled in his chest, warm and pleasant, and streamed through his veins. "A woman I'm…"

He paused, his thumbs slowing to a stop on her flushed cheeks.

…falling in love with.

Face warming, Will glanced at Andi, the question in her eyes reflecting his own surprise at the strength of emotions running through him. He swallowed hard, set the overwhelming realization aside and refocused on Taylor's face.

"A woman I'm glad chose the same path as me and my daughter this weekend," he finished quietly.

Taylor's tears slowed. "I'm glad, too. Things may be rocky, but I'm very thankful I've had the chance to meet both of you. I just hope I didn't give you too hard a time the first couple of days."

A grin fought its way to his lips, the small action a slight relief from the intense emotions swirling within him. "Nah. You've challenged me—kept me on my toes. I promise you this trip wouldn't have been the same without you. I'd have been stranded on my own for two days with no one to brave the snake, mudslide and bears with."

Andi scooted closer to them, a note of intrigue replacing the sad, fearful tone in her voice. "There was a snake? And a mudslide?"

Slowly, Taylor smiled back at him, tears drying on her cheeks as she glanced over at Andi. "There's been a little bit of everything on this mountain."

"And there's more waiting on us," Will said, his smile fading at the thought of Andi's and Taylor's injuries and the hike and climb that lay ahead. He inspected the bleeding wound the bear had left behind on Taylor's thigh, curled his palm around her shin and squeezed. "Let's get you cleaned up. It's time we found a way out of here."

TWELVE

Headstones were not a good sign.

Taylor stopped in the center of a small cemetery, her sweaty skin prickling under the cool shade of thick trees towering around the overgrown space.

"This can't be right." Andi, her limp more pronounced, hobbled out of the thick tree line and bit her lip as she stared at the weathered grave site. "What's a graveyard doing in the middle of nowhere?"

"It's historic." Taylor bent, rubbed her tired eyes and inspected an aged headstone. The elements had taken their toll, leaving black tinges on the edges of the stone, and green algae had spread across its center, obscuring most of the markings. "From the late 1800s to early 1900s, probably."

Will, standing several feet ahead, surveyed the tangle of trees, shrubs and foliage obscuring the terrain that lay before them. "We're in deep backcountry. No telling what we'll stumble across." He glanced back at them, concern in his dark eyes. "Keep your eyes and ears open. Stick together and keep talking. We've got a lot more ground to cover."

And after that, they'd have to climb five thousand

feet to reach the crag and hope the rescue helicopter returned at just the right time. It was a long shot at best, but there was no alternative.

Taylor rubbed her weary eyes. Three hours ago, they'd sat by the stream for a little while, washing their wounds, refilling the empty water bottles and collecting themselves after the bear attack—and her grief-stricken confession over Preston's death.

She stilled, waiting for familiar emotions to assail her at the memory—guilt, shame and condemnation. But…they didn't come.

Instead, a sensation of exhausted relief had replaced the turmoil that had clamored inside her for years, and the brief unsettled feeling she'd experienced at the sight of the headstones began to ease. It was as though confessing her actions out loud had helped lighten the heavy burden she'd carried for so long, and Will's reassurance that she could be forgiven had nourished the hope that struggled to bloom within her heart, allowing it to grow and unfurl fully in her chest. It had stayed with her during the two hours they'd hiked after leaving the campsite and made their way to the ravine, though their progress had been slowed by injury, hunger and exhaustion.

But even now, that hope resurfaced as she joined Will in examining the imposing path that lay ahead, the miles that separated them from a chance of being rescued and the ever-increasing ascent to the rocky outlook.

"We can do it," she said. Just not alone.

I believe there's nothing we could ever do or not do that would cause Him to abandon us.

"Yeah." Will smiled—tired but sincere—and looked at Andi. "How you holding up?"

Andi lifted her chin and smiled back, but it was forced. "I'm good. Let's keep going."

"Not quite yet." Taylor crossed the clearing and eyed Andi's shin. "You're bleeding again."

Bright scarlet blood had seeped through the make-shift bandage wrapped around her leg, and it had begun to trickle toward her injured ankle.

Taylor crouched beside Andi, wincing as her tight muscles screamed in protest, and carefully began peeling off the soaked cloth. "Lean on me so you don't strain your ankle and let me know if it starts to hurt too much."

Andi flinched and a cry of pain left her lips, but when Taylor paused in removing the dressing, she looked down at Taylor and motioned for her to continue.

After peeling off the blood-soaked dressing, Taylor grabbed a bottle of filtered water from the dry bag she carried and, watching Andi's face for signs of discomfort, poured it carefully over the wound, washing away bits of dirt and the trickle of blood.

"You're good at this," Andi said, placing a hand on Taylor's shoulder for balance and peering down at her injury.

Taylor paused then, satisfied the wound was clean again, returned the water bottle to the dry bag and ripped another strip of cloth off the bottom of her shirt. "I've had a lot of practice."

A tense silence filled the space between them. Then Andi asked softly, "Because of your husband?"

Grimacing, Taylor nodded, then proceeded to wrap the strip of cloth around Andi's shin.

Andi squeezed her shoulder gently, stilling her movements. "I'm sorry. I wish that hadn't happened to you."

Taylor looked up and smiled. "Thank you."

Andi leaned closer. "I wish things had been different," she said. "For all of us."

Taylor slowly tied the fabric into a snug knot. "What kinds of things?"

Andi glanced at Will, who walked to the other side of the graveyard and ducked between a tangle of trees to study a different route through the ravine. "Did he tell you about my mom?"

"A little."

"That she left us?"

Taylor stood. "Yes."

Andi released Taylor's shoulder and looked down at her bandage. Her fingers picked at the fabric, testing the knot. "Did you know your mom when you were my age?"

"No. I never met her."

Andi looked up again, her brown eyes seeking Taylor's. "What about your dad?"

"I never knew him, either."

She was silent for a moment, then said, "My dad told me last night that he thought you might be on your own. He said he tries to remember that everyone struggles with something, and that it's important to save room in his heart to be kind and help others when he can." Face flushing, she winced. "I'm sorry I haven't been more welcoming to you lately."

Taylor smiled gently. "It's okay. You're pretty lucky,

you know? Having a dad like yours. He loves you very much."

The sadness in her expression eased as she glanced across the clearing again, one corner of her mouth lifting in a small grin when Will reemerged from the trees. "Yeah. He's pretty fantastic. Even if he does get on my nerves sometimes."

Taylor laughed. "I'm guessing that's usually what happens when dads are looking out for their daughters. I'd be worried if he didn't get on your nerves once in a while. Wouldn't you? At least that's one way you know how much he cares."

The little mouth hitch turned into a full-blown, pleased grin. "I suppose."

Will, sipping from a bottle of water, halted midstep in their direction, lowered the bottle and narrowed his eyes at Taylor. "She's not sharing more disastrous moments from our camping trips, is she?"

Nope. She's just proving even more what a wonderful dad—and man—you are.

Heart skipping, Taylor kept that pleasant thought to herself, cocked her head to the side and grinned. "How many disastrous moments were there?"

Will smirked. "More than I'd care to revisit."

"Then you better keep us moving before Andi has a chance to remember another one." Taylor motioned toward the overgrown paths behind him. "Which way do you think is the straightest shot to the outcrop?"

"Hard to tell," he said. "But my best guess would be the one on the left. There's a narrow trail that winds down the mountain a ways, and I can hear water moving farther down the path. We need to refill the water bottles again, and that might be a good place to do it."

"I'm starving," Andi said. "How much farther do you think it'll be until we make it to the outcrop?"

"Don't know. Might have a better idea when we reach the bottom of the trail." Will frowned, tipped his head back and looked at the sky. "But it's taking us longer than I planned, so we may need to regroup when we reach the stream. Decide if we want to chance tackling the outcrop today or camp one more night."

Taylor glanced up, too, noting the slow swing of the sun toward the western part of the sky. Unless the outcrop was right around the corner, the chances of them reaching the crag today were pretty slim.

"Might not be a bad thing if we don't make it today," Taylor said. "It'll be a strenuous climb, and a good night's rest will help us all, I think."

Nodding, Will lifted his chin at Andi. "How's your leg?"

Andi smiled. "Good. Taylor changed the bandage and fixed me up."

"And your ankle?" Will's brows rose. "I don't want you keeping pain a secret, okay? If you're hurting, you'll tell me, right? That way we can—"

"Stop and rest," Andi finished for him, her smile widening. "Yes, sir. I promise."

A slow grin spread across Will's face. "Immediate compliance. Now, that's a first." His brown eyes settled on Taylor. "Whatcha been teaching my kid?"

Taylor shrugged. "Nothing. As a matter of fact," she added, winking at Andi as she recalled the advice he'd given her, "I think she's learning from you."

A look of pride entered Will's expression, and he held her gaze a moment longer before ducking his head and motioning for them to follow. "We better get going.

Sooner we reach the bottom of the trail, the sooner we'll get full water bottles and a breather."

Taylor watched him stroll toward a narrow dirt path, her attention clinging to the wide set of his shoulders and muscular profile beneath a splash of sunlight through the thick trees. For such a strong man, he was patient, considerate, and maybe even had a bit of a sensitive side, judging from what Andi had shared. Andi was indeed lucky to have him as her father. And any woman would be lucky to have him in her life at all.

Her cheeks warmed and, catching Andi's eyes on her, she held out her arm. "Why don't you lean on me? It'll make the walk downhill easier."

Andi hesitated, but nodded gratefully and curled her arm around the bend in Taylor's elbow. "Thanks."

They followed Will down the winding dirt path, Andi leaning on her as they stepped over knotted roots and ducked beneath low-hanging branches. The descent was steeper than she'd anticipated, and soon beads of sweat began trickling over her temples and down her cheeks.

"How much farther?" Andi asked, her breath catching, the limp more noticeable.

"We're almost to the creek," Will said, glancing back at them.

True to his word, Will lifted a thick branch out of the way, motioning for them to proceed, and once they cleared the trees, sunlight flooded a damp moss-covered bank, and the gurgling rush of water arose in the humid summer air. Due to recent rains, the water moved high and fast.

A shudder ran through Taylor at the memory of the

river's strong pull, sucking her beneath the surface. "How deep do you think it is?"

"Five, six feet, maybe," Will said, joining them on the bank. "There's a clearing on the other side." He pointed to a thick log that had fallen over the deepest part of the swift creek, forming a crude but somewhat stable bridge to the other side of the bank. "Normally, I'd say that'd be a good place to cross, but all things considered…" His gaze lingered on Andi's leg and he shook his head. "Maybe we should try swimming across instead? Or maybe finding another place to cro—"

"No," Andi said quickly. "I don't want to go back in the water yet. I'm so tired, all I want to do is crash for a while. I can make it across the log."

Taylor glanced at Andi, who leaned more heavily on her arm. The young girl's expression was determined, but her lips pressed into a thin line as though she were in pain. "What about your ankle?" she asked softly. "That log isn't a flat surface, and you'll need the use of both feet to stay balanced all the way across."

Andi frowned and glanced down at her injured ankle. "If I hold on to you, I think I could stay balanced long enough to make it across."

"Might be easier in the water," Will said. "You could hold on to the log, and Taylor and I could help y—"

"Please, Dad." Her hand tightened around Taylor's arm as she stared at the water rushing past them. "I don't want to go back in the water yet. I can do it if Taylor is okay with helping me." She looked up, her eyes searching Taylor's. "What do you think?"

Taylor studied the vulnerable shadows in her eyes and the hint of hope fighting its way into her expression. She smiled, all too aware of what Andi was feeling. That pressing need to strike out and prove herself. To move on. To reach for something better.

For so many years, Taylor had felt empty—almost dead inside. But lately, especially after her confession to Will and his reassurance that God would never abandon her, she was beginning to feel more capable than she had in a long time. And during this trip, she'd begun to feel alive—truly alive—for the first time in her life.

Taylor smiled. "I think we should go for it."

Will planted his right foot on the center of the log, reached out his left arm and carefully glanced over his shoulder. "You ready?"

Andi slipped her arm around his and nodded. "Ready."

She didn't sound ready. Her breath had quickened, her eyes darted over the water rushing beneath their feet and her hand clamped on to his upper arm. From the bank, the creek looked deep but unintimidating. Perched on the log, however, the scene was very different. Water, flowing fast several feet below them, crashed against stones, spraying their bare legs and arms. The steady roar of the current grew louder once they stepped onto the log, and the opposite riverbank—which had seemed no more than fifteen or twenty feet away while they stood safely on the ground beside the river—now looked as though it lay two miles away.

Will leaned forward an inch or two and glanced at Taylor, who stood on the other side of Andi, their arms entwined. "Taylor? You still up for this?"

She glanced his way, her blue eyes bright and blond

hair shining beneath a hint of sunlight that broke past the tall trees lining the creek. "Let's do it."

He stilled, savoring the sight of her excited expression. It was mesmerizing, almost—the slow change in her demeanor that had begun to gradually appear over the past couple of days. He'd first noticed it when she'd rescued him from the river after the mudslide. Instead of breaking down in tears or losing her temper with God as he had, she'd pointed out how God had helped them and encouraged him to see the brighter side of their situation. Two nights ago, a note of hope had entered her voice as they'd watched elk graze in the meadow near the lean-to they'd constructed. And last night, she'd stood for hours with him under the sparkling night sky, admiring the stars, finding common ground with his painful past and sharing her fears.

Sometimes I can't understand why He doesn't answer. Why He doesn't help us when we need Him so badly.

He'd wondered then if she'd be able to hold on to that little bit of hope he'd glimpsed in her eyes and heard in her voice two days ago. He'd wondered even more after she'd broken down with guilt and shame by the stream hours earlier. But with every step they'd taken along the mountain over the past hours, her tears had dried, her head had lifted and her eyes had looked up—not at the mountain peaks, he thought, but perhaps farther beyond. To something, or someone, even more beautiful and a thousand times more powerful.

Those rough waters are good at pushing people closer together. Closer to God, too.

Will smiled. Good ol' Jax. As much as he hated to give the man credit, he had to admit Jax had been right so far. Not only did it seem like Taylor was beginning to heal on this mountain, but his daughter was arm in arm with him, leaning on and trusting him, and it seemed Taylor might be, too.

"Take it slow at first," Taylor said, her eyes clinging to his as she adjusted her grip on Andi's arm. "One step at a time, okay?"

Will's smile grew. "You got it," he said softly.

Will refocused on the log, its surface speckled with splashes of creek water that sparkled in the sunlight, and carefully took a step forward. The wood felt slick beneath his shoe and he stiffened, maintaining a steady footing.

"All right, Andi," he said. "Like Taylor said, take it one step at a time, okay? And hold on to us as much as you need to."

A heavy breath left her parted lips and she nodded. "Okay."

She took one step and shifted her weight forward, teetering for a second on one leg.

Will steadied her with one hand. "It's not too late to change your mind. We can always turn back and—"

"No." She dragged in a steady breath and offered a tight smile. "Thank you, but I can do it. We're all tired, and this is the fastest way across."

Pride rushed through him, quiet and comforting. It'd been a long time since Andi had set her pain aside and thought of others besides herself. This was the confident, caring young woman he'd always known she was at heart.

She nudged him, the tension in her grip easing slightly as she laughed. "Come on, Dad. You're holding up the train."

He chuckled. "Yes, ma'am."

Will stepped forward again and Andi followed slowly, squeezing his arm tight as she shifted her weight and regained her balance. Taylor waited until Andi was steady on the log, and she'd follow, moving slowly along the log and supporting Andi with her hand on her elbow.

They continued across the log, one small step after another, the swift creek below them roaring loudly when they reached the center of the log, drowning out Will's voice as he guided Andi and Taylor's praise as she complimented Andi on her progress.

By the time they reached the last quarter of the log, the sun had dipped farther in the sky, Andi had stumbled twice and her arm shook in Will's hold.

"We're almost there, baby," he said, eyeing the length of the log, then the bank. "Three feet, maybe four, and we're there."

She nodded jerkily, refocused on the log and took another step. Her foot slipped across the wet bark and her arms flailed wildly in his and Taylor's grip.

Andi squealed, rocking back and forth within their hold. Will firmed his grip on her, bent his knees and squatted down a few inches to regain his balance. Taylor followed suit, and moments later, the swaying stopped and they stood as one again, steady and balanced, cold creek water spraying their faces and necks.

Taylor's soft laughter rang out above the water. "And to think, you almost backed out of this trip, Will."

Panic receded from Andi's face and she smiled. "Good thing I talked him back into it."

Lips quirking, Will cocked an eyebrow. "Y'all

wanna hold on to that thought until after we reach the bank? We still have a couple feet left to go."

Grins still plastered on their faces, they nodded.

Hiding his own smile, Will resumed the slow pace toward the bank and they followed, eventually making it safely to dry ground.

Andi sagged against him in exhausted relief. "Thank goodness that's over."

Will bent low, scooped her up in his arms and hefted her snug against his chest. "Let's get you somewhere where you can rest for a while." Glancing over his shoulder, he called back to Taylor as he walked, "There's a soft patch of grass on the other side of the clearing. I'm gonna get Andi settled and get a fire started. It's too late to tackle the last stretch to the overlook, so we'll camp here for the night and head out first thing in the morning."

Taylor shifted the dry bag she carried off her shoulders, lowered it on the ground and began rummaging inside. "I'll fill the water bottles at the creek, then join you."

Thanking her, Will strolled across the clearing, squinting against the glare of the late-afternoon sun as it slowly lowered behind the treetops. The sporadic chatter of birds began to slow, a rhythmic chorus of crickets began and a cooler breeze drifted over the creek and across the clearing.

Squatting, Will gently eased Andi to the ground, removed her shoes and checked her injuries. Her ankle was puffy—which was to be expected after such a long hike—but the bandage on her leg was in great shape and would last through the night without needing to be changed.

"Taylor did a good job fixing you up," he said, sitting on the grass beside Andi.

"Yeah." She wiped sweat from her eyes and peered down at her bandaged wound, a sad note entering her tone. "She said she's had a lot of practice."

Anger sparked in Will's gut and he curled his fingers into the thick grass, forming fists. His eyes sought Taylor's graceful form as she walked near the creek, crouching down and filling one water bottle, and then another. After filling the last bottle, she sat down on the bank, and when a crow flapped its big wings overhead, she looked up and smiled as it soared past.

He frowned, his chest aching at the thought of another man putting his hands on her. Hurting her. How could Preston have done it? How could he have married her, professed to love her and harmed her in such a way?

That kind of anger and violence he'd never understand. And Taylor deserved so much better. She deserved a man who appreciated her sharp mind and generous heart. Who respected her thoughts and beliefs. Who'd protect her and cherish her. A man like…

"You like her a lot, don't you?"

Andi was staring at him now, her narrowed eyes traveling slowly over his face.

"Yeah," he said softly, meeting her direct gaze head-on. "I do."

Andi studied him a moment longer, then turned away, her attention settling on Taylor in the distance. "I know I said that I wanted it to just be you and me." She picked at the grass, her fingers trailing through the long blades. "But some of today was kinda nice, you know?" She frowned. "Not the bear or Taylor being sad and all, but after. When she helped me on the hike. And when you were both helping me get across the creek. That was kinda nice." She glanced at Taylor again. "Working together like that, it was kind of like being a…"

"Team?" Will bit his lip, studying the play of emotions across Andi's face.

"Maybe. But it felt like more than that. It felt like…"

"Family?"

Andi looked at him then, her eyes meeting his, the same longing that throbbed in his chest reflected in her sad smile. "Yeah," she said, her voice hesitant. Surprised. "It felt like family."

THIRTEEN

Sunlight coaxed Will from a deep sleep. He blinked slowly against a thin ray of golden light that strolled across the grassy clearing, traveled over his feet and legs, then up his chest to settle over his cheek.

Inhaling, he stretched his arms overhead and flexed his legs, loosening his sore biceps and calves. His fingers bumped something soft and he rolled his head to the side to find Andi curled into a ball, sleeping deeply, beside him. Taylor, her cheek resting on her hand as she lay on the other side of Andi, still slept, too.

Smiling, Will refocused on the sky above them. The day was just getting started, the sun having only just begun peeking above the mountain peaks, and a burst of color painted the sky in hues of gold, pink and purple. A light mist hovered over the clearing, leaving his skin cool and relaxed, and he fought to keep his eyes open, the exhausting events of the past several days threatening to drag him back to sleep despite the lofty goal they'd planned for today.

Hours earlier, after Taylor had refilled the water bottles at the creek and rejoined him and Andi in the clearing, he'd built a fire and they all three had scavenged some nuts and berries in the bushes along the tree line, taking great care to stick together and keep an eye out for bears. Thankfully, the excursion had been uneventful, and by nightfall, the fire was flickering brightly beneath the stars. Bellies full and eyes heavy, they'd stayed up a while longer, lounging in the soft grass and pointing out constellations in the heavens. Andi had drifted off first and Taylor second, leaving him alone with his thoughts for another hour until he'd finally succumbed to sleep, as well.

Strangely enough, last night had been one of the most peaceful rests he'd ever had. A velvet sky full of stars, Andi's deep, peaceful breathing as she slept—the sound just as comforting now as it had been years ago when he'd checked on her in her crib at night—and the knowledge that Taylor was nearby, a part of their journey, had set his mind at ease. His prayers for a safe hike to the outcrop today had come easy, and sleep had sneaked up on him even more easily.

So much so, he didn't want to move at all from his grassy bed, despite the fact that they needed every drop of daylight they could capture for the journey to the outcrop.

His eyes fluttered closed and he'd almost drifted into a light sleep again when a soft drumlike beat whispered in the distance. The beating of wings. A hawk, maybe? Or a crow? It was too early to be an ow—

Will bolted upright, the earth tilting for a moment until his eyes focused on the misty clearing, swift-moving creek, then the mountain range that rose before him. He tilted his head, listening intently.

The sound receded, then renewed again, the steady rhythmic whirl very faint but discernible.

"Chopper." He shot to his feet, shook Andi awake first, then Taylor. "Up! Get up. We've got to get going."

He grabbed the water bottles that were scattered on the ground near the blackened remains of the fire and shoved them in the dry bag.

"What's wrong?" Andi, sitting up, rubbed her eyes.

"The helicopter's out." He stilled, motioning toward the mountain range in the distance as Taylor sat up and pushed her blond hair out of her face. "You hear that?"

Taylor tilted her head and eyed the sky. "Yeah. But it sounds like it's going in the other direction."

"Probably." He bent over the dry bag and secured it closed. "That's why we need to get going."

Taylor frowned and shook her head, a sleepy expression on her face. "So we're changing the plan? We're going to follow the helicopter instead?"

"Nope." Will stood and slung the dry bag over his shoulders. "We're going to the outcrop and we're going to climb to the crag."

Andi pointed toward the mountains. "But the helicopter's going that way." She swiveled around and pointed behind her. "And you said the outcrop's in that direction, right?"

"Yep." He nudged the charred wood of the previous night's fire with his shoe to make sure it had completely burned out. "If the rescue chopper's flying a full route today, it should pass back over this area in a little while. When it does, we need to be at the top of that outcrop, visible and ready to signal for help."

"How do you know it'll come back?" Andi asked, peering up at him.

He hesitated, glancing over his shoulder at the empty—and now silent—sky. "I don't. Not for sure."

Eyes lowering, she bit her lip. "What if we hike all that way and it doesn't show up?"

"It might happen, but I don't think it will," he said through stiff lips, hoping the uncertainty moving through him didn't emerge in his voice. "This is our best shot at getting help. We need to..." He spread his hands, searching for words. Searching for strength he wasn't sure he had left to ensure they made it safely out of the ravine and up another mountain for a rescue that may or may not come through for them. "We just have to..."

"Have faith." Taylor stood. "We have to have faith that it'll return. It almost found us once. We just have to believe that, this time, it'll show up again and get us out of here. That when we get to the top of that crag, we won't be alone." She met his eyes and smiled, the warm look of gratitude in hers lifting his spirits. "We'll keep talking to God and have faith that He'll answer."

Will nodded, admiring the hopeful light in her eyes and determined expression despite the dark circles of exhaustion under her eyes. "Yeah," he whispered. "He'll answer."

"Okay," Andi said, standing slowly. She winced as her injured ankle took her weight. "Let's go to the outcrop."

Will's heart sank as he eyed her ankle. Purple and red bruising had spread across the pale swollen flesh, wrapping around her ankle and marring her puffy heel. He knelt beside her, cupped her calf in his palm and gently lifted her foot, inspecting it closely.

It didn't look good. As a matter of fact, it—

"I'm fine." Andi's hand squeezed his shoulder. "I can make it to the outcrop."

He glanced up, a sweet mix of pride and admiration running through him at the determined tilt of her chin and confident set of her shoulders. "It's obvious you're in pain, Andi. And it's a long hike from here to the outcrop."

"I promise, I won't slow you down."

"I'm not worried about that," he said, easing her foot back to the ground. "I'm worried about you injuring yourself even more." Sighing, he eased back on his haunches and studied the rugged landscape in the distance. A sense of urgency spiked through him as he glanced at the still silent sky. "I'm familiar with these mountains and have a better shot at getting there faster." He glanced at Taylor. "If Taylor agrees, you and she could stay here and I'll hik—"

"No." Andi shook her head, her long brown hair spilling over her shoulders. "I don't want to split up again. What if something were to happen to you? What if—?"

"I'll be fine."

"But I won't know that for sure." Her voice broke and moisture glistened along her lashes. "I don't want to separate again. I won't know where you are, if you're okay or if I'll ever see you again." She shook her head. "I'd rather my ankle hurt during the hike than to sit here wondering whether you're okay or not."

Will rose and cupped her face in his hands, sweeping his thumbs gently across her cheeks. "Okay. We'll go together." He glanced at her shoes. "Let's see if we can get your shoes on. You're not hiking barefoot."

It took several minutes to get Andi's shoe on her injured foot. The swelling from her ankle injury had traveled down to her heel and toes, and after loosening the shoelaces and gingerly testing different angles, Will and Taylor finally managed to get the shoe in place and laced tightly enough that it was secure. Then they looped one of Andi's arms through one of their own and, positioned on either side of her, they helped her take her first slow steps of the morning across the clearing to loosen her tender muscles.

When they made it to the tree line, Andi's pace picked up and Taylor smiled. "There. I think we've gotten a steady rhythm. Just don't go running off on us."

A weak laugh burst from Andi in between heavy breaths. "There's absolutely no chance of that."

The first mile through thick woods and thorny brush was hard, but when they emerged from the ravine and reached the base of the mountain Will had spoken of, the imposing trail winding up the rugged mountain to the exposed outcrop seemed grueling…and almost impossible to surmount.

During the initial hike, Andi had leaned more heavily against Will, but now she practically sagged on his arm. He eyed the increased swelling of her ankle and the stubborn jut of her jaw. Her face was beet red and sweat soaked her shirt, but she stared up at the outcrop, an eager light in her eyes as she tilted her head to the side.

"I don't hear anything," she said. "How long do you think it'll take them to come back around this way?"

Will surveyed the blue sky. The sun had risen high above the mountain range as they'd hiked from the clearing to the outcrop, warming the air to a humid heat. There wasn't a cloud in sight…or any signs of a helicopter. Only the whistle of the breeze as it swept over mountain peaks punctuated the stillness surrounding them.

"I don't know." Will hefted the dry bag more securely on his right shoulder. "But at least we're in a clearer space. Hopefully, it'll swing by on our way up and catch sight of us."

Though he had to admit, he was beginning to have his doubts. The longer the day wore on, the less chance there was of the pilot returning.

"Let's keep going," Taylor said firmly, stepping onto a crude dirt path that led toward the outcrop. "The sooner we get there, the sooner we can rest."

The encouraging note in her voice spurred them on and they hiked another mile up the snakelike trail of dirt that wound around the mountain, higher and higher into direct rays of the hot summer sun, Andi's steps slowing more and more with each step.

A hawk circled overhead, its sharp cry ringing across the mountain range. Just below it, jutting out from around the bend in the trail, was the outcrop, its bald face rising up almost like an arrow pointing at the sky, each rugged ridge leading to the summit more perilous than the one before.

Andi looked up, sweat streaming down her blazing red face, her chest heaving on ragged breaths. "Are we...almost...there?"

"You are," Will said firmly. Halting midstep, he tugged Andi to a stop, too, then led her a few steps to the left and helped her lower to a seated position, her back resting against a smooth stretch of rock wall. "There's no way you're climbing that outcrop. You need to rest."

"But I—"

"No arguments." Will shrugged the dry bag off his shoulder and withdrew a bottle of filtered water. "Here." He unscrewed the cap and pressed the bottle to her lips, holding it steady as she drank from it slowly between heavy breaths. "You stay here, keep sipping that and rest."

He moved to stand and she reached out with a shaky hand, halting him. "Stay…stay here with me."

Heart breaking at the sound of fear in her voice, Will squatted down beside her and tucked a wet strand of hair behind her ear. "I've got to climb the outcrop, Andi. The best chance we have of being spotted is on that crag."

"Then let me go." Taylor eased down beside them, glancing from him to Andi. "I can make the climb, and you can both stay here."

Will shook his head. "It's a steep climb, Taylor. Shorter than the wall we scaled by the river, but it's more dangerous. There aren't as many big holds and you'll have to pivot more than—"

"Are you saying I can't do it?"

He paused, the slight twitch of her lips dragging a laugh from deep within his worry-laden chest. "No, I know better than that. And even if I didn't, I'd know the repercussions would be enough to keep me silent on it." His smile slipped and he leaned closer to her, saying softly, "I'm just worried, is all. You've got to be as exhausted as we are and you'll be climbing blind."

"So would you, if you went. At least this way you can stay with Andi." She reached out and squeezed Andi's shoulder. "Don't worry. I'll get us some help, and no matter what happens, your dad won't leave you."

Andi lowered the water bottle with a shaky hand, her expression crumpling and tears spilling over her lashes. "You'll be careful, won't you?" Her chin quivered. "You'll come back to us?"

"Of course." Taylor leaned over, wrapped her arms around Andi and hugged her tight, smoothing a hand over her hair. "As soon as the helicopter comes back or when the sun starts to set—whichever comes first—I'll climb back down and stay with you both."

A sob shook Andi's shoulders. Will's heart warmed as Andi hugged Taylor back.

"Be careful," Andi said brokenly.

"I promise," Taylor whispered before releasing her and standing.

Will stood and walked with her, saying over his shoulder, "Stay put, Andi. I'll be back in a sec."

They rounded the corner and stood at the base of the outcrop, staring up at the steep trail of rock.

"Trust." Will cleared his throat, struggling to steady the tremor in his voice. "Free-climbing isn't about—"

"Physical strength," Taylor finished for him, facing him. "I know. A lot of what's needed," she continued softly, placing her hand gently on his chest, her warm touch settling directly over his heart, "is here."

Emotion rolled through his chest, strong and pleasant, making his breath catch. He covered her hand with his own and squeezed. "Please be careful. Take your time."

She nodded, her blue eyes lowering to his lips. "I will."

He dipped his head, pressed his forehead to hers and closed his eyes, savoring the feel of her presence. She pressed closer, her chin lifting and lips brushing his.

He covered her mouth with his own, kissing her back softly, trying his best to transfer every bit of strength he had left to her, praying for her safe return.

A soft sigh of pleasure left her and he raised his head, his eyes searching the dark blue depths of hers. "You're not alone. I'll be right here if you need me."

Nodding, she slid her hand from his chest and stepped back, then walked to the base of the outcrop, felt for a secure hold and hoisted herself onto the lowest ledge.

Will's throat tightened as he watched her sweat-slicked arms and legs lift her weight higher and higher, her muscles flexing as the wind whistled past the sharp edges of the crag above.

"You know how precious she's become to me," he whispered on a quiet prayer to the silent sky above. "Move the mountain for her. Please get her there safely."

Taylor curled her fingers around the sharp edge of stone, wincing as it cut the tender flesh of her palm. She looked over her shoulder at the drop below, a sense of dread snaking through her at the sight of hard rocks and thorny brush. But that was nothing compared to the summit of the outcrop. The crag was little more than a narrow wedge jutting out from the mountain itself, planted atop the mountain she, Andi and Will had climbed, almost five thousand feet above the ground.

Look up.

The deep tones of Will's voice whispered through her mind and she faced the huge stone in front of her and inhaled slowly.

"Keep looking up," she reminded herself. "That's where I'm headed."

Or at least that was where she'd been heading for the past half hour. Only, with each foot she climbed, she left Andi and Will farther behind, and soon they were out of sight, and she was on her own.

She rested briefly, perched there on the side of the outcrop, her hands holding the ledge above her and her toes planted on the ledge below, and rolled her lips, recalling Will's kiss. The feel of his tender kiss still lingered on her lips, warming her skin and sending a rush of strength through her chest, lifting her spirit.

You're not alone.

She looked up again and focused on a small wisp of a cloud in the distance, its white contours flexing with the wind's current, stretching and shifting along with the breeze across the sky. A heavier gust of wind swept over the mountain. Then silence settled, her raspy breaths the only sound on the ledge.

Arms trembling, she pressed closer to the rock's face. She wasn't alone—she'd truly begun to believe that. If only He'd speak or send a sign…anything so long as it offered reassurance and gave her the strength she needed to ascend the remaining feet of imposing stone.

Sweat stung her eyes and she blinked hard, wincing as her eyes burned. Thoughts muddled in her mind, tangling together in phrases and half-formed sentences, the toll of the past few days sinking past her skin, through her muscles, and seeping into her bones, making her body feel heavy and sluggish.

Fatigue and soreness washed over her. Her thighs shook and a cramp knotted in the sole of her right foot, forcing her to curl tighter to the rocky face to which she clung, and she bit back a pained cry.

"What did your pops used to say, Jax?" She forced herself to speak, to ask the question out loud and regain her focus. "On the bank, what did you mention he used to say?"

Her disjointed thoughts, whirling together, began to part, easing away from each other, and one memory solidified in her weary mind.

When the world broke a man, all he had to do was come to God's land and let Him know he's here.

"That's all I need to do, right?" she asked, grabbing the thought and holding on to it. Centering it in her mind. "I just have to let You know I'm here."

Sucking in a strong breath, she tightened her grip on the ledge above, pulled hard and hoisted her body onto the next landing.

"It's taken me a long time to get this far." Voice trembling, she continued praying. "And I'm hoping You'll help me along a little bit further."

The next good hold was to the right, at least three feet away, and she'd have to shift her weight to one leg to reach it.

"I'm asking for another chance," she prayed softly. "A chance to get my feet under me and start over."

She lifted her right leg, shifting her weight to the side, and balancing on her left foot, she focused on the ledge up ahead, homing in on the most secure place to grab.

"Please forgive me for not trusting You. Please help me find a way forward."

Inhaling, she held her breath and lunged upward, her hand landing in the right spot—the perfect place she'd homed in on—and her right foot settled on a small, safe rock two feet above her. She immediately dragged her left leg up, balanced on both feet and regained her bearings.

A swift breeze swept over the outcrop, cooling her overheated skin, and she tipped her chin up, breathing deeply. Just feet above her, the crag jutted out over her head, a smooth bare shelf of rock that offered an unimpeded view of the mountain range and skyline. But the next move would be tricky. There was only one choice to make—a straight upward lunge toward the shelf, quick grab and pull…or a longer, unpredictable route around the crag with the hope that the path, unviewable from this angle, would be clear enough to scale to the summit.

A cut on her palm began to bleed, coating her skin with blood, causing her hold to slip. She scrambled with her left hand, pulling harder and leaning to the left, her obliques screaming at the abrupt movement.

"I'm here…" she whispered, her legs aching. "Please help me. Which way do I go?"

Her grip slipped again, her right hand losing its hold, and she flailed briefly, the tips of her toes straining to maintain their balance on the lower jut of rock and her left hand clamping down on the rough rock beneath her fingertips.

"Please—" Her voice broke, a sense of dread sinking her spirit, weighing her down even further. "Which way?"

A soft throbbing sound echoed in the distance. The rapid beat mingled with the pounding of her heart, drawing closer and growing louder. Faint cries peppered the air, the sharp calls barely discernible, but the sound drifted up the mountain, reaching her ears, speeding up her heart.

The helicopter!

She rolled her head carefully to the left and there it was, just a small dark speck in the blue sky, but headed in the direction of the outcrop. Glancing over her shoulder, she hoped to catch a glimpse of Andi or Will, but saw nothing but jagged ledges and a spine-snapping drop to the ground below.

The shouts returned, so very faint and far away that they barely carried on the breeze, but she heard them all the same. Heard Andi and Will urging her on, even though she couldn't see them.

Adrenaline spiking, she dragged her wet hand over her soggy shorts, managed to wipe most of the blood away, then eyed the thrust of the crag above her.

"I'm here," she shouted, the sound hoarse. Weak.

The whip of helicopter blades drew closer, whirling louder, faster.

Lunging upward, Taylor grabbed the crag with her right hand, then left, and yanked, hauling herself up and over the sharply angled ledge, her legs dangling precariously in the air for a few moments as she dragged her lower body onto the smooth landing.

"I'm here!" Muscles seizing and body throbbing with pain, she shoved to her feet, lifted her arms high above her head and waved. "Over here! We're over here!"

The dark speck drew nearer and nearer, increasing in size, the distinctive shape of the helicopter sharpening as it approached.

Hot tears streaming down her cheeks, Taylor reached higher and waved her arms faster, hope flooding her heart as the helicopter flew over her, then circled back, slowing as it headed toward the crag, then hovered above her.

Dropping her head back, she smiled heavenward, the rhythmic throb of the helicopter's blades pounding in time with the beat of her heart as hope flooded her soul and filled her eyes with a fresh surge of happy tears.

God hadn't abandoned her. He was right here with her, had been all along—even during her darkest times—residing within her heart and leading her to a safer place and better life. He'd led her here, to safety and strength. To Will and Andi.

FOURTEEN

"Do you know where you want to go?"

Taylor swallowed a hefty swig of cherry-flavored soda, savored the sweet fizz of carbonated water on her dry tongue and opened her eyes.

A nurse stood in front of her, writing notes on a clipboard. He stopped writing, tucked the pen behind his left ear and smiled. "Slight dehydration, minor lacerations and no broken bones. You were lucky, all things considered." He crossed his arms, the clipboard tucked against his chest. "Dr. Hamilton's cleared you, so you're free to go. I can buzz the front desk if you want? They'd be happy to call a cab for you and you could be on your way in less than ten minutes to wherever it is you'd like to go."

Taylor stared at him for a moment, absorbing his words, letting the moment sink in. For the first time in her life, she'd spent no more than half an hour in a doctor's presence and been cleared to leave in less than that amount of time with a smile and well wishes.

No one had questioned her endlessly about the cuts on her leg and hands. There'd been no skeptical glances or intense stares full of pity. Just a quick examination and wound cleaning, brief surprise and sympathy for the disastrous rafting trip she'd endured and the cold can of cherry-flavored soda she'd requested from the hospital cafeteria's vending machine pressed into her bandaged palm.

All in all, it was the best experience she'd ever had in a hospital. And not once had her skin clammed up or her hands shaken while sitting on the narrow hospital bed in close confines with the male doctor and nurse.

"...anything else?"

Taylor blinked and shook her head, refocusing on the nurse. "I'm sorry. What did you say?"

"I asked if you had any questions or needed anything else before we get you checked out."

She tipped the can up, drained the last bit of soda and grinned. "Could I have one more of these, please? Or will I be overcharged and sent a horrendous bill later?"

He grinned back. "Oh, you've done this before, huh?"

"Yeah." She tensed, but the memories that briefly moved through her mind were not nearly as painful as they had been in the past, and her smile remained.

"Don't worry. There's a gentleman waiting for you in the lobby. He's footing the bill." The nurse turned and headed for the door, saying over his shoulder as he left, "Take your time. The soda and your friend will be waiting for you when you're ready."

Her heart skipped. *Will.*

After the nurse left, Taylor grabbed her shoes by the chair, put them on, left the hospital room and made her way down the hall to the lobby. It wasn't very busy; the late-afternoon crowd that filled the waiting room had thinned out since she, Andi and Will had arrived in the emergency room several hours ago.

It'd taken a little while to load everyone into the rescue helicopter, and the flight to the nearest hospital had lasted around forty-five minutes. When they'd arrived, Andi had been taken back immediately and Will had gone with her. Taylor had been taken to a different room later, and she had yet to hear how either of them were doing. But maybe Will was waiting for her right now.

Taylor scanned the waiting room, skimming over at least a dozen empty chairs and several strangers before her gaze settled on a familiar face.

"There you are," Jax said, standing. He held a can of cherry-flavored soda in one hand and a hesitant smile creased his cheeks. "I was just about to go back there and rustle up a doctor with some answers." His good humor dimmed as he took in her appearance, and he grimaced. "Well, that's if you wanted me to. Wouldn't blame you if you didn't want to see or talk to me."

She studied his face, long gray beard and embarrassed expression, and bit back a smile, so grateful he was still in one piece, alive, healthy and standing tall.

"Can't say I've ever let a rafting customer down so badly before." He picked at his jeans, rubbed his flushed forehead. "I won't blame you if you kick me in the shin. You can kick me in both shins if you want. It was my fault y'all got stuck out there with no—"

Laughter burst from her lips. She walked across the room, threw her arms around him and squeezed. "It's so good to see you, Jax."

He rocked back on his heels for a moment, then slung his arms around her and hugged her back. "Well, now…" He choked up a bit. "This is a surprise, but I'll take it."

She laughed once more, then released him and stepped back, drinking in the safe and sound sight of him. "I'm glad you made it out of the river safely. What about Be—?"

"Beth and Martin are fine. Just fine." He dragged in a deep breath and shook his head slightly. "Though I still have no idea how we managed to crawl out from under that raft and out of those rapids."

"I bet you were praying."

Jax stilled and studied her face. "Yeah." He nodded slowly. "Yeah, I was."

Taylor grinned. "That'll do the trick. A little prayer goes a long way. It's something I learned on your rafting trip."

He raised an eyebrow. "Did you now?"

"Yep. Among a whole host of other things."

Jax watched her closely a moment more, then held out the can of soda and smiled. "I believe you ordered this?"

"I did." She accepted it, popped the top and took a long sip, then sighed with gratitude. "Thank you so much. You have no idea how good this tastes after days of drinking filtered river water."

He gave a knowing smirk. "Oh, yeah, I do. Had to make do with it myself for a while a few years ago when I was stuck in a similar predicament." He held up a finger, retrieved something from his chair and held it out. "I believe this belongs to you."

"My camera." Taylor picked it up, her fingers seeking out familiar placements as she tilted it to and fro, checking for damage. She turned it on and immediately a photo of the river appeared in the digital frame. More pictures popped up as she scrolled through, the last photos she'd taken from the banks of Bear's Tooth River, the rapids crashing below. "Amazing," she said softly. "Nothing looks cracked or broken, and everything seems exactly as it should be."

"Yep. You packed it well in a dry bag and we found it floating a couple miles downriver the first day we went searching for y'all. Just a shame you didn't have it with you while you were stranded out there. If nothing else, I bet you came across some fantastic sights." A serious note entered his voice. "By the way, did you find what you were looking for out there?"

"Indeed," she said, laughing. "As a matter of fact, I got a very close-up view of the falls the first day when I plunged over them." Taylor smiled wider, her heart filling with so much hope it spilled over, sending a peaceful sensation through her. "And I found something else I didn't even know I was looking for."

"Well." Jax shrugged. "Maybe next time you take a trip, you'll be able to snap a few pics of an even better view. Got any ideas where you want to go next?"

Yeah. She sure did. And the photos she imagined in her mind weren't of waterfalls or rivers, but of two people who'd become very important to her.

She shook her head. "Doesn't matter where I go next." The more important consideration was with whom. "Things turned out well on this trip, though," she continued. "Better than well, actually, considering what happened. How'd you, Beth and Martin make it off the mountain?"

"Chopper," he said, smiling. "Found us hiking up the riverbank the second day. And believe me, it wasn't a moment too soon. Beth enjoyed the raft well enough, but she sure ain't no happy camper when it comes to the kind of camping we were forced to do. First thing Beth did when we made it back to dry land was rent a hotel suite with a Jacuzzi. Don't think she's left that room yet. But that's understandable, considering it rained on us for hours that first night before we managed to find a bit of shelter."

"Same thing happened to us. Will and I spent the first night in a cave…" Her voice trailed off as she glanced around the lobby again, searching for the sight of him. "Where is Will, by the way? And Andi? Do you know if she's okay?"

Jax nodded and held up a comforting hand. "Yeah. She's all right. Came out with a banged-up ankle—which I suspect you already know. They had to stitch up a cut on her leg, and she's dehydrated, so they hooked her up to some fluids. Gonna keep her for at least one night to make sure she's good to go."

Taylor hesitated. "And Will?"

Jax tilted his head and studied her expression, a slow smile appearing. "He's with Andi. Doing fine, by all accounts." He gestured toward double doors on the other side of the room. "They're in a room down that hall. I only got back there once to check on them. Then the doc shooed me out to sew up Andi's stitches. Said no more visitors except family."

She bit her lip as a nurse opened the double doors and exited the hall, peering between the gap in the doors for a better view of the hallway. "I'd just like to see them. Make sure they're both okay. Do you think they'd let me in for a sec?"

Jax grinned, a mischievous look sparking in his eyes. "Oh, I think I can find a way to get you in."

Will shoved his hands in his pockets and stared out the small hospital room window. Night had fallen and stars sparkled brightly in the sky above the parking lot outside. He ducked his head a bit and grinned, his cheeks warming at the remembered feel of Taylor's hand inside his own, her palm pressing tight to his.

And even more comforting was the memory of Taylor sticking close by Andi's side as they'd traveled in the helicopter to the hospital. Despite her own lingering pain and exhaustion from the past few days, she'd put Andi's needs before her own, holding her hand during the flight, speaking softly when Andi had become nervous and walking by Andi's side from the helicopter into the hospital up until the moment the nurse helped Andi into a wheelchair and wheeled her down the hall.

When Andi had been wheeled into a room, helped into a bed and examined by a doctor, his focus had turned solely to Andi's well-being. He'd watched as her injuries were tended to and listened carefully to directions as to how to care for the wounds and replace the bandage on her leg. He'd been overjoyed when Jax had joined them, safe and sound, and stifled his laughter as Jax had grumbled when the doctor urged him out of the room. Then he'd sat by Andi's bedside for over an hour, smoothing a hand over her hair like he'd used to do when she was a little girl, until she'd fallen asleep. Once assured she'd drifted off into a peaceful sleep, he'd eased to the window to stretch his legs.

Now his thoughts returned to Taylor, and he longed

to slip out of the room and seek her out. Verify for himself that she was safe and well.

But he wouldn't leave Andi. Not when there was a chance she'd wake up without him here. Not to mention…there was this nagging feeling in the back of his mind. This unsettling concern that maybe the feelings he'd begun to hope Taylor had for him may have been a result of circumstance. A fluke, even. Just one of those things that happened under extreme stress or unusual circumstances.

Maybe here, back in his small hometown of Stone Creek, Taylor wouldn't feel the same. The rural community was probably a great deal different than the places she'd lived and toured as a travel photographer. And who knew how long she'd stay?

His gut hollowed, an uneasy sensation flowing through him. For all he knew, she may have already left Stone Creek. She might've checked out of the hospital, caught a cab and traveled straight to the airport.

No. He shook his head. That was something Heather would've done, not Taylor. But even so…what if she didn't feel the same way about him? What if the intense emotions she stirred within him were one-sided? It'd been so long since he'd dated, let alone fallen in love, that he—

The door creaked open. He turned around to find Taylor peeking around the door.

"I'm sorry," she whispered, glancing at Andi's sleeping form. "I didn't mean to wake her or intrude." She started backing away. "I'll just slip out and—"

"No," he whispered back. His heart beat faster as he crossed the room and eased the door open a bit more. "Please come in."

She hesitated for a moment, then slipped into the room and stepped back as he shut the door behind her.

"How'd you get past the stone-cold guard?" he teased.

Taylor grinned. "I've got connections." Concern darkened her eyes. "Do you mind? I don't want to disturb Andi or—"

"No, not at all. I'm happy you came." He kneaded the back of his neck, weighing his words. "Matter of fact, I was just thinking of you."

A blush bloomed along her cheekbones. "You were?"

He nodded. "How'd your doctor visit go? Everything okay?"

"Yeah. It was short and sweet. Best hospital visit I've ever had. It was a breeze compared to..." The blush in her cheeks darkened to a deep scarlet and she looked away, her gaze settling on Andi. "How's she doing?"

"Good." Will glanced at Andi, who still slept peacefully, hoping to distract himself from the raw emotions that surged within him at the mention of the abuse Taylor had endured from her ex-husband. "She's doing really well. A few stitches today, and she'll be checked again tomorrow morning. If she's rehydrated and still doing well, they say they'll release her to come home."

"That's great news." Taylor placed a can of cherry soda gently on the table beside Andi's bed, then lifted another can toward him. "I brought you both something. Well, Jax did, actually. He's provided me with a steady supply of soda, so I thought I'd share."

Will smiled as he took the soda. "You saw Jax?" At her nod, he added, "He was worried about you and felt awful for what happened. I told him it wasn't his fault but—"

"I told him the same thing, so maybe it'll finally sink in." She held his gaze, her blue eyes clinging to his. "Actually, I thanked him."

"For the trip?"

"Yeah," she said softly. "If it hadn't been for his ad highlighting the falls, I'd have never joined this trip or met you and Andi."

He waited, searching her expression, then studied her soft smile. Pleasure stirred in his chest as he remembered the kiss they'd shared on the outcrop, a surge of tenderness moving through him along with the desire to protect and comfort.

"I'm glad we met, too." He lifted his hand, sifted his fingers through the soft fall of her hair and trailed his fingertips across the freckles scattered along her cheek. "And I was hoping you'd feel the same after all we've been through."

She leaned into his touch, curling her hand around his and closing her eyes briefly, then rose on her toes and brushed her lips across his stubbled cheek. "Thank you."

He forced his eyes open—they had drifted shut at the soft touch of her mouth—and tried to focus on her words. "For what?"

"For saving my life," she whispered.

He brought her hand to his lips, kissed her wrist gently and smiled. "We saved each other."

Sheets rustled across the room and he lowered their clasped hands and slowly released her, then strolled across the room to Andi's bedside.

Her eyes fluttered open and she focused on him, a sleepy smile appearing. "Hey, Dad."

"Hey." He smoothed her hair back from her forehead. "How you feeling?"

Andi tilted her head back slightly and stretched her legs a little, flinching when her injured leg flexed. "Sore, but okay otherwise." She rolled her head gingerly to the side and eyed the IV that delivered fluids through her arm, glanced down at her legs and then noticed Taylor standing across the room. "Taylor." Her eyes widened a bit. "You came."

Taylor nodded and crossed to the other side of the bed. "Of course. I told you I would, and besides, I wanted to make sure for myself that you were doing okay."

Andi gestured toward the sheet, frustration briefly crossing her expression. "If it wasn't for my ankle and stitches, I'd probably walk on out of here tonight."

Taylor smiled. "Let's not rush it, okay? We're just glad you're doing better, and one night in the hospital won't hurt as long as they're taking good care of you, which I can see they are." She motioned toward the overstuffed chair by the bed. "May I?"

Andi nodded.

Taylor sat, then grabbed the soda from the table and held it up. "Feel like a taste of cherry soda?"

Laughing when Andi nodded eagerly, she popped the top, lifted the can to Andi's lips and waited patiently as Andi lifted her head and took a sip.

Andi licked her lips and issued a sound of pleasure. "Mmm. That tastes wonderful." A heavy sigh escaped her. "If only I had a double cheeseburger to go with it."

Will chuckled. "I'll run down to the cafeteria in a

minute and see if they're still serving. If not, I'll ask Jax to pick us up a bag of burgers from one of the fast-food joints around the corner." His stomach growled at the thought of food and he rubbed it. "Way I feel right now, I could eat about three of 'em."

"Taylor?" Andi fiddled with the hem of her sheet, then asked, "Will you stay?"

Will's breath caught at the vulnerable note in Andi's voice and he moved closer, placing his hand on hers.

"Do you…?" Taylor glanced up at him, concern flashing in her eyes. "Do you mean here in the hospital tonight?"

She nodded, then added, "And maybe in Stone Creek? Just for a while?"

Will tensed. "Andi, I don't thi—"

"There's a lot more to do here than people think," she rushed out. "There are lots of rapids and hiking trails. And there's a big park downtown. If you catch it just right, you can see three dozen lightning bugs in one place. It's pretty amazing."

Taylor hesitated. "Well, I—"

"And we could go camping," Andi continued. "You, me and dad. We could take you to Badger's Crossing and you could see the place for yourself and—"

"I don't think you're going to be up for camping anytime soon," Will said, squeezing Andi's hand gently. "And—" as much as he hated to acknowledge it "—Taylor probably has plans to travel to another location. She wasn't exactly on vacation during our trip— she was working."

The excitement shining in Andi's eyes dimmed and she nodded reluctantly. "I know. It'd just be nice to do something together again—without the drama," she added on a small laugh. She looked at Taylor again and issued a sad smile. "I understand if you can't stay. For a second, I just thought maybe—"

"You have any good fishing holes around here?" Taylor asked, leaning forward and propping her elbows on her knees.

"Yeah," Andi said. "At least a dozen."

"Any waterfalls near these fishing holes?"

"Tons." Andi perked up, planted her hands on the mattress and shimmied upright a couple of inches. "And there are really great views of rapids from the banks of the river near our house. I could show you all of the best places. You'd have enough great shots to sell to at least ten magazines."

Taylor pondered this, tapping her chin with her fingertip. "What about hotels? You know of any good places to stay that'll have a reasonable rent for a couple weeks? I have to be careful. Can't afford a suite with a Jacuzzi on the pay from my photo gigs."

"A Jacuzzi?" Will tilted his head and grinned.

"I'll tell you later." She smiled, the excited gleam in her eye coaxing a surge of affection within him. "Would you mind if I stayed a little while longer? Hung around you two for an extended work-vacation?"

"No," Will said softly, his voice catching with happiness. "I wouldn't mind at all." He held her gaze for a moment longer. Then, catching Andi's eyes on them, he cleared his throat. "Guess I'll go check on those cheeseburgers."

"Would you bring us back some more cherry sodas?" Andi asked, her smile wide.

He motioned toward the can in Taylor's hand. "You haven't finished the one Taylor brought you yet."

"But I will." When he raised his eyebrow, she shrugged. "Dad, we've all been deprived. You eat three cheeseburgers and I'll drink two cherry sodas."

"Guess you got a point." Smiling, he opened the door, but he stopped abruptly, inches from the nurse who was entering the room.

The nurse glanced at Taylor, then frowned at Will. "Visiting hours are over. Only family members are allowed."

Will moved to speak, but Andi beat him to it.

"Taylor is family," she said, grabbing Taylor's hand as she made to rise from her chair.

Will met Taylor's eyes and the same surge of affection sweeping through him was reflected in her eyes. "Yeah," he affirmed. "Taylor's family."

EPILOGUE

Taylor lifted her camera, zoomed in at just the right angle and said, "Smile as though you spent several days stranded in mountain backcountry and just spotted a rescue helicopter in the distance."

Andi, standing on a popular overlook in the Great Smoky Mountains National Park, propped her hands on her hips and laughed. Will slung his arm around Andi's shoulders and grinned, his handsome features proud as he looked at his daughter.

"Or," Taylor added, snapping another photo of father and daughter beneath the bright summer sun, "smile as though you just graduated from high school."

Andi threw her arms out wide and tossed back her head, her long brown hair rippling in the breeze.

Hours earlier, she and Will, dressed in their Sunday best, had sat in the bleachers of Stone Creek High School's football stadium on a Saturday morning and cheered Andi on as she'd walked across the stage and received her diploma. Taylor had run out of tissues to mop up her tears of joy, and even though he'd tried to hide it, Will's eyes had glistened in the early-morning sunlight as he'd watched his daughter, elegantly dressed in her cap and gown and heels, stride confidently off the stage and back to her seat, waving at him in the stands along the way.

It had been slow going one year ago as Will and Andi had rebuilt the trust between them. After leaving the hospital, Andi had been eager to go home—something that had surprised, and pleased, Will more than he'd been comfortable admitting to Andi. But he'd shared his joy with Taylor, and she'd delighted in watching Will and Andi's bond renew over the three weeks she'd spent renting a motel room in Stone Creek and touring the local fishing holes with them both.

Taylor smiled as she moved a few steps to the left for a different angle and snapped several more pictures of Will and Andi. She'd loved every minute of the three weeks she'd spent with Will and Andi a year ago...and she'd fallen more in love with Will every day that had followed.

She'd exchanged the motel room for an apartment and relocated to Stone Creek, spending her free time with Will and Andi and taking Andi along with her on photography gigs whenever possible. Andi was a quick learner and had a natural talent with the camera. Over the ensuing months, she and Will had grown closer, taking Andi on rafting and camping trips, cooking evening meals together at his house and sitting outside under the moonlight, admiring the stars and recalling moments from the trip down Bear's Tooth River that had changed the course of their lives in the best ways possible.

"Now, you two," Andi said, jogging across the grassy overlook and reaching for the camera. "Let me take a few of you."

Taylor hesitated as she handed Andi the camera. "But it's your day, Andi. The purpose of this camping trip is to celebrate your achievements. I'm putting together a portfolio for you, and I want a lot of pictures of you and your dad to—"

"And I want a lot of pictures of the two of you," she stated firmly, giving Taylor a gentle nudge. "Now, get over there and practice your smile."

Taylor laughed as she joined Will. "Would you look at that? She graduates high school and thinks she's the boss now."

"I am the boss," Andi teased, grinning. "At least for the weekend. Then my celebration is over and it's back to normal." She snapped a picture, then paused. "Or a new normal, rather, seeing as how I've decided to attend Tennessee State in the fall."

"Oh, that's wonderful," Taylor said, smiling up at Will. "Why didn't you tell me? You knew I was anxious about that." She glanced at Andi. "I was hoping you'd decide to stay in state so you could visit more often."

Andi grinned, a suspicious light sparkling in her eyes. "Oh, I plan on sticking close to home this summer."

"Then we can take that rafting trip we've been planning." Taylor began an itinerary in her mind, listing all the locations she'd planned to photograph along the trip. "I really want to get some shots of the falls near—"

"I hope we'll be too busy for a rafting trip," Will said, wrapping his arms around Taylor's waist and drawing her close.

Andi continued snapping pictures, the soft clicks of the camera repeating rapidly in the background.

Taylor frowned up at Will. "What do you mean?"

"I mean that I'm hoping that we'll be too busy planning our wedding to take a rafting trip," Will said softly.

Taylor stilled, her breath catching as she searched his eyes.

He smiled down at her, his expression softening as he opened his palm. A diamond ring glittered in the sunlight and tears of happiness flooded her eyes.

"I love you, Taylor," he whispered. "And I can't imagine my future without you in it."

The soft snick of the camera continued, and Taylor, tears of joy streaming down her face, glanced at Andi. "You knew about this, didn't you?"

Andi smiled, her own eyes glistening. "Yes. And I fully expect to be your maid of honor."

Taylor laughed. "I wouldn't have it any other way."

"Does this mean you're saying yes?" Will asked, cradling her face in his hands and wiping away her tears.

"Yes," she whispered. "I love you, Will."

He kissed her softly, right there on the overlook beneath the wide sky, amid the impressive mountain range. Moments later, Andi propped the camera on a large boulder, set the timer and joined them on the overlook, wrapping an arm around each of their waists and smiling into the camera as it clicked, snapping a picture—the first of many for a new family full of faith and love.

* * * * *

Karen Kirst was born and raised in East Tennessee near the Great Smoky Mountains. She's a lifelong lover of books, but it wasn't until after college that she had the grand idea to write one herself. Now she divides her time between being a wife, homeschooling mom and romance writer. Her favorite pastimes are reading, visiting tearooms and watching romantic comedies.

Books by Karen Kirst

Love Inspired Suspense

Explosive Reunion
Intensive Care Crisis
Danger in the Deep
Forgotten Secrets
Targeted for Revenge

Love Inspired Historical

Smoky Mountain Matches

The Reluctant Outlaw
The Bridal Swap
The Gift of Family

Visit the Author Profile page
at LoveInspired.com for more titles.

TARGETED FOR REVENGE

Karen Kirst

To appoint unto them that mourn in Zion, to give
unto them beauty for ashes, the oil of joy for mourning,
the garment of praise for the spirit of heaviness;
that they might be called trees of righteousness,
the planting of the Lord, that he might be glorified.
—*Isaiah* 61:3

This is dedicated to the women who took a chance
on my first book about an undercover outlaw. Who
could've guessed that would lead to a twelve-book
series? And when the historical line closed,
you let me try my hand at bombs and explosions.
Thank you to Love Inspired editors Emily Rodmell
and Tina James for guiding my publishing career.

Acknowledgments

This book wouldn't have been possible without the
invaluable insight and input from Sergeant Jeff Duren
of the Hendersonville Mounted Police Unit.
Thank you, Jeff, for your willingness to help
with my fictional world. More important,
thank you for your service to the community.

Any mistakes are purely my own.

ONE

Tessa Elliott was used to looking over her shoulder. Searching crowds for that one familiar face had become a habit during the four years she'd been in hiding. But she wasn't as diligent as in the beginning, and the meaning of the librarian's remark didn't immediately register.

"A man was asking for me?" Tessa repeated, angling away from the children seated on the patterned carpet. "Did he give you his name?"

"No, I'm afraid not. He looked like a visitor from Atlanta," she said. "He was dressed in a three-piece suit. His accent wasn't local, though."

Dread congealed in her stomach. "Did he have black hair? And a scar above one eyebrow?"

"Come to think of it, he did have a scar. He's awfully handsome. Polite, too. Is he a friend of yours?"

Tessa slipped on her cross-body canvas bag. "Did you tell him where I live?"

Mrs. Smith looked down her crooked nose at her. "I wouldn't do that. I did tell him you and Lily are regulars at the children's story hour."

She turned a full circle, searching the stacks for an

intimidating figure she'd learned to fear from a young age. "When was he here?"

"Not long after we opened," she said. "Are you in some sort of trouble, Tessa?"

He'd been in town for three hours already? Maybe longer?

"I—I have to go." Rushing forward, she scooped Lily into her arms. Her surprised cry caused the children's librarian to halt her story and the other children to stare.

"Mommy, I want to stay!"

"We're going on an adventure, ladybug." She hurried through the double doors, only to stop and scan the parking lot and surrounding streets for hulking vehicles with blacked-out windows. There were mostly dusty pickup trucks and minivans. She dashed to her battered Toyota sedan and got Lily secured in her car seat.

"Why can't the 'venture wait until after the story?"

Tessa met her three-year-old's gaze in the rearview mirror. Dark curls formed a halo around her pale, round face.

"I know you're upset to miss story time, but this can't wait."

"I didn't get a snack."

"I'll get you one at home."

She sped through the picturesque Georgia town and prayed the Southern hospitality she'd found so comforting hadn't led Dante straight to her door. At least Mrs. Smith had had the good sense not to share her address. In her neighborhood, she drove past her rental house three times before she was satisfied it was safe to enter.

If Lily hadn't needed to use the potty, she would've left her in the car only long enough to grab the emergency travel bags she kept in her bedroom closet. Instead, she ushered her into the quiet house and deactivated the alarm. Blood surged through Tessa's veins, throbbing erratically at her neck, rushing through her ears and making her light-headed.

"We need to get on the road."

Lily did a pirouette in the hallway, her shoulder-length nut-brown curls flaring. "Where are we going?"

Tessa's throat threatened to close up. If her brother had tracked her down, she had only one choice. She must go to Lily's father, Mason Reed. "You'll see soon enough." Lightly tapping her nose, she flicked on the bathroom switch. "Hurry, okay?"

Tessa strode to the opposite side of the house, past the kitchen and into her bedroom, then jerked the bags from her closet. Over the years, she'd periodically switched out Lily's clothes for bigger sizes. The last time had been around Easter, so most of the clothes would be season-appropriate. She grabbed the accordion file from the desk, the one containing legal documents, including the birth certificate Mason had never seen or dreamed existed.

The sound of a male voice startled her. Had Dante or one of his guards somehow gotten in? She'd drilled Lily not to open the door, not for any reason.

Dropping everything, she ran to Lily's bedroom.

"I want to see you today," the man said. "Maybe at the park. What do you think, Lily?"

Lily danced around the speaker and video-surveillance apparatus. Seeing Tessa in the doorway, she grinned. "Mommy, my friend wants to see me. Can we play at the park?"

Tessa gripped the doorjamb for support and stared

at the dresser, where she'd placed the popular security feature right after Christmas.

"What do you say, Mommy?" the deep, disembodied voice mocked her, even though she'd remained out of its view. "Can we play?"

That voice had featured in her nightmares.

Dante had not only found them, but he'd also invaded their sanctuary by hacking into their security system. Battling nausea, she waved Lily over to the door. Taking her hand, she hustled her to the garage and buckled her in. Then she retrieved the bags from the hallway outside her room. As the garage door was going up, she got behind the wheel and started the engine.

"Lily, how long have you been talking to your friend?"

She bounced her pair of sparkly stuffed ponies through the air, completely unaware of the tension in Tessa. "Don't know."

"Since Christmas?"

She shook her head.

"Easter?"

"Uh-uh."

Tessa gave up. How long her Mafia prince of a brother had been in contact with her daughter wasn't the point. The car screeched out of the driveway, then they sped to the neighborhood entrance, earning a glare from Mr. Peabody as he shuffled to his mailbox. Once her absence became known, would he tell her friends he'd seen her leave in a hurry?

She felt a pang of remorse. Lisa, Barbara and several other neighbors had befriended her during her lonely, fright-filled pregnancy. Lisa had been by her side during Lily's birth. They had brought her meals and watched over Lily so Tessa could catch up on sleep. The women had been her support network, yet they hadn't known her entire identity was a lie. Now they would be left with questions that probably wouldn't be answered.

Tessa was barely able to keep from blasting through every red light between them and the interstate exit. With only three intersections to go, she noticed a dark Cadillac Escalade easing out of the library parking lot on their right. A second, identical one trailed the first.

Her fingers dug into the wheel. The bright April sun glinted off their windshields, searing her eyes. The light turned green, and she gunned it. The SUVs followed at a distance. As she drove through the last intersection and entered the long, deserted stretch between the town proper and the interstate, they sped up.

The one directly behind her bore down on her sedan and tapped her bumper.

Lily's chatter stopped. "Mommy?"

"It's all right, ladybug."

She put more pressure on the gas pedal. The car may have looked rickety, but thanks to Joey's expertise over at the local garage, the engine was in good shape. Thick stands of lofty pines formed natural walls on either side of the two-lane road. If she lost control, her car would be no match for them.

Please, Lord, I need Your help.

She'd become a believer soon after fleeing New Jersey. Her personal relationship with Christ meant everything to her. He was her protector, her best friend, her counselor. She trusted the Scriptures and, in them, He promised to never leave or forsake her.

The SUV struck her car again, with more force this time. The wheel jerked. The back end lurched, pointing her hood toward the road's edge and the grass between asphalt and unyielding trees. Her palms were slippery, and she had trouble righting the vehicle. Lily began crying in earnest.

Up ahead, a semitruck loaded with logs was chugging onto the road. If she could make it in time, he would block the SUVs.

Sending up another fervent prayer, she stomped on the gas pedal. The trees outside became a blur. The trucker saw her and blasted his horn. The logo plastered on the driver's door got larger and larger. Sweat dripped beneath her collar, and she couldn't catch her breath.

At the last second, she swerved. Entered the oncoming lane. A red sports car stared her down. Honked and flashed their lights. She wasn't going to make it. Mason's face flashed in her mind. He would never meet his daughter.

Tessa pushed the old car to go faster. "Please, please, please—"

Finally, she cleared the semitruck and jerked back into the right lane with seconds to spare. The sports car was a blur as he zipped by in the opposite direction. The rearview mirror gave her the news she'd prayed for. The SUVs were stuck behind the truck. She had mere minutes to disappear.

Tessa zoomed past the interstate exit. Dante would expect her to take it. Several miles past the exit, she turned into a truck stop and parked behind the building. Sweaty, shaky and not entirely sure they were safe, she twisted in her seat and worked on calming

Lily. Long minutes passed before the little girl's sobs quieted. A juice box and pack of fish-shaped crackers helped restore calm.

"I don't like this 'venture," she mumbled, stuffing crackers into her mouth.

"We're going to the mountains," she told her in the brightest voice she could muster. "To Tennessee. It's beautiful there. You're going to love it."

"Do they have story time?"

She smiled. "I'm positive."

That wasn't all. Serenity, Tennessee, was where she'd met and fallen in love with a police officer. Those months with Mason Reed had been blissful, a brief span of stability and normalcy far from the reaches of her Mafia family. Until he'd left her with no explanation, of course, breaking her heart in the process.

Would he reject her again? Or would he agree to protect her and their daughter?

Mounted Police Sergeant Mason Reed sat astride his equine partner, Scout, and surveyed the scores of people who'd turned out for the annual spring event. He used to like the hot-air-balloon festival. Now, it was a raw reminder of his gullibility.

Beside him, Foster "Silver" Williams hefted a disagreeable sigh. "I know that look."

Mason didn't bother sparing him a glance. "You must have a smudge on your sunglasses."

"No smudge. This is the look you get every year around this time. Don't think I don't recall the significance."

Silver, nicknamed such because his hair had gone gray prematurely, had been with Mason the day his world had disintegrated. He and Tessa were supposed to have met up at the hot-air-balloon festival. Her brother had shown up instead.

"It's been almost four years. Time to let it go." Shifting in his saddle, Silver waved his gloved hand across the horizon like a wand. "Women can't resist the uniform or the horse. You should use them to your advantage."

Silver's cream-colored gelding, Lightning, swished his tail and bobbed his head, as if in agreement. A reluctant smile curved Mason's mouth. "There's a woman out there who will make you regret that cavalier attitude one of these days."

"I'm not a commitment kind of guy," he said, shrugging. "And I don't pretend otherwise. You, my friend, pine for home and hearth, and there's no reason why you can't have it. You were with her how long?"

He inhaled deeply. "Eleven months." And five days, to be exact.

"Eleven months is not enough time for her to qualify as the love of your life. I say put the past behind you, once and for all, and start searching for your forever girl."

Mason had dated off and on. Nothing had stuck. Some had complained he was emotionally closed off. He had Tessa to thank for that. Because of her betrayal, he hadn't been able to trust anyone new.

His radio chirped, and Serenity's other two mounted police officers, Raven Hart and Cruz Castillo, checked in.

"How's things at your end?" Mason asked.

"Uneventful," Raven said, her voice crackling over the radio.

"That's what I like to hear. We'll head your way in a few."

Raven and Cruz had chosen to patrol the fields where the balloons were tethered until their release at sunset. The blue-green mountains rose to sloping, gentle peaks in the distance, offset by a jewel-blue sky. Mason and Silver were covering the more densely populated area around Glory Pond, where paying customers could ride paddleboards and canoes. At the far end, Black Bear Café offered indoor and outdoor seating. A temporary stage had been set up beside the expansive brick patio, and plucky bluegrass tunes intertwined with laughter and crying babies. A bicycle-and-boat-rental shop was situated in the shelter of old-growth trees. Picnic tables were interspersed in the welcome shade. Beyond the trees, food trucks were parked in the cement lot between the pond and town square, offering everything from gourmet grilled-cheese sandwiches to mochi ice cream.

He and Silver had stationed themselves beneath the tallest trees for a temporary reprieve from the heat.

A towheaded girl of about ten approached. "Excuse me, sir, may I pet your horse?"

Mason leaned forward and slid his hand along Scout's neck. "Scout would be offended if you didn't."

She giggled and gingerly touched his nose. "How old is he?"

"Six. A farm up in Gatlinburg donated him to our unit. He's a Tennessee Walker."

She admired his chestnut body and flaxen hair. Scout had an easygoing disposition, and he lapped up the affection. Not far away, a couple waited and watched with fond smiles. The loneliness inside Mason throbbed like a dull headache that never quite went away. He angled his face so that Silver wouldn't notice and comment. His partner and friend, for all his swagger and smooth talk, was surprisingly intuitive.

Silver handed her a pair of small business cards. "Each horse on the mounted patrol unit has one," he explained. "Their picture is on the front, and their bio is on the back."

"Neat. Thank you."

"You're welcome."

Her parents beckoned her, and she skipped away. He watched the trio weave through the crowd and stop at a lemonade vendor.

Mason sensed Silver's keen gaze on him.

"That's it," he declared. "I'm creating an online dating profile for you."

"You wouldn't dare."

"Why not? You're obviously not going to look for love on your own…" He sat straighter in the saddle, the hollows in his cheeks more pronounced.

Mason looked around for signs of trouble. "What?"

"It can't be—" Silver snapped his mouth shut. His gloves creaked and strained over his bunched hands. Lightning nickered.

Mason didn't see anyone who'd indulged in too much alcohol. No physical altercations brewing. Serenity was tucked into the mountains of East Tennessee and was one of several gateway towns to Great Smoky Mountains National Park. Because of that, their population swelled April through October, bringing unique challenges to local law enforcement. Millions of visitors traveled through their town each year. Some drove through, stopping for a meal or to fuel up, while others took advantage of the various campgrounds, cabin rentals and motels. Not all were law-abiding citizens.

At the moment, he didn't recognize any laws being broken. "I can't read your mind, you know."

Muttering under his breath, Silver pointed to the cluster of blue canopies offering a range of kids' activities. The nearest one was face-painting central. His gaze probed the occupants, eventually landing on a woman standing apart from the group. Average height and weight. Casual but neat attire. She was a woman whose appearance—black hair, olive skin and striking features—would draw second and even third glances.

He'd recognize her anywhere. Her hair was thicker and fuller, the glossy curls sliding over her shoulders as she searched for someone or something. Sunglasses covered her eyes, but he knew the curve of her cheek, the straight line of her nose, the generous mouth almost always primed with shell pink gloss.

He almost fell off his horse.

What was Tessa doing here?

She bent and hefted a little girl into her arms, a girl with matching ringlets and dark eyes.

His skin stretched too tightly over his cheekbones. His teeth ground together. Denial spiraled inside, pulsating white-hot through his veins. Tessa was married. She had a child. She'd moved on. Suddenly, he was furious at himself for letting her steal four years of his life.

"I can handle this," Silver drawled. "I'd be happy to, in fact."

He would never admit it aloud, but he considered the offer. He didn't want to hear about Tessa's wonderful life, her devoted husband and child.

The decision was taken out of his hands the moment he noticed men closing in on her. A pair of muscle-bound men in black clothing, telltale bulges at their hips hinting at firearms. Tessa noticed and tensed, gathering her daughter closer to her.

"They're not here to see the balloons, I gather," Silver commented.

When one made a grab for the little girl, Mason urged Scout into action.

"Out of the way!"

He alerted the people blocking his path of his intent, and they quickly accommodated him and Scout. He had to repeat the command multiple times. The last thing he wanted was for an innocent bystander to be stepped on or knocked off balance.

Silver and Lightning were close behind. Over the radio, his partner alerted Raven and Cruz.

Tessa's scream unleashed a wave of alarm through the crowd. The goons noticed the horses' rapid approach and took off. Silver thundered after them.

Mason hauled Scout to a halt and slid to the ground.

Tessa's shoulders eased when she saw him. There was no flash of recognition. When they'd dated, he'd been a patrol officer. She wouldn't know he'd accepted a position with the mounted-police unit.

"It's okay, Lily." Silent tears streamed down the child's cheeks, and her tiny shoulders shook with sobs. "You're safe. The police officer is here. He'll help us."

He took Scout's lead with one hand and her elbow with the other. "Come with me, Tessa."

His voice, and that he knew her name, must've registered, because she whipped up her head to focus fully on him. Her lips parted. Her eyebrows descended behind her glasses. "Mason?"

"This way."

Using his body as a shield, he hustled them through the curious onlookers, past the pond and to the Serenity mounted-police tent. He secured Scout to an oak tree and led Tessa inside. It was spacious enough to accommodate twenty-five people or more, and the white canvas provided much-needed privacy. A couple of tables had been set up to hold snacks and drinks. He slid out a folding chair and pointed. She complied without a word.

He removed his glasses and helmet, threading his fingers through his damp, rumpled hair. She watched him, her body taut and coiled, her arm curved protectively around the girl.

"Why are you here, Tessa?"

Her pallor became more pronounced. She, too, removed her glasses. Her hazel gaze slammed into him.

"I came to find you."

TWO

Suspicion chased disbelief across his rigid features. Surely the anger swirling in his brown eyes wasn't directed at her? He was supposed to have greeted her with an apology, or at least a blush of shame for what he'd done to her. Tessa was light-headed from the high emotions battling for supremacy.

He had grown more handsome with time. Slightly over six feet, he was sleek power in a deceptively trim frame. He had bronze skin, molten eyes the color of a rabbit's pelt and rich, thick brown hair.

After too many long, lonely years, mere inches separated her from the man who'd ripped the sun from her sky. She was supposed to despise him. She hadn't ever learned to do what she was supposed to, though. If she had, she would've done her father's bidding and married one of his Mafia associates. She'd have been like her mother, bearing children into a legacy of violence.

His upper lip curled. "What could you possibly want with me?"

This wasn't the thoughtful, kind man who'd wooed her with home-cooked meals, horseback rides and random gifts of chocolate. This wasn't the man who'd plagued her dreams, the man she'd wept buckets of tears over. Her Mason wasn't capable of such an ugly expression. With that intense darkness enveloping him, he could have blended right into her Mafia family.

A shudder rippled through her. "My brother wants me dead. I caught him conspiring to kill a police officer and tried to prevent it."

Tessa licked her dry lips, wishing she could unsee the photos Dante had shoved in her face. Despite her best efforts, she hadn't been able to save Officer Fisk.

Mason folded his arms over his chest, an action that pulled the crisp, blue-black uniform tight across his shoulders. "How many brothers do you have? Because the one I met didn't strike me as a cold-blooded killer."

Dizziness washed over her. "You met Dante? When?"

He gave a minuscule shrug. "Doesn't matter. Go on."

"I approached Officer Fisk. He asked if I'd be willing to record evidence of their plans."

"Their?"

"My father and Dante. There are things you don't know about me, Mason."

He stared at her for long moments, then his gaze slid to Lily. "Clearly."

The possibility that Lily could be his daughter obviously hadn't entered his mind. He must think she was married or divorced. Tessa began to question her decision to come to him. He'd left her without a word, not even a text message or email. Why would he care that she was in danger? She wasn't even convinced he'd protect Lily. Sure, he'd mentioned having children someday. But it was clear he hadn't wanted any with her.

She stood up so quickly spots danced before her eyes. "This was a mistake."

His hand was gentle on her shoulder, steadying. "Hold on. Let me get you a drink."

Mason strode to the tables and made his choices. He brought back a bottle of water and orange juice. "Does she like this kind?"

Sinking to her seat, she took the juice from him. "Would you like some, Lily?"

Her daughter had plastered her cheek in the curve of Tessa's neck. Now, she lifted her head and reached out, peering shyly at Mason from beneath her curls.

"I like horses," Lily blurted.

He acted surprised she was talking to him. "You do?"

"Mommy bought me lots of horse books. Tillie's pink. Her sister's name is Toni, and she's purple."

His wide gaze assessed Lily, and Tessa wished she could read his thoughts. Did he see anything of the Reed family in her? Most people said she resembled Tessa, but there were certain gestures that reminded her of Mason.

"My horse's name is Scout," he said. "He helps me do my job."

Lily sat up. "Can I ride him?"

"That depends. Scout's particular about who rides him, but I'll tell you a secret." Lowering his voice, he said, "His favorite snack is peppermints."

Lily clapped her hands together. "I like peppermints, too."

His lips curved into a semblance of a smile. Tessa's heart flip-flopped.

There was movement at the tent entrance, and Mason's hand instinctively reached for the gun at his waist. Another officer entered, and Mason relaxed. "Well?"

"They jumped into a waiting SUV. We lost them. The sheriff's department will be on the lookout."

He removed his helmet. Sweat dampened his gray hair. The color should've been odd on a man in his late twenties, but combined with his fair complexion, angular features and vivid violet eyes, it gave him a unique look.

She'd met Mason's friend several times and liked him, despite his seize-the-moment, live-for-today approach to life.

"Hello, Tessa." His smile was more feral than charming. "What brings you to Tennessee?"

His tone conveyed he wished that she'd stayed away. She dismissed the objection forming on her lips. She wasn't here for answers or apologies. Lily's future was at stake.

"Lily, would you like to watch a video on my phone?"

She nodded and accepted the juice bottle. After settling her at the table in the corner, Tessa rejoined the men in the middle of the tent.

"I'm in trouble. My last name isn't Elliott. It's Vitale. You may have heard of my father, Antonio. His nickname is Bloody Tony."

Silver grunted and pinched the bridge of his nose. "Who hasn't heard of him?"

Mason's hands slipped from his hips. "You didn't think it was necessary to tell me this before? Did they know you were dating a cop?"

"No! Not until the very end. I wouldn't have put you in danger, not for anything in the world." His eyes darkened, and his jaw twitched. "I didn't know what my family was until I was thirteen. I would've run away then if I could have. When it was time for college, I convinced my father to let me come to Tennessee. I adopted the surname Elliott and didn't share many details of my past. I was supposed to go home every summer, but after the first one, I made sure I had an internship to keep me in Knoxville. I defied my father again after graduation when I got an apartment and job here. He and Dante had decided I should marry the son of another powerful family. The marriage would've cemented our families' alliance." She grimaced. "Dante would've come immediately to fetch me, but he was tied up with pressing business. That's why you and I had almost a year together."

He passed a weary hand over his face.

Silver paced closer. "Is Dante's goal the same as it was back then?"

"Dante wants me dead. He will take her to New Jersey once he's dealt with me."

Mason's watchful gaze fell on Lily. "How long have you been on the run?"

"Since the early days of my pregnancy." He actually winced. "At the police's request, I agreed to wear a listening device and try to gain a confession. My father's health was ailing, and he's always had a soft spot for me. I thought I could get him to talk about the plans for Officer Fisk, something that would hold up in court. Dante was tipped off by my sister, Francesca, and burst into the room. He would've killed me right then and there if Father hadn't intervened. I was locked in my bedroom for days. Dante showed me the photographs of Fisk's body, and he promised to do the same to me.

By that time, I knew I was expecting. I had to escape. I wound up in small-town Georgia, and that's where we've been until yesterday."

Tessa could see the puzzle pieces start to fit together, could see him go ghostly pale beneath his tan. His eyes flashed to hers, as sharp as a rapier.

"How old is she, Tessa?"

"She turned three last month."

Silver bowed his head, squeezed his friend's shoulder and left the tent. The air became stifling, the cheery cartoon voices of Lily's video at odds with the anger and shock rippling through Mason.

"Is she mine?" he growled. "Or the other guy's?"

"What other guy?" she whispered, her brow puckering. "You were the only one."

Mason felt as if he might rip apart. Tessa may have been unfaithful, but she wouldn't keep his child from him.

"Look, I know the truth. Dante came to me and explained everything. He showed me the photos of you and your part-time boyfriend." His police-issue boots were uncomfortably tight, the bulletproof vest digging into his ribs. "Or was I the part-time one?"

"That's why you left without a word?" Her fingers dug into the spot over her heart, leaving imprints in her hunter green shirt. "Dante showed up at my apartment and demanded I go with him. When he saw a photograph of us on my mantel, he started asking questions. He was livid when he found out you were a cop. He threatened to hurt you, Mason. I tried to buy some time so I could tell you everything. Before I could, you'd left town."

"You were kissing another man in that photo."

"Are you sure it was me?" she challenged. "Give me your phone."

"What?"

"Take out your phone and search Francesca Vitale."

Mason did as she said and stared at the brunette on his screen. "Your sister?"

"She and I were close as children. Not anymore. She ratted me out when I was trying to help Fisk. You don't think she could've curled her hair and kissed someone just to serve Dante's purposes? He wanted me home, and he employs unusual methods to get what he wants."

And now, according to her, he wanted her dead.

He thrust his fingers through his hair and closed his eyes. He hadn't seen the woman's face, only a side view. Francesca looked enough like Tessa that it would've been easy to mistake the two. Since Tessa hadn't told him the truth about her family, he'd had no reason to doubt Dante's account.

But you're a police officer. Aren't you supposed to sniff out the bad guys?

"You didn't cheat?"

"No," she choked out.

He closed his eyes and prayed he wouldn't embarrass himself and fall to the ground in a dead faint. Slowly, he opened his eyes and looked at the little girl perched on the folding chair. His *daughter*.

"Did you know? When you left?" he murmured, his voice sounding like sandpaper.

"It wasn't until I was in New Jersey. When I finally figured it out, I tried to think how I could tell you. Keep in mind, I had no idea why you left or why you refused to talk to me."

"That's no excuse," he countered, swiping the air with his hand. "I missed her birth, her first words, steps, everything."

"I'm sorry, Mason." Her eyes begged him to understand. "Try and consider it from my point of view. My father, Antonio, and Dante don't think twice about killing someone they view as a threat to their plans. You were better off not being involved. Safer."

"Then why come to me now?"

"Because, if Dante succeeds in killing me, you can take her somewhere safe and raise her to be a decent human being."

THREE

Tessa was a bundle of nerves as Mason navigated the congested streets. Her most treasured memories of Tennessee were rooted in this town. Nestled in a picturesque valley amid lush, forested mountains, Serenity was magazine-worthy. They passed the central, parklike square framed with shops, cafés and the early twentieth-century courthouse.

Pangs of nostalgia were swallowed whole by Dante's vendetta. Was he watching them even now?

Silver had retrieved their belongings and Lily's car seat from Tessa's vehicle. The Serenity PD was working in conjunction with the sheriff's department in the search for her brother. Silver and the other mounted police officers would stay and manage the event while Mason got them to a safe place.

"Are you still living in the riverside duplex?" she asked.

"I bought a house last year."

Tessa glanced over, taking in his profile and marble-cast body. She could've bounced a nickel off his forearm—he was clenching the wheel with that much force. He wasn't happy with her. All this time, he'd believed she'd betrayed him. That he'd doubted her loyalty, that he'd accepted without question her flawed character, made her want to shake him. But part of the blame rested on her shoulders. He hadn't known her brother's true nature because she hadn't been forthcoming about her past.

Now he had another reason to despise her—keeping their child a secret.

Lily hummed a popular church hymn in the double cab's second row, clutching her ponies to her and staring at the passing scenery. Her lids were growing heavy.

"Does she do that a lot?" he asked quietly.

"Hum when she's sleepy? Yeah."

He sighed. "My mom has said I used to do that when I was little."

"Oh."

The hurt in his voice brought tears to her eyes. Sliding lower in the seat, she stared out the passenger window. She couldn't wish away his hurt, couldn't undo her decisions.

They left the town center behind and headed deeper into the foothills that marched alongside mountains and acres upon acres of protected forests. His spicy scent filled the truck cab. The traces of horse and leather were new, but not unpleasant.

A couple of miles later, he flicked the turn signal and guided the truck onto a ribbon of pavement. His driveway was a straight shot through the woods. The trees thinned to a clearing, revealing a white farmhouse with a red metal roof, shutters and front door. A wraparound porch invited visitors to enjoy a respite from the hot days. White and yellow rhododendron bushes brushed against the large windows. A flagstone path led around the house to a storage shed. It could've been a calendar photo for the month of April.

Once out of the truck, she studied the large willow tree trailing wispy fingers over the shed and a bubbling creek meandering to the woods. From here, she could see the top tip of a blue-green mountain.

"It's beautiful."

"It suits me." He avoided her gaze, gesturing to the house with his keys. "There are some things that still need attention, but everything works."

Tessa lifted Lily out of her car seat and, shifting her slumbering weight, climbed the porch steps. Mason went ahead of her and unlocked the door. She was glad she wasn't walking into a space rife with memories. Being near him was difficult enough.

Inside the foyer, she was met with ivory walls, shiny, mahogany floors and the bottom half of a staircase. To her left, sunlight drew colored diamonds across the planks and a cream throw rug. A round-armed denim couch faced the brick fireplace. A cloth ottoman stood in place of a coffee table, and the antique globe light fixtures could've been original to the home. On their right, shadows draped a formal study, allowing her a vague glimpse of a masculine desk, chair and built-in bookshelves.

Mason paused, looking uncertain. "She still takes naps?"

"Not every day. But we caught snatches of sleep in a roadside motel overnight. Yesterday and today's events have exhausted her."

"Do you want her on the couch? Or I have a guest bedroom upstairs."

"The bedroom will work."

His dark gaze seemed to soak in Lily. "Will she mind if I carry her up?"

Tessa took a step toward him. Lily didn't stir as she transferred her to Mason's arms. The sight of her daughter's pink, plump cheek resting against his broad chest, with her curls spread over his uniform, made Tessa's heart swell. This reunion hadn't been planned, but it was right.

He carried her to the second-floor hallway and turned left. There were four rooms in all, two bedrooms on this end and another bedroom, possibly the master, shared the other end with a hall bath. He went inside the room that looked out over the rear of the property. A fluffy, powder blue rug was splashed over the refurbished floorboards and anchored with a white frame double bed. A white coverlet with dainty blue sprigs topped the mattress. Matching curtains hung at the windows. A single dresser was stationed against the outer wall and a mirror above it. The furnishings were sparse, but the home was welcoming.

Mason placed her on the bed and covered her with a quilt. He didn't immediately move away. He gazed down at her for multiple heartbeats, then he bent and brushed a kiss on her forehead. Feeling like an intruder, Tessa retreated to the hall.

Taking their relationship beyond the proper boundaries hadn't been part of God's plan. She hadn't realized it then. Now that she had a personal relationship with Christ, she basked in His forgiveness and the promise of new mercies each morning.

Downstairs, he led her through the living room to

the kitchen, which ran the length of the house. A new fridge was out of place in the worn work area. The cabinet paint was peeling, and some of the doors hung at odd angles. The sink was stained with rust. At the far corner, a rough-hewn table and chairs sat in front of a window with a forest view.

"Coffee?"

"Yes, please."

He rummaged through the cabinets and removed a pair of mugs. Once he had the machine set to brew, he pointed to a room out of sight and around the corner from the table.

"I'm going to get out of this gear. Milk's in the fridge. Sugar is in that jar. Help yourself."

Tessa hesitated. In the past, she'd been completely at home among his belongings. They'd often cooked together in his cramped duplex kitchen. Actually, she'd done the prep work under his direction, and he'd done the cooking. Her mouth watered just thinking about his spaghetti Bolognese.

He returned wearing a black Serenity mounted police cotton shirt, faded jeans and scuffed tennis shoes. A streamlined, black-and-white watch cradled his wrist. His hands were bare of other jewelry. With a start, she realized he could be in a serious relationship and that her sudden appearance might cause trouble.

She licked her dry lips. "Is anyone going to be bothered by my presence here?"

He arched a brow. "Besides me?"

The verbal shot wasn't his style. At her grimace, he lowered his gaze.

"It didn't occur to me that you might have a wife

or fiancée. I was focused only on getting away from Dante."

"There's no one," he said flatly.

Tessa hated that his answer pleased her. This trip wasn't about reuniting their family. It was about surviving Dante's vengeance.

Mason poured them both coffee, fixing hers as she'd preferred before, half milk and two dashes of sugar. He walked the length of the kitchen and gestured to the table. She sat and cupped the mug between her hands. He stared out the window…formidable and untouchable.

"I know you have questions," she ventured. "I'll answer them to the best of my ability."

"Tell me about Lily."

"She's spunky. Sweet. She gets cranky when she's hungry."

He grunted. "Like you."

"I make sure to keep snacks with us," she said. "Her favorite food at the moment is grilled chicken. She likes any type of fruit. She dislikes green beans and refuses to try mashed potatoes or macaroni and cheese."

He finally turned his gaze on her. "I thought those were standard fare for kids."

"I thought so, too."

"How do you support yourself? Was she born on time? Were there any complications? She looks healthy. Is she?"

Tessa blinked, and he inhaled sharply. He pulled out the chair opposite and lowered himself into it. "I have a hundred questions. I don't even know where to start."

"Ask me whenever they come to you." She pressed her palms to the warm mug, hoping he didn't notice her nervousness. "The pregnancy was uneventful. I didn't gain as much weight as the doctor would've liked—"

"You didn't have enough money for food?" His eyes were so very dark, his eyelashes thick and inky black. She wished he'd look at her like he used to, when he'd thought she was interesting and beautiful and fun.

Those days are gone forever.

"It wasn't that. I just found it difficult to eat. My worry about being found didn't help the nausea any." Tessa had spent the first months reeling from Mason's abandonment and the fact she was, by all definitions, a fugitive. "Lily arrived a week before her due date, but she was perfect. No health concerns. Normal weight."

"I'm glad you were both okay," he said solemnly.

"When I left New Jersey, I took jewelry I'd received over the years and sold it piece by piece. It was enough to cover room rentals and food. Once I settled on Walton, I found a small home to rent for a decent price. And I started working when she was three months old. I got a job at our church's day-care program so that I could have her with me."

His eyebrows winged up. "You go to church?"

"This may surprise you, but my priorities have changed. My life is now centered around my faith in Jesus."

"I try to live the same way." His gaze roamed her face, regret twisting his features. "I wish I could say the same about when we were together." Before she could comment, he said, "What are her favorite things to do?"

"She loves to color and paint. Anything that's messy, really. She wants to learn how to bake cookies, and not the premade, tear-apart kind. I've promised to find someone to teach her when she gets older. I take her every week to the library's story hour." Her smile faded. "That's where we were yesterday when Mrs. Smith tipped me off."

"How do you think he tracked you down?"

"I don't know for sure." She hadn't accessed her old social-media accounts and had paid cash for literally everything.

"I wish you'd have come to me back then. We could've figured it out."

"I did what I thought was best for you," she said, knowing he would never understand. He hadn't lived her reality, hadn't seen what Dante was capable of. "And for our unborn child. If Dante found me here, he might've killed you out of spite."

His fingers balled. "Yet you risked untold dangers by heading into the unknown. I'm a cop, Tessa. I could've found a way to protect you."

"Cops are his favorite targets."

The words were automatic, a whisper of the past. Their truth had faded enough for her to choose this town, this man, as her safe haven. Too late, she remembered Fisk's terrible death. She pressed her hand to her mouth.

"I should've gone west, not east." Shoving out of her seat, she lurched to the window, leaned on the sill and drew in deep breaths.

He came up behind her. "What did you say?"

She pressed her forehead to the cold glass and closed her eyes. "I didn't stop to pray or consider. I heard his voice on the surveillance system, and I panicked. That's what he wanted. To keep me from making the right move."

"Tessa, coming here was the right move. If you hadn't, I would still be in the dark about my child."

"But at what price?"

Tessa's fear was palpable. Fear for *him*. Kind of difficult to swallow after all these years of thinking she'd played him for a fool.

He didn't know if he was angrier at her or himself. He hadn't been looking for a relationship that long-ago afternoon when he'd come upon Tessa's vehicle, her tire busted and no spare in the trunk. Her unruly curls and winsome smile had enchanted him. As he'd taken her in his cruiser to the nearest automotive-parts place, he'd become intrigued by her. She was passionate about her work pairing foster kids with loving couples. From that one conversation, he'd glimpsed her heart for service, and that mirrored his own life path. By the time they'd returned to her car and gotten the tire patched, he'd known she was someone special. His instincts had been right. She was not only kind and quick to defend the weak, but she also had a zest for life. He'd fallen for her, plain and simple.

Tessa was the only woman who'd inspired thoughts of wedding rings and lifelong commitment. Near the end, she'd gotten distracted and anxious, and he'd panicked. He'd made the mistake of thinking that taking the next step in their relationship would fix things.

When Mason had believed she'd been unfaithful, he couldn't see her or talk to her without damaging her with his words. He'd been that decimated.

He should've given her a chance to explain.

"It's too late to switch courses," he said. Her silken hair was a curtain around her face. He prayed she wouldn't break down, because he wasn't sure he'd be able to resist holding her. "Tell me what I need to know about your brother."

Her shoulders lifted and fell. "There's no mercy in him. No compassion." She faced him, her eyes telling tales of a sinister history. "He thrives on other people's misfortunes. Once he sets his mind to something, he won't be dissuaded."

"You said your father stopped him from killing you."

"Our father is the only person Dante will heed. His health is failing, however. I've kept up with Vitale news through local papers and social-media accounts. I don't know that he could stop this. I don't know where I stand with Father anymore, not after I acted against them."

Mason was having trouble understanding how such a family operated and how it could've produced Tessa.

"He's five years older than me," she continued. "Seven years separate him and Fran. He disdained spending time with us because, in his mind, he was more worldly and important. While Fran and I were playing with puppies in the garden, he was being molded into the Vitale second-in-command. It wasn't until I stumbled into one of their retaliation kills that he started paying attention to me." She pressed her lips together and smoothed her hair behind her ears.

"It wasn't the kind of attention you wanted."

Her eyes awash in misery, she shook her head. Mason was tempted to cup her cheek and smooth his thumb across the soft, freckle-dusted skin. How could she have hidden this part of her life from him for so long?

He shoved his hands in his pockets. "How old were you?"

"Thirteen." She closed her eyes. "I came to the receiving room in search of Father. I'd won some certificate at school… I can't remember now what it was. Father and his men didn't see me, but Dante did. He shoved me behind the couch, covered my mouth and made me watch as they stabbed that man again and again. It wasn't a slow death," she whispered bleakly.

Mason blew out his breath and switched his attention to a bluebird perched on the feeder outside. He'd let a ruthless killer convince him that Tessa was the one without morals. He'd basically driven her back to that place of torment, and she'd been carrying his baby.

His eyelids pricked. Tessa had been vulnerable and alone.

Lord Jesus, thank You for keeping Your hand on them. Thank You for bringing Lily into my life. Please help me to be the kind of father You want me to be. Help me keep them safe.

There was much, much more he needed to know, but he couldn't digest any more at this moment. Before he could suggest she rest for a while, the window to their right exploded. Glass shattered. The distinct whistle of a bullet registered, followed by Tessa's scream.

Mason grabbed her. Shoved her beneath the table and slid into the space with her.

"You hurt?"

Her eyes were panic-stricken. "No. You?"

Another shot whizzed inside, digging into the Sheetrock behind them. The shooter was on the move, getting closer.

"Stay here. I'm going outside."

"Mason, don't." She seized a fistful of his shirt.

He placed his cell in her hand. "Call Silver."

Then he snagged his pistol from the counter and went in search of the enemy.

FOUR

Mason crouched in the screened-in porch and searched for the glint of a rifle scope among the trees. The sun's angle was unfortunate, and the slanting rays made his unprotected eyes water. He shifted to ease a leg cramp, and a bullet pierced the screen near his head, pinged off the patio table and burrowed into the wood siding.

Above the drumming of his heart, he heard sirens echoing off the mountains. An engine revved out of sight. A blur of black caught his eye. Before he could take aim, a door slammed and tires burned against pavement.

He shoved through the porch door and rushed to the corner of the house, pressing close to the facade. Peering around the edge, he glimpsed the tail end of a Cadillac Escalade as it sped down his driveway.

Mason retraced his steps. Inside the kitchen, glass bits crunched beneath his sneakers. A honeysuckle-scented breeze seeped through the open fissures and stirred the curtains. The chairs around his table were disturbed and the space beneath was empty.

"Tessa?"

After looking in the utility room and first-floor bath, he strode the length of the house, checking other windows for damage. She wasn't in the living room or the office. The front door was secure. His pulse began to gather speed. Had they lured him out back on purpose? Had they gotten to her? To Lily?

He pivoted and was about to scale the stairs when her ballet flats tapped down the wooden treads. She'd had at least two dozen pairs when he'd known her, and these were black with a subtle sparkle. Next, her tailored black pants came into view, a silver band around her wrist and finally her scoop-neck shirt and slinky earrings. Her features creased with worry when she saw him.

"Are you okay? I was upstairs when I heard the second shot."

His grip on the pistol eased slightly. "I'm good. Lily?"

"Still asleep." Reaching the foyer, she held out his phone. "Silver promised to send help. Did you see Dante?"

"There was one shooter in the woods. He heard the sirens the same time I did. I didn't get a good look at him, but I saw a single SUV."

Moving into the living room, he stationed himself at the edge of the picture window and monitored the yard while he contacted police dispatch. One of the mounted-police-unit trucks pulled through the trees and parked behind his. A low-slung black Corvette jerked to a stop farther down the drive.

Tessa had come to stand beside him, close enough that her particular scent, a blend of vanilla and cinnamon, taunted him.

"I need to brief my unit."

Nodding, she turned her attention on the officers exiting the truck. Mason tucked his Glock in his rear waistband, about to trade the cool interior for the balmy evening. He descended the porch steps, meeting Cruz and Raven halfway. They were still in uniform but had left their helmets in the truck.

Silver's car alarm chirped, and he pocketed his keys as his long strides ate up the tender green grass.

"What's going on?" Cruz looked from Mason to the house. The newest member of the unit, he had transferred from Texas last year. He'd shared snippets of his previous life, although not enough to gain a clear picture.

"Full disclosure. The woman inside the house is Tessa Vitale, daughter of Antonio Vitale. You may have heard of him."

Raven whistled. "Bloody Tony. What's she doing in our neck of the woods?"

The tips of Mason's ears burned. He didn't relish revealing his private business, but these three had his back, no matter what. "I knew her as Tessa Elliott. We were once in a serious relationship, and she's returned requesting my protection. Apparently, Antonio is in poor health and is slowly relinquishing his duties to his heir, Dante." He explained her involvement with the unfortunate Officer Fisk. Their expressions darkened with dismay. "The little girl with her, Lily, is my daughter." Saying it out loud for the first time choked him up. Staring at his boots, he used the ensuing silence to mentally regroup. "I understand you're as shocked as I am."

"She didn't tell you?" Raven demanded, outraged on his behalf.

He lifted his gaze. "Tessa and I have a lot to work through. I know I can count on you to treat her with respect."

Cruz inclined his head, a silent show of support. Raven clamped her lips together. Silver's gaze was probing, solemn. Then his famous grin flashed, and he looped his arm around Mason's shoulders. "This makes me an honorary uncle, right? I'm going to spoil her rotten."

Mason actually smiled. Inside the house, he left the others in the living room and followed the sound of tinkling glass. Tessa was sweeping up the broken bits and didn't look up at his approach.

"I'll take care of that later." His voice was gruffer than he'd intended. Her presence in his home was throwing him off-kilter.

She propped the broom against the wall. When she came near, he said, "I told the others about our connection and about Lily."

"I figured." A flush worked its way up the slender column of her neck.

"They have to know the facts if they're going to help."

"I understand, Mason."

Tessa remained at the room's edge, using the armchair as a shield. Cruz and Raven sat on opposite ends of the sofa, and Silver leaned against the fireplace, arms crossed. Awkward tension hung in the room. Silver offered a quiet greeting. The other officers merely nodded in reaction to his introductions. Mason retrieved his laptop from his office and brought up

Dante's image. Sour resentment rushed to the surface. This man had orchestrated his and Tessa's breakup. If not for him, Mason might've had a chance to attend his daughter's birth, to be involved in her early years.

Wrangling his focus on the matter at hand, he set the laptop on the ottoman and jerked a finger at the image. He hadn't changed much in the intervening years. Whipcord-lean and well over six feet, Dante carried himself like a prince and dressed like one, too.

"This is Dante Vitale. Thirty-one years old. Has a distinguishing scar above his left eyebrow. He's unmarried?"

"That's right," Tessa confirmed. "He's had an on-again, off-again relationship with a woman named Shelly Miles."

"New Jersey is home base. How many guards does he usually travel with?"

"Four. Bruno Esposito is the one who sticks like glue to my brother. He's a Mack truck." When Mason searched more images and angled the screen toward Tessa, she nodded. "Bruno's the grizzled one. Don't let his age fool you. He's in better shape than I am. And he's been in the Vitale service for decades. He won't hesitate to sacrifice himself for my brother."

"Do you recognize anyone else?" Cruz asked her.

Tessa leaned forward, resting her hands on the chair's curved top, and studied the screen again. "The short guy on the end, the one with the mustache, is James Lisowski. He's a follower, not an original thinker. I don't know the others."

"The license plate I glimpsed was from Georgia," Mason said. "I'm guessing Dante likes to travel in style."

"My father owns a private plane. They probably flew down and then rented vehicles."

Raven flipped her long black braid behind her shoulder. "They'll dump the Cadillacs. The tags make them easy to spot."

"Or they'll switch out the plates for locals and remove the rental stickers," Cruz said, rubbing his jaw.

Mason caught Silver's gaze. "What are you thinking?"

Uncrossing his arms, he pushed off from the mantel. "This guy's got wads of cash at his disposal. He can get his hands on weapons, getaway vehicles, you name it. He can pay for information or dirty jobs. That makes him more dangerous than most." His violet gaze fell on Tessa. "You're going to require twenty-four-hour protection."

Although what he said hadn't been an accusation, Tessa flinched.

"Let me be clear about something," Mason said, making eye contact with each of them. "I'm not asking any of you to go above and beyond the usual job requirements. We have our patrols and other cases. I don't expect anyone to put in extra hours on this."

Silver rolled his eyes. "Don't be so dramatic, brother. We're in this with you, one hundred percent."

Raven jutted her chin. "I'm willing to do whatever needs to be done."

Cruz left the couch to clap Mason's shoulder. "There's no doubt in my mind that you'd stick your neck out for us. I'd do no less for you, Sergeant."

"Thank you," Mason said gruffly, catching Tessa's touched expression.

"I'd like to thank you, too," she said. "I appreciate your willingness to help."

Raven and Cruz were all business, acknowledging her with solemn nods.

Raven swung her head, her long braid sliding along her crisp uniform. "Let's go, Cruz. We've got to see to the horses."

"I'll take guard duty tonight," Cruz offered.

"Already called it," Silver announced, smirking.

Cruz planted his hands on his utility belt, a teasing challenge in his eyes. "I didn't hear you call it."

"Then you weren't paying attention."

A disgruntled noise escaped Raven. She hooked her arm through Cruz's and tugged him toward the door. "When will you two stop acting like teenagers?"

Mason observed Tessa watching the interplay between his teammates. She must be aware of their loyalty to him and that they weren't thrilled with her. But she wasn't in a position to care whether they liked her or not. She was desperate for help, and that desperation had driven her to him.

He wished she'd come for different reasons, like his right to know he was a father. Despite the circumstances she'd found herself in, he couldn't completely let her off the hook. He wasn't sure he'd be able to forgive her, and that was a problem. Because they were going to have to work together to keep their daughter safe.

Yesterday morning, Tessa wouldn't have dreamed she'd be sharing a meal with Mason. As the years had passed, she'd thought of him often, reliving their many happy moments together. What she hadn't allowed herself to do was envision a reunion. It was too fraught with regrets and disappointments. Now, she was seated in his living room, and the reality was much worse than she'd feared.

He was painstakingly polite to her. When he did look at her, his face was a calm sea, while his eyes were twin hurricanes. They whipped at her, threatening to topple her. *How could you do this to me?*

Her reasons for staying away had seemed so right and solid when hundreds of miles separated them. Face-to-face, her logic disintegrated like a sand dune in gale-force winds. She hadn't calculated the depth of his hurt. She'd wounded *Mason*, the one person she never would've chosen to hurt, not in a million lifetimes.

The salted fry turned to dust in her mouth. Gulping orange soda—apparently Silver's idea of a proper drink for adults and toddlers alike—she begged God to stall her tears until she was alone.

I'm drowning here, Lord. Drowning. What have I done?

"I ordered chicken tenders, too, in case she didn't like burgers," Silver said, gesturing to Lily's plate.

Lily had taken off the bun and torn the patty into pieces. She hadn't eaten much. She'd awoken crying from her nap. The unfamiliar surroundings had scared her. Coming downstairs to find a roomful of uniformed officers hadn't helped. Cruz and Raven had quickly made themselves scarce, and Silver had contacted a meal-delivery service.

Mason had retreated to the kitchen, rid the floor of glass and nailed plywood over the broken window. For safety reasons, he'd set up a portable table in the living room, tucked between the wall and the couch. They'd be able to see anyone coming up the drive.

"Lily, would you like some chicken?" Tessa asked.

She shook her head and scooted her chair even closer to Tessa's. Lily hadn't spent much time around men, especially men in uniforms with badges and guns.

"I ordered pie for dessert. Does she like pie? It's pecan," Silver said. "Does she have any allergies?"

Mason had spoken very little during the meal, aside from saying a brief prayer of blessing. He was seated on her left, at the head of the table.

"Fortunately, no." Tessa looked across the table at Silver. "You've thought of everything. Thank you."

"You're welcome." His unusually colored eyes seemed to take her measure.

Tessa was glad for Silver's company, despite his reservations. He kept the meal from being conducted in complete, miserable silence. She noticed his habit of wearing long sleeves and leather gloves year-round hadn't changed. Her curiosity stirred. When she'd asked Mason the reason, he'd gotten a funny look and declined to answer.

"When are we going home, Mommy?"

Silver's hand stopped halfway to his mouth, the burger dripping juice onto his plate, and he snuck a furtive glance at Mason. Tessa didn't look at him. She couldn't.

"I'm not sure yet." She hadn't yet considered what exactly to tell Lily or how to explain their current circumstances.

Mason cleared his throat. "You don't want to leave before you see the stables, do you? We have six horses. You can help me feed them."

Lily's expression brightened. "Tonight?"

"My friends, Cruz and Raven, are already getting them tucked in. I thought we could go in the morning and feed them breakfast."

"Can I give them mints?"

Mason smiled. "They'd like that."

"What are their names? Are they boys or girls?"

Lily listened as he explained about the horses in their care. Tessa used the distraction to hand her daughter bits of meat and fries, which she ate without complaint. When they were finished, Silver retreated to the study to make phone calls.

Tessa cleared the wrappers and napkins, while Mason put leftovers in the fridge. Lily trailed behind him.

"Will you color with me?"

His brown eyes reflected surprised pleasure. "Do you like to draw? We could use blank paper and pens."

"There are crayons and coloring books in Lily's travel bag," Tessa suggested.

"I'll get them from the truck."

"Yay!" Lily bounced on her toes.

As soon as Mason brought in the bags, Lily dug in hers and removed almost all of the items until she found the crayons and books. Toddler-sized clothes and socks, along with baby dolls and toys, were now strewn across his floor. Tessa recalled he liked to keep things tidy, but he hadn't been obsessive about it. He patiently encouraged Lily to replace her unwanted things, helping her along the way. When the pair moved to the table and began coloring together, Tessa felt out of place. Unneeded. In Mason's mind, unwanted.

You don't have the right to feel sorry for yourself.
Besides, he deserved Lily's undivided attention.

Tessa carried the bags upstairs and, for lack of anything better to do, transferred their belongings to the dresser drawers. There was no way of knowing how long they'd be staying, but she didn't think he'd mind. When she finished, she waited in the open doorway, letting their mingled voices waft up the stairs and over her.

Lord Jesus, please protect us and lead law enforcement to Dante. Please give Mason a chance to form a lasting bond with Lily.

She thought about asking God to not let Mason hate her, but it seemed selfish.

Retrieving her Bible from the top drawer, she spent the next half hour reading through her favorite Psalms. She heard the study door open and close, and Silver's voice as he addressed Mason. The front door creaked and boots thudded on the porch.

Mason and Lily came looking for her not long after.

"Mason's a good colorer, Mommy," Lily said as she scampered onto the bed.

"Is that so?" Tessa closed the heavy book and placed it on the nightstand.

"Guess what? He used the glitter crayons."

Mason remained on the threshold, his hands in his pockets. He looked as uncertain as she had felt earlier. He took note of the Bible, and she could tell he was still adjusting to the fact she was a believer. She could say the same about him. As wonderful as their relationship had been, it hadn't been built on God's standards. Without Him as their foundation, they wouldn't have found lasting happiness together.

Tessa stood to her feet. "She usually takes a bath before bed. Do you mind?"

"Of course not." He twisted toward the hall. "There are fresh towels and washcloths in the linen closet."

"I didn't see Ducky in my bag," Lily announced.

"I'm afraid we left him at home."

"I can't take a bath without Ducky!"

Sensing the brewing meltdown, Tessa plucked her off the bed. "Ducky wouldn't want you to sleep in Mason's nice clean bed without washing off the dirt first. He'd be sad if you did."

She contemplated that. Mason slowly nodded. "Maybe we can find a friend for Ducky in one of the stores here."

"Can I take the new friend back home with me?"

His features shuttered. "That's a possibility."

Tessa felt like they were navigating emotional land mines. They couldn't make plans for the future until they'd dealt with the present.

Mason left them to their own devices. After Lily had bathed, brushed her teeth and climbed into bed, she asked if he could read her a bedtime story. Tessa found him downstairs on the couch, his laptop on his lap.

"Sorry to disturb you. Lily's requested that you read to her."

He closed the laptop. "Is that part of her bedtime routine?"

"It is."

"Books were a big part of your life."

"They always have been." They'd been her escape when life became difficult. "I've read to Lily since she was about six months old. Story time at the library is a long-standing tradition."

He looked at her, his gaze unreadable. "I'm glad you're passing that passion on to our daughter."

He gave her a wide berth and ascended the stairs. Tessa couldn't resist following him. He hadn't asked her to stay away, so she didn't.

"What are we reading?" Mason got comfortable on the bed, stacking pillows behind his back and stretching his legs out.

Lily's damp curls kissed her pink nightgown, and her cheeks were rosy from the warm bath. She snuggled close to him and handed him the book. "The horses are named Tillie and Toni."

"I remember you told me about them earlier today." He opened the book to the first page and began to read.

Tessa hovered in the hallway, thrilled with the sight of Mason and Lily together, like a father and daughter should be. She was also ensnared by the soothing cadence of his velvet-wrapped voice.

Lily must've found his voice just as soothing, because she fell asleep before the end. Mason gingerly got to his feet and, leaving the book on the nightstand, joined Tessa.

He pulled the door almost closed. "How did I do?"

"You're a natural."

"She keeps reminding me this isn't her home."

"Kids her age don't like change. Our departure was rushed and fraught with danger. Dante almost succeeded in running us off the road, and I had to skirt a log truck to put distance between us, in the process playing chicken with a sports car."

His face hardened. "You didn't tell me."

"I didn't have a chance to in the handful of hours we've been here."

He pinched the bridge of his nose. "I didn't mean to put you on the defensive."

"I'd say you're handling everything amazingly well."

"I want to tell her the truth about who I am."

"Okay."

"We'll tell her together, when the time is right. After the danger has passed."

"Dante won't be easily defeated or distracted from his goal."

"We'll be ready for him."

Tessa wanted to believe Mason, but he had no idea the depth of evil he was up against.

FIVE

Mason had been awake since two in the morning, when he and Silver had switched guard duty, but he was wired. It could be the gallon of coffee he'd downed. More likely, it was because his mind wouldn't rest. He had a daughter who was in serious danger of being abducted and an ex-girlfriend with a target on her back. His enemy had been groomed for crime since birth.

Muddling matters was the very real resentment clamoring for attention. Every time he thought about Lily's birth, her first birthday party, her first words—all the major milestones he'd missed—his heart spasmed with pain. Tessa had professed to love him. But if she really did, she wouldn't have robbed him of precious time with his daughter.

He *should* take his hurt to the Lord and ask for healing. Right now, he wanted to wallow in his anger, because forgiving Tessa meant what she'd done was okay. And it wasn't. Not by a long shot.

Mason drove past the courthouse. Tessa was hunkered against the passenger door, her focus on the lush green landscape that typified a wet spring in the Smokies. She had been withdrawn this morning, content to let Lily's chatter fill the silence. In the past, he would've pulled her into a hug and rained kisses over her face until her trilling laughter erupted. She must've sensed his attention, because she shifted away from the window and looked at him. She'd donned a fitted black jacket over a cotton-candy-pink shirt and the same black pants and sparkly flats from yesterday. Her lips were shiny with her favored gloss. Silver cross earrings shimmered at her ears. The striking combination of her dark, riotous hair and gold-green eyes against her olive skin made him feel as if he'd been kicked in the chest.

His fingers tightened on the wheel. She still affected him. An annoying state of affairs, that.

"What day is it?" Lily asked.

"Sunday."

"I want to go to church."

Tessa sighed. "I wish we could, ladybug. Maybe next Sunday."

Mason was glad Lily didn't press the issue. While he would've liked to take her—and possibly Tessa, as well—to his church, it wasn't safe. He usually attended services after feeding and grooming the horses. This morning, he'd be in a meeting with his immediate superior, Lieutenant Hatmaker. Hatmaker had called last night and shared his extreme annoyance that Mason and Silver had left the event prematurely. While he had a right to his opinion, Mason was in charge of the horses and his officers. He'd made the only decision open to him—get Tessa and Lily to safety. Fortunately, the man in charge of patrol division, Lieutenant Polk, would also be in the meeting. He hoped they could review the case and agree on a plan of action going forward.

"Here we are," he said, pointing to the unit stables. They were located on the far side of town, beyond the firehouse and police headquarters. While not as large as the state's other units, the facility was more than adequate for both the horses and officers.

"I don't remember this being here," Tessa said.

"It's new, only open eighteen months. The old site was several miles outside of town and fairly run-down. We had several fundraising events to raise money. Private donors also pitched in."

The parking lot was enclosed by a tall, chain-link fence. Mason got out and unlocked the gate, then drove close to the building's side entrance. Silver had followed them from the house, and he took care of locking the gate.

"Why are the horses outside?" Lily strained to see the large paddock that ate up much of the property.

Mason liked her boundless curiosity and wonder over seemingly simple things. She was a bright, beautiful child. Of course, she took after her mother.

"They spend each night in the paddock, as long as the weather cooperates."

"Can I go inside there with them?"

"How about you and your mom watch as Silver and I lead them inside? Then you can help us feed and groom them."

She seemed satisfied with that as he released the restraints and hoisted her into his arms. Her weight was slight, her hair springy and soft, and she smelled like the syrup they'd doused their waffles in. He closed his eyes briefly to drink in the experience. When he opened them, he found Tessa watching him and Lily. He couldn't pin down one singular emotion in her wide eyes. He only knew that she was aware of what her choices had cost him.

Good. She *should* feel guilty and ashamed.

Will that really make you feel better?

Not comfortable with his thoughts or their exposed position, Mason directed Tessa and Lily to stand just inside the stables' wide pass-through while he and Silver led the horses into the central area, a long, spacious aisle lined with stalls.

"It's time to groom the horses and give them a quick checkup." Mason positioned Scout in the middle of the aisle and attached ropes to his head collar. They waited as he gathered the grooming kit from the tack room.

Farther down the aisle, Silver was executing the same routine with Lightning.

Halfway through his routine, Mason noticed Lily was getting antsy. He started explaining the things he was checking on Scout.

"You check his teeth?" Her eyes got big. "Like a tooth doctor?"

"Like a dentist, exactly. A horse with a sore tooth can become very cranky." Beckoning Tessa closer, he said, "Have a look for yourself."

Adjusting Lily higher on her hip, Tessa approached and petted Scout's strong neck. "You do this every day?"

"Before we head out on patrol and after we return. If we find anything beyond our ability to treat, we call in the vet."

"I remember how much you enjoyed riding. Now

that your job involves horses, do you find time to ride
for fun?"

He and Tessa had been frequent customers of area
riding stables. Their favorite was located in Cades
Cove, inside the national park. "Not as often as I'd
like." He snagged a dandy brush. "Do you want to
brush him?"

"You don't mind?"

He held out his arms to Lily, who willingly came
to him. He placed the brush in Tessa's palm and got
out of her way. She was almost finished when Mason
heard a feminine gasp coming from the side hallway,
where the offices were located.

He turned and saw his sister staring at them with
mouth agape.

Tessa slowly lowered the brush. "Candace."

Candace's eyes narrowed. "What brings you back
to Serenity, Tessa?"

"I, ah—"

"Let's go to the break room, sis," Mason interrupted,
lowering Lily to the ground.

Leaving Lily with Tessa, Mason took hold of Candace's arm and steered her the way she'd come. She
resisted, and her head swiveled over her shoulder.

"Why aren't you at church?" Mason said, urging
her forward.

Her blue gaze pierced him. "When my brother texts
and asks if I have any spare toddler books at the day
care and possibly a bath floaty, I get suspicious."

He flicked on the break-room light, ushered her inside and closed the door. She slapped a cloth bag on
the nearest table and jammed her hands on her hips.

"Why is she here, Mason? And why does that little girl have your eyes?"

"You think Lily has my eyes?"

She made a flustered sound. He might have inherited his mom's looks, but his sister had gotten her high spirits.

"Tessa sought me out because she needs protection from her brother." He explained her unfortunate family ties. "And, yes, Lily is my daughter."

"But she cheated on you."

"No, she didn't. That was a ruse to get me to leave her."

"She could be lying, you know."

"I believe her, Candace."

She thrust her hand through her pale hair, mussing the short strands. "She does look like you."

"The timeline is right."

"I can't believe you're a dad." She slapped her hand to her chest in typical dramatic style. "And I'm an aunt. Mom is going to flip! Have you told her?"

"I was planning on calling her sometime today." It wasn't a conversation he was looking forward to having.

"Promise me something," Candace urged. "Don't fall for her again. When you and Tessa were together, you were happy—insanely happy. I was jealous of what you guys had, in fact. But afterward…" She closed the distance between them and placed her hand on his shoulder. "Mason, I can't let you return to that bleak place."

He had no intention of letting that happen. "No need to worry. Tessa and I had our chance, and we blew it."

* * *

The rectangular office space wasn't meant for this many people. Officers in and out of uniform crowded around the boardroom-style table. Mason wielded a marker in front of a dry-erase board at the room's far end. Leadership was an easy mantle on his shoulders. He looked official in his Serenity PD T-shirt, which had a bear logo over his heart, cargo pants and military-style boots. His holstered weapon rested against his waist.

Tessa remained at the room's edge, seated apart from everyone, her chair straddling the open doorway. From this vantage point, she could see into the break room, where Candace was entertaining Lily. The petite blonde, opposite from Mason in looks and temperament, was clearly enamored with her niece. It made sense, since Candace loved kids. So much so that she'd opened her own day care.

Tessa and Candace had once gotten along like sisters. Indeed, Tessa had thought that someday they'd be family. Candace had refused to take her calls following the breakup, and Tessa had eventually stopped trying. While she accepted that their friendship likely wasn't going to be restored at this point, she was thrilled for Lily. Her daughter would benefit from having a law-abiding family.

"Tessa?"

With a start, she realized everyone was staring at her. The mounted-police unit had been joined by Lieutenant Hatmaker, whose attitude suggested the milk in his coffee had soured, and men from the patrol division—Lieutenant Polk, Officer Bell and Officer Weiland.

Mason's eyebrows were raised. "We need more insight into Dante and how he operates," he said. "Does he dole out orders, or does he like to get his hands dirty?"

"A little of both, I guess. He lets his guards round up the target. If it's someone he wants to deal with personally, he has that person brought to a specified place." Her throat went dry. "He likes to toy with his victims."

Silver pushed his laptop to the center of the table. "The photos of Officer Fisk were leaked online. Is this Dante's handiwork?"

Tessa kept her gaze on her lap, her stomach churning. Those images were burned into her brain, and she had no desire to be subjected to them again. "Yes."

Ominous silence filled the space. She could feel their horror being directed at her. Her own sibling had committed atrocities against an officer. How could she be normal?

Cruz was the first to speak. "Where would he choose to stay when far from home base?"

She forced her gaze up. "A hotel is not ideal, with security cameras and witnesses. I'd say he would scout out a private residence and either pay for someone's silence or seize it."

"He'll find a place convenient to Mason's," Raven announced to the group. "I'll compile a list of nearby residences, focusing first on the rentals."

"Call my assistant Lindsey," Silver instructed. "She'll help you with the rentals I own."

"Will do."

Lieutenant Polk, a pleasant-faced gentleman, stated that he, Bell and Weiland would visit the homes in Mason's vicinity and warn residents to be vigilant. Other officers would contact local business owners.

When everyone began to file out of the room, Lieutenant Hatmaker squared off against Mason like an irate bulldog.

"This personal issue better not overshadow your other duties, Reed," he snapped. "If I see that it becomes a problem, I'll take my concerns to the chief."

Mason squared his shoulders. "My officers and horses are my top priority, as is protecting every member of this community. Dante Vitale is a threat to everyone in Serenity, not just Tessa. No one is safe with him running free."

Hatmaker's gaze flicked to Tessa, and he seemed to dismiss her out of hand. "Then we need to make sure he's caught soon."

He stalked into the hallway and joined Polk and the others. Mason closed the door behind him and rested against it.

"Is he always like that?" she asked.

"He has his days," he sighed. "We don't always see eye to eye. I have to do what's best for mounted patrol, and he's working on behalf of the department. Our goals sometimes clash, and we have to find ways to compromise."

Catching Dante was crucial for so many reasons. Tessa walked over to the board and reread the case notes. He came to stand beside her.

"I used to pretend I was adopted," she mused. "That I had a regular family somewhere."

"Did Dante ever hurt you?" His voice was like gravel.

The question threw her. She thought about her

bruised and swollen throat after he'd strangled her, the slaps and pinches he'd doled out that their father knew nothing about.

"Tessa." Her name was a jagged whisper on his lips. His fingers closed over hers, warm and comforting.

Tears sprung to her eyes. She hadn't expected compassion from him.

"It wasn't severe."

"Doesn't matter," he growled. "It's still abuse."

She merely nodded, the words on the board blurring.

"Did your mother know?"

"She lives in fear of both my father and Dante. She wouldn't have dreamed of intervening."

His fingers flexed on hers, then let go. "Did he torment your sister, too?"

Tessa finally met his turbulent gaze. "Growing up, Fran idolized Dante. That fed into his ego." She toyed with the jacket buttons on her sleeve cuffs. "My mother did help convince Father to let me attend an out-of-state university. I'm grateful for that."

"You said you chose UT Knoxville because a childhood friend vacationed in the Smokies."

"That's true. It only took one prospective college visit to convince me." She smiled, thinking about her freshman dorm room. "Some might think changing out a mansion for a cramped dorm would be a rough adjustment. That wasn't the case for me. I loved everything about campus life, mainly because it wasn't tainted by my Mafia roots. I went home that first summer because it was expected." The good memories dissipated. "It was a nightmare. Dante and my father were pressuring me to spend time with their chosen groom, Leo Girardi. He was the oldest son of another

Mafia family. My father believed our marriage would seal a lifelong alliance."

Mason's mouth became pinched, and his gaze could have cut through metal. "You mentioned your parents wanted you to marry a family friend."

"That was Leo. I went on a few dates with him long before I met you. We were never engaged. In fact, I didn't spend a significant amount of time in New Jersey after that first summer. I flew in for holidays, but I made sure I had summer internships lined up after that. When I graduated, I was supposed to return home. I defied them. I had already been offered a full-time position with Family Connections."

"The private foster agency where you worked."

"I had interned with them the summer before my senior year, and I saw the director's heart and passion for the kids. I liked everything about their process, and I was thrilled to be an official member of the team."

"You miss it."

"I do. I can't explain how it felt when we made a successful placement. Knowing that hurting kids were going to a loving home, to live with people who'd been trained and equipped to help them adjust and thrive, gave me purpose." She lifted one shoulder. "On the other hand, I feel blessed to have a daughter to raise. I can't imagine life without Lily."

His unreadable gaze shifted to the board. "How long before Dante demanded your return?"

"A year. Dante started sending threatening emails and texts. I tried to reason with him. He didn't want me around, not really. Why not let Fran marry Leo? The only reason he didn't come for me sooner was because Father's health was failing. Dante had to establish his authority in his place. By then, you and I were together." Her chest became tight. "I couldn't leave you. I wouldn't have…"

There was a knock on the door. Sighing, Mason strode over and yanked it open. "Yes?"

Candace didn't look the least bit abashed for interrupting them. "Lily wants a snack. Mind if I get something from the vending machine?"

Mason looked at Tessa. "Is that okay with you?"

"Of course."

He left the door ajar, a sign he was done rehashing the past. "The hardware store opens in an hour. I need to buy a new window. Cruz volunteered to be our lookout today."

"You have loyal friends."

"The best a guy could ask for."

Mason joined the other officers, and Tessa went to the break room. Not surprisingly, Candace didn't stick around for long. When it was time to leave, Silver and Cruz walked with them to Mason's truck and waited until they were buckled in. Cruz got into his personal vehicle, a beat-up Jeep Wrangler. Silver let them out of the gate and waved them off.

Conversation was sparse during the short ride to the edge of town, where Benson's Hardware was located. She and Lily remained in the truck and Cruz in his Jeep while Mason shopped. He emerged twenty minutes later with the window.

"We're fortunate they had it in stock. A trip down to Maryville wouldn't be ideal."

"How much was it? I'll repay you."

Backing out of the space, he shot her an incredulous look. "No way."

"Replacing your window is the right thing to do."

"I appreciate the offer, but I'm not taking your money. In fact, once this is over, we'll have to sit down and have a long chat. I plan to support her."

Anxiety stung her like a thousand fire ants. Would he take her to court and attempt to get full custody? Worse still, would he try to keep Tessa's visits to a minimum?

She averted her face and tried to push aside those worries. Mason had always been a fair person. She had to believe he hadn't changed in that aspect.

They left the hardware store behind and passed several touristy shops. One in particular held special memories.

"The Village Tinker is still in business?"

"I go in there at least once a week for fudge."

She studied his profile. She missed his smile, his laugh, his good opinion of her.

"Rocky road?"

He glanced over. "It's the best."

"You never even tried butter pecan," she protested, falling easily into their friendly argument over the confection.

"I didn't have to. I know what I like." His focus shifted to the rearview mirror, and he tensed. "We've got company."

In the reflection, she saw an Escalade speeding through the curves and bearing down on Cruz. Before Mason could call his friend, a loud popping sound reverberated off the steep terrain that hugged the right side of the road. The Jeep swerved and sped toward the rocky, earthen barrier. Tessa gasped, certain Cruz was going to smash his vehicle head-on.

"Mommy?" Lily tossed her book on the seat and tried to look out the rear window.

Cruz righted the Jeep at the last second, but it wobbled and flipped onto its side, skidding along the asphalt. Tessa clapped her hand over her mouth.

Mason barked instructions into his phone, clearly in contact with police dispatch. He gunned the engine, taking the turns at increasing speeds. His truck was in good condition, but it wasn't made to handle curves.

Lily began to cry, her soft whimpers making Mason's face harden to stone. He slammed on the brakes and jerked the truck onto a skinny side road almost hidden by trees. Tessa reached back to hold Lily's hand. When she did so, she saw the SUV gaining on them.

"Mason."

"I know."

The dense woods thinned on their right. Through the gaps, a rain-swollen river gushed over jagged rocks and fallen logs. The truck bounced over an old wooden bridge. Lily's cries grew louder.

Beyond the bridge, the trees gave way to a sloping, grassy bank. The Escalade slammed into the truck's rear corner, sending it skidding.

"Hold on," Mason yelled, forearms bulging as he fought the wheel.

They were jolted again, and this time there was no correcting their trajectory. The truck bumped and careened down the bank. Tessa braced her hands on the dashboard. She held her breath.

The roiling, greenish brown water rushed at them, swallowing the hood and battering the windshield. They were either going to be swept downstream or shot by Dante's minions.

SIX

A bullet demolished his driver's-side mirror. The river slammed his side of the truck, the water level reaching almost to his window. The force was such that he couldn't get his door open. He used the arm controls to roll his and Tessa's windows down.

"I'm going to draw them away." Mason unholstered his Glock. He'd counted the driver and one passenger. Only one SUV was present, suggesting Dante had remained in his hiding spot and sent half his team after them. "Get her out of that seat and stay down!"

Tessa unbuckled her belt and, twisting around, reached into the back seat and began to unfasten Lily's restraints. "Shouldn't we try to get to shore?"

Another bullet whizzed by and dug into his hood. They were aiming at him. Good.

He eyed the water's movement, the churning currents fed by recent rains. If Tessa slipped on a rock or accidentally let go of Lily…

Out of the corner of his eye, he saw the passenger get out of the vehicle. The short, stocky one with a mustache Tessa had identified as James.

"Backup is on its way," Mason said. "Just sit tight."

Praying that was the right advice, he leaned his upper body out of the open window and got off a shot. James scampered to the opposite side, using the Escalade's bulk for cover. Mason lurched into the water and sucked in his breath. Icy needles pricked his exposed skin. Staying low while also keeping his pistol dry, he fought the current, his sodden boots and pants weighing him down.

The driver remained in the vehicle, but James released a volley of shots, so close he could feel the spray as they skimmed the water. He leaped onto the bank. Going up on his elbows, he got off his own shots. Glass shattered.

Mason began crawling along the bank, away from the truck. A hail of gunfire followed him, as he'd hoped. Where was backup? He prayed Cruz wasn't harmed.

He kept an eye on his truck. From this angle, it looked secure. Leaving Tessa and Lily hadn't been his first choice. If Dante and his other guards showed up, there'd be nothing Mason could do to stop them from taking the girls. Worse would be a stray bullet finding either of them.

He couldn't hear the reassuring sound of sirens above his own thundering heart, along with the river surging between its banks and successive gun blasts.

A flash of black between the trees and the flare of a well-tuned engine heralded his partner's arrival. The men noticed, too, and James slid into the SUV. They raced past Mason, headed in the opposite direction.

Mason should've waited until he was certain they were gone. Instead, he jumped to his feet and sprinted for the truck. Silver beat him there, wading into the water and scooping Lily into his arms. Tessa climbed out of the passenger-side window unassisted. She took a single step toward the bank. Silver shifted Lily to the crook of one arm and held out his other hand. Their fingers brushed. Tessa's feet were swept out from beneath her, and she lost her balance. A cry pierced the air before she disappeared beneath the water.

Everything inside him rebelled. "Tessa!"

He blew past Silver and, resetting the safety, left his pistol on a rock. The churning river tossed her as if she was in a giant washtub, pushing her mercilessly along. Tessa resurfaced, searching for something— anything—to grab hold of. He ran along the bank, gauging the terrain, hoping to guide her to an outlying rock or fallen log to hang on to. Ahead, the woods took over.

But that option was no longer viable, so Mason waded in. The water was deep, cold and menacing. If he wasn't careful, he'd wind up in need of rescue, too. He used the current to his advantage, adding his own strokes to buoy himself closer to her.

She was sucked under again, and his own lungs spasmed.

He pushed harder, resisting the urge to try to find purchase on the rocks.

Ahead, he saw her head pop up. Her body slammed into a car-sized boulder. Her fingers scraped along the uneven surface, scrabbling to grasp anything. She wasn't successful in stopping her forward progression, but it bought precious seconds.

Mason brought his boots down and leveraged himself toward her. Tessa extended her arm. He snapped his hand around her wrist like a handcuff and refused to let go.

The river swept them farther along. Debilitating cold seeped into his bones.

"Over there!" Tessa pointed to where the river curved, and massive tree roots were exposed in the bank's edge.

Mason steered them both toward the tree. As the water became shallower, his hand scraped along the bottom. He hardly registered the tiny cuts and gouges on his palm.

Together, they half swam, half limped the remaining feet to safety. They collapsed onto the sliver of rocky dirt beside the tree, lungs heaving and muscles trembling. Overhead, the sky was a delicate blue traced with wispy clouds.

Mason sat up and threaded his wet hair off his forehead, then scanned Tessa for obvious injuries. Her hair was plastered to her head, and her lips were nearly blue. "You scared me."

She opened her eyes. "*You* were scared? I'm not sure I would've made it if you hadn't jumped in."

Groaning, she pushed herself into a seated position. That's when he noticed the blood trickling down her cheek.

"You're bleeding." Gingerly moving aside the sopping tendrils, he exposed a deep gash near her temple.

"How bad is it?"

"You'll need antibiotic cream and possibly stitches."

"It could've been worse." Her gaze darkened. "You put your life at risk."

"I couldn't let you drown."

"I meant drawing the gunfire to you. Dante wants you out of the way. No sense making it easier for him."

"He's not going to get what he wants. Not this time."

Mason's fingers were featherlight where he held her hair away from the gash. His face was close enough for her to see the tiny droplets shimmering on his skin.

"Do you remember when we hiked to Laurel Falls and I sprained my ankle? You carried me on your back all the way down to our car." He'd been patient and attentive, and hadn't complained once.

Shared memories and old feelings shimmered between them.

"Yeah, I remember." Pulling his hand away, he thrust his fingers through his hair and left it in spiky tufts. He got to his feet and held out his hand. "Silver will come after us if we don't return soon."

Tessa gladly accepted his hand. She was beginning to feel the aftershocks of an acute adrenaline rush. Her legs were like gummy candy left in the hot sun too long. Thanks to the cloudy day and her cold, wet clothes, she was beginning to shiver.

Mason held tightly to her hand, just as he had in the water. Her rising panic had dissipated the moment he'd latched on to her.

"Do you think someone has reached Cruz by now?" she asked.

"Yes."

Whether that someone would help or harm was the question. Dante hadn't participated in this attack, leaving them to guess his whereabouts.

"What are you going to do for a vehicle?" she asked.

"Drive a unit truck until I can deal with insurance and go to the dealership."

"I'm sorry—"

"Don't apologize." The pressure on her hand increased, and he shot her a sideways glance. "You're not responsible for Dante's choices."

Back at the site, Mason retrieved his gun from where he'd left it. A pair of Serenity PD officers had arrived, their cruiser lights flashing. Lily was seated in the passenger seat of Silver's Corvette. The door was open, and when she spotted Tessa, she scrambled out and ran to her. Tessa plastered on a reassuring smile, crouched down and ruffled her hair. Lily looped her arms around her neck.

Silver gave them a once-over and wrinkled his nose. "I'd offer you a ride home, but neither of you are coming near my car." His gaze snagged on her, and he frowned. "Tessa, should I summon an EMT?"

Her hair hid her head wound, so he must've seen traces of blood on her face. "As long as Mason has a first-aid kit at home, I'm good."

Mason studied her. "Are you sure that's wise? You took a beating in there."

"Positive. I've got scrapes and bruises, the same as you."

He rolled the hem of his shirt and tried to squeeze the excess water from the material. "Any word from Cruz?"

"He texted a few minutes ago," Silver replied. "He's going to the hospital to get his wrist examined. His Jeep is toast."

"That Jeep was a gift from his grandfather."

"Maybe it can be salvaged."

Mason turned to survey his half-submerged truck. "I've got to get our phones out of there. Lily's car seat, too."

"I'll give you a hand," Silver said.

While the men retrieved their belongings, the officers blocked the road and informed her the crime-scene unit was en route. Officer Bell showed up and offered to take them to the station, where they could pick up Tessa's Toyota. No trackers had been found. Bell would then follow them to Mason's, where he'd help sweep the property. Silver volunteered to stand watch the rest of the day until Raven could relieve him.

As soon as they were cleared to enter Mason's house, Silver ordered them to change while he rustled up something to eat for Lily. A hot shower chased away the river's chill and soothed Tessa's aches and pains. Her lingering anxiety was another story. By coming to Serenity and seeking help, she'd put more people in danger—innocent people who were important to Mason.

Her worries must've been written on her face. When he appeared at her bedroom door with a first-aid kit, his countenance immediately clouded.

"What's the matter? Is your head hurting? I knew you should've gone to the hospital."

"I'm fine." At his disbelieving stare, she added, "Physically, I'm fine."

He gestured to the patterned armchair in the corner, angled to take advantage of the window view. "Let's get your wound tended."

She got comfortable and knotted her hands in her lap as he placed the box on the stamp-sized side table and rifled through the contents. He smelled wonderful, like a pine-filled meadow in spring. He looked better than wonderful—better than all her lonely imaginings. He'd changed into another pair of worn-in jeans and a Great Smoky Mountains shirt. The sunflower-yellow cotton was the perfect foil for his brown hair and eyes. If only she had the right to caress his cheek, smooth his hair, hold his hand...

She wove her fingers more tightly together. "How long have you been with the mounted police?"

"I joined about six months after we broke up."

Funny, she didn't recall an actual breakup. He'd just disappeared without a word, and she'd had to deal with it.

"You were content with patrol. Why the change?"

"The opportunity came up, and I craved a challenge." He gently shifted her hair, his gaze intent on her wound. "I don't see any debris in there. Can you hold your hair out of the way?"

"That's good, because I don't relish the idea of you digging for any." Tessa hid a wince when he smeared on ointment with a Q-tip. The bruised flesh was tender.

"Sorry." His breath fanned over her forehead. "I'm afraid you're going to have a scar."

"My hair will cover it."

He straightened. "It's not too late to take you to the hospital. Or a walk-in clinic, at least. It's a deep cut."

"No, thanks."

"Afraid of needles?"

She thought of the epidural procedure and shuddered. How she'd longed to have Mason with her, holding her hand and coaching her. He was such a strong, calming presence.

"I avoid them when possible."

He opened a large bandage and positioned it with care. "We'll have to keep an eye on it. If there are any signs of infection, you won't have a choice but to be seen."

"What about your hands? I saw some cuts earlier."

He held them up. "Nothing serious."

She pointed to one in the groove of his palm. "That one could use a bandage." She stood and moved out of the way, then pointed to the chair. "Switch places."

"Yes, ma'am." Mason sat down and balanced his hand on his knee.

Tessa swabbed the same ointment he'd used onto the worst of his cuts. "Silver was working patrol in Knoxville when I was living here. When did he decide to join this unit?"

"About a year after me. He sold his place there and bought land in Serenity. Raven joined around the same time. One officer retired and another transferred to the Nashville unit, so we had two positions to fill."

She searched the box for a small bandage. "Is Raven from here?"

"She and I went to high school together. She's several years younger, though."

She picked out a bandage, then ripped off the paper and pressed it into place. "Cruz moved here from Texas?"

He nodded. "We got approval to add a fourth officer, and he was the most qualified applicant."

Tessa closed the box. "You all seem to get along."

"Considering how much time we spend together, I count that as a blessing." He pushed out of the chair. "The horses are our partners, too. I've grown to love working with them. And being on horseback lets me interact with the community on a deeper level."

She gave him a tentative smile. "I'm happy for you, Mason. You have a nice home. A satisfying work environment. Friends and family who love you."

Although he'd said there wasn't a significant other in his life, she couldn't help wondering if he'd had any serious relationships. The thought made her slightly ill, which wasn't fair. He deserved to be happy, to be loved and adored. Preferably by someone without dangerous ties to organized crime.

"Did you have a support network in Georgia?"

"I became close with several women in my neighborhood. I also made friends at church. The women I worked with at the day-care program were genuine and kind. However, I couldn't forget I was a fraud. I couldn't forget for a moment that I was being hunted."

"Did you—" He started to sidestep her. "Never mind."

She put a forestalling hand on his biceps. "Did I what?"

"It's none of my business."

"You want to know if I dated?"

A muscle in his jaw ticked. "Like I said, none of my business."

"No, I didn't."

His gaze was skeptical. "Why not?"

"I had Lily to raise. She's my priority."

"Plenty of single parents manage to balance their children's needs with their own."

"Are you upset that I didn't have someone in my life?"

His mouth tightened. "I didn't say that."

Did he want her to confess that he'd ruined her for other men? That the mere thought of dating made her break out in a cold sweat?

"All the excitement this morning has made me hungry," he said, brushing past her and stalking over to the door. "Let's go see what Silver thinks qualifies as a healthy meal for our daughter."

Tessa nodded, relieved he'd taken some of the tension with him. She breathed in air not scented with his skin and reminded herself that reconciliation wasn't the goal. Their own hurt and disappointment couldn't get in the way of protecting Lily.

SEVEN

Mason was startled awake sometime in the night. He snagged his phone and fired off a text to Raven, who was outside patrolling the perimeter.

All good?

He got a thumbs-up emoji in response. The coiled tension inside slowly uncoiled. Then she sent him another text.

Are you in the kitchen? Light's on.

No. I'll check on it.

Shoving out of bed, he crossed to the door and opened it. He heard the rough slide of the rickety silverware drawer and the suctioning sound of the fridge door being pulled open. A high-pitched voice was followed by a shushing sound. After confirming the guest bedroom was unoccupied, he padded down the stairs in his T-shirt and pajama pants.

He found Tessa at the counter emptying chocolate

packets into mugs. His sudden appearance startled her, and she knocked one into the sink.

"Mason, I'm sorry we woke you," she said in a hushed voice. Her curls were a soft, disheveled cloud around her face. She was as beautiful as ever, and he was tempted to pull her into his arms and kiss her.

Lily rushed over to him. "I had a bad dream."

He crouched to her level and pushed a curl off her forehead. "Hot chocolate is the best cure."

Tessa was using a paper towel to wipe up the spilled powder. "I hope you don't mind. I found the box in your pantry."

"Not at all. Make yourself at home."

She nodded and looked away. "Would you like some?"

"I'll fix myself coffee." It was half past two. "I'll be relieving Raven soon."

Lily yawned. She shifted closer, wrapped her arms around his neck and rested her head on his shoulder. "Do you have marshmallows?" she asked sleepily.

Tessa observed them, her worry plain. Mason could relate. What effect would this upheaval have on Lily? She was too young to understand why she'd been ripped from her familiar world and dropped in the midst of dangerous situations. He desperately wanted to tell her that he was her dad, but he wasn't sure when the right time would be.

Hugging her close, he said, "I don't have any, but they're going on the top of my grocery list."

"I like the pink and green ones."

"You'll have to tell me what else you like."

She lifted her head. Her eyes were big and dark in her pale face, and her eyelashes were thick and spiky, like his. "Pancakes and ice cream. Oranges. Grapes. Breadsticks." She rattled off a dozen other items, and Tessa hid a smile.

"That's a lot to remember. You and your mom can write everything down in the morning, okay?"

"Will you take me to Ed's?"

"Who's Ed?"

"He makes pizza."

Tessa poured milk into the mugs. "It's an Italian restaurant. We have lunch there every Sunday. Their pizza is top-notch."

"Ah. Well, we have some pretty good pizza here, too."

Lily's brow wrinkled. "Ed gives me free ice cream."

He wondered if Tessa had thought ahead to what would happen once Dante was no longer a threat. Surely, she wasn't planning to return to Georgia. But would she want to live here in Serenity? This was his hometown. As a law-enforcement officer, he was widely known. She might not feel welcome or comfortable here, especially once the gossip mills latched on to the fact he had a surprise daughter.

His phone buzzed. "Raven's heading inside." He relayed the text. "I've got to go upstairs and change."

He patted Lily's back and stood. After setting the coffee machine to brew, he hurried to his room and changed into black cargo pants and a long-sleeved dark cotton shirt. Back downstairs, he sat at the table and began lacing up the old pair of utility boots he'd dug out of the closet when Raven entered the kitchen.

"Coffee's brewing," he told her. "Want some?"

She took in the scene and shook her head. Tessa offered her hot chocolate, which she also declined.

"I brought water." Unzipping a bag she'd left on the counter, she took out a bottle and twisted the lid open. "I'm going to bunk on the couch. Good night."

"There's an extra guest bedroom upstairs," he said to her retreating back.

"This is fine."

Tessa's gaze trailed after the female officer. When she switched her attention to him, he read the concern in the hazel depths. Putting others at risk was a problem for her. When she'd headed for Serenity, she hadn't known she would be dealing with his entire unit.

The bathroom door closed, and the sink faucet turned on.

"Lily and I will take our hot chocolate to the bedroom so we don't keep her awake."

"Raven operates on very little sleep."

Her eyebrows met. "Oh."

"She lost someone close to her, and now she says nights are her enemy."

"I'm sorry to hear that."

"Do me a favor and don't let on that you know. It's a sensitive subject."

"I understand."

She watched as he slid his service weapon into the security holster attached to his utility belt. He double-checked that he had spare ammo and a full case of pepper spray. His flashlight battery was low, though, and his backup batteries were at the stables.

"What about you and the others? Your job requires quick decisions. I don't like to think about you working on limited sleep."

"It's true this job demands a lot—physically, mentally and emotionally. We're trained to deal with a number of stressors, lack of sleep being one of them."

Mason cooled his coffee with milk and guzzled it before heading for the door.

"Be careful, Mason."

The simple words hauled him into the past. He'd worked second shift then, so they'd spent afternoons together. Before he'd headed to work, she'd framed his face and kissed him sweetly on the lips, bidding him to be careful. Without fail.

His hand on the knob, he didn't turn around. He didn't want her to see how hard this was. Having her around, in his home no less, was cracking the ice around his heart and releasing memories that seared him.

With a nod, he let himself out of the house, making sure to engage the lock. The air had a distinct chill, not unusual for April in the mountains. The half-moon bathed the trees in filmy light, enough that he wouldn't need his flashlight for most of the route he'd take around the property. He headed past the shed and leaped over the stream, which was rippling and gurgling along its shallow path.

He stopped and turned to observe the house. The kitchen light winked off, and he pictured Tessa and Lily navigating the stairs, anticipating their chocolate treat. When he'd bought the place last year, he'd known it was too big for one person. He'd hoped that one day he would meet someone to make him forget Tessa. That wasn't a fair expectation. Maybe that's why he hadn't had more than a handful of casual dates. He couldn't come to a relationship with an open heart and mind. Now that Tessa had barged back into his life, he was even less optimistic about his ability to move beyond the past.

The light from their bedroom spilled into the night. Finding that one person to share his life with was no longer important. He had a child to raise. He would focus on making up for the years he'd lost.

As Mason parked the borrowed unit truck close to the stables early Monday morning, Tessa recognized the willowy brunette hovering in the entrance.

Her stomach dropped. "Your mom is here."

He killed the engine and removed the keys. "I meant to prepare you. She called right after my alarm went off this morning. Candace apparently wasn't acting like herself yesterday, and Mom gathered it had something to do with my absence at church."

"She knows everything?"

"Yes."

Tessa mentally braced herself. Mason wasn't the only person affected by her decisions. His mom, Gia, and Candace must've believed, like him, that she'd been unfaithful. Her innocence on that charge didn't negate the fact she'd kept Lily a secret. She had hurt Mason, plain and simple. She deserved their anger and recriminations. And she would bear them, because of Lily. If she had any say, her daughter wouldn't have ties to Tessa's family. Gia and Candace would have to fill the void. It was too much to hope that Tessa could also claim that benefit.

Mason unbuckled his seat belt. "You can't blame her for being impatient to meet her only grandchild."

Tessa winced at the reproach in his voice. "Of

course not. I want Gia and Candace to form a strong bond with her."

He flicked a glance in the rearview mirror. Lily was subdued this morning, content to look through her books.

"That won't happen if you go back to Georgia," he asserted in a low voice. "If you try and take her away again, you'll be in for a fight."

Tessa's head reared back. Mason's jaw was hard, his body stiff.

"I wouldn't do that to you."

He searched her face, picking away at her with his fierce gaze, leaving her sore and exposed. Their present interactions in no way resembled what used to be. He hadn't spoken to her in anger, hadn't directed his frustration at her. Unlike the men in her family, Mason had treated her with a fond regard, underscored with respect. As their bond had grown stronger, fondness had deepened into something more, something rare and precious. She had believed they would be together forever.

But then he'd lost faith in her. And in the midst of her crisis, she'd run away from him instead of to him. Time wouldn't heal their wounds, and it made her feel like giving up.

"Are we gonna see the horses?"

Lily's voice sliced through the thick, tension-choked air. Mason's chest expanded on a ragged sigh, and he pulled the door handle, popping open the door. "There's someone I'd like for you to meet first."

Mason walked with Lily, her tiny hand in his large one, and Tessa followed a few steps behind. The smells of hay, earth and horseflesh washed over her. She could hear companionable chatter and activity in the central stable area.

"Lily, this is my mom. Her name is Gia."

Gia's eyes were suspiciously bright and eclipsed only by her smile. "Hello, Lily."

Lily shifted closer to Mason and leaned against his leg. Tessa's heart fluttered. That she had taken to him so readily made this transition easier for everyone.

"She didn't get a good night's rest," he informed Gia.

Gia's forehead creased. "Poor darling. I'm not surprised, all things considered."

Mason ushered them into the break room and closed the door. "I wish we could've met at my place or yours, but it's not safe. In fact, you should have an officer escort you home."

Gia finally looked at Tessa. "Mason told me about your troubles. You did the right thing coming here. He's the best person to offer you protection. If there's anything I can do to help, let me know."

Tessa's white-knuckled grip on the plastic chair loosened. She'd expected to be blasted or berated. The school nurse was a confident woman, someone who could handle whatever life threw at her with poise. Tessa had quickly grown to admire her fortitude. Mason thought Gia was too quick to speak her mind, but that trait was balanced by her fairness and generosity of spirit. She was also a fabulous cook. Mason and Tessa had enjoyed many Sunday-evening suppers in her home. Candace had been there, too, and it had been the closest to normal Tessa had ever experienced.

Gia had approved of their relationship, but she'd let them know they needed God as their foundation. Tessa wished now she'd heeded the other woman's wise advice. Her troubles had eventually driven her straight into God's arms, however. She didn't regret that part of her past.

Silver knocked on the door and, poking his head in, addressed Mason. "We've got a lead."

Tessa would've liked to go with him, but Lily reached for her, clearly not in the mood to be left with a stranger.

Tessa dropped into a chair and pulled Lily onto her lap. Gia settled on the opposite side of the table and clasped her hands on the smooth top. The ceiling lights shimmered over her brilliant gold-and-diamond wedding ring set that Mason said she'd refused to take off, no matter how many years had passed since her husband's death.

Her brown gaze soaked in everything Lily. "She's a beautiful child."

"I know my decisions don't make sense to you."

"I am hurt," she admitted. "And shocked. I didn't see this coming."

"I owe you an apology."

"Mason explained the initial misunderstanding between you two and why you didn't seek him out." Her gaze was full of compassion. "I was a single mother for most of Mason and Candace's teen years. I worked hard to create a safe, loving environment for them. I can imagine the fear and uncertainty you grappled with. If I had been in your shoes, I might've made the same choice." The creases at the corners of her eyes became more pronounced. "My son changed after you left. There was a long stretch of time when I wondered if he'd ever recover. This unit, the horses and training, brought him back to life. I won't lie—I'm worried how your reappearance will impact him. I can't bear to see him suffer again."

"That's the last thing I want, Gia."

Before the other woman could respond, Tessa's phone rang. She fished it out of her purse and frowned at the unknown number. She chose not to answer. Instead of a voice mail, a text came through. A photo of a couple she didn't know, tied and gagged.

Her throat closed up.

"What's wrong?" Gia said.

A second text came through. Answer my call, darling sister.

Shoving the chair away from the table, she lowered Lily to the floor. The phone began to ring. A video-chat request, no less.

"Lily, I need for you to stay with Gia for a few minutes."

"But, Mommy—"

Gia stood. "Is it okay if I show her the horses?"

Tessa nodded her assent before hurrying into the hall and bursting into the conference-style office they'd used the day before. Mason was there with Silver, Officer Bell and a deputy.

"Dante's calling. He has hostages, I think. I have to answer."

Mason surged out of his chair and strode over.

She swiped the screen and was greeted by her brother's deceptively serene face. "What have you done, Dante?"

"Is that any way to greet your only brother?" he chided, his smile at odds with the glitter in his black eyes.

"How did you get my number?"

He shrugged. "I had Jorge fly down to Georgia and search your house. You really should go paperless, Tessa."

"Who are those people?"

"The Pascals? They're my reluctant hosts." He began walking through what looked like a cabin. The rustic furniture and decorative nods to black bears and the mountains told her he was nearby. The view flipped to reveal the couple in the photo. "Say hello to my sister. Oh, I forgot, you're indisposed."

The man and woman were both fair-haired. They were strapped to dining chairs and seated side by side. Gags prevented them from speaking, but their eyes broadcast their terror. Blood trickled along the man's temple.

They looked like nice people. Somewhere, there were family members who loved them. Perhaps children and grandchildren. They were in danger through no fault of their own.

"Please don't hurt them." She started trembling from head to toe.

Mason's hand came to rest on her lower back, his fingers curving around her waist.

"I'll let them live if you agree to turn yourself over to me."

She'd known that was coming. Sticky, slimy dread wound through her.

"Okay. I'll do it."

"That's not going to happen," Mason growled. Reaching up, he twisted the phone so that Dante could see him. "You're not going to lay another hand on Tessa."

Dante's smile was cold enough to freeze a mountain waterfall in summer. "Sergeant Reed, I can't say it's a pleasure to speak with you again. Let me get this straight—you're saying Tessa's life is more important than these people's?" Turning the video on them, he said, "Did you hear that? Local law enforcement isn't willing to save you. You should've chosen another place to vacation."

There was movement and a sudden, charged blast. The woman's muffled screams stabbed Tessa. The man's face contorted as blood formed a blossoming stain on his thigh.

Beside her, Mason went rigid. Around the table, Silver and the others jumped to their feet, ready to respond.

"You've made your point," Tessa gasped. "Where and when? Tell me, and I'll meet you."

"Noon. I'll text you the location right before." His mouth became an ugly slash. "And, Tessa, bring my niece."

The call ended. A terrible silence descended.

"You're not going to him," Mason declared, his eyes flinty.

"Those people are in danger because of me."

"You're not sacrificing yourself. I won't allow it."

EIGHT

Mason could feel the other officers' surprise. His customary equanimity had splintered. And no wonder. Tessa had just offered herself in trade.

"What other option do I have?" she cried, her voice quaking. "That man will die for sure if I don't, and the woman, too. Dante will shoot her out of spite."

"What about Lily?"

Her hands fisted. "He can't have her."

"I meant would you leave her without a mother? And when he realizes she's not with you, what will he do to the Pascals then?"

Silver edged past the other officers. "That name sounds familiar. Show me the photo?"

She pulled up the text and let him peruse it. "The angle doesn't show any defining architectural features."

"You think this could be one of your cabins?" Mason said.

"It's possible."

Mason tried to get a handle on his emotions while his partner contacted his assistant.

"Lindsey, I need you to check the rental roster and

tell me if we have anyone by the name of Pascal." His forehead crimped, and his gray hair slid into his eyes. He flicked it away impatiently. "Their wedding anniversary? You told me last week?" Silver paced the narrow distance between the door and the table. "I *do* listen to you. How else would I have recognized the name?"

Tessa leaned into Mason. "He has cabins?"

"About forty," he murmured. "Scattered across two counties. Some are in Serenity, but the majority are in Pigeon Forge and Gatlinburg."

Silver ended the call and scowled. "Lindsey is being her usual irascible self. Did you know she accused me of taking her for granted?"

"The Pascals?" Mason prompted.

"I was right. They're a last-minute booking. Florida residents here celebrating their anniversary." He shifted past them and wrote the Serenity address on the board. "Deputy Stark, we have three hours until the meetup with Dante. Is that enough time for SWAT to organize?"

"It'll have to be." He left the room already issuing instructions into the phone.

"You plan to ambush Dante and his men?" Tessa asked doubtfully.

"We'll have the element of surprise on our side. He doesn't know we're aware of his location."

Officer Bell rubbed his hands together. "Weiland and I will provide support."

"Our unit will be there," Mason said. "In case we have runners."

Lieutenant Hatmaker wasn't going to be pleased with this new development. Like any other reasonable law-enforcement officer, he disliked bad press, anything that called Serenity PD's competency into question. Hatmaker took it a step further, however. In his mind, they were in competition with other departments to be the best, to be above reproach, to be infallible. He sometimes forgot he was dealing with human beings in police uniforms. Perfection was unattainable.

When Bell and Silver left the room, Tessa made a soft appeal. "Are you sure you have to go?"

"That cabin is surrounded by forest. Our horses can access areas patrol cars and the SWAT armored vehicle can't."

"I have a bad feeling about this."

"If everything goes according to plan, your brother and his goons will be in custody before lunch. Cruz can stay behind with you."

It was the best option. Cruz's wrist had been badly sprained. Chasing criminals through the mountains would pose a threat to his recovery. He could fire a weapon if necessary, though.

"I'm in charge of this unit," he explained. "I can't knowingly send them into danger without me."

She crossed her arms over her middle. "I pray Mr. Pascal survives."

Tessa discussing prayer in any format was unusual. Mason took comfort knowing they shared a common faith in God. That was one positive that had come out of their breakup.

He squeezed her shoulder. "I'll join you in that prayer."

Mason left her to find Cruz and make his request. The officer was already in the locker room getting ready to suit up. He wouldn't have chosen to be left out of the action, but he agreed that watching over Tessa and Lily was the best option.

"Thanks, Cruz."

"I'm happy to do it."

Mason, Silver and Raven worked quickly to get their horses loaded into the trailers. His mom insisted on remaining at the stables. Tessa didn't seem to mind, so he didn't argue the point.

When the others were in the truck and ready to go, he crouched before Lily. He finally understood what officers with wives and kids went through. His chosen career posed significant risks. Even a routine traffic stop could prove deadly.

"Can I have a hug, ladybug?" He'd heard Tessa using the nickname, and it rolled off his tongue with ease.

She wrapped her arms around his neck. "Are you going to ride Scout?"

"I am."

"I gave him an apple. He's my friend."

"I'm sure he liked that." He smiled and lightly tapped her nose. "I'll see you in a little while." Standing, he turned to Tessa. "I'll call you with an update as soon as I can."

She looked so anxious he almost offered her a hug.

Cruz gave him a thumbs-up as he left the building. Mason climbed behind the wheel, and they began the twenty-minute ride through twisting, mountainous roads. They were in almost constant contact with Bell and Deputy Stark. SWAT was estimated to arrive in another half hour. Because the mounted police were playing a support role, they would take care not to let their presence be detected.

Silver got on the phone with Lindsey again and

verified that the property next door to the Pascals' rental was unoccupied. The land parcels were large and wooded. Mason turned into the specified driveway and parked the truck at the far end, using the generous, three-story structure to further obscure their presence.

As they unloaded the horses and rechecked their gear, Mason had to work at maintaining his composure. That frustrated him. His equine partner, Scout, depended on him. His human partners did, too. They depended on each other. They were a cohesive team, and if he let himself be distracted, he could make a mistake that could cost someone their life.

Officers Bell and Weiland arrived mere minutes before SWAT. The highly efficient team fanned out across the property next door and got into position. Silver had sent them floor plans of the multilevel luxury cabin earlier, so they'd have time to plan. Silver, Raven and Mason mounted their horses and remained on standby.

Minutes ticked past. The temperature was pushing seventy-five degrees, and his uniform absorbed the sun like a sponge. Sweat trickled between his shoulder blades.

He glanced over at Silver, who wore his long-sleeved uniform shirt and gloves. How the guy managed to look as cool as a Popsicle he had no idea.

The woods were a serene vista. The smell of a charcoal grill and sizzling beef carried on the breeze. When would the sounds of invasion break the spell?

Scout's flesh rippled with tension. Mason's anxiety was leaking into his horse and making him antsy.

Raven cocked her head, listening. "Either this is the most peaceful takeover ever or we got the wrong address."

Silver cocked a brow. "Lindsey make a mistake? Not likely."

Bell's voice crackled over their radios, letting them know he was returning. They watched for his familiar form on the road. He jogged the length of the driveway.

"They're gone," he said, panting. "Dante must've had someone watching the stables and was informed of our visit."

"The Pascals?" Raven demanded.

"Inside. The woman's unharmed. We have an ambulance on the way for Mr. Pascal."

Mason was on the verge of splintering apart. "He's going after Tessa."

Silver reached over and took Scout's lead. "Go."

The instant his boots hit the ground, he began sprinting for the cruiser. "You and me, Bell."

The other officer did an about-face and hurried after him.

How long of a head start had Dante had? They hadn't encountered the SUVs on the drive up the mountain, but side roads were plentiful. Once seated in the passenger seat, he called Cruz.

Bell buckled in and started the engine. "Anything?"

"Voice mail."

"That doesn't mean he's in trouble."

Mason punched in Tessa's number. Then his mom's. No response from either of them.

Bell took the curves at excess speeds. "Remember, cell signal is spotty in these mountains."

He gritted his teeth hard enough to make his jaw ache. His mom, Tessa and Lily were sitting ducks. What if they didn't reach them in time?

* * *

Tessa paced the length of the aisle. Three horses observed her from their stalls. The past hour and fifteen minutes had crawled past. Why hadn't Mason reached out?

"I'm going to speak to Cruz," she announced, stopping short.

Gia waved her on. "Go ahead. Lily and I will keep Iggy company."

Iggy, a good-humored quarter horse, was enjoying the attention. Tessa wished the majestic creature could distract her from the constant wondering and worry.

God has this under control, remember? Worrying won't change the outcome. You have to trust His plan.

Tessa strode to the short, broad hallway where the break room and offices were located. Cruz was in the smallest office, seated at the lone desk, and was watching the security feeds. One camera was angled at the main entrance and parking lot. The other showed the paddock.

He looked up at her approach. A purple bruise on his chin was the only indication, other than his bandaged wrist, that he'd been in an accident. "I haven't had any updates."

She sagged against the doorjamb. "Shouldn't we have heard something by now?"

Rubbing his hand over his short black hair, he leaned back in the swivel chair. "Not necessarily. Every case is different. SWAT is running the operation, not us. Now, if the perps leave the cabin for the forest, Mason and the others will pursue them. That could take a while. Besides, cell reception isn't reliable in these mountains."

If Mason was in trouble, he might not be able to get a message to her.

Cruz gave her a sympathetic smile. "Mason doesn't take unnecessary risks. He's a professional."

"I believe you." What no one else seemed to want to believe was that Dante shouldn't be underestimated.

Cruz's gaze returned to the cameras, and he shot upright in the chair.

"What is it?"

"We've got company," he said intently, nodding to the man using pliers to snap the gate's lock. One Cadillac was waiting behind him. "You, Gia and Lily— get to the tack room and don't come out."

He ushered her out of the office. When she hesitated, waiting instead to watch him test the front-door lock, he urged her to hurry.

Tessa tamped down her rising horror and rushed into the center of the building. Gia immediately noticed something was off.

"We have a situation," she said, trying to keep her voice even. Scooping up Lily, she beckoned for the other woman to follow. Gia didn't ask questions. Nor did she comment when Cruz stormed past and used a key to unlock a cabinet stocked with weapons. Tessa regretted not learning how to use a gun. Then she could have helped the officer instead of leaving him to defend the stables alone.

Gia entered the long, narrow, windowless room first. Tessa closed the door behind her and searched for something to block it.

"It smells, Mommy."

Lily wiggled to get down. Tessa released her and followed her to the far corner, where Gia was standing, her hands clasped at her waist. The lines around her mouth were more pronounced.

"Cruz has some police business to take care of, and he asked us to wait here. I'd like to pray for the police officers who work to keep us safe. Want to join me?"

Lily took her hand and held out her other one to Gia, who didn't bother hiding her surprise.

"I think that's a great idea," Gia murmured, her voice choked with emotion.

Tessa offered a prayer for safety without giving details that would alarm Lily. God knew them, anyway. Lily went second. Her prayer was very brief, as usual, and precious. While Gia was praying, the muted sound of gunfire and splintering glass greeted them. Her hold on Tessa's hand tightened.

The door was rammed open, the thick wood thudding against the wall shelving. Tessa spun around and shielded the others.

"Bruno!"

The loyal Vitale employee hadn't changed much over the course of four years. He was still a bull of a man, with massive fists that could break a person's face.

"Don't make this harder than it has to be," he said, holstering his gun.

"Bruno, please. I have a daughter now." She backed up, and Lily grabbed onto her legs. "Dante is like a son to you, right? You would do anything to protect him. I can't let you have her. But I'll go willingly with you."

Gia made a noise of protest. Bruno didn't spare her a glance as he advanced into the room. Like Dante, this man didn't know the meaning of compassion.

"Dante wants you both."

Tessa glanced around, desperate to stop him. She seized a pitchfork and wielded it in front of her. Lily began to cry softly.

Bruno stopped. A vein in his neck bulged. Sighing, he took out his gun again and aimed it at Gia.

"Put it down, Tessa, or she dies."

"Don't, Tessa," Gia said softly, sadly.

Shifting in front of Gia, she glared at him. "Put the gun away."

"You first." He gestured to the pitchfork.

Her stomach in knots, she let it fall to the floor.

"Come over here," he ordered.

Tessa reached down and, easing Lily's hands free, gently pushed her toward Gia. "I love you, ladybug."

When Lily almost lurched forward, Gia wrapped her arms around her and held her fast.

"Mommy!"

Her heart splintering, Tessa approached Bruno. His mitt-sized hand latched on to her upper arm. The blast of gunfire coming from the main entrance told her Cruz was being kept busy with the other goons.

"Let the child go," he said.

"No!" Tessa tried to shove him out the door. "I said I'd go with you. He's not getting anywhere near her!"

He didn't budge, just trained the gun on Gia. When Gia didn't react, he jammed the barrel into Tessa's skull.

"This one's death certificate is already signed. You insist on being stubborn, and you shorten her life."

Her mouth opened, and her gaze snapped to Tessa's, apology and tears filling the brown depths. She let go of Lily, who shot across the room to hold on to Tessa.

Bruno scooped her up as if she weighed nothing,

lodged her beneath one arm and pushed Tessa through the door. She stumbled, and he caught her in a bruising grip, forcing her toward the side entrance.

"Stop!" Cruz's command volleyed down the aisle. She managed to look over her shoulder. He was crouched inside one of the empty stalls, his weapon ready.

But he wouldn't take a shot, not with Tessa and Lily in the way. Frustration was carved into his face.

Bruno marched into the lane between the stables and the paddock. Bright sunshine hampered her view. She tried to think of a solution. If she fought back, Bruno or one of the others would likely shoot her and take Lily.

Her vision cleared enough for her to make out the waiting Cadillac, angled close to the building. Another one was idling on a side street beyond the paddock, where her brother was no doubt watching. The blood in her veins threatened to dry up as their unwanted reunion loomed. Would he take his time killing her, or would he show her mercy?

The crunch of boots on gravel behind them was accompanied by a sharp command. Mason and Bell emerged from the stand of trees edging the paddock. At the same time, Cruz eased out of the building, his weapon aimed at Bruno.

"You're not leaving here with them," Mason said with steely calm. His gaze didn't flicker to her or Lily, and his expression was a closed book.

Bruno's fingers dug into her flesh. He whirled, his head swiveling to take in all the officers. In the distance, the second SUV peeled out and disappeared onto a secondary road.

Bell spoke into his radio and set the deputies on Dante's trail.

Mason continued to edge closer. "You're outgunned. There's no reason for this to get ugly."

The driver shot at Cruz, who dove to the ground. Bruno released her. Tessa's hands closed over Lily, who was screaming at the top of her lungs. To her relief, the much larger man didn't fight her. He pounded after the vehicle.

Tessa scooped Lily into her arms and ran for shelter. A shot rang out, followed by a grunt and a thud. Tires screamed against the pavement.

There was a scuffle. Tessa didn't wait around to see the outcome. She entered the stables, believing they'd be safe, when strong arms closed around her like a vise.

NINE

"Thank the Lord you're okay," Mason breathed, his lips catching her hair. His heart thundered against his ribs.

Tessa melted against his chest, her arm coming around his waist, fingers tangling with his utility belt. Tremors worked through her body. Her breathing was ragged.

He would've been content to hold her all day, or at least until they'd both recovered from that close call. Lily had other ideas. Plus, his mom wanted to see for herself that no one was harmed.

"Oh, Tessa, I'm so sorry," she gasped, taking her hands. "I didn't know what to do."

"It's okay."

"What happened exactly?" Mason asked, dreading the answer.

His mom launched into a detailed explanation. "Tessa was very brave."

Mason couldn't speak. He hated it when violence was visited upon innocent civilians, much less people close to him.

"How did you know to come back?" Tessa asked, tucking Lily close to her side.

"Dante figured out our plans. When we got there, they were gone."

Had he ordered one of his goons to surveil the stables? Had he hacked Tessa's phone and listened in to their conversations? Although that would take serious skill, Dante had the means to make it happen.

"The Pascals are being taken to the hospital," he informed them. "I'll call and get an update later. We'll go home soon." It was nearing lunchtime. While he was new to this dad business, he'd already learned that Lily benefited from frequent and timely meals. "Stay inside while I check on things."

Mason walked outside in time to see Bruno being loaded into an ambulance. The deputies would accompany him to the hospital and stay there until he was ready to be transferred to the county jail.

Cruz ambled over. "You guys got here in the nick of time. I almost lost control of the situation."

Meaning, Tessa and Lily almost got taken on his watch. "Leaving you alone was my call. What happened falls squarely on my shoulders." He gestured to the building. "How are the horses?"

"Spooked, but okay. I'll show you the damage to the building."

They walked around to the front, where Mason assessed the busted gate lock and the obliterated main entrance. Fixing that was a priority.

"I'll take care of all this," Cruz said. "Go be with your family. They've had a traumatic morning."

He didn't correct Cruz. Tessa wasn't technically

family. As the mother of his child, however, she was automatically in his circle of important people.

When Raven and Silver returned, he helped them unload Scout, Lightning and Thorn, and settle them inside. Silver left to meet Lindsey at the cabin and determine if there had been any property damage. Raven and Cruz would remain at the stables and oversee the necessary repairs. Officer Weiland agreed to accompany Mason and the others to his home. Before they left, Mason called around to several alarm companies and found one available to install a system in his home that day.

His mom asked to spend the afternoon with them. She might be as tough as nails, but this was enough to rattle anyone. They had a quiet lunch in the kitchen with the curtains drawn. Afterward, his mom volunteered to show Lily how to bake cookies. He recognized the attempt to distract the little girl and appreciated it. If he wasn't preoccupied with the escalating threat, he would've participated.

Mason found Tessa on the screened-in porch. Seated with her back to the wall, staring at nothing in particular, her fingertips slowly polishing the mug's surface, she looked fragile and hollow. The opposite was true, he knew.

She looked over at him. "I know I'm not supposed to be out here. I just needed five minutes of fresh air, blue sky and birds singing."

Of normalcy. A reminder that there was good in the world. "I get it." He pulled out the chair next to her and sat. The screen across from them still bore evidence of the henchman's bullet. "Bell just got here. He and

Weiland are at the end of the driveway. The alarm company should be here any minute."

"A cost you weren't planning on."

"It's worth it. I hope you understand about your phone. Let me know if you need to make any calls while you're waiting to get it back." He'd given the phone to Deputy Stark. Their department was larger and had the capabilities to determine if it had been compromised. "You're welcome to use my laptop anytime."

"Anything that will help prevent another scene like today, I fully support. Any updates from the hospital?"

"Mr. Pascal is out of surgery and is expected to make a full recovery. Silver has already pledged to refund their rental fees and travel expenses. He'll also cover any out-of-pocket medical expenses."

"I'm sad their memories of East Tennessee are tainted. At least they survived." She swallowed hard. "What about Bruno?"

"No need for surgery. The bullet went clean through his shoulder."

"Bruno is important to Dante. I don't know how he'll react to him being taken into custody."

"The sheriff's department has increased security."

"They won't get any information out of him," she warned.

Mason nodded in deference to her personal knowledge. "It's one less man to contend with. Maybe rattling Dante is a good thing. He'll be more likely to make a mistake."

"Or do something rash." Her eyes were twin tombs. "I don't want to contemplate how Lily will be treated if he were to take her to New Jersey. His hatred for me would bleed into that relationship. My sister betrayed me, so I have no hope she'd stick up for my child." Her fingers latched on to his arm, and she crowded his space. "No matter what happens to me, promise you'll move heaven and earth to keep her out of his clutches."

His mom's words scrolled through his mind. Bruno had said Tessa's death certificate was already signed. Figurative words, of course, but no less chilling. When he'd come out of those trees and seen her and Lily seconds away from being ripped from him, Mason had been desperate to save them both.

As if of their own volition, his fingers slowly and reverently traced a line from the bandage on her temple to her jaw. Her eyes flared with surprise. Beneath that, he recognized loneliness and longing.

She'd been alone for so long, shouldering explosive secrets. He'd been alone, too, and not because he relished the bachelor life. Because she'd taken away his right to decide.

Tessa must've sensed the shift in his mood, because she lowered her gaze and removed her hand from his arm.

"I don't want you to worry," he said gruffly. "Lily's well-being is my top priority." Scooting out his chair, he said, "We should go inside."

Tessa still loved him.

That first year without him had been a nightmare. The fear that Dante would track her down. The worry about her unborn child and how ongoing stress would impact the pregnancy. The separation from Mason— missing him, aching to see him, talk to him, hold him. When she'd brought their daughter into the world without him, she'd made a conscious choice. No more mourning what she'd lost. She had to pour all her energy into raising Lily and creating as normal a childhood as possible. Out of a need for self-preservation, she'd buried her love for Mason.

Those moments with Bruno, when it seemed she would soon be reunited with her brother, she'd released the lock on her feelings. She'd allowed herself to fully feel again. Why wouldn't she cherish what they'd shared if she was on her way to die?

But she hadn't died. Mason had rescued her. And he had held her so tightly and tenderly. Just now, he'd caressed her face and regarded her with affection. Like old times.

What did it gain her, though? Fresh hurt. Fresh pain. Fresh rejection. Not because of Dante's actions, but her own.

Certain she couldn't keep her turmoil hidden, she murmured an excuse to him and Gia and slipped upstairs. In the privacy of the bedroom, she poured out her heartache to Jesus and took comfort in the Scriptures' promises. God loved her. He wouldn't leave or forsake her.

Tessa was physically and mentally spent. When Gia brought a sleepy Lily upstairs, Tessa opted to take a nap, too. The sound of a vehicle woke her more than two hours later. She left Lily tucked beneath the blankets and padded downstairs. Through the living-room window, she watched the security company van get swallowed by the trees as it disappeared down the drive.

"Feel better?"

Tessa finger-combed her hair off her forehead and

gave Gia a perfunctory smile. "I will after I've had a cup of coffee."

"I just made a pot."

Gia poured a cup for Tessa and retrieved the milk from the fridge. She then returned to her cutting board and continued dicing onions and tomatoes. The curtains were drawn, and needles of sunlight poked around the edges.

"I'm not usually a nap taker," Tessa said, sipping the rich brew. The house was silent, and she wondered what Mason was doing. "Has the security company already installed the system?"

She nodded. "He was quick and efficient. He will have to come back later and do the upstairs windows. Mason wouldn't let him disturb you and Lily."

"Oh."

"After what you've both been through, you've earned the rest."

"Thank you for entertaining Lily. Actually, I've been meaning to find someone to teach her to bake."

A genuine smile curved her lips. "She's a delightful child. You've done an excellent job with her."

Her cheeks heated. "Thank you. I had support from the community."

"You made friends, I hope?"

"At first, I kept people at a distance. But when my pregnancy became apparent, women in my neighborhood started popping by unannounced. They brought me books, maternity clothes and baked goods. I blame my weight gain on Barbara Roland's caramel brownies." She smiled, remembering how Barb and the others had become her tribe. She wondered if she'd ever see them again.

Gia's gaze flicked past her shoulder. "Are you going to stand there all day or are you going to help me make salsa?"

Tessa didn't need to turn around. Her stomach flip-flopped as Mason slowly traversed the room and came to a stop beside her. How much had he heard? She glanced at him, relieved to see his expression wasn't shuttered like before.

She glanced down at her wrinkled scoop-neck shirt and pants, wishing she'd taken a moment to change before coming downstairs. Her hair was no doubt in wild disarray, the default hairstyle she'd been born with.

"Was anyone with you during the delivery?" he said, washing his hands and retrieving an extra knife and cutting board.

"Lisa, my next-door neighbor, is a pediatric nurse. She volunteered, and I accepted."

As he diced the vegetables, his movements were both careful and precise. He had tanned, strong hands, thick wrists and corded forearms. His watch face caught and refracted the overhead light as he worked. Tessa was reminded of the countless meals they'd prepared together, sometimes just the two of them and sometimes with Gia and Candace.

"Were there any complications?"

"None."

Tessa got the feeling he wanted to ask more pointed questions but refrained. Later, when the time was right, she'd give him the opportunity to delve more deeply into Lily's birth.

Gia's perceptive gaze bounced between them. "Tell me about how you came to be a believer, Tessa."

"I was a regular patron at the library, both before

and after Lily's arrival. Mrs. Smith, the head librarian, invited me to church. I was both fascinated and confounded by her faith. She talked about God like He was a dear friend. It was a natural thing for her to bring Him into daily conversations." Her father and Dante thought believers were weak. "My circumstances drove me to a place where I was in desperate need of peace, and I eventually recognized God was the true source. I also had much to be forgiven for, and it comforted me to know He was willing and able to forgive me."

Gia swiped at her eyes. "These onions," she muttered.

They shared a smile that buoyed her spirits. She felt Mason's gaze on her.

"I'm happy you had a support system," he said. "More important, I'm happy you found God."

"When did it happen for you?"

"A year or so after we broke up." His spiky lashes swept down to hide his eyes. "I pretty much hit rock bottom."

Now *she* was ready to cry. At least she'd had Lily to focus on. "That must've been hard."

"Hard for this mom to watch." Gia's voice was raspy.

"Good came out of it," he pointed out. "I'm a changed man."

Lily's wobbly voice called for Tessa.

Mason immediately put down the knife. "Do you mind if I go?"

"Of course not."

He quickly washed his hands and went upstairs. Tessa set aside her coffee and took his place at the cutting board.

"He's enamored with her," Gia noted fondly. "He's

talked about having children off and on through the years."

"He'll be a wonderful father."

Reaching across the counter, she squeezed Tessa's hand. "God will see you through this, Tessa. He brought you, Mason and Lily together for a reason."

Without faith, it is impossible to please God. That was one of the first verses she'd memorized, and she'd repeated it to herself whenever fear threatened to overtake her. Now that Dante knew her whereabouts and was launching an all-out campaign to ruin her, fear was her greatest enemy.

He wasn't just gunning for her anymore, either. Mason was in his crosshairs.

TEN

Mason was in his study that night fielding texts from his sister when Tessa came searching for him. He waved her in and offered her a seat. Instead, she hovered by the door.

"Am I interrupting?"

He placed his phone on the desk. "Candace wants details about what happened this morning." She was nosy and pushy, but he couldn't imagine life without her.

"She's right to be worried about you."

"She's worried about all of us. My guess is she's also jealous that Mom got to spend the day with Lily, and she didn't."

Her lips curved into a semblance of a smile. "Lily's asleep. I didn't think she'd be tired after her long nap, but these last few days have been chaotic."

"I've heard Candace say that kids like routine, especially at that age."

As a brand-new father of a three-year-old, he felt at a distinct disadvantage. He had little experience with kids, and the amount of knowledge he needed to do this right was overwhelming.

"Gia was really helpful today. I'm glad she came over."

He was glad, too, because her presence had been a buffer. It bothered him how quickly he'd gone from anger and distrust to awareness and yearning. He couldn't afford to be attracted to Tessa, because he couldn't continue to throw up barricades. They were co-parents of an innocent, vulnerable child. A team. He had to treat her as a friend, not an enemy.

"Do you mind if I use your washer and dryer in the morning?" She pinched the material of her wrinkled shirt and pulled it away from her body. "I didn't bring many clothes with me."

"Of course not. Use whatever you need." Her disheveled appearance didn't detract from her soft, inviting presence. She took his breath away, no matter what she wore or how her hair was styled. "If you think of anything you'd like from the store, let me know."

"Thank you." Tessa gestured to his open laptop. "Anything new?"

"Bruno is settled in at the county jail. He'll be in the medical area until he's ready for general population. Raven renewed her efforts to warn area residents."

"I'm afraid the Pascals aren't the only ones who will be hurt by him."

He shared the same concern. "We've got a lot of people working on this."

She pulled a flash drive from her pocket. "I thought you might want to see Lily's baby pictures. I keep copies on my computer, so you're welcome to keep this."

"Thank you." Mason immediately inserted it into his laptop.

"I'll say good-night then." She turned to go.

"Why don't you stay?" he blurted. At her raised brows, he said, "You can give me a running commentary."

She hesitated. "If you're sure…"

He reached out with his foot, hooked the chair leg and tugged it closer. She sat down and clasped her hands in her lap.

The first photo knocked him back. Wearing a soft pink, flowing dress, Tessa was pictured outside a brick building with budding dogwoods all around. Her smile was wide, teeth showing, her eyes dancing at the camera. Her curls had been tamed into an elaborate, upswept style. His gaze zeroed in on her bulging stomach.

"I forgot about this one," she said quickly. Leaning across him, she would've clicked the next photo if he hadn't seized her wrist. She froze, and he did, too.

Her bones were delicate beneath his fingertips, her skin as soft as he remembered. Her hair tickled his chin as she angled her face toward him.

He allowed his gaze to roam her features—features he hadn't been able to oust from his mind. The sweeping, elegant eyebrows, the earnest, intelligent eyes, the straight nose and full lips.

His mouth went dry. His hearing dulled until he could only detect the *pound, thud, pound* of his heart.

He wanted to kiss her. He *longed* to kiss her.

"I can't."

Her brows slapped together. "Can't what?" she whispered.

Oops. He hadn't meant to say that aloud. Instantly, he released her and shifted away. "Nothing. Ah, how far along were you in this photo? Where was it taken?"

She audibly swallowed and left his personal space.

"I was about seven months. Lisa, my neighbor, also attends the same church. She talked me into splurging on this dress, and she insisted on taking my photo after service that day. For Lily's sake."

He stared at the screen. "You look radiant."

"I didn't feel anything other than awkward, but thanks."

Mason moved on to the next one, and was overcome for a different reason.

"She was beautiful from the start, wasn't she?" Tessa murmured. "She weighed seven pounds and three ounces at birth."

"She didn't have much hair."

A light trill of laughter filled the room. "That didn't last."

They continued through dozens of pictures. Some evoked a deep, emotional charge, while others made him laugh out loud. Tessa answered his questions at length. He knew she regretted her choices and their impact on him. That didn't erase the complicated mix of emotions he was feeling. It also didn't answer a question that haunted him—if she could go back in time, would she make the same choices?

When his phone buzzed, he noticed the late hour and the caller's identity at the same time.

"What's up, Silver?"

"We have a problem."

Mason listened to his explanation with growing unrest. As soon as the call ended, he answered Tessa's unasked question.

"Bruno escaped."

"What? How?"

"Silver's not sure of the exact details. We know that

two prison employees have been hospitalized. The jail is on lockdown until they review footage and complete the investigation."

Tessa buried her face in her hands. He twisted in his chair and cupped her shoulders.

"It's an unfortunate setback, but we have dozens of men searching for them. Who knows? This could all be over tonight."

ELEVEN

At first, Mason thought the alarm pulsing through the dark house meant someone had triggered the new system. He was reaching for his pistol when he smelled smoke.

Bolting out of bed, he quickly dressed, tucked his weapon in his rear waistband and tried unsuccessfully to get Weiland on the phone. The door wasn't hot to the touch. He entered the hallway and immediately started choking. Wispy fingers of smoke licked at the ceiling.

Dropping to all fours, he crawled toward the stairs and yelled Tessa's name. Where had the fire originated? Why wasn't Weiland answering?

When he reached the stair railing, a wall of heat slammed into him, sucking the breath from his lungs and drenching him in sweat. Irate flames ate at his front door.

His sense of urgency intensifying, he bellowed for Tessa. He inhaled acrid smoke, and his voice disintegrated into hacking coughs. Going on his belly, he crawled military-style, feeling as if he was clambering through mud. Another bout of coughing stalled him.

Why hadn't the shrieking alarm roused them?

Their bedroom door loomed before him. What would he find behind the wooden barrier?

Mason lunged for the knob and twisted. Complete darkness greeted him. He flicked the light switch and got nothing.

"Tessa?" He hurried toward the bed. "Wake up!"

As his eyes adjusted, he saw that the bed was empty. Had to be a trick of the shadows. He swept his arm across the mattress.

Denial rose in his throat. She wouldn't have left on her own, wouldn't have left him to burn inside this house.

The curtain at the window rippled, admitting a shaft of fresh air. Open. The window was open. His hands gripping the sill, he leaned out and scanned the yard. The movement activated the battery-operated security light, and his stomach dropped at the sight of the industrial ladder in the grass.

Dante had come for them.

He thought he heard screaming. If he didn't figure out a way to get out of this house, Tessa would soon be dead and his daughter would be in the Mafia prince's clutches. Getting her back through legal means might be impossible, thanks to Dante's influence.

Mason searched the house's exterior for anything he could use to climb down. Finding nothing, he returned to the hallway, only to double over when his lungs seized. The smoke had thickened. He couldn't go down the stairs. Couldn't get to the ground from Tessa's room.

What now?

Dear God, help me so I can help them.

* * *

Tessa struggled against her captor's rock-hard grip. A few steps ahead, James had Lily wedged against his shoulder like a slab of beef. Her arms were outstretched toward Tessa, and her fear-filled cries startled birds from their homes as they passed under the branches. His high-beam flashlight sliced through the trees and underbrush, lighting the path, but it wouldn't catch the attention of Officer Weiland. She'd seen his prone body beside his cruiser. She didn't know whether he was merely unconscious, or worse.

Mason wasn't coming, either. She managed to twist enough and get a glimpse of the farmhouse. The upstairs windows were black, sightless eyes, and orange-yellow flames flickered in the first-level windows like an evil, mocking smile. The tacos Gia had made for supper threatened to come up.

"Mason!" The anguished cry got her nothing but mocking laughter.

"He's a goner," her captor sneered, jerking her over the uneven ground. "And you will be soon. You deserve it after all the trouble you've caused the boss."

Tears threatened, and she blinked them away. Grief wasn't her friend. Right now, she had to focus on escape. Her life depended on it.

"Where are you taking us? Where's my brother?"

The vise on her arm became punishing, and she tried to pry his fingers loose. The goon, who was well over six feet, stopped short, hauled her against him and captured her other arm. She tugged and pulled, but to no avail. His crude laughter washed over her, even as his grip became crueler. Any second now, she expected to hear her bones snap.

"We're wasting time, Vince," James called without stopping. "The fire department will be here soon."

Vince brought his face close to hers. "Not in time to save Sergeant Reed," he taunted.

She kicked him square in the shins, and he growled his displeasure. "If it had been up to me, I would've made his death a lot messier. Like yours is gonna be."

"Let's go." James's command cracked the night.

Vince's cruel eyes bored into hers a beat longer, then he started dragging her at a punishing pace.

Defeat was inevitable. She was no match for these men. How was she supposed to get herself and Lily free?

Her heart beat out a rhythm of regret. Tessa hadn't wanted to admit that escaping Dante was out of the question. No one escaped his wrath, not forever.

A two-lane road dissected the woods. Waiting there was a different vehicle, an older Suburban in place of the Escalades. No sign of Dante, Bruno or the fourth guard.

Tessa balked. This couldn't be the outcome.

"Let me hold her," Tessa called to James. "I can calm her. You don't want to present an out-of-control child to Dante, do you?"

He stopped beside the rear door and turned around, considering. Lily whimpered and squirmed. Tessa's body vibrated with adrenaline. Should she run once she had Lily in her arms? Was it worth the risk to them both?

Vince surprised her by agreeing. "You're driving, James, and I'm not wrangling that sniveling brat on the way."

"Fine. Get in." James opened the door and pointed

to the row seat. The dome light spilled onto the ground. Lily's round face was mottled, her lashes drenched with tears. "Then I'll give her to you."

Tessa's only opportunity shriveled, and so did her heart.

I failed to keep our daughter safe, Mason. I'm so sorry.

Vince yanked her forward. In the next second, the iron grip on her arm fell away. A gasp stirred the air. He hit the ground in a quivering, contorted form. Tasered. By whom?

Out of the shadows, a figure in black emerged.

Joy and relief crashed over her. Mason had gotten out. He'd come for them, their very own personal hero. *Thank You, Jesus.*

He looked ferocious and unpredictable, with his hair in wild disarray, his features obscured by soot and his hands wielding a Taser and a pistol. Lily's crying resumed, and Tessa saw James mentally run through his options. Any second now, he was going to use Lily as a shield or a bargaining chip. She didn't think, just acted.

Screaming out her rage and fear, she charged and grabbed Lily's waist. Startled by the outburst, James let go. Tessa ran for the trees on the opposite side of the road, a good distance from the guns but still within view of Mason.

A single shot reverberated through the night, and she flinched. Mason dove to the ground. The Suburban's engine rumbled, and tires spun out. Mason discharged his weapon but failed to disable the fleeing vehicle.

Tessa remained where she was as he bent to check the prone man's pulse. Clearly finding none, he stalked across the road, his boots beating out a furious rhythm, his body as rigid as a flaming arrow. She involuntarily took a step back even as he wrapped his arms around them both, his careful embrace at odds with the emotions he held in check.

Little by little, she rested against him, taking solace in his unsteady heartbeat and heaving breaths. He reeked of smoke, but she didn't care.

"You're angry."

"Yes."

"At me?"

"What?" His hands cupped her upper arms, and he eased back to look at her. "No, of course not."

His voice sounded terrible, like he'd inhaled a sack of burning embers.

"I couldn't warn you. When I woke up, one of them—James—was already climbing onto the ladder with Lily, and the other one had a gun. He ordered me outside. I—I had to stay with her. And I know what I did just now was risky, but I couldn't stop myself. I just knew he was going to toss her into the back and drive away."

"I'm not angry, Tess." He cradled her cheek, his thumb sweeping over her cheekbone. "I've been operating on the assumption that I was going to be too late." He ceased speaking and took a moment to gather his thoughts. "I'm proud of you. You kept your cool. Didn't panic. Not many people in your predicament could've done that."

Tessa wanted him to hold her again, but he turned toward the road. "James shot and killed his partner rather than deliver him into our custody."

"His name was Vince. Maybe they didn't want to risk another jailbreak?" She felt terrible about the loss of life, despite his ill intentions toward them. "I saw Weiland. I think he's dead."

"I checked on him. They knocked him unconscious. He'll have a nasty headache, but he should be fine."

Mason dissolved into a fit of coughing. Tessa stood by, feeling helpless.

"You have to go to the hospital."

He straightened. "I'm okay."

"How did you get out?"

"When I discovered you and Lily were gone, I made my way back to my room and climbed out onto the porch roof. I shimmied down a column and used the railing as a foothold. I heard Lily crying and figured you all were in the woods, so I decided to try and cut you off via the road."

Sirens alerted them to the first responders' impending arrival. They made their way back to the driveway entrance and were met by Weiland. He was upright, using the car as a prop, but obviously in pain.

The stench of burning wood carried through the trees, and Tessa could see the orange-yellow flames dancing with glee. Before she could dwell too long on Mason's enormous loss, the fire trucks and ambulances rolled in, trailed by Silver and Cruz. Mason would've led them to the slain man, but Silver witnessed him have another bout of coughing and ordered him into a waiting ambulance.

"We'll take care of this," Silver reassured him, no trace of his usual droll wit. "And I'll personally see that Tessa and Lily are kept safe."

An EMT was already at Mason's side.

Mason gave her a half-hearted wave. "I'll text you."

"I don't have a phone."

"Right." He winced. "I'll contact Silver as soon as I can."

She watched as he was led to the nearest ambulance. Firefighters were swarming the scene, shouting commands to each other and working to save the house. If it could be saved. Lieutenant Polk and some other officers arrived, and Silver quickly consulted him and Cruz. He then retrieved the car seat from the borrowed unit truck and hustled Tessa and Lily to his car.

"Where are we going?" she asked.

"I would take you to my place, but I'm in the middle of renovations. Lots of dust and tools that make it unfit for a toddler." The engine purred, and he maneuvered the Corvette onto the dark road. "I have an unoccupied cabin that is isolated and accessed by a single lane. Easy to defend."

The dashboard clock glowed. Half past three. "My presence is seriously messing with your unit's sleeping habits."

Not to mention putting them in harm's way and causing destruction to their private property. Even their workplace hadn't gone untouched. She swallowed down rising panic.

"We need to be tested sometimes," he said, maneuvering a sharp turn with ease. "Pushed to our limits. Besides, I like the adrenaline rush."

He flashed a lopsided grin, and she could see how Serenity's female population could be dazzled. Since first meeting him, Tessa had sensed that his flippancy was a deflection technique. Mason wouldn't betray his friend's secrets, however, and she didn't know Silver well enough to pry.

The smooth ride lulled her into an exhausted silence. She couldn't keep track of the turns and twists as they climbed higher into the mountains. There were fewer residences here. Finally, he turned onto a wooded lane that led to a single cabin shrouded in darkness. The absence of trees behind it, coupled with an ocean of twinkling stars, suggested they were on top of the world. Their only neighbors would be black bears and other wildlife.

Silver told her to stay put while he went through flipping on lights. Satisfied, he escorted her and a half-asleep Lily inside and told her to pick a room. He'd be bunking on the couch. Cruz would be there later and could take one of the other four rooms. The place was both grand and welcoming, with high ceilings and wooden beams overhead, a stunning stone fireplace, floor-to-ceiling windows and plush throw rugs. She had no doubt it would be spectacular in daylight. Right now, she wanted nothing but sleep.

Tessa chose the master suite. Once she got Lily tucked beneath the comforter, she ducked out to the living room. Silver was lounging at the kitchen bar, typing into his phone. He had fingerless gloves on tonight. Less formal than the ones he wore with his police uniform, they were a soft tan material. His long-sleeved cotton shirt came over the gloves so that not even a strip of skin showed.

He looked up at her, and she knew that he knew what she was thinking. His unusual violet eyes seemed to dare her to put voice to her questions. Then, his lips quirked in that typical grin.

"I've just had a text from Mason. He's at the hospital waiting to be seen. Not patiently, I might add."

She rested on the couch's fat arm. "I don't know how long he was trapped in the house."

"He's going to be fine. You all are."

"His house was set on fire because of me."

"Not you." He set his phone on the counter and faced her. "Your brother."

"Details."

"Mason has his priorities straight. He values people above anything else. Trust me, he's not thinking about what he's lost tonight. He's thinking about what he didn't."

Mason didn't leave the hospital until late Tuesday afternoon and the doctors were satisfied the oxygen delivered by mask was enough. He'd argued against having a tube stuck down his throat, especially since his chest X-ray and blood work were normal. They gave him a sack of inhalers and pain meds and made him promise to return if he experienced shortness of breath.

Raven picked him up and drove him to Silver's cabin refuge in the sky. He bid her goodbye and climbed the steep steps, surprised when he experienced a bout of light-headedness. He paused at the top and sucked in air, then winced. The inside of his throat felt as if he'd swallowed needles.

Silver answered his knock with a lift of his pale brows. "They didn't let you shower?"

"I was hooked up to oxygen all day." He detested feeling weak, especially now. "Where's Tessa?"

He probed the interior for a sign of her or Lily. He'd been here once before, when his friend had first purchased it as a foreclosure. Silver had transformed the place.

"They're in the pool."

"The interior pool downstairs? I thought you were going to get rid of it."

"Lindsey argued to keep it."

If Mason hadn't felt like a strong wind could push him over, he would've interrogated his friend. Silver had a lot of first, second and occasionally third dates with a woman before moving on. He had no permanent female ties in his life, other than with his assistant. Mason had once asked if he felt anything personal for Lindsey, and he'd quickly shut him down. Theirs was a professional relationship, he'd insisted, nothing more.

"Where did they get swimsuits?"

"Lindsey went to Uncle Ollie's Outfitters. She got the suits, towels and some clothing for them both. Toiletries, too. But you three will have to do some serious replacement shopping in the next day or so."

He glanced down at his filthy clothing. "Do you have anything I can change into?"

"I've got a spare set of clothes in my car. Meanwhile, I'll throw yours in the washer."

"Thanks, brother. For everything. I've asked a lot of you in recent days."

"I'll find a way for you to repay me," he said with a grin.

Mason's quiet laugh turned into a short bout of coughing. Silver's grin was wiped clean.

"Did you leave the hospital against medical advice?"

When he could speak again, he said, "I have my discharge papers right here."

Silver returned with a cold bottle of water. "Take care of yourself, Mason. Those girls need you."

He took long, grateful chugs. "I'll be as good as new in a day or two."

"You think Dante's going to give you time to recover before he launches his next assault?"

"That's the problem. We've been playing defense too long. It's time to start canvassing local shops, bars, restaurants. You know how chatty the locals can be. Someone, somewhere, has to have seen something that can lead us to where he's holing up."

"Patrol unit can help with that. I'll also reach out to Deputy Stark. He said the sheriff's department is willing to help in whatever capacity necessary."

This wasn't the sheriff's department's case, and he appreciated their cooperation. The additional manpower was crucial, especially since he and his unit were focused on protecting Tessa.

Mason kneaded his forehead. The nurse had said his headache was caused by carbon monoxide. "I'm going to shower."

He needed to see Tessa and Lily. In the long hours inside that isolated hospital room, he'd replayed the scene with James and the now-deceased Vince. Once again, he'd almost lost them.

Silver showed him to a room separated from the others. "This cabin has two master suites. Tessa chose the other one."

Mason strode between the sitting area and fireplace and placed the sack of meds on the king-size bed. "How's she doing?"

She'd amazed him with her courage and determination, facing off against those thugs.

"She blames herself for everything that's happened."

Silver leaned against the door frame. "I have a feeling she's a flight risk."

His knees gave out, and he sank onto the mattress. "She wouldn't."

"Guilt is a powerful motivator, my friend. Our current troubles, combined with your tangled past, are enough to send her packing. Have you told her that you forgive her?"

He clamped his lips together.

"Have you made sure she knows you *want* to protect her? That she made the right decision coming here?"

Mason racked his brain. Had he?

"She still loves you," he stated matter-of-factly.

Silver couldn't possibly know that. "We share a child together. Of course we care about each other's well-being."

"There's no 'of course' about it. Plenty of people who share children despise each other."

Mason couldn't feel that way about Tessa. He could be angry with her, frustrated and hurt because of what she'd done, but he could never despise her.

"We're not getting back together."

He couldn't even let his mind go there. All he could see down that route was heartache. He wouldn't be surrendering his heart to Tessa again.

TWELVE

After a long, hot shower, Mason was ready to sleep for days. Instead, he donned Silver's plain polo shirt, too-long pants, which he rolled up at the ankles, and socks, and followed feminine voices to the downstairs pool. Pausing at the glass door, he watched Tessa choose a sandwich and baby carrots from a platter, then place it on Lily's plate. The patio-style table was framed by a giant window with a view of the mountain ridges marching into the horizon. Lily was wrapped in a neon-pink-and-yellow towel, her curls in disarray and her skin flushed from her recent swim. Tessa wore a demure white wrap of some sort over her swimsuit.

Lily said something, and Tessa smiled in response. That smile was like the one she used to give him, and it made him yearn for those dreamy, uncomplicated days. Things had been easy between them then. Falling for her had been the most natural thing in the world. Who wouldn't love a woman like her? At first, he'd been attracted by her beauty and the sweetness she radiated, but he'd soon discovered her character was worth pure gold. She stood up for the weak and vulnerable and hated to see anyone suffer. If she could help someone, she did. Plain and simple. He'd been challenged by her generosity and spurred to renew his commitment to his community. Their personalities complemented each other, and it hadn't taken long for him to start thinking about spending forever with her.

Tessa glanced up, noticed him there on the other side of the door and stilled. Instantly, the strain of the past days had her in its grip. Her worry for him was written in her expressive eyes and her full, trembling mouth. Despise Tessa? Impossible. Exactly what he felt for her, he was afraid to examine. One thing he had to make clear—they were far from enemies.

He pulled open the door and was hit with a wave of humid air, heavy with chlorine. The tickle in his throat thankfully didn't progress into another coughing fit. Tessa didn't move as he walked around the pool's edge and made his way to them.

Lily grinned at him. "I got to swim!"

Mason sat in the chair beside Lily. "Maybe I can swim with you later."

"Yes, please!" She waved a carrot in the air. "Mommy, can we swim with Mason?"

He hid a grimace. Mason wanted her to know he was her father, but so far, the right opportunity hadn't presented itself.

Tessa was seated opposite him. Her gaze seeming to absorb him, as if she hadn't expected him to ever return from the hospital. Was she as tormented by flashbacks as he was? For a while last night, she'd believed him to be stuck inside his burning house, succumbing to the smoke and flames.

"Maybe we can later." She gestured to the platter.

"Are you hungry? Lindsey was here earlier, and she stocked the fridge."

His stomach growled in response. "I hadn't realized I was until I sat down."

He snagged a sandwich and a canned soda, and he and Tessa ate while Lily chattered about her pony books and the library back home.

"There's a nice library here," he told her. "I'll take you there someday soon."

Her eyes brightened, and she sipped her juice. "Do they have Tillie and Toni books?"

"It's possible. If not, there's a huge bookstore over in Pigeon Forge."

Tessa's lashes swept down, and her mouth looked sad.

"It's your mom's favorite store," he informed Lily. When Tessa's head whipped up, he added, "Used to be, anyway. I took her there at least once a week. I browsed the magazines while she poured through the science-fiction section."

He met Tessa's gaze, and they simply stared at each other, remembering. Their habit was to order coffee at the in-store café, then chat for a while before going their separate ways through the store.

"Mason took me to used bookstores all over this area. No matter how far away it was, he'd take me without complaint."

"Remember the one in Tellico? We drove for hours, only to learn it had shut down months prior." He chuckled, remembering her chagrin.

"I should've done my research," she agreed wryly, rubbing at the condensation on her soda can.

"The Snack Shack we found by the river made up for it. They had the best hot dogs and fries I've ever had."

She leaned forward. "Remember that cheese dipping sauce?"

"I could've taken home a tub of that stuff." He rubbed his stomach. "I wouldn't mind eating there again."

The flush of delight showed in her twinkling eyes. "I wonder if it's still in business."

Lily dropped her carrot on her plate. "I want fries."

"Maybe I can take you to the Snack Shack someday soon."

"Mommy, too?"

He sensed Tessa's gaze on him. He'd begun to think of them as a package deal, but when this was over, he and Tessa would be parenting separately. They would have to work out a shared custody agreement. In his opinion, the best solution was for Tessa to find a place to live here in Serenity so they could both spend the maximum amount of time with Lily. But would she want that?

Honestly, the whole idea saddened him. When he'd dreamed of his own family, it hadn't looked like this. But he and Tessa had to find a way to make this work.

"Your mom is welcome to come with us."

He risked a glance at her, and she was preoccupied with her food, picking at the crust instead of eating.

"Say yes, Mommy!"

"We'll see." Tessa avoided his gaze. "For now, finish what's on your plate. Miss Lindsey brought brownies for us."

Lily's energy kept the tension at bay. After the meal, Mason and Tessa carried the leftovers upstairs. Silver was snoozing on the couch, so they quickly hustled Lily into the master suite. He would've left them to their own devices, but Lily begged him to watch a show with her.

Once Lily had changed into dry clothes, she hopped onto the bed and patted the mattress. Mason joined her, using the mound of pillows as a prop, and he settled in to watch her favorite shows on her device. He was keenly aware of Tessa seated across the room by the fireplace, flipping through a magazine. She cut a lonely figure. If they were a true family, she'd be huddled up with them. He and Tessa would pretend to be interested in the kid's cartoon while sharing secret looks. Maybe he'd tuck her hair behind her ear. Knead her tense shoulders. Tickle her palm and make her laugh.

You're not together. You can't think such things.

She had changed into jeans, flip-flops and a Smoky Mountains shirt, clearly purchased from the tourist shop. Her hair was woven into a thick braid that allowed him a clear view of her defined cheekbones, jaw and delicate ears. While he was watching, she fished out her lip balm and applied it. Did she use the same brand? The shiny kind that tasted of coconut when he kissed her?

He closed his eyes against the pain of the past.

"Are you sleeping?"

He opened his eyes and found Lily's face hovering close. Tapping her on the nose, he shook his head. "I wouldn't dream of it."

Although, now that he had a full stomach and was propped on a soft, inviting bed, the hours of sleep he'd lost were catching up with him. He made it through one half-hour episode before he had to get up or fall asleep in their room.

Pushing to his feet, he padded to the fireplace. "Can we talk?"

Tessa looked up, wariness and concern at war in her hazel eyes. "Go to bed, Mason. Whatever it is can wait until tomorrow."

"It's not even eight o'clock."

Setting aside the magazine, she stood up. "You're about to fall over. Your body needs rest."

"You'll be here in the morning, right?" he prompted, Silver's warning resurfacing.

Her brows crashed together. "I'm not going anywhere."

"Good. That's good." She was right. He needed a clear head when he told her what was on his mind. "Good night, Tess."

"Good night."

Tessa set the flour and sugar containers on the counter, then searched the lower cabinets for a mixing bowl. For a rental cabin, the kitchen was well-stocked. She was learning Silver didn't do anything halfway.

"You're up early."

Crouched and peering into the cabinet, she twisted on her heel and almost toppled over.

Although dressed in his own clothes again, scruff darkened his face and his hair was mussed. She snagged the bowl and carefully stood, aware that her heart rate had tripled—not because he'd startled her, but because he wasn't the in-control, focused, author-itative police officer right now. He was an extremely handsome man with no barriers in place…half-asleep, rumpled and approachable. She yearned to close the distance between them and snuggle into his warmth and strength.

"I, ah, couldn't sleep." She glanced out the wall of windows, where the sky was a delicate purple. "I thought I'd make pancakes. Lindsey asked for a grocery list yesterday, and she delivered. Did I disturb you?"

"No, I slept like a rock." He went to the coffeemaker, situated beside the fridge, and perused the various flavors. "I can't remember the last time I had pancakes. I usually grab some yogurt and a banana before work."

"I'm making enough for everyone." Tessa resumed her preparations, trying to ignore the magnetic pull he had on her. When they were a couple, she'd reveled in how he made her feel. She'd been free to be affectionate with him then. "Silver was already awake when I came in here. He took coffee out to the officer on duty."

He was pouring his coffee when he noticed the tin can Tessa was preparing to open.

"Beets? What...?"

"Lily likes pink pancakes. They're what make the pancakes pink."

"You can't be serious." He came to stand close beside her. "Hiding beets in a pancake? That's just wrong. The grocery store has food coloring, you know."

"This is the healthy alternative. Kids are notoriously picky. These recipes help parents sneak in nutrition. You'd be amazed at what you can hide avocado in. There's even a recipe for black-bean brownies I've been wanting to try."

"I just lost my appetite," he grunted, sipping his coffee.

"You're not even going to try them?" Her eyebrows winged up. "They're actually decent."

"Decent is not the quality I expect from my pancakes, Tessa. Mouthwatering, butter-soaked, fluffy. That's my style. That's normal breakfast food."

Smiling at his mock outrage, she dumped the beets into the blender and hit the button. She expected him to take his coffee to the seating area or possibly join the other men outside. Instead, he rounded up a skillet and spatula for her, then set out the eggs and maple syrup. It reminded her of the times they'd cooked together.

She remembered suddenly that he had wanted to talk to her, and she accidentally dropped an egg. It cracked on the polished wooden floor, the insides oozing perilously close to Mason's sock-covered feet.

He snagged several paper towels and cleaned up the mess.

She washed her hands and faced him, arms folded against a sudden chill. "Are you planning to try for full custody?"

His eyebrows hit his hairline. "Where did that come from?"

"You had something on your mind last night. After our talk about the Snack Shack, I gathered you wanted to establish alone time with Lily. I'm fine with that. What I'm not okay with is you taking her away from me."

He set down his cup with a thud. Cupping her shoulders, he looked her square in the eyes. "I'm not going to do that, Tess. You have my word."

She couldn't think with him so close, his eyes delving deep into her soul, his hands keeping her from flying apart.

"I need to ask your forgiveness," he stated thickly. Her jaw dropped. "For what?"

"Believing your brother. Doubting you. Being stubborn and self-pitying to the point I refused to even talk to you."

Tessa couldn't stop her hands from gripping his sides, above his waist, where sleek muscle met his thick work belt. "Where did you go? I pestered your coworkers and your mom and sister for a full week. I went to the police station. Candace's day care. No one would tell me anything."

"Into the mountains. The backcountry."

"You went *camping*?"

She'd pictured him on a beach somewhere, possibly with a beautiful woman on his arm, one he'd left her for.

"Hiking through the forest alone seemed like a good escape. I didn't realize my mistake until I was out there. I couldn't escape thoughts of you. We spent so much time together in these mountains." The skin around his eyes went tight. "Things might've been different if I'd only given you a chance to explain. I'm sorry."

"Oh, Mason, I'm sorry, too. I hate that I hurt you." A sob worked its way up her throat, and she was hard-pressed to contain it. The tears wouldn't be checked, however. They slid down her cheeks and under her chin.

He pulled her close and wrapped his arms around her. She went willingly, eagerly seeking comfort and release from the guilt that had become part of her daily existence. Mason let her cry without reservation. He was a sturdy support, tenderly caressing her back in a rhythmic, soothing motion. She wept for past mistakes, lost time and what might've been.

When her tears were spent, she lifted her head and caught him discreetly dashing moisture from his own eyes.

"We're going to be okay," he declared huskily. "We were a good team before. We'll be an even better team now because we both want what's best for our daughter."

Tessa let out a shaky breath. He wasn't insinuating that they would be a couple again. Their history was too mangled to overcome. But they could be wonderful co-parents.

The fact that she longed to frame his face and pull his mouth down to hers proved it wasn't going to be easy…not even close.

THIRTEEN

"Will we be anywhere near a grocery store?" Tessa buckled into the unit truck's passenger seat and propped her cross-body purse on her knees.

"If black beans are on your list, the answer is no."

"I'm not going to make healthy brownies, especially after you acted like my pancakes were poisoning your body."

Mason smiled, opting not to tell her they weren't as terrible as he'd pretended. He'd wound up eating those ridiculous pink pancakes in order to appease his daughter. She'd offered him some in that musical voice, her big eyes fastened on him, and he hadn't been able to refuse. Tessa had found the exchange amusing, of course. He'd made a show of adding an extra helping of maple syrup, silently daring her to comment. Her smile had only grown wider.

Mason was getting used to shared meals. While he had a standing invitation to eat at his mom's and the unit had frequent cookouts, he ate alone when at the farmhouse. He liked listening to Lily's chatter, and he liked observing how Tessa interacted with their daughter. She was a good mother—loving, patient and a pro at fending off impending meltdowns. He wouldn't have managed on his own as well as she had.

Don't forget this togetherness will end as soon as Dante is in custody. This family facade will splinter into Daddy-Lily time and Mommy-Lily time.

He couldn't allow his past feelings for Tessa to confuse matters. He was over her. Had been over her for years. Just because holding her made him feel whole again didn't mean they could pick up where they left off.

"Did you see Silver's face when I told him the ingredients?" he said.

His friend had dug in to a full stack without knowing what gave them the pink hue.

A full-bodied laugh bubbled up in her throat. "For a second there, I thought he was going to be sick." Watching the cabin grow smaller in the rearview mirror, her humor faded. "I hope leaving Lily was the right decision."

"Silver will manage just fine until my mom gets there."

Lily had very little to entertain her, and all three of them were in need of clothes. He'd decided a stop in town could be arranged, as long as they didn't linger. Officer Bell would accompany them while another officer remained to guard the cabin. First, he had to meet with the insurance adjuster and stop by the stables.

Despite having Bell as a police escort, Mason remained on the lookout for suspicious vehicles. When he turned into his driveway, his thoughts were yanked from potential threats to the destruction of his home. He left the truck without a word. Tessa did the same, remaining next to the vehicle while he slowly walked around the ruined structure. The fire chief had told him that between the fire and the water damage, it couldn't be saved. He would have to rebuild.

I know what Your Word says, Lord. You work all things together for my good. This doesn't feel good, though.

He'd poured a lot of time, energy and money into making the old farmhouse a comfortable home. His off-duty hours this past year had been dedicated to updates and repairs. His mom and sister had helped him paint the entire first floor. He'd watched countless video tutorials in order to repair the upstairs bathtub. He'd added the screened-in porch himself. All that work, for nothing.

I have no choice but to praise You, Father. You are good all the time, no matter what. You've protected us from evil. You saved us from the fire. That's what matters.

A glance around reminded him that the property itself had been the selling point, not the house. It was a gorgeous piece of land in a good location. He still had the trees, the creek and the mountain view. He could envision Lily running through the yard, a puppy yipping at her heels.

When he rejoined Tessa, her sadness was almost palpable. "Are you okay?"

"I will be." He'd work with an architect to design an even better layout, a home with his child in mind. "You know that verse about God making beauty from ashes? Lord willing, I'll have a new and improved home one of these days."

"Where will you stay until then?"

He shrugged. "I could rent a camper and stay here

on the property or rent one of Silver's cabins. My mom's is an option, too."

Any response was swallowed up by the insurance agent's arrival. Again, Tessa gave him space, taking refuge in the truck cab while he and the agent discussed the next steps.

When he climbed behind the wheel, he angled toward her. "Promise me you won't leave town. You're not alone anymore. We're going to face Dante together."

Her startled gaze slid from his to roam the damaged structure outside the windshield. Her thoughts weren't hard to decipher. He expected a tally of his losses and the close calls, the reasons why coming here had been simultaneously beneficial for her and detrimental to him. Instead, she looked at him and nodded.

"I promise."

He swallowed his hastily prepared arguments. "Good."

Officer Bell, who'd been waiting at the driveway's edge, waved as they pulled onto the road. At the stable gates, he punched in the code Cruz had messaged to him. Dante's attack had helped them identify weaknesses around the stables, and they'd responded with intensified security measures. Once he'd parked the truck, he and Tessa hurried to the front entrance and entered another code. The lock deactivated, and he pushed open the new, bulletproof glass door. Music filtered through the building, punctuated by conversation.

Cruz and Raven were grooming their horses. They both looked surprised to see him.

"I thought you were supposed to rest today," Raven

chided, her long braid swinging in defiance. Her horse, Thorn, seemed to send him a baleful glare.

"Too much to do," he responded. The dip between Tessa's eyebrows deepened, and he felt compelled to explain. "The chest tightness is almost gone. I feel almost fully restored after a full night's sleep."

Her concern didn't immediately fade, and he had to admit it was nice to know she cared that much.

Hearing his voice, Scout moved to the door of his stall and whinnied. Mason greeted his partner with a hearty pat and a peppermint. Tessa asked Cruz about his wrist.

"It's mending just fine."

"What about your Jeep? Silver mentioned something about possibly being able to repair it?"

Mason turned and caught the negative shake of Cruz's head. "It was on its last legs. I'll go vehicle shopping when I get the chance."

"I need a truck. Maybe we can go together," Mason chimed in. "What's the plan for today?"

"Patrolling the square and Glory Pond," Cruz responded. "We're going to show Dante's picture around and see if we get any tips."

He prayed they received solid leads. Dante and his men would continue to spread their destruction. Mason was troubled by James's ruthless actions. Dante's goons were willing to turn on each other, and that didn't bode well for the citizens of this town.

"I may join you on patrol tomorrow." He led Scout out of his stall. The horses were used to a certain routine, and these past several days had been anything but.

"Not a good idea." Raven had that obstinate set to her chin. "You have to stay with Tessa and Lily."

As the unit's senior officer, he had the final say. He respected his fellow officers, however, and took their opinions into consideration.

"You do have a target on your back," Tessa reminded him.

He didn't like to think of the cases and other responsibilities that were taking a back seat because of his personal problems. He also felt like he owed his officers and the patrol unit, along with countless deputies, a huge debt of gratitude.

"We'll take it on a day-to-day basis."

Raven didn't have a response to that, which he accepted as agreement. She and Cruz went to the locker rooms to change, and he located his grooming tools.

"Want to help?"

Tessa eagerly accepted the curry brush and went to work while Mason gathered a bucket and muck fork. He was inside Scout's stall when Cruz poked his head in.

"We're headed out. Want us to wait for you?"

"Bell is out there. We've got to make a quick shopping run after this."

"I forgot to mention that the Houston Falls High School principal called yesterday. He had questions about Friday."

Mason had forgotten that his unit was to take part in a regional event. Various law-enforcement agencies and first responders would be on the school campus for a meet and greet with students and citizens of the community. "We'll have to skip this year."

"Skip?" Lieutenant Hatmaker's voice drew them both out of the stall. He was in uniform and had taken off his hat. Thumping it against his thigh, he stared at them in disbelief. "You can't be serious. Serenity's mounted-police unit attracts scores of interested students, teachers and parents. You bring positive press to our department. You can't skip."

Tessa stopped in midstroke and leaned into Scout's bulk, disquiet covering her features.

Raven had hold of the truck keys, and they jingled as she approached. "Are you aware that Mason's home burned down the other night?"

"I heard." He looked at Mason. "I'm sorry that happened. Were you able to save any of your belongings?"

His grip tightened on the muck rake. "I haven't gotten permission to enter yet." The fire chief was supposed to contact him. Mason held out hope that a few mementos, like family photographs and his father's Bible, could be salvaged.

"At least you survived." Hatmaker's attention flickered to Tessa. His nose pinched, as if he was annoyed by her very presence. "And since you didn't suffer life-threatening injuries, you won't have a problem fulfilling your obligations."

Cruz took a step forward, a vein bulging at his temple. "This wouldn't have anything to do with the fact that the host school's principal is your brother-in-law, would it?"

"You're out of line, Castillo."

Mason put a staying hand on Cruz's shoulder and addressed Hatmaker. "What about our Mafia problem?"

"The campus will be crawling with law enforcement. Your man would be an idiot to try something then."

Mason noticed Tessa's scowl and eye roll. She had lived with the villain and was intimately acquainted with his arrogance and audacity. But once Hatmaker settled something in his mind, it would take the force of dynamite to change his mind.

"We'll be there," he said, feeling Cruz's shoulder bunch with annoyance.

"Good." His fingers tightened on the hat. "Now that we have that squared away, how about you explain exactly how the stables came under attack. Did you sign off on the security upgrades?"

Cruz shook off Mason's hand and took a step forward. Mason grabbed his arm. "You and Raven go ahead and patrol. The horses are probably getting antsy."

His jaw clenching and unclenching, he nodded and stormed out of the building. Steam practically spewing from her ears, Raven pivoted on her heel and followed.

"Tessa, do you mind finishing up with Scout? Take all the time you need."

Mason took Hatmaker through the scenario, literally walking him through the stables and taking extra time in the tack room, emphasizing the danger to Tessa, his mom and Lily. Just as these men had no qualms hurting Mason's family, they wouldn't hesitate to hurt innocent bystanders. But Hatmaker seemed unfazed. While Mason agreed a last-minute withdrawal would be unfortunate, the potential for violence couldn't be ignored.

Before the lieutenant left, Mason broached the subject once more. "The chief is aware of our participation on Friday, I assume?"

He pulled on his hat and stared at Mason from beneath the brim. "He is aware, and he and I are in agreement. This is an event we can't afford to miss."

Schooling his features, Mason bade him goodbye and rejoined Tessa as she was returning Scout to his stall. She'd finished the mucking for him.

"He didn't change his mind, did he?" She gave Scout a final pat.

"Unfortunately, he doesn't often change his mind about things. You and Lily will have to come with me. There won't be anyone to guard the cabin. Don't worry, we'll work out a plan."

"I trust you."

Mason registered several things at once. They were alone. She was very close, and her face tilted up, her golden-green eyes wide and clear. Her lips shone with her favored gloss. Was it his imagination, or did he smell coconut?

Reaching out, he plucked straw from her hair, taking his time while doing so. The strands were fine and springy. He outlined the fresh bandage with his fingertips. "How's this healing? Any sign of infection?"

Her eyes were transfixed on his face. Was she leaning toward him? "It's, ah, fine. Just fine."

Scout chose that moment to demand attention, butting Mason's shoulder with his face. Tessa blushed and ducked her head. Mason didn't know whether to be disappointed or relieved. *Relieved,* his cautious mind urged. *Kissing Tessa? Big mistake.*

"We should go. Bell's waiting."

Without a word, she accompanied him into the overcast day. Bell was waiting in his cruiser, and he gave them a thumbs-up.

There was no traffic on the secondary street. Everything seemed serene, but he couldn't shake the feeling they were being watched. He stayed close to Tessa as he walked with her to the passenger-side door and ushered her inside.

"Mason—"

A distinct whistling pierced the air. The door window exploded. He lunged for her, shoving her down on the truck seat and shielding her with his body.

Above his frantic heartbeat, he heard Bell return fire and shout on the radio for backup.

"Mason."

He shifted the bulk of his weight onto the seat's edge, looked down and got a nasty shock.

Blood seeped through her shirt.

"You're hurt." He tugged aside her collar to inspect the damage. There was a deep wound right below her collarbone and too much blood for him to guess the cause. "Have you been shot?"

"N-no, I don't think it's a bullet wound. The pain would be worse." Her ravaged gaze snagged him. "Right?"

The volley of bullets had stopped. Staying as low as possible, he pulled the door closed and rummaged in the dash compartment. He got a fistful of fast-food napkins and pressed them against the wound. She gasped and went paler.

"I'm sorry, sweetheart. We have to slow the bleeding." He took her hand and pressed it against the napkins, which were already turning a deep crimson.

Bell brought his cruiser alongside the passenger side and rolled down his window. "You guys good here? I have to look for the shooter."

"Tessa's hurt. I'm taking her to the hospital."

"I'll follow you through the gate."

When Tessa made to sit up, he put a restraining hand on her shoulder. "Stay put."

If there was a bullet lodged inside, movement could jar it and nick a vital organ or artery. He climbed over her on shaky legs and started the engine, aware that the curvy road to the hospital would be its own nightmare. They had at least a forty-minute drive, and that was if he was doing average speed. He would have to drive below the limit in order not to jar her. But by then, she could bleed out.

Please, God, don't take her away. Lily needs her. I'm afraid I do, too.

Tessa was lying in an awkward position, one leg bent with her ballet flat propped on the bench seat, and the other braced on the floor. Wind whipped through the busted window. Forested hills hemmed them in on either side, and she watched the trees flash past.

The searing pain around her wound site was severe, but it was limited to the surface. She could breathe unhindered, and she was alert.

"Silver, is my mom there yet?" Mason demanded in a terse tone. "Good. Keep her and Lily away from the windows, and be ready to defend the cabin. We don't know how many Dante is working with. He could've flown in more of his own people or hired local criminals."

He guided the truck through a series of tight, high turns, and Tessa's stomach cramped. She closed her eyes and inhaled the earthy, mossy air in an effort to keep the nausea at bay.

The shooter had to have been surveilling the stables

and would know Lily wasn't with them. Dante could use this opportunity to try to snatch her.

Mason ended the call. "Silver will guard her with his life."

When she didn't answer, he lightly touched the top of her head. "Tessa? You with me?"

"I'm going to sit up now."

"Don't."

She grabbed the headrest and pulled herself into a seated position. The nausea intensified for a few seconds, but she closed her eyes again and willed away the panic.

"Lay back down before you pass out."

The tendons in his arms stood to attention where he gripped the wheel. His dark eyes were stark.

"These curves are making me sick," she said, keeping the napkins snugly in place. "Sitting up will help." When he started to protest, she said, "Mason, the wound site is the only part of me that hurts. I must've gotten grazed by the bullet or stray glass."

"You're still going to the hospital."

Tessa couldn't argue the wisdom of that, even though she'd rather be on the way to Silver's cabin. Being apart from Lily right now was not ideal. When anxiety threatened to overwhelm her, she started praying. God loved Lily even more than Tessa did, which was tough to wrap her mind around. He had a plan for her daughter—a future and a hope. If she didn't cling to His promises, fear would consume her.

The road evened out, and they entered a picturesque valley with emerald green fields and soaring, blue-green mountains. The smooth ridges were dotted with cabins. Campgrounds, shops and mom-and-pop restaurants welcomed visitors.

She lowered the sun visor and used the mirror to evaluate the wound. Carefully lifting the napkins, she saw that the uneven gash was no longer oozing blood.

"How bad is it?"

"Deep enough to require stitches," she sighed. "I'm not about to poke around to find out if something is embedded inside."

"We may have to postpone the hospital visit." Mason checked the side mirrors and frowned. "That sedan has been following us since the outskirts of Serenity."

"Didn't you say this two-lane road is the main link between Serenity and Pigeon Forge?"

"True, but this is a top-of-the-line Cadillac with a rental sticker. Could be nothing, but my gut's telling me otherwise."

As they approached another steep set of curves, this time headed down into the outer limits of Pigeon Forge, the sedan sped up. Tessa twisted in the seat for a better look and recognized the driver.

"That's James," she exclaimed.

He held out his phone. "Call 911. Stay on the line with them."

Tessa did as he asked, relaying pertinent information while Mason navigated the curved roads with increasingly excessive speed. Perspiration dampened her nape beneath her hair, and that sick feeling in her stomach returned.

As they came around the last kink in the road, the sedan bumped into the truck's bumper, jolting them.

Mason kept the vehicle steady. The next hit shuddered through the cab, knocking Tessa sideways into the door. The phone slipped from her fingers and sailed through the open window. She reached out in vain as the truck left the road and the tires caught on bits of gravel.

Mason jerked the truck into a hard right, careening between two ramshackle buildings onto a cracked, paved road. A billboard that was partly covered with ivy advertised a tourist attraction. A high, kudzu-choked hill hugged one side of the road. On the other, spindly trees were all that stood between the road and a deep crevice.

"I lost your phone."

"They have our last location," he responded. "This road dead-ends at an abandoned water park."

"What happens when we reach the dead end?"

Mason's gaze penetrated hers. "We ditch the truck and lose them on foot."

FOURTEEN

The property owners had erected a chain-link fence around the water park to keep out trespassers. Not to be denied, someone had used wire cutters to open a make-shift entrance, where a welcome banner and turnstiles stood. Mason punched the gas and aimed for that opening. The truck's front end split the fence wider, and the jagged metal fingers scraped like nails along the sides.

In the rearview mirror, he saw the sedan emerge into the parking area and hurtle toward them.

"Time to bail."

Slamming on the brakes, he brought the truck to a stop mere feet from the old pay booths. Tessa's seat belt dug into her wound, and she cried out. Waving off his apology, she popped the door latch and scrambled out. Mason met her at the front bumper as he un-holstered his weapon. He grabbed her hand and they started running.

Instead of going straight ahead through the littered corridor that was lined with lockers and bathrooms, he led her to the left, and they darted between trees, overgrown brush and what once had been a baby pool.

Brackish green water in the shallow basin tainted the air with a nasty stench.

Shouts sounded behind them. James had brought a friend, maybe two.

Up ahead, debris littered the cracked pavement. They were forced to slow their pace and dodge slabs of wood, probably from the half-dismantled stairs that used to lead to a lifeguard lookout. A bullet dug into the cement near his feet.

They had to find cover. It had been over a decade since he'd been to the water park, and he wracked his brain trying to remember the layout. There was an indoor pool somewhere beyond the spiraling tube slides. That could be their answer.

Tessa pointed to the cement slides ahead. "Now what?"

Woods formed a natural barrier beside the slides, and the fence was beyond that. He didn't have wire cutters and no way to know if there were other man-made gaps.

"We keep going."

Releasing her hand, he took the left slide while she took the right. The cement runways attached to the ground weren't too steep, but there were cracks with roots and grass jutting out, making traversing them while running a tricky maneuver. The slant shifted by varying degrees before dumping into a large basin.

At the slide's edge, Tessa stopped short and grimaced at the ankle-deep water that hid any number of allergens.

Footsteps pounded far above, and he saw James motion to someone out of sight.

She lowered herself to a seated position.

"Try to keep that wound covered," he advised, wriggling down into the basin and hurrying to her.

Curving an arm around her waist, he assisted her down and glanced at her shirt. He didn't mention the fresh blood matting the material to her skin. They'd have to deal with it later.

Their mad dash toward the concrete steps made water splash up. Tiny droplets sprayed over his arms and legs. His peripheral vision picked up movement to their right, and he saw a bald, muscular suit-clad guard advancing from the cluster of food huts and metal tables.

Mason searched for proper cover and decided on the bathroom structure a few yards from the concrete steps. With a hand on her back, he put himself between Baldy and Tessa, urging her up the stairs and across the expanse. When he saw the guard prepare to shoot, he got off a shot first. It went wide, but the guy interrupted his pursuit to duck behind a table.

Once they reached the breezeway, he felt somewhat better. They again had to dodge debris, this time tiles that had been ripped out of the ceiling. Someone had sprayed graffiti on the lockers, and broken bottles and metal cans littered the ground.

On the other side of the breezeway, they realized they were hemmed in. Thick black bars, part of the original structure, had been installed to link the bathroom building with the child's pool area. Probably to contain the children so parents didn't have to worry about them wandering off. His midsection aching, Mason gazed at the enclosure.

"Over there." Tessa indicated an area of collapsed fence.

To reach it, they'd have to wade through knee-high water and duck under bridges linking four domed play structures.

"We're going to be hooked up to antibiotic IVs after this," she sighed, forging ahead.

Their rushed progression disturbed the algae and stirred up broken bits of bark and leaves. Mason held his Glock high above the water. It was their only defense, and he couldn't let the ammo get wet. Halfway through the pool, they were shot at again.

Tessa lurched through the water and ducked behind the nearest play structure. Mason wasn't far behind. Putting her between the structure and his body, he scanned the periphery. The direction of the shot suggested it was Baldy. The breezeway was visible from their vantage point, and it was empty.

Where was James? Were there others descending upon them?

He and Tessa were both battling fatigue. She was injured, and his lungs hadn't fully recovered from the smoke. Law enforcement would investigate the areas immediately surrounding their last communication, but this was a large county. No telling how long it would take authorities to respond to their distress call.

One thing was certain—they had to keep moving.

"Let's get out of this area," he said. "Go to that next structure while I cover you."

"You'll be right behind me?"

"Yes."

She pursed her lips and blew out a breath. "All right. Here I go."

Tessa lunged through the water, and no responding shot came. Mason waited until she had reached safety to follow her. The goon shot at him. The bullet pinged off the bridge inches above his head.

She seized his arm and pulled him out of sight.

A gurgle of distress left her lips just as James appeared in the breezeway. Mason put his hand on her back. "Go!"

James raised his weapon. Mason discharged his first and managed to clip the guy.

Tessa hauled herself onto the grimy ledge and called to him. He was the target of another spray of bullets from Baldy's direction. When he got close, she grabbed his forearm and gave him a boost up. Water sluiced from his pants and shoes. From this vantage point, he finally spotted the building he'd been looking for.

As they climbed through the gap, he explained that they would try to get to the indoor pool. They could better defend themselves there while they awaited backup.

Taking her hand, he led the way through the underbrush. Scarred, uneven pavement stood between them and the dull gray gym-like building. The exterior was pitted and crumbling, and more than half of the high windows had been punched out. The side-entrance door hung on its hinges. They would enter there.

"Ready to run?"

She nodded somberly.

He touched her cheek, distracted by her soft skin. "I want you to fix your eyes on that building. Don't look back, and don't worry about me."

"Not worry about you? Impossible."

Mason was overtaken with the urge to kiss her. *Not the right time. Not the right move.*

"Now!"

They took off, sprinting as fast as their legs could carry them. He heard the shots, felt one whiz past his ear. Mason was convinced they didn't want to kill them yet, but only wanted to wound them in order to capture them for Dante's demented purposes. Not exactly a comforting prospect. Although, he wasn't sure how committed they were to capturing them at this point. He and Tessa had evaded them for days. They were down one man, and now Bruno and James had sustained wounds.

Tessa stumbled. He caught her arm and prevented her from falling. Ahead, the gloomy interior beckoned. What would they find inside?

As they ducked under the heavy door, he heard James and his cohort shouting to each other. Tessa went first. Once inside, he hefted the door and propped it into an upright position. Because a thick layer of clouds hid the sun, there was little light coming through the high windows.

Tessa paced a few yards away. "How long until the police get here?"

"Hopefully not long." He was short on ammo, outgunned and outmanned. Their enemy had the advantage.

Mason strode the length of the cement wall. He had to check the main entrance—

A cascade of rocks striking the pool floor coincided with Tessa's scream, followed by a thud. One second, she was standing nearby, the next, she'd disappeared.

"Tessa!"

He ran to the edge of the giant pool, careful to avoid the section that had given way under her weight. She was lying on the bottom, cement chunks and tile shards in a haphazard pattern around her. Her eyes were closed, and she wasn't moving.

The fall had jarred every bone in her body. Her left ankle seemed to be the only serious injury, and she was certain it was only a sprain.

"Tessa?"

Opening her eyes, she saw Mason sprawled on his stomach and gripping the rounded ledge.

"I'm okay. I may have sprained my ankle, that's all."

His relief was temporary. "The ladders are missing, and there aren't steps for you to climb out on. Can you stand up and come over here?" He sat up and removed his belt. "I'll try and pull you out."

Tessa gingerly got to her feet and couldn't contain the hiss that escaped once she put weight on her ankle. This was seriously going to slow them down. One positive? The new injury distracted her from the pain in her chest. She was beginning to think there was something lodged in her wound, probably glass that would have to be removed by a medical professional.

Hobbling over to the pool wall and looking up, she realized how far the distance was between her and Mason. She surveyed the rest of the basin. Although cloaked in milky shadows, she could tell the pool was all the same depth. Diving platforms were spaced out across the far side.

"Grab the belt." Mason had gotten into a crouched position and was bracing his weight against that rounded lip that had crumbled like sawdust under her. Would this section hold?

Tessa wrapped the belt around one wrist and got a secure grip with her other hand. She tried not to think about the men outside and how any minute they were going to breach the building.

Mason began to hoist her up. Almost immediately, the lip where his tennis shoe was braced disintegrated. A large chunk barely missed her cheekbone, and she let go.

"It's not going to work," she said.

The tension on the belt eased, and he lowered her to the ground so she could free her wrist.

He glanced at the broken door they'd entered through. "I'm going to walk around the pool and try and find another way out."

Tessa's gaze followed his progress, her trepidation intensifying the farther away he got.

"Got something."

He bent to pick up whatever it was he'd found, and he didn't see the far door swing open. Tessa called out a warning. Before he could react, James struck him over the head.

Mason slumped to the ground.

She willed him to get up, to speak, to do *something*.

Footsteps registered behind her, and she got a whiff of citrusy cologne that made her gag. She lifted her gaze and felt what little courage she'd had shrivel like a grape in the sun.

His smile was as cruel as ever, the promise of retribution in his black eyes striking fresh terror inside her.

He crouched at the pool's edge. "Hello, Tessa."

FIFTEEN

Those who didn't know Dante wouldn't guess from his appearance that he was a monster. Tall and physically fit, he had the face of a model and the bearing of one born into power and prestige. He wore his black hair slicked off his forehead in a wave, highlighting his patrician features and full, sculpted mouth that could so effortlessly twist with cruelty. The scar above his eyebrow—sustained during a knife fight when he was a teen—gave him just enough mystery to draw in others, who would be unaware that he was the deadly spider and they were the prey caught in his web.

"You've caused me no end of trouble, little sister," he stated calmly. "You will have to pay for that."

He called to his goons. "Get her out."

James and the other man brought over a silver ladder that looked as if it used to be attached to the cement. Together, they held it in position so that she could climb up. With no other choice, Tessa slowly ascended the unstable rungs, trying not to put weight on her injured ankle.

At the top, James clamped onto her arm and shoved her toward Dante. He caught her wrists, stopping her before she slammed into his chest. His razor-like gaze scraped over her.

"The years have not been kind to you."

His nearness made her skin crawl. "You should've stayed in New Jersey. I'm not a threat to you."

"You made yourself a target when you sided with a cop and sought to incriminate us." He smirked. "I'm sure you're aware that I don't let betrayal go unpunished, not even when it originates in my own family." With a sound of disgust, he pushed her away from him. She stumbled into the wall. "Bring Sergeant Reed to the vehicle."

"Please, Dante, leave him out of this. Mason isn't important to the family."

"Not important?" His brows winged up. "Sergeant Reed is the father of the first Vitale grandchild. That makes him very important." Gripping her chin in a bruising hold, he said with a touch of temper, "It was really bad of you, Tessa, to keep Lily's existence a secret. Father was devastated when he learned of your duplicity. I'm going to make it up to him, though. I'm going to take her to him."

Tessa couldn't speak. Her worst nightmare was coming true.

James and the other man trundled past them, dragging an unconscious Mason out of the building. Dante waved his arm with an exaggerated royal flourish to indicate she should walk ahead of him. Outside, she wasn't met with the reassuring whir of sirens or the sudden arrival of the authorities. During the too-brief trek to Dante's vehicle, she kept hoping and praying for a rescue that didn't come.

The men stowed Mason in the trunk, securing his

wrists and feet with thick rope. Dante pushed Tessa into the back seat and slammed the door. He stalked around the vehicle and slid into the vacant space beside her. The trunk lid closed with a thud. She knotted her hands together and pressed them against her stomach. In his unconscious state, Mason was unable to defend himself. He could have a concussion or worse.

James got into the passenger seat and the bald one got behind the wheel. As they bumped over the neglected road, Tessa prayed they'd encounter the police. But the dilapidated buildings and half-hidden billboard came into view and, beyond them, the main road. The vehicle headed left, in the direction of Serenity, but they soon turned off onto a secondary road.

The deeper into the cove they drove, the harder her heart thumped against her rib cage.

"Is Father aware of your reasons for being here?"

"He knows I'm on a mission to collect the evidence you have on Officer Fisk's death and that I'm here to retrieve his granddaughter."

"I don't have any evidence. I told you that in the beginning."

"I don't believe you." He fiddled with his diamond cuff links. "Sergeant Reed will provide the incentive you need to talk."

"You're not planning on leaving either of us alive." The certainty chilled her to the bone. "What will Father do once he learns the truth?"

"You turned against us. Why should he care? You know, you could have had an unparalleled life, yet you threw it all away."

"I didn't want that life!" she blurted. "I never wanted

it. If you hadn't forced me to return home, if you'd let me live my own life, none of this would've happened."

His expression turned vicious, and he wrapped his fingers around her throat, applying enough pressure to stop air from entering.

"Are you suggesting *I* am to blame for your treachery?"

She clawed at his fingers. Her vision turned black as her lungs stretched to a bursting point.

His phone chirped. With his free hand, he checked the caller's identity. "Saved by the business you despise," he drawled, releasing her to answer the call.

"Jack, this had better be important."

Tessa sucked in air and huddled against the door, as far away from Dante as she could possibly get. The window was cool and smooth against her hot skin. She wanted to close her eyes and give in to her misery, but she had to stay alert and remember the route they were taking. She couldn't give up hope. She had to fight to stay alive...for Lily.

As the tires ate up the miles, they left civilization behind and entered what could be part of the national park it was so wooded and isolated.

Dante ended his call and she stiffened, expecting him to pick up where he'd left off. Instead, he ignored her, his long, elegant fingers tapping his knee.

The car began to slow. A bright spot of color in the green-and-brown vista drew her gaze. The older, red-brick home was well maintained, with ivy creeping up the walls and wide, welcoming windows. The mailbox had the name *Johnson* printed on the side.

"Where are the owners?"

The driver parked the car and opened her door. She

got out, and when Dante unfolded his frame on the other side, he smirked at her across the roof. Sunlight broke through the clouds behind him, shining on his hair and throwing his eyes in relief.

"Out of town."

Tessa trailed the men to the rear of the car and gulped down a moan when she saw Mason's unmoving form. He looked to be simply asleep. When they removed him from the trunk, she saw a thread of blood between his hair and shirt collar. She hated the feeling of helplessness that engulfed her mind, body and soul.

Would they die here today?

The inside of the house was clean and homey. Before she could look around for anything that might serve as a makeshift weapon, they marched her down the stairs and into a basement. This unfinished space was nothing like the first floor. Half the walls were made of dirt, and the others were cement block. There wasn't a single window. A sparkling front-load washer and dryer were out of place, as were the cabinets fitted with brightly colored fabric-organizer boxes.

James lowered Mason to the ground. He groaned, but his eyes remained shut. They propped him up against a foundation pole and wrapped thick rope around his shoulders to secure him. His head was bowed, his upper body held upright by the rope.

When they turned to her, she took a step back, only to encounter her brother's chest.

He guided her to the other pole and ordered James to bind her to it. As the rope wound around her upper body, she appealed to Dante one last time.

"Please, leave Mason out of this. I'll go home with

you. I'll do whatever you say, I promise. Just don't hurt him."

He sniffed, as if she was emitting a foul stench. "You're of no worth to us any longer, Tessa."

Mason's head felt too heavy for his body. His vision, when he first opened his eyes, was blurry. When it cleared, he got a nasty dose of reality. They were at the Mafia prince's mercy. Not a good place to be. But they were alive, and he was intent on keeping them that way.

Tessa was close enough that their feet almost touched. Above her shoe, the flesh was pink and swollen. The blood on her shirt was dark, the torn material matted to her body, hinting that the wound had crusted over. When Mason's gaze landed on the fresh welts on her neck, fury funneled through him. He strained at the ropes, struggled to free his wrists and ankles.

Crouched beside her, Dante twisted toward Mason. "Ah, Sergeant Reed, you're awake. Welcome to the reunion."

"Get away from her."

Dante laughed, and the other men in the room joined in. Tessa's gaze begged him not to bring their wrath down on him. He closed his eyes and tried to calm the raging beast inside. What had he learned early on in his training? Out-of-control emotion would get him, his fellow officers and innocent civilians killed.

"I'm glad you're awake. I was about to outline my plans for Lily."

Mason's eyes snapped open.

Dante's self-satisfied air grated. "Once I'm done with you two, I'm going to take Lily home with me. I will raise her as if she were my own daughter." Ignoring Tessa's squeak of protest, he said, "I'll make sure she doesn't turn out like her mother—ungrateful and small-minded. No, Lily will be more like her Aunt Francesca, who understands the value of the Vitale legacy. Who knows? One day I may marry her to a business associate. Unlike her mother, she will do what's best for the family."

"You won't be able to get to her," Mason informed him. "My unit will guard her with their lives."

His expression turned mocking. "I captured you and Tessa in a matter of days. I'll have Lily before the week is out. Once I do, I'll make sure she forgets you both. Day by day, week by week, year by year, I'll erase her memories of you."

Mason made the mistake of looking at Tessa. Tears streamed unchecked down her cheeks, and he felt them like rivers of burning acid over his heart.

God, I can't fail her. I can't fail our daughter. Please don't let evil win.

Dante angled back to Tessa. "Sister dearest, it's time for you to give me the information I seek. You recorded that long-ago conversation with Father. You know, the one that incriminated us for planning Officer Fisk's death? Where is it? On a flash drive? Laptop?"

Her lips trembled. "There is no recording, Dante. Not in my possession. Fisk was listening in with his equipment. I was supposed to get the confession while he did the rest. You burst in before Father admitted his guilt."

The skin around his eyes tightened, and the veins at his temples bulged. He lifted a hand in a silent signal. Tessa's eyes widened as James stalked across the room and stood over Mason. He'd removed his dress shirt, but had been wearing a white cotton shirt underneath. His partner had stitched him up where Mason had clipped him.

James balled his fingers into an impressive fist, hauled back and slammed it into Mason's face. Fire exploded in his cheek, and the force of the blow whipped his head to the left. His existing headache grew by leaps and bounds, but he forgot it when James's boot connected with his ribs. Once. Twice. Three times. Mason felt the instant the bone gave under pressure.

Tessa's pleas bordered on hysteria. He'd give anything to remove her from this equation, to spare her from her brother's callous disregard for human life.

"Stop, Dante! You have to believe me. There is no evidence to be found! Didn't you check Fisk's belongings?"

He heard her gasp. Mason lifted his head. Dante's hand cupped her throat, poised to cut off her air supply.

"Do you remember when I made you watch Skinny Walter's murder?"

Her hands fisted on the cold cement. She swallowed convulsively.

"I will make you watch Sergeant Reed's death if you don't tell me. It won't be merciful, I promise you."

"Boss, Bruno's upstairs," James interrupted. "He's got the food you asked for."

Dante ignored him. "Tessa, I had one of my men search your place in Georgia. He didn't find anything, which leads me to believe you brought it with you. When I finish my meal, I expect you to have a different answer. Understand?"

At her nod, he finally removed his hand and stood. He left the basement, closing the door at the top of the stairs and locking them in.

SIXTEEN

"Oh, Mason…" Tessa's voice was thick with sorrow and regret. "If I could change the past—"

"You're not to blame for his actions. Frankly, how you managed to escape his clutches in the first place is a mystery." He shifted to get a better look around, unable to mask the pain vibrating through his midsection. As long as his busted rib hadn't punctured a lung, he'd be okay. "We have to find a way out of here."

"How? There's no window. No weapons that I can see. Neither of us have a phone." She rested her hands on her lap, and her brow furrowed. "Hold on."

Tessa dug into her pants pocket and fished out a small silver object.

"Why do you have nail clippers in your pocket?"

She turned the clippers this way and that. "I trimmed Lily's fingernails this morning…" Her eyes widened, and she began to clip at the thick rope holding her fast to the pole. "If I can get free, I can untie you."

"We might have a chance." A slim one, but he wasn't going to discourage her.

Mason understood that if they did succeed, it would be God's will that they do so. He understood what

Daniel must've felt in the lion's den, what Shadrach, Meshach and Abednego had felt entering that fiery furnace. Death was almost certain. Yet, God had other plans. Even though his and Tessa's situation seemed impossible, He had the power and authority to make a way of rescue.

The boards creaked overhead as the men walked around. Occasionally, laughter would interrupt their conversation. How they could enjoy a meal, as if they weren't about to commit murder, was beyond him. In his line of work, he'd encountered plenty of selfish, angry people who committed crimes for various reasons. Many of them had become slaves to drugs and alcohol, and addiction drove their actions. He hadn't come across any that killed for sport. Unfortunately, Dante appeared to enjoy hurting others, and he paid his henchmen to do his bidding.

Watching Tessa chip away at those ropes, he realized the self-righteous anger he'd been nurturing since she'd returned was gone. The bitterness was gone. The past couldn't be changed, his part or her part. Without those emotions to fuel his reactions, he was left with feelings for Tessa that had survived the breakup, feelings he couldn't let overrule caution and sound judgment.

"Got one." Tessa strained against the remaining strands. When they didn't budge, she started in on another one.

Mason silently cheered her on while reexamining their surroundings. There wasn't much that he could see that would help them fight their way out.

The minutes it took for her to free herself felt like days. He listened to the activity upstairs, trying to gauge how long they would linger over the meal. He didn't want to imagine Dante's reaction if he caught them in the middle of an escape attempt.

Tessa gave a small cry of triumph when she wriggled free. Hurrying over, she worked on untying his wrists. It took longer than it should have.

"My hands are sweaty," she lamented, trying again to undo the knot.

"You're doing fine."

Finally, she succeeded. He instructed her to work on the knots tying him to the pole while he freed his ankles. The awkward angle exacerbated his rib pain. He gritted his teeth and worked faster. A chair slid across the floorboards in the room above them, and he wondered if that signaled their meal was over.

The knob jiggled. He and Tessa both froze. Someone called out, and footsteps moved away from the stairs. Her fingers flew into a frenzy. He felt the rope give way.

Moving around to his side, Tessa placed an arm around him and helped him to stand. His head felt too light for his body, and the room listed to the right.

"Mason?" she whispered, pressing close against him.

"I'm fine."

Opening his eyes, he managed a tight smile. "We need a weapon."

They quickly searched the space around the laundry organizer unit. Tessa motioned for him to follow her beneath the stairs. On the other side, there were numerous shelves that held jars of homemade jams and soups. In the corner, he located a broom. He whacked it against his knee, and the wooden handle snapped into two pieces.

"Mason, look." Standing at a point by the middle of the cement wall, Tessa went on her tiptoes and tugged on a swath of thick fabric. As it fell away, a ground-level well-type window was revealed. That window evoked the first smile he'd seen on her face in ages.

Excited now, she retrieved a metal bucket from the corner, then turned it over, climbed up and shoved at the window. At first, it didn't budge.

"Is it unlocked?"

"Yes. It's just stuck." Tessa wouldn't give up. Nor would she let him help. The window began to open, inch by inch.

Sweat dampened the back of his neck. Would the men hear the occasional squeaks and investigate? As soon as the thought entered his mind, the upstairs door opened and closed. Someone began to descend into the basement.

Tessa whirled around and nearly toppled off the bucket. Mason put his finger to his lips. Wielding one half of the broken broom handle at chest level and gripping the other at his waist, he crept over to the stairs. Baldy got to the bottom and, noticing they weren't where he'd left them, turned to alert the others. It was the opening Mason needed.

He jabbed the handle into the man's stomach, knocking him back several steps. He used the second piece to whack his temple area with all the force he could muster. Baldy crumpled to the ground, unconscious but alive. Mason relieved him of his phone and weapon.

At his urging, Tessa climbed out first. He wriggled through and joined her on solid ground. Every breath delivered stabbing pain that radiated through his upper body. His head throbbed, making it difficult to concentrate.

She folded her hand into his and gazed at him with those beautiful hazel eyes—she was looking to him for direction. Tessa trusted him with her life.

He swiftly evaluated their surroundings. "We'll stay with the tree line," he said, pointing to the natural property border that curved around to the only road access. Once they had reached the relative safety of the woods, he said, "Did you see other homes during the ride in? Do you remember how far we are from the main road?"

"Several miles." She frowned at him, concern and doubt written on her face. "This house is the last on this road. The owners must like their privacy."

He squeezed her hand and released it. He fished the goon's phone from his pocket. "Password protected. No surprise there. I can't make a personal call, but I'm going to try to reach the authorities."

He hit the emergency link and dialed 911. They continued walking while he spoke to the dispatcher. Tessa's limp became more pronounced, and he shortened his strides.

Distant shouting announced their absence had been discovered. Tessa seized his arm, and he informed the 911 operator that he would have to put him on mute. At the sound of an approaching car, they crouched behind some underbrush. Mason removed Baldy's revolver from his waistband.

Through a slender gap in the plants, he saw the sedan cruising at maybe five miles per hour. All the windows were rolled down, and Dante, Bruno and James were scouring both sides of the road, guns glinting in the sun. Baldy was slumped in the back seat, his eyes closed.

Tessa uttered faint snatches of a prayer.

The car jolted to a stop not far from their hiding place. And then the sirens echoed off the peaks above and through the cove. The timing couldn't have been more perfect. Dante ordered James to drive.

Neither Mason nor Tessa dared breathe as the sedan disappeared from sight. The minutes ticked by. The sirens grew louder.

"Are they really gone?" She twisted toward him, hopeful yet wary.

Mason put away the weapon, then slowly got to his feet and inched to the road's edge. "They're really gone."

With a joyful exclamation, she limped over to where he stood and threw her arms around his neck. Mason wrapped his arm around her lower back and buried his face in the curve of her shoulder.

The enormity of their close call threatened to overwhelm him. He'd been shot at before, by pumped-up drug users and petty thieves determined to avoid jail time. This encounter with Dante was on a different level. This was personal, and the man was cruel. No matter what, Mason had to prevent him from getting to Tessa again.

Mason lifted his head. She'd grown more beautiful during their time apart and, right now, there was no fear, no guilt, no wishing for a do-over. She was looking at him like she used to, like he filled her life with joy and meaning. He'd forgotten how easily she could make him feel like a superhero.

He carefully placed his hands on either side of her

face, and then he kissed her full on the lips. Gently, sweetly, shyly. She leaned into him, and his ribs spasmed.

Mason pulled away as the first cruiser approached. After placing the gun on the ground, he held up his hands. He recognized the officer behind the wheel—Officer Jolene Hammond. She was quickly joined by two others. After getting the details, she stayed with them while the others pursued Dante. He borrowed her phone to call Silver. His friend had been trying to contact him and was audibly relieved to hear they were safe. Silver reassured him that Lily was as happy as a lark because Gia was catering to her every whim. The statement made Mason smile. His mom was born to be a grandmother.

An ambulance arrived and whisked them both to the hospital. Tessa was subdued during transport, and he couldn't get a read on her. Was she overcome with fatigue? Shock? Or was it the kiss?

When they were alone, Mason would have to tell her nothing had changed. The moment of tenderness had been the result of intense gratitude that they'd escaped Dante's clutches. He didn't regret the kiss—it had been a healing balm after a harrowing day. He did regret any confusion his actions had caused her. He didn't know what she envisioned for her future, didn't know how she felt about him. One thing was for certain—friendship was the best they could hope for.

SEVENTEEN

Tessa counted the ceiling tiles to keep from drifting off. She couldn't close her eyes. If she did, she'd see Dante's sneering face again. She'd relive the terror of watching his goon hurt Mason.

There was a knock on the tiny corner room the ER staff had stuck her in. The security guard posted outside announced the visitor and waited for Tessa's assent to admit her.

"Candace."

The blonde strode inside, closed the door and hung a nondescript backpack on the doorknob. Her face was a study in concern. "I brought you a change of clothes."

"Have you seen Mason?" Tessa scooted upright. "How is he?"

She perched on the lone chair and propped her purse on her knees. "I was with him just now. The doctor wants to keep him for one night, not only because of his head injury and busted ribs, but because of his recent smoke inhalation. As you might've guessed, my brother is insisting he will recuperate faster at home." Her shadowed gaze held Tessa's. "How are you?"

Her fingers skimmed the bandage poking out from

the hospital gown. "Happy they got the glass out of my wound relatively quickly. It needed a couple of stitches." She gestured to the foot of the bed. "My ankle is merely sprained."

"He told me what happened. I'd be a puddle on the floor right now. You're a strong woman."

"I'm a mess. I'd be a bigger mess if not for my faith." God was her protector, her strength, her everything.

"It's interesting that you and Mason both embarked on your faith journeys after your relationship imploded."

"God used our hurt and disappointment to draw us to Him."

She cocked her head to one side. "Do you think there's a chance for reconciliation? You still care about each other. Don't try to convince me otherwise."

Tessa's cheeks heated as she recalled Mason's kiss. It had been the best of kisses and the worst of kisses. She'd sensed his iron-clad restraint as he held back four years' worth of emotion. For her, that kiss hadn't settled anything. It had spawned questions she was afraid to get answers to.

"I can't answer that right now."

Candace smiled. "That's not an outright no."

"You wouldn't mind if Mason and I…?" She couldn't put voice to her words. A second chance with Mason? Tessa hadn't let herself entertain the possibility. Even now, she was afraid to hope.

"Do I have reservations? Not as many now that I know everything that transpired between you. My brother was the happiest he's ever been when he was with you. These past years, he's been going through the motions. Not professionally—his career challenges him and gives him great satisfaction. His personal life is another story. He's never gotten over you, Tessa. And now, you share this amazing little girl. Surely you could work things out."

"You're excited to be an aunt, aren't you?"

"I admit I have a personal stake. If you and Mason are together, I get more time with my niece."

Tessa felt her mouth stretch into a smile. "I've missed our friendship, Candace. Do you think we could start over?"

"I'd like that."

The nurse arrived and gave Tessa instructions on wound care. Before she had a chance to change, Mason showed up in a wheelchair. The right side of his face was battered and bruised.

"Are you ready to go see Lily?"

His slight smile and easy tone couldn't distract her from his careful, solemn demeanor. Was that due to his physical discomfort? The weight of their shared trauma? Or regret that he'd kissed her?

"Shouldn't you stay the night?" she asked.

"No, I shouldn't. My ribs are cracked, not broken. My internal organs are fine."

"What about your head? You lost consciousness for quite a while. Do you have a concussion?"

"Tessa, I'll rest easier at the cabin. Rest equals faster recuperation."

"Have you heard from the Pigeon Forge PD?"

"Dante got away." His nostrils flared. "We're going to blast these guys' faces across social media and air them on the local news. Silver even mentioned paying for a billboard. By tomorrow, the tips will be pouring in."

Tips took time to sort through, however. And Serenity's law-enforcement entities were stretched thin. This was the beginning of the tourist season, and Tessa's predicament couldn't be their sole focus.

Pigeon Forge PD escorted them from the hospital to the mounted-police truck parked at the abandoned water park. Candace had driven her own vehicle to the hospital, which left Tessa to drive the truck. Her injuries weren't as severe as Mason's, and she hadn't been given pain medication. One of the officers volunteered to continue with them the rest of the way, and they gladly accepted.

At the cabin, Silver and Cruz's welcome was grim. That Silver couldn't find anything to joke about was telling. His eyes smoldered violet fire as he took in Mason's battered face and the bruises on her neck.

Lily heard the commotion at the door and streaked through the living room like a comet. "Mommy!"

Tessa hoisted her into her arms and reveled in the sweet show of affection. *Thank You, Lord Jesus, for bringing us back to her.*

"Guess what? Mimi and me made lots and lots of cookies!" Lily played with Tessa's curls. "And we made castles out of Play-Doh and watched shows."

Mimi? Her gaze found Gia, who was traversing the spacious living area as she wiped her hands on a kitchen towel. "I hope that's okay. I didn't explain any details."

"It's fine. Thank you for entertaining her all day."

"It was my pleasure." Tessa shifted, and Gia got a full glimpse of Mason. She gasped.

"Mom, I'm fine," he inserted, moving forward to

kiss her cheek. The climb up the steep porch stairs had taken its toll. He was in pain and trying to hide it.

"After we heard about the 911 call and the loss of contact, I prayed for you both nonstop."

Lily leaned sideways in her arms and reached for Mason. He smiled and would have taken her weight, but Tessa shifted away. "Not a good idea. Let's sit on the couch."

When they were settled, Lily climbed onto his lap and touched his face. "You have a boo-boo."

He took hold of her fingers and pressed a kiss to them. "It will heal. Have you had many boo-boos?"

"No." She shook her head. "Mommy doesn't let me climb up the slide. She makes me slide down like I'm 'posed to."

He chuckled, then grimaced. "Your mom is one smart lady."

"Will you build a Play-Doh stable with me?"

"That's a great idea. First, I have to wash up, and then your mom and I need to eat something."

Gia gestured behind her. "I assembled lasagna earlier. I'll put it in the oven to bake. Lily can help me with the salad if she'd like."

Lily scrambled off Mason's lap. Candace entered the cabin and intercepted her.

"Where are you going so fast?"

"Cooking with Mimi."

Candace's eyebrows were swallowed by her bangs. "Mimi, huh? Do you mind if I help?"

Lily nodded and grabbed her hand. Together, they went to wash up and gather the vegetables.

Mason lightly touched Tessa's hand. "We need to

tell her the truth as soon as possible, before my mom and sister do it for us."

"Tonight?"

He considered the idea. "Tomorrow morning after breakfast. We'll both be refreshed."

"Okay." Tessa wasn't sure how much of the conversation Lily would understand, but she was ready for her to know Mason's true role in her life.

"You and I should talk, as well."

Her stomach lurched. "I think I know what you want to discuss, and it can wait until we're no longer in danger."

He appeared to be on the verge of disagreeing. Then he thought better of it.

"I want you to know that I wouldn't dream of hurting you again."

He obviously regretted that moment in the woods. "I know, Mason. I feel the same."

"We're on the same page then."

"Yes."

Were they really? Honestly, she hadn't ever stopped loving him. If she was offered a second chance with the love of her life, she'd snatch it. But he wasn't looking to be with her again, and she couldn't blame him.

Mason tucked into the mouthwatering meal his mom had prepared, content to absorb the conversation around him. The shower had washed away the grime and loosened his muscles, and, while the medication had merely taken the edge off his discomfort, he felt well enough to sit with his family and friends and thank the Lord for his blessings.

Silver, Cruz and Raven occupied one side of the

rustic table. Candace and his mom were seated at either end. Lily was in a booster seat between him and Tessa. A wrought-iron globe chandelier cast a broad circle of light over the serving bowls, dinnerware and glasses. The meaty, tomato-rich aroma melded with his mom's tangy homemade salad dressing and garlic knots. After a solemn prayer of thanks offered by Gia, everyone dug in.

Mason was pleased to see that Lily was willing to try most foods. The more time he spent with her, the more he came to appreciate Tessa's mothering skills. She'd managed to keep their daughter safe in a town where she had no roots and no family. Not only that, but she'd also given her a normal upbringing.

Over Lily's head, he studied Tessa's profile. She had also showered and changed into fresh clothes. Her glossy black hair had been tamed into a tidy French braid, and tasteful earrings sparkled at her ears. Since he'd known her, she hadn't gone for flashy or expensive. She'd grown up surrounded by luxury, but she'd turned her back on that life out of principle. That said something about her character.

She glanced up and caught him staring. For a moment, they got lost in each other, reliving that moment of rejoicing in the aftermath of ugliness. He would like to tell her she was the strongest woman he'd ever met. He would like to ask her exactly where she'd gotten the courage to defy the mighty Vitale family.

The invisible connection was broken when Lily tugged on Tessa's sleeve and asked for more juice. He looked away, only to encounter the combined focus of Silver and Cruz. Their disquiet was obvious. Silver, especially, had reason to worry. He'd had a front-row seat to Mason's implosion following Tessa's departure.

He gave a brief shake of his head, a silent signal that he was fine.

After the meal, Tessa and Candace whisked Lily to the master bath for her bedtime routine and his unit cornered him outside on the balcony. Cruz propped his body against the corner post while Silver paced. Raven dropped into the chair beside him.

Light from the dining room combated the hazy, purple-tinged dusk cloaking the woods on either side of the cabin. The mountain peaks in the distance had become smudged, indistinct shapes.

"What happened out there?" Silver said. "I want a bullet-point list."

Fingers of fatigue whispered over him. This day ranked up there as the second worst of his life, and he wasn't eager to explain the gory details. But his partners were putting their lives on the line for him, Tessa and Lily, and they deserved to know exactly what sort of enemy they were dealing with.

He inhaled a lungful of honeysuckle air, trying to ignore the unhappy response in his rib cage. The others were quiet as he relayed the facts with as much professional detachment as he could muster. They didn't immediately respond. Their silence added an ominous weight to the otherwise innocent night.

Cruz crossed and uncrossed his ankles. "I've come across his type before, back in Texas. Our department lost three officers before we managed to capture the guy."

Silver ground his teeth. "We're not losing anyone. I've reached out to a private security firm with a stellar reputation and hired two of their men. They start in the morning."

Mason didn't have the energy to launch a proper protest. "You hired them without consulting me?"

"We need the assistance. We're spread too thin."

Mason couldn't afford private security. "It will cost a fortune."

"I'm footing the bill."

"I can't let you do that. I have a home to rebuild and a truck to replace. There's no telling how long before I could repay you."

"I don't want to be repaid."

"Foster—"

"Whoa." He halted and held up a gloved hand. "Stop with the parent-given name, will you? We can't keep going on little to no sleep, and we can't monopolize the patrol unit or the sheriff's deputies. Let me do this."

His friend shelling out loads of money for Mason's benefit wasn't fair.

"Think of Tessa," he urged. "And your daughter."

Dante's sneering face flashed into his mind. "I owe you, brother."

Their phones buzzed simultaneously. Raven got to hers first. "Social-media blitz is a go," she said. "Dante and his henchmen won't be able to buy a pack of gum without looking over their shoulders."

"I'm still waiting on my billboard contact to return my call," Silver said, scrolling through his phone. "I'd like to get their faces in a high-traffic area."

"Mayor Chesney will have something to say about that," Raven said. "Advertising the presence of Mafia criminals is bad for tourism."

"Tourists getting taken hostage and shot by said

Mafia criminals is also bad for tourism," he returned with an arched brow.

"I'd like to hear you say that to the mayor's face," she said, softly laughing.

"Did the Pascals get back to Florida yet?" Mason asked.

"Lindsey put them personally on the plane."

The sliding glass doors swooshed open, and Lily padded out in her pajamas. She searched the semidarkness and zeroed in on him. He set aside his phone and put his hands out to frame her tiny waist, lest she decide to leap into his arms.

"You smell good enough to eat," he teased, deliberately sniffing her hair. "Is your shampoo scented with lemons?"

She giggled. "No, silly, not lemons."

"Hmm." He sniffed her sleeve. "Is it watermelon?"

"Nuh-uh." She braced her hands atop his.

He smelled her cheek. "I know. It's pancake syrup."

"No, it's apples!"

"Ah, apples. Why didn't I think of that?" He spotted Tessa, who was standing near the sliding doors and watching them with a tired smile.

"You're off to bed, huh?"

"Candace is going to read me a book."

"You'll have to tell me about it over breakfast."

"Okay." Lily surprised him with a kiss on his cheek.

His partners bade her good-night and watched as she reentered the house. Tessa offered a half wave and followed her inside.

Mason closed his eyes and asked God to grant her dreamless, restorative sleep. He didn't like to think what the hours ahead might bring. Each time he worked a tragic car accident or took part in a search-and-rescue operation that morphed into body recovery, he replayed the events in his head for days. He envisioned the victims and relived the relatives' grieving reactions. After what he and Tessa had been through, there would be flashbacks and memories that refused to budge.

"I'm going home." Raven's announcement brought him out of his private reverie. Looking down at him, she placed her hand on his shoulder. "Get some rest."

"That's my goal."

She jabbed her finger at the others. "You two, don't keep him out here much longer. He's practically falling asleep where he sits."

Cruz pushed off the post. "I'll walk you out."

"Aren't you the gallant one," she quipped, nudging his shoulder.

He looked dubious. "I've never been called anything close to that."

They entered the cabin, their banter trailing behind them. Silver assumed Cruz's former spot and crossed his arms as he regarded Mason with a hooded gaze.

"Should I be worried?" he drawled.

"My lungs and ribs will heal."

His friend's expression didn't change. "I like Tessa. Always have. But she has the power to send you back into the abyss. I don't want to see that happen."

Mason pushed his fingers through his hair and tried not to think about that kiss. "I'm not the same man I used to be."

"Because of your faith, I know."

If they hadn't spoken about spiritual matters before, Mason would've missed the hint of challenge in Silver's voice.

Resting his hands on the chair arms, Mason said, "You can't measure God's characteristics as a Heavenly Father against your earthly one."

"Easy for you to say. You hit the dad jackpot." He fisted his gloved hands.

Mason searched for the right response. Lewis Reed had had his share of faults, like everyone else, but he'd been a hero in Mason's eyes. Following his early passing, it had taken Mason a long time to work through his grief. He still missed him. Silver hadn't been so fortunate, with either of his parents, and he bore the scars to this day. His childhood trauma stood between him and a lasting, personal relationship with God. Mason prayed that someday, Silver would lay his burdens down at Jesus's feet and find healing.

"I'm not interested in discussing my messed-up family," Silver inserted.

"I can't give you the answers you're searching for." He didn't know exactly what was happening between him and Tessa. While they hadn't discussed the kiss outright, she'd seemingly agreed with him that it hadn't been the best idea. They'd waded through enough hurt, and they were both intent on maintaining peace for their daughter's sake.

Something clicked in his mind, and he turned the tables. "Is my experience with Tessa the reason you've avoided commitment?"

A sardonic laugh burst forth. "No, what it did was cement my decision to stay single. Emotional entanglements are the last thing a guy like me needs. Besides, I would make a woman miserable long-term."

"That's a convenient lie you've told yourself, brother."

Silver's phone buzzed. He fished it from his pocket and skimmed the message. "Lindsey has a pressing question about a reservation. I have to call her."

"I'll give you some privacy."

As he trudged to his bedroom, fatigue dogging his steps, Mason wondered what the future held for Silver and if his friend would remain stubbornly alone for the rest of his life. Would he choose the safety of solitude or would he take a chance on someone?

His own future was a huge question mark, as well. The idea of Tessa settling down in Serenity and eventually marrying someone else made his chest ache and his stomach churn. As he tested the front-door lock, he glanced down the hallway toward her room. Just like in the past, he found himself wanting to spend every minute with her. An alarming prospect.

He comforted himself with the knowledge that he didn't have to make any decisions regarding the future right now. They had an enemy to overcome first.

EIGHTEEN

Tessa jerked upright, lungs heaving, as she tried to get her bearings. The night-light in the bathroom bathed the bed and dresser in a triangle of light. She wasn't in that dank basement anymore. Her pajama shirt clung to her clammy skin. Nausea roiled through her middle. Threading her curls off her face, she studied Lily's peaceful form beside her and tried to shake the vestiges of the dream.

Folding back the comforter, she slid out of bed. Her sore ankle protested, and she hobbled into the bathroom, where she splashed cold water on her face and pulled on the wrap that matched her new striped pajama shirt and pants. Wide-awake now, she slipped on her sandals, crept through the silent cabin and emerged into the night. The air carried the scents of honey and flowers' perfume. Crickets' chirrups performed a woodland symphony. Stretched out above her, sparkly diamonds patterned the canvas of black sky. God's handiwork never failed to amaze her.

"Hey."

She jerked toward the source of the greeting, her hand flying to her chest.

"Sorry. I didn't mean to startle you."

There was no mistaking Mason's voice. As her eyes adjusted, she was able to discern his body from the shadows. He was lounging on the hand-carved bench tucked between twin planters.

Tessa circled the wrought-iron table to get to him. "You can't sleep, either?"

His legs were stretched out, ankles propped on one another, and his arm rested along the benchtop. "I got a couple of hours' worth. I was hoping you'd fare better than me."

She sat without asking permission and clasped her hands on her lap. "I had a bad dream."

Mason was quiet for long moments. "I was hoping you wouldn't. Want to talk about it?"

Her mouth went dry as she thought about what had unfolded at the water park and inside the redbrick house. "Not really."

His arm left the bench to curve around her shoulders. He moved with care, no doubt to protect his ribs from sudden movements. Or maybe he didn't want to startle her again. Either way, she liked the contact. She liked being close to him.

"I am sure of one thing," she muttered.

"Yeah? What's that?"

"I'm going to avoid basements for a while."

"Good idea." She heard the smile in his tone.

They soaked in the serene night, content to draw comfort from each other's presence. She assumed he found her closeness comforting. He kept his arm around her as if it was the most natural thing in the world. Occasionally, his fingers whispered over her shoulder, the soft caress unhurried.

Sitting there together, Tessa was hurtled into the past…to a time when they were in sync, when their lives were effortlessly entwined.

"You were amazing," he murmured. "I always knew you were strong and resourceful. I didn't know how strong until yesterday."

"I was petrified." She shuddered, remembering the beating he'd suffered. "I thought I was going to watch you die."

Mason shifted and tucked her against his side. She rested her cheek against his chest and inhaled his heady scent. The cotton fabric stretched across his muscular torso was soft against her skin. His heart pounded a reassuring rhythm. When he smoothed his hand over her unruly hair and kissed the top of her head, she closed her eyes and sighed. This was as close to perfection as she could get.

She didn't dare speak or move, lest she shatter the moment. Minutes stretched by, and she relaxed into him. The tension ebbed from her.

"I have an idea."

She opened her eyes. "Tell me."

"You need rest. I'll sit outside your room until you go to sleep."

She reluctantly lifted her head and shifted out of his half embrace. "That's a thoughtful offer. You need rest, too. More than I do, in fact."

"I want you to drift off with the assurance that you're safe, I'm safe and Lily is safe." Leaving the bench, he held out his hand. "Come on."

Not wanting him to strain his ribs, she stood on her own and then fitted her palm against his. Once inside with the door secure, he chose a cushioned chair from the entry area and scooted it down the hallway. He stationed himself across from her door and pulled out his phone.

Tessa rested her hand on the knob. "You're really sweet for doing this."

"What can I say? I'm a sweet guy."

The screen light allowed her to see his grin and shining eyes. His busted face, too. Her heart squeezed with tender fondness for this brave man. The renewed sense of solidarity between them filled her with gratitude. He might never love her again, but she had hope she'd win his good opinion and respect.

Bracing her weight against the chair, she bent and brushed a kiss on his noninjured cheek. His skin was part smooth, part prickly, advertising his need for a shave.

His forehead furrowed. "What was that for?"

"For being you." Swallowing the lump in her throat, she said her good-night.

Beneath the covers again, she fell asleep within minutes of her head touching the pillow. What seemed like a short time later, she was awoken by Lily's lilting chatter. Sunlight peeping around the curtains assured her that morning had arrived without a single bad dream.

Lily bounced on the bed. "Look, Mommy! Mason made us pancakes!"

Tessa sat up and spotted him near the room's fireplace, setting a tray on the coffee table. The aromas of rich coffee, spicy sausages and something fruity brought her fully awake. He straightened and turned, white teeth flashing in his beard-shadowed face.

"I made the good kind of pancakes," he said with a wink. "No surprises."

Lily slid off the mattress and pattered over to him. "Will you cut mine? And pour syrup?"

His smile turned protective and proud as he gazed down at her. Smoothing his hand over her curls, he nodded. "I'll work on that while your mom gets dressed."

Choosing a chair that had its back to the room, he began readying Lily's breakfast. Tessa hurried into the bathroom and chose from her meager belongings— another tourist-geared T-shirt, jeans and sandals. She looked in the mirror and grimaced at her reflection. Her skin was paler than usual, giving her freckles center stage, and there were circles under her eyes. There was nothing to be done about it, so she put on her shiny lip gloss and applied curl-taming gel to her mane.

Tessa joined the others and reached for coffee. He'd prepared a trio of plates piled high with fluffy pancakes, sausages and strawberries. "How did you have the energy for this? Did you get any rest at all?"

Having gotten Lily settled, he got comfortable with his own plate in his lap. "I stayed in the hallway for about thirty minutes, until I heard you snoring. I—"

"I do not snore."

Eyes sparkling, he forked a strawberry. "Eat your pancakes, Tess. Tell me those aren't superior to your pink—"

She cleared her throat and inclined her head toward Lily, who was currently licking maple syrup off her fingers and absorbing every word.

He smirked. "She obviously likes them."

"Why are you in such a good mood?"

He looked over at Lily. "Because we're about to have a momentous conversation."

"Keep her age in mind, okay? I'm not sure how much she'll understand. I don't want you to be disappointed."

"I won't be." Anticipation buzzed through him. He'd initially decided to wait until the danger had passed, but yesterday had reminded him that the future wasn't guaranteed.

Tessa was perched on the chair behind where Lily sat on her knees, hunkered over the coffee table. Tessa balanced her breakfast on the fat cushion arm and found a safe spot for her coffee mug on the small table beside it.

She dipped a slice of sausage in the syrup and shot him a tremulous smile. "I'm happy and relieved this day has come."

Lily quickly finished her breakfast and would've shot off to watch her favorite show if Tessa hadn't called her back. "Mason has something he'd like to talk to you about."

She draped over his chair. "What is it?"

Butterflies fluttered in his chest. He set aside his plate and took her small, plump, slightly sticky hand in his. "Lily, have you ever thought you might like to have a dad?"

She bounced on her toes. "Tommy Hamilton doesn't have a dad."

From across the coffee table, Tessa clarified, "Tommy is in her library story group."

"Maggie's mom went to heaven," Lily said, her eyes big.

"Is Maggie also in your story group?"

"She's at church."

"I see. Well, your mom and I are old friends…" He paused to collect his thoughts and decided to just come out with it. "Lily, you don't have to call me 'Mason' anymore. I'm your dad."

She ceased bouncing and blinked up at him. "You are?"

His heart swelled with the drive to protect this tiny human. "Yes, ladybug, I am."

"Will you make me yellow pancakes every morning?"

He chuckled. Before Tessa ducked her head to hide a smile, he saw that her eyes were suspiciously bright.

"Not every morning, but as often as I can."

"Will me and Mommy live with you?"

He licked his lips. "Do you remember that there was a fire at my house?"

"Uh-huh. It's broken."

"That's right. My house has to be fixed. After that, you will stay with me a lot."

"But what about Mommy?"

Mason avoided looking Tessa's way. Did she feel as sad about managing two separate households, with Lily bouncing between, as he did? "Well, we'll have to figure that out. As soon as we do, we'll let you know."

"Can I watch my show now?"

"Not with those dirty hands," Tessa said, standing. "I'll help you get the syrup off."

While they were in the bathroom, he sipped his coffee. Lily's response hadn't been as jubilant as he'd expected, but he reminded himself she was only three.

There was a knock on the door, and Silver poked his head in. "We've had a sighting."

Mason abandoned his coffee and went into the hallway. "Where?"

"We got a call from a concerned citizen in the Bear Ridge neighborhood about an hour ago. I'm meeting Lieutenant Polk and a couple of patrol officers. I'll report in as soon as I know something." His violet gaze shifted behind Mason, to the remnants of their breakfast. "How did it go with Lily?"

"Good. She didn't pose as many tough questions as I thought she might." He hooked his thumb toward the bathroom. "Give me a moment to tell Tessa I'm leaving."

"You're not going."

Silver was his best friend, which gave him the right to express his opinion. But Mason outranked him. Before he could speak, his friend cut him off.

"In this situation and with your injuries, you'd be a distraction, not an asset."

Mason didn't like what he was hearing.

"You know I'm right," Silver persisted. "Put yourself in Tessa's shoes. After everything that happened yesterday, is she going to be comfortable alone with my newly hired private security guards standing over her?"

"Fine, I'll sit this one out. I expect regular updates."

"You got it."

He relayed the development to Tessa when she and Lily emerged. Her tension abated somewhat when he told her he was staying. Silver had made the right call, after all.

"Are you up for a shopping trip?"

She had gone to clear her and Lily's plates from the coffee table. Instead, she straightened and stared at him. "Shopping? Now?"

"We'll stay local. There's a shop in the square that has everything you and Lily need to replenish what you lost in the fire."

"Are there toys?" Lily asked, her eyes alight with excitement.

He bent to her level and chucked her chin. "If that shop doesn't have toys, we'll search until we find some."

She clapped her hands together. Tessa was still uncertain, gauging by her expression.

"We'll have professional bodyguards with us the entire time. I'll be armed, as well."

"We are running low on toothpaste and other toiletries."

"This excursion is for clothes and shoes. You might even find the slipper-style you like so well."

"Ballet flats," she corrected, grinning.

"Yeah, those things."

As soon as the breakfast dishes were cleaned and put away, they got acquainted with Silver's hired guards, Tyson and Angus, and were soon driving down the mountain to the heart of Serenity.

Lily radiated excitement. She'd been mostly confined indoors since their arrival. The promise of a new toy was also at the forefront of her mind.

The square was usually bustling on beautiful spring days, and this morning was no exception. Mason waited for a parking spot to open directly in front of the Mint Julep Boutique. Tyson and Angus scored one nearby a few minutes later. Once the men were stationed out front, Mason ushered Tessa and Lily inside the feminine, colorful shop. He greeted the owner, Sally Decker, and took great pleasure in introducing

Lily as his daughter. Sally didn't attempt to hide her surprise, and he knew the word would spread through Serenity like wildfire. He didn't mind. It would save him from repeated explanations. He took Lily to the toy-and-book area to allow Tessa time to peruse the clothing.

Lily's mission seemed to be to handle every single stuffed animal and book in stock. This was Mason's first shopping excursion with a toddler, and he found her enthusiasm charming, though it was no small task to replace everything just so. He made sure to face the shop door and windows, occasionally checking on the hired bodyguards. Silver had vouched for their professionalism, and Mason trusted his friend's instincts.

"I want this one." Lily clutched a white-and-pink unicorn to her chest and looked at him with pleading big brown eyes. "This one, too." She snagged a board book from the shelf. He was certain that with time and experience, he'd learn to say no to her. For now, he couldn't help but succumb.

"What do you say, Lily?" Tessa interjected. Several items of clothing were draped over her arms, and a pair of child-sized sandals dangled from her fingers.

"Please, Daddy?"

His gaze jerked back to Lily's round face, his heart skipping with joy over one simple word. "Yes, you may have those two things. Let's go pay."

He and Tessa wrangled over who should foot the bill. In the end, she acquiesced, probably because other patrons had entered the shop and could eavesdrop.

Emerging onto the sidewalk, he made eye contact with the guards. Angus gave him a thumbs-up.

"Look, Mommy, a fountain." Lily pointed to the parklike square across the street. "Can we go see it?"

The square was bustling with folks congregating on benches, enjoying donuts and coffee, and others walking their dogs along the brick paths. To the left and right of the Mint Julep Boutique, tourists and locals strolled along the sidewalks, their purchases swinging at their sides. It was a normal scene on a day with lovely weather. He looked at the beautiful woman beside him and wished the three of them could explore like a regular family. But the threat hadn't gone away.

"I'll bring you here again, I promise. For now, we should return to the cabin."

Lily started to pout. Tessa said, "We can ask Mimi if she wants to come over and swim. What do you think about that?"

"Okay."

Tessa locked gazes with him. "You didn't buy yourself anything."

"I'll stop in a store down the road. Won't take me five minutes to get what I need."

He made arrangements with Tyson and Angus, and they followed closely during the brief drive to the Village Tinker. Tessa's eyebrows lifted. "This is where you're getting clothes?"

"I'm not difficult to please." He winked.

Inside, he breezed through the clothing section, snagging the bare necessities, then hurried to the real reason he'd come here. Back in the truck, he produced a large white box. Tessa wet her lips.

"Is that what I think it is?"

Lily leaned forward, only to be snagged by her booster-seat belt. "Can I see?"

"Lily, your mom and I used to come to this very store and buy their homemade fudge."

He opened the lid with a flourish, and the scents of rich, buttery caramel and chocolate filled the cab. Lily's eyes got huge as they took in the confectionary slabs.

Tessa immediately reached for her favorite, butter pecan. Her eyes closed in bliss as she tasted the first bite. "This hasn't changed a bit. Sweet perfection."

Mason chuckled. "Not as perfect as rocky road."

He handed Lily a piece of both. "Next time, I'll take you inside and let you choose a flavor."

In the middle of enjoying a second piece of fudge, his phone chirped. Tessa's enjoyment faded as he read the text.

"The tip didn't pan out," he told her, mourning the dip in her mood. Her gaze darted to the store and parking lot.

Mason tucked the purchases on the seat between them and put the gear in Reverse. Dante wasn't in the Bear Ridge neighborhood, as suspected, which meant he could be anywhere.

NINETEEN

Despite Mason's misgivings about the unit's involvement in the community outreach event, Lieutenant Hatmaker's stance didn't alter. They couldn't bow out. Mason and the others debated whether to leave Tessa and Lily at the cabin with the private security guards, Tyson and Angus, or to keep them with them. Because of the distance between Serenity and the neighboring city of Pigeon Forge, they decided on the latter.

Tyson and Angus had commandeered one of the stadium locker rooms for their use, and that's where she, Lily, Gia and Candace were supposed to stay until the community event was over. Restless and dogged by worry, Tessa had paced the smelly, oppressive room until Angus had had enough. He'd offered to accompany her for a quick peek at the mounted-police unit, to put her mind at ease, he'd gruffly said.

She remained in the cool shade created by the bleachers rising above her on either side. Behind her, a long tunnel led to the interior restrooms and snack bar. Angus stood slightly behind her shoulder, ready to shield her at any hint of trouble. As much as she disliked Lieutenant Hatmaker's attitude toward Mason, she had to agree with his assessment of today's threat level. Dante was arrogant, but he wasn't stupid. Even he would have second thoughts about trying something in the midst of this law-enforcement extravaganza.

The bleachers on this side of the high-school football field were mostly empty, as the event attendees were busy roaming the turf and drifting from one organization to the next. Students and faculty were joined by hundreds of citizens of all ages who'd come to learn about and interact with law enforcement and emergency services. Children got their pictures taken in shiny fire trucks. EMTs let volunteers practice wrapping and stabilizing pretend broken bones. The SWAT armored vehicle was obviously a crowd favorite.

The biggest draw of the day, though, was the mounted-police unit. The foursome and their respective mounts were mere yards away from this access point, and they were an impressive sight in their official Serenity PD gear. The equine officers' manes were in elevated, elegant braids along the crests of their necks. Their navy-and-silver saddle pads bore the department symbol and their individual names. Reflective breast-collar covers and leg wraps glinted when struck by the sun's rays.

Raven and Cruz interacted with attendees from their saddles, their two-toned helmets matching the saddle-pad colors. Silver and Mason stood with their horses and handed out bio cards. Due to his healing ribs, Mason had chosen not to get into the saddle. The fact that he was required to be here at all bothered Tessa. While he'd come to breakfast that morning looking rested, he hadn't been able to completely hide his discomfort. He'd reassured her he was recuperating nicely, and she had no choice but to believe him.

Watching him now, handsome and debonair in that blue-black uniform, mirrored shades and tall boots, she prayed for God's protection to continue. He had experienced tremendous losses since her return, both in material goods and his health. Yet he hadn't blamed her. Hadn't descended into self-pity. He'd focused all his energy on keeping her and Lily safe. She would've fallen for him if she hadn't loved him already.

"Time to return to the lair," Angus said.

"Can we swing by the snack bar on the way? It's almost suppertime."

Angus agreed. Tessa splurged on pizza, nachos and other not-so-healthy snacks, enough to share with everyone. Gia and Candace's lively personalities made the evening bearable. They doted on Lily, and she soaked in the attention like a thirsty forest lapping up a spring shower. Their two-member family had grown with their dash to Tennessee, and both Tessa and Lily had benefited.

It was growing late when Mason strode through the door and told them the event was winding down. His bruises had deepened to a dusky purple. The swelling had gone down, however. After quickly downing two slices of pizza, he hugged his mom and sister goodbye. Gia's vehicle was parked in a different area, and the pair would not be accompanying them to the stables.

Holding hands, Mason and Lily preceded Tessa onto the field. Tyson walked beside her, while Angus brought up the rear. Silver was waiting for them. He stood between Scout and Lightning and had both horses' leads. At the far end of the field, Raven and

Cruz were riding their mounts into the grassy section where the unit trucks and trailers were parked.

Their group joined the mass exodus as attendees headed for their cars. Law-enforcement agencies were packing up their tables and tents. A handful of food vendors were also clearing out. When they reached the trucks, Mason immediately buckled Lily into her seat and urged Tessa to get in.

"Is something wrong?" she asked.

"No, I just don't want to take any chances." His gaze was hidden behind the sunglasses. "I'll be back as soon I help them get the horses settled."

The hired guards paced around the truck and didn't enter their own vehicle until Mason was behind the truck's wheel. They pulled into the departing traffic first, followed by Mason, and then in the second truck, Raven, Cruz and Silver.

The trip over had taken roughly forty-five minutes. Due to the volume of traffic surrounding the school, Tessa settled in for a longer return route, content to listen as Mason recounted the event highlights.

"I'm sorry you had to miss it," he said finally, glancing over.

"Who knows? Maybe I'll get to go next year."

"I'd like that." He wiped his forehead with his sleeve and adjusted the air vent. "You and I haven't had a chance to make plans or even discuss our options."

Options? Like an apartment for her somewhere in town, convenient to his home and work? She watched the stream of people navigating the metal-and-chrome sea. The school's flag waved gently in the breeze. The setting sun reflected in her side mirror, and she got her sunglasses from her cross-body bag.

Would she be successful at building a new life in Serenity like she had in Georgia? Could she handle living in the same town with Mason, loving him from afar and watching as one day he wooed and won someone else's heart?

Tessa forced her mind from the morose thoughts. What good would come of thinking about a future when her present was balanced on a knife's edge?

When she didn't respond, Mason let the matter drop. Lily began humming as they entered Wears Valley Road, a sure sign she'd be asleep before they reached the stables. As they neared the dilapidated buildings and old water-park sign, Tessa's stomach cramped.

Mason sensed her distress and, reaching out, closed his hand over hers. "The memories won't ever go away. They'll lose their potency, though."

"I hope you're right, because I feel sick every time I picture them carrying you unconscious through the park and stowing you in the trunk."

A tortured look stole over his face. "Trust me, I get it. I would erase those images for you if I could."

She squeezed his hand. "I know."

As expected, Lily was asleep when they pulled into the stables' lot and parked. Tessa suggested staying inside the truck with her, but Mason shot down that idea. They had to unload the horses, remove their gear and brush them down, not to mention dole out their overdue supper.

Tessa carried her inside and got comfortable in one of the break-room chairs. She would've liked to help the officers, but they had a certain routine and would accomplish that faster without her underfoot. Fishing her phone from her pants pocket, she settled in to watch her favorite music videos.

At first, she didn't pay attention to the loud voices coming from deeper in the building. Then, a shot rang out, and she flinched. The door was flung open, and Mason filled the doorway, his jaw tight and his eyes hard.

"Dante's men are out there, and they're spraying the building with gasoline. They're going to burn us out and pick us off, one by one."

His cunning enemy had chosen to act when the bulk of law enforcement was in another town, packing up from the event or driving the twisting, winding connector road they'd taken. His unit had contacted dispatch. That didn't guarantee help would arrive before their stables were burned to the ground, just like his home.

"What's the plan?" Tessa asked, hurrying after him into the building's central area and shifting Lily's slumbering weight higher on her shoulder.

"You're riding into the mountains," Cruz answered for him. He'd led Iggy into the aisle and was putting a saddle on her.

Thankfully, they'd gotten the horses unloaded and inside before Dante's crew descended. Now, they had to find a way to save them.

Tessa stopped short of bumping into Mason. "Is that true?"

Again, someone else interjected. "It's your best option." Raven was stuffing water bottles and snacks into a backpack. "You'll exit through the rear door, which he won't be expecting, and ride through the trees until you can cross the road into wooded terrain. From there, you can skirt neighborhoods and keep out of sight. He would have a tough time pursuing you, even if he somehow spotted you."

From the side paddock entrance, he heard a distinct pop, followed by return fire. Tyson and Angus were out there trying to take out the goons with the hoses.

Mason was torn between the desire to stay and defend his unit, and getting Tessa and Lily out of harm's way. Part of being a good leader was learning when to delegate responsibility. Silver and the others would do everything within their power to prevent loss of life and damage to the facility. There was only one choice to be made.

"We'll need a sat phone." After retrieving one from the office, he joined Silver beside Scout's stall and stuffed it into his saddle pack.

"He could track your location with that."

"I'll keep it turned off unless there's an emergency." Mason strode to the weapons closet, used his key to unlock it and retrieved a rifle and ammo to go along with his pistol.

Cruz coaxed Iggy through the rear door. Mason looped his rifle sling over his head and, after motioning for Tessa to follow him, led Scout outside. This was a rarely used exit, and the strip of ground behind the building was uneven and overgrown.

Tessa coughed in reaction to the wall of gasoline fumes. Silver eased Lily from her arms so that she could climb onto Iggy's back. Raven rushed out and stuffed the snack supply inside his saddlebag. She held up a blanket.

"Found this in my locker. Use it to create a child wrap once you're far enough away. It'll make travel easier." After zipping up the bag, she hurried back inside. Cruz wasn't far behind.

"I'm going to head for the abandoned campground, Camp Smoky," Mason told Silver. "We can rendezvous there tomorrow morning."

"Good plan."

"Stay safe."

"Back at you."

Once Mason was astride Scout, he caught Tessa's gaze. "You ready?"

"I am."

He was grateful she was an experienced rider, because this wasn't going to be a fun trip. They were heading into residential areas fraught with unknown factors. At least his horses were trained to work through the unexpected.

They picked their way through the overgrowth of ferns and other greenery. At the point where the woods met the two-lane road, he waited for an opening in traffic before signaling to Tessa. A diagonal approach to the opposite lot led them through high grass and to another copse. They rarely conversed during their journey. Mason had to stay alert to potential pitfalls, and Tessa was concentrating on guiding her horse while keeping a snug hold on Lily. He would've liked to give her a break, but he had to be ready to fire a weapon at any moment.

When they encountered a group of tweens and teens kicking a soccer ball in a dense neighborhood, Mason urged Scout to keep riding. It wasn't their usual habit to ignore or avoid people in their community, and his equine partner was confused. But he followed Mason's directives and continued deeper into uninhabited territory.

The sun dipped behind the mountain ridge above them, cloaking the forest in a hazy shroud. Lily's distressed voice shredded the stillness, and Mason tugged on the reins and waited for Tessa and Iggy to come alongside.

He could barely make out their features, and the small clearing they were in was a blend of indistinct shapes.

Tessa rubbed Lily's tummy and murmured reassurances.

"I want to go home." She was trying to twist around and face Tessa. No wonder she was frightened, waking up to find herself far above the ground, balanced on a large animal. In the dark forest, no less.

"I know, ladybug, but Scout and Iggy are taking us on an adventure. Your daddy's here with us, and he's going to make sure we get to our destination. We're going to spend the night in a campground."

Lily clutched her mom's shirt. "I'm hungry."

"Raven packed us some snacks," Mason said, dismounting and using his flashlight to check the options in the backpack she'd tucked into his saddlebag. He wished he'd brought his pain meds, but quickly dismissed the thought. His mind needed to be sharp and clear. "Animal crackers or cheese squares? Or would you like a granola bar?"

"'Nola bar."

He removed the wrapper and handed it to her. While she ate, he gave Tessa a bottle of water and snagged one for himself.

"How are you?" he softly asked.

"Not too shabby." She shifted in the saddle and took another long drink. "You must be hurting."

"It's manageable."

"I guess it wouldn't be wise to use the sat phone and check on things?"

"Unfortunately, no." He couldn't stop thinking about his officers, human and equine, and wondering how they were faring. "If my calculations are correct, we should reach the camp in another hour."

Before she could respond, the sounds of revving engines, like angry bees, rocketed over the high crest above. Dirt bikes zoomed straight for the clearing. The bikes' lights flashed over them, temporarily blinding them and startling the horses.

Mason couldn't make out distinguishing features, body shapes or sizes. Were these joyriders out for an adrenaline rush, or were they locals hired to do Dante's bidding?

TWENTY

Tessa could feel Lily slipping from her grasp. Mason reached over and seized Iggy's reins, holding the horse steady as the trio of dirt bikes hurtled past them and disappeared into the thickening darkness.

She wrapped her right arm around Lily's middle and tugged her close. Her little body was shivering, despite the warm temperature. "It's okay, sweetheart. They're gone."

Tessa's heart was racing. For a split second, she'd thought Dante and his men had tracked them somehow and rented special equipment to reach them. While they had probably determined she and Mason weren't at the stables, they had no way of knowing their destination.

When Mason was convinced that Lily and the horses had calmed enough to resume their journey, he removed something from his saddlebag, snapped it in half and handed the glowing orange stick to Lily.

"Hold on to that, okay?"

She waved it around, clearly enamored. Mason reclaimed his position in the saddle. Tessa gave Iggy free rein. Horses had excellent night vision, especially with the full moon and stars acting as night-lights.

The rest of the trip was uneventful. With Lily's hunger assuaged and a new plaything to occupy her, she was content to rest in the circle of Tessa's arms. Occasionally, an owl's repetitive call would filter through the trees. Openings in the canopy above revealed wedges of star-studded sky.

"See the lake?" Mason said over his shoulder.

The terrain had leveled off about a mile back, and Tessa scanned the horizon, her eyes catching on the shimmering, reflective surface straight ahead.

"The lake marks the entrance to Camp Smoky," he continued. "There are multiple cabins rimming it. Beyond those are the old gymnasium, cafeteria and larger boarding structures used for big groups."

"Where will we stay?"

"The cabins are in bad shape, but one of the larger dorms will probably work. The owner doesn't live in the state anymore. He pays someone to tend the grounds. Patrol comes up here on a routine basis to check for uninvited guests."

"Like us, you mean?"

"Not quite," he replied, a smile in his voice. "Unless you hid a spray-paint can in your pocket."

Remembering the water park's dilapidated state, she suppressed a shudder. "Is there electricity?"

"Unfortunately, no."

"Then we won't be able to see s-p-i-d-e-r-s or m-i-c-e."

Laughter rumbled in his chest. "That's the first time anyone has spelled something at me."

She smiled. "It's a fact of life with a toddler."

"Noted." The horses ambled past the lake and along a gravel drive. "I'll check out our sleeping quarters.

It won't be the most comfortable night, but we can cling to hope that Silver will bring fresh pastries for breakfast."

Moonlight enabled her to make out the basic details of the structures. The heart of Camp Smoky was laid out in a circular pattern, with a large, semiwooded area in the middle of a ring of buildings. The cafeteria was a long, low cabin with a porch running the length of it. A chapel anchored one end of the circle, while a building that Mason said used to house miniature golf rental equipment and a general store was at the other.

After passing the chapel, Mason halted before a tall structure and passed his flashlight over it. Set back from the gravel circle, the cement building was painted a drab color. A generous wooden, ground-level porch had two sets of stairs leading to the upstairs deck.

"Why are there so many doors?"

"The dorm is separated into four sections on the first floor, to be used by different groups. There's a shared restroom with showers and toilets in the rear of the building. Upstairs, there's a maze of separate quarters."

Woods created a mysterious backdrop behind the buildings on this side of the camp. She tried to imagine children spending happy summer days here and couldn't quite manage it.

They dismounted and tethered the horses to the post-and-rail fence. She and Lily waited on the porch while Mason tested windows. He found one that was unlocked, slid it open and climbed inside. She could see his light move through the space. Seconds later, the door swung open.

"Would you believe there are still mattresses in the bunks?"

"How long has this been closed to campers?" She entered the tight space and surveyed the floor-to-ceiling wooden bunks, three beds high.

Mason got on his knees and searched the slots underneath. When he didn't spy any critters, he began shaking out the thin blue mattresses.

"I'm not sure exactly. Two years. Maybe three."

They ate by aid of an upturned flashlight. Afterward, Mason urged her to get some sleep while he kept watch outside. Lily clambered onto one of the lowest bunks and clutched her orange glow stick.

"Watch this, ladybug." Wrappers crinkled. Plastic snapped. In a matter of seconds, he'd placed glow sticks around the room. Yellow, blue, orange, red. They created a fluorescent display that dispelled the grim atmosphere.

She giggled and sighed into her arms, which she was using as a makeshift pillow. "Pretty, Daddy."

Tessa snagged his hand, pulled him close and hugged him. He hesitated, then lightly ran his hand over her hair before cupping her nape. The weight of his palm was warm and familiar.

He hadn't had a chance to change out of his uniform, and the starched fabric was pulled taut over his bulletproof vest.

"What's this for?" he murmured.

"You're amazing, that's all."

"Because of glow sticks?" he asked good-naturedly. "If I'd known how easy it was to impress you, I would've brought those out days ago."

Tessa forced her arms to release him. Going forward, she couldn't give in to random hugs and spontaneous shows of affection. Their dire circumstances had forged a new bond between them. She was certain he felt it, too—this renewed sense of solidarity and the knowledge they could depend on each other. The broken trust had been repaired.

Her love for him refused to be confined to the deepest, most hidden part of herself. Tessa understood what that meant for her—a life of longing for something she could never have, a life of loneliness and heartache. No other man could take his place.

Tessa would do what was best for Mason and their daughter. Over time, she would come to accept that her role in his life was that of a co-parent and friend, nothing more.

"You're a wonderful, thoughtful father, Mason." Emotion leaked into her voice.

His rugged features were encased in multicolored light, allowing her to see his shy smile. "Thank you, Tess. That means a lot coming from you. You make parenting look easy."

"I've had practice. You, on the other hand, know instinctively what to do. Glow sticks don't impress me. You do."

He rocked back on his heels. Before she added to her sentimental confession, she found a spot beside Lily.

"Sweet dreams." His voice was a soft caress.

She closed her eyes and ordered the wishes and dreams inside her to die a swift death.

He checked his cell phone throughout the night. Every time, he was met with a no-service message. The temptation to turn on the sat phone was great.

Were the stables intact? The horses safe? His officers unharmed? Had Dante slipped through their grasp once again?

The continuous loop of his thoughts returned to Tessa. So much had changed since she'd stormed back into his life. He would do anything for her, including taking a bullet for her. That had been true four years ago, and it was true today.

He walked along the platform that linked the building to the gravel drive and greeted Scout and Iggy. Across the grassy expanse, faded neon lights could be seen through the window of the girls' room. Was Tessa asleep? If not, was she thinking about him? About her and him together?

Absently rubbing his aching side, he studied the sky transforming from deep navy to shimmery lilac. She hadn't indicated in the slightest that she wanted a do-over with him. All she wanted was his forgiveness and his promise they would raise Lily as a cohesive team. He was fine with that. Perfectly satisfied.

They couldn't re-create what they used to have. To think they could was arrogant and foolish.

Why, then, did the thought of living on the fringes of her life make him want to put his fist through a wall?

Mason's mind refused to rest as dawn broke. His gaze strayed often to the gravel drive in anticipation of Silver's promised arrival. But his friend didn't show, and the sun climbed ever higher. Lily emerged from the room shortly after eight o'clock. Bright-eyed and bursting with energy, she skipped through the grass and wrapped her arms around his legs.

"Morning, ladybug." He smoothed her curls. Gazing into her precious face, he again thanked God for the opportunity to be a father. "How did you sleep?"

"Mommy said I had a dream about a ship."

Tessa joined them, her smile edged with fatigue. "She rolled and thrashed as if she were on a ship's deck."

She pulled her hair into a ponytail and applied a fresh layer of lip balm. "No sign of Silver?"

"Not yet." He stood as Lily bounced away.

Her hazel gaze swept him from head to toe. "Why don't you lie down for a while? I'll let Lily stretch her legs and keep an eye out for him."

It was a tempting offer, especially since he hadn't gotten his usual boost of caffeine. "If I go to sleep now, you may never pry me from the bunk. He should be here soon."

Unless things had gone south…

"Hey." She touched his arm, righting his focus. "I'm worried, too, but we can't lose faith."

"Mommy, I gotta go potty." Lily danced around Tessa.

"Let's go in those trees over there."

While Tessa was taking care of things with Lily, Mason opened a new bottle of water, chugged half the contents and splashed the rest over his face. A sudden flurry of birds exiting the woods near the cafeteria had him reaching for his pistol.

Seconds later, the report of a rifle echoed through the camp and a high-velocity bullet hurtled straight for him. He dove to the ground as the fence railing above him exploded in a shower of splinters.

He saw Tessa and Lily walking back, oblivious to the danger. One of the building's stairways stood between them.

"Get inside!" he yelled.

Another shot dug into the dirt near his boots, and he crawled away from the girls. Like he had during the river incident, he would draw the enemy in a different direction. How Dante had located them was a troubling mystery.

He heard Lily's plaintive cry as Tessa scooped her up and pounded across the porch to safety. As soon as the door slammed shut, he continued his fast crawl through the grass. When he reached gravel, he got to his feet and sprinted for the octagonal ball pit on the far side of the lane, then leaped over the knee-high panels. Hitting the cement, he used the panels for cover as he surveyed the woods beyond the basketball court.

The crunch of tires on gravel distracted him. The familiar logo painted on the truck and trailer penetrated his adrenaline high, and he offered up a prayer of thanks.

He signaled to get Silver's attention. The truck came under fire, so Silver stopped and opened his door. Raven was in the passenger seat. From this angle, he could see her prepping her service weapon and speaking into her radio.

Mason's yell reached him, and Silver acknowledged the warning. There was a blur of movement in the woods. A man who looked like James left the trees, skirted the basketball courts and disappeared behind another dorm. He couldn't be allowed to escape. His route would circle around the dorm, volleyball court and chapel, leading him to the dorm where Tessa and Lily were hiding.

Silver pursued the mustached man. Mason left the ball pit and returned to their dorm. No one answered his summons, so he kicked down the door and strode through the room, calling for Tessa.

The bathroom stalls were vacant. He walked down the line of showers, yanking open the curtain dividers one by one, his heart sinking like a stone when he failed to find them and there was no response to his calls.

"Mason?"

He whirled, expecting to see Tessa. In his rising panic, he'd mistaken the owner of the voice.

Raven stood beside the sinks in full gear, her weapon ready and her expression a mixture of fierce determination and compassion.

"They're not here," he rasped.

Dante had gotten to them. He'd taken the two people on this planet that he couldn't live without. His lungs squeezed, and he felt like he was going to suffocate.

"I lost the love of my life," she said. "I won't let that happen to you." Stalking to the exit door, she ripped it open. "Let's go get them back."

TWENTY-ONE

"Cat got your tongue, sis?"

Tessa didn't waste her breath begging for mercy. Tenderness and compassion had been drilled out of her brother. She held Lily close and sent her desperate pleas to God.

They'd left the dorm behind and, with Bruno bringing up the rear, marched beneath the shade trees that separated the dorm and chapel. A Suburban was parked near the chapel's rear exit and rusted air-conditioning unit. There were three of them here—Dante, Bruno and a third man tasked with killing Mason. What did that mean for the mounted police officers?

"What happened last night? Did you burn down the stables?"

Dante's answer was a scowl and flaring of his nostrils, which gave her hope. Maybe the fire department had arrived in time. Maybe the others had defended their headquarters until Dante and his crew had been forced to give up.

"How did you find us?"

"Social media can be a useful tool. You and Sergeant Reed captured the attention of a group of kids playing soccer. They took photos and posted them online. We got a map of the area and checked several places before coming here." He leaned in and spoke to Lily. His signature citrusy cologne enveloped them. "I'm your Uncle Dante. Do you remember me talking to you through your video system in Georgia?"

Lily's arms tightened around her neck. Tessa would've put distance between them, but Bruno was behind her, a large gun pointed at her spine. The humidity and intensifying heat from the sun weren't responsible for the sweat popping up on her skin. She was trying not to reveal her terror to her daughter, but it was growing more difficult by the minute.

"I heard you like horses. I have lots of horses at my home in New Jersey, and I'm going to take you to see them. You can learn to ride. Your Aunt Francesca also loves horses and will be your teacher. What do you think about that?"

When Lily didn't respond, he touched her shoulder. Tessa flinched. Fire ignited in his eyes, and he held out his arms.

"Give her to me."

Tessa shook her head. Her insides were quaking. This couldn't be the outcome. Dante couldn't win.

"Don't make this difficult for her," he growled. He wasn't thinking of her, though. He was worried about having to handle a toddler-sized meltdown.

Tessa glanced around. The chapel blocked her view of the wooded recreational area in the middle of the inner circle. There was no sign of Mason. Was he unconscious somewhere, felled by a bullet?

Would this abandoned campground be her final resting place?

She took a trembling breath. "Ladybug, I want you to go with Uncle Dante for a little while."

Lily burrowed closer. Tessa smoothed her hair and kissed the top of her head.

"I love you, Lily."

"Enough." Dante rolled his eyes and took her daughter from her.

Her heart shattered as Lily arched her body to try and reach Tessa.

"Calm down," Dante commanded. He opened the rear door while trying to corral Lily. "Why don't you sit in here—"

"Daddy!"

Dante spun around and Lily wiggled free. She ran to Mason, her short legs pumping with all their might. He had left the cover of the trees between the dorm and chapel, his rifle trained on Dante.

Time slowed. Tessa's frantic mind couldn't decide between fight or flight. Just as Lily reached Mason, Raven strode out of the trees. Holstering her pistol, she caught the toddler and hustled her along the chapel's long exterior.

Dante lunged for Tessa and shoved a gun to her temple. "Now we have a problem."

Mason's stance didn't falter. "There's a simple solution." He held the rifle steady, and his body was locked into offensive mode. "Free Tessa and turn yourself in."

Bruno inched closer to his boss. "What's the plan?"

Speaking loudly enough for Mason to hear, he said, "Tessa is my ticket out of here. I'm not giving her to you." His fingers dug into her upper arm, and she whimpered. "I'm going to do what I should've done long ago—rid the Vitale family of its black sheep.

Mark my words, Sergeant Reed, I'll be back for my niece. Next time, you won't see me coming."

Mason's gaze didn't stray to her once. His expression remained shuttered. How could he be so calm?

"I can't let you leave, Dante. You're going to serve time for your crimes."

Dante began to laugh his cruel, self-satisfied laugh, the one that instilled fear in her, the one that signaled he'd won.

There was a sharp report, and his laughter was cut off. He grunted and fell to his knees. A second gunshot, this one much closer, hit Bruno. The large man slumped against the Suburban and would've fired at Mason if he hadn't received another bullet in the arm.

Mason and Silver descended on the injured men and gathered up their weapons, then flipped them on their stomachs and slapped on restraints.

Through it all, Tessa stood immobile, afraid to move or even breathe. Was the danger truly over?

"James?" Mason barked at Silver.

Breathing heavily, his gray hair sliding into his eyes, he gave a thumbs-up sign. "Trussed up like a Christmas goose."

"Where's the fourth one? Baldy?"

"In the county jail. Snagged him last night before the others bolted," Silver replied. "We didn't suffer any losses."

Mason's gaze found Tessa. The almost predatory fierceness in the brown depths slowly faded as he acknowledged she was unharmed.

"Is it over?" she whispered.

His throat convulsed. "It's over."

Dante thrashed and spewed threats, reclaiming Mason's attention.

"I'm going to find Raven and Lily," Tessa told him.

She needed to be far away from her deranged brother. More than that, she needed to be with her daughter.

He merely nodded, effectively dismissing her. Tessa understood that he had to be in police mode right now, but she craved his reassuring embrace. She'd almost lost Lily forever. She'd had a gun shoved at her head. She'd stood between two men who'd been taken down by officers.

She wanted his arms around her and his reassurances that everything would be okay, that their renewed friendship would remain strong. She wanted much more than that, but wanting more made her feel greedy.

Mason had forgiven her and had let her back into his life. Wasn't that enough?

As she reunited with Raven and Lily, her mind turned to the future. How long would Silver let her and Lily stay in the cabin? Where would Mason stay? Would he expect her to leave Lily with him while she retrieved her belongings from Georgia?

Would he expect to have a say in where she and Lily lived? Would he put in a good word for her wherever she applied for a job?

As soon as backup arrived, Raven drove them to the cabin, where Gia awaited. While Lily greeted her grandmother, the officer took Tessa aside.

"Want my advice? Eat something, take a long bubble bath and try to relax. Mason will be tied up for a while."

She took a deep breath and nodded. Her pulse

wouldn't settle, despite the knowledge they weren't in danger anymore.

"Thank you again for everything."

Her gaze turned assessing. "You don't look relieved."

"I am."

Raven obviously wasn't convinced. "You and Mason will figure things out. Don't waste the second chance you've been given." Her smile was sad. "Not everyone gets a second chance."

With that, she climbed into the vehicle and left. Tessa spent part of the morning doing as Raven had suggested, indulging in a full breakfast prepared by Gia and taking a restorative bath in the luxurious master suite. They had lunch on the covered deck overlooking the mountain ridges dancing into the horizon. By midafternoon, she was wondering if Mason even planned on returning to the cabin. When Gia offered to put Lily down for a nap, Tessa gratefully accepted. She took a stack of magazines from the living room out to the deck and got comfortable on the bench.

Sometime later, the glass door slid open and Mason emerged.

"Mason."

Tessa jumped up, not caring about the magazine fluttering to her feet. Judging by his clean clothes and freshly washed hair, he'd been here long enough to shower and change. Or maybe he'd done that at the stables, which, Raven had informed her, had not suffered any damage. Fire crews and a sheriff's deputy had arrived in time to save the day.

He closed the door and strode toward her with purpose. He was wearing yellow again, one of her favor-

ite colors on him because it paired perfectly with his
tan skin, and dark hair and eyes. As usual, his handsome, rugged appearance had a devastating effect on
her equilibrium. How was she supposed to pretend that
friendship would satisfy her?

"I didn't hear you arrive—"

He framed her face with his calloused hands and
brought his mouth down on hers, stealing her words
and wiping rational thought from her mind.

Tessa wrapped her arms around his waist and locked
her hands behind him, both to keep him close and to
maintain her balance. His lips were firm and searching, his fingertips gentle as they slid into her hair and
cupped her head. It had always been like this between
them—instant connection, a heady combination of
emotion and attraction. Mason was her normal, her
safety net, her family.

Beneath her hands, his back muscles quivered. He
lifted his head and gazed at her with hope-brightened
eyes. "I still love you, Tess."

Happiness bloomed inside her, chasing away the
darkness of the past four years.

"Oh, Mason, I never stopped loving you," she whispered, her smile stretching from ear to ear.

His mouth curved into a dazzling, teeth-flashing
smile that weakened her knees. He was looking at her
with unabashed love and acceptance, not like before.
Better than before. There were no more secrets between
them. Mason knew the true her, Tessa Lenore Vitale.

He removed something from his pocket and, swallowing hard, placed it in the palm of her hand. "I
bought this for you a week before things blew up in
our faces."

Tessa stared at the tiny velvet bag. "You kept it all this time?"

"I couldn't bring myself to part with it."

Her fingers trembling, she removed the hard, round object and blinked at the gold band topped with a shiny diamond.

"It's lovely."

He took her hand and went down on one knee. "You're the only woman I've ever wanted for my wife," he said gruffly. "What do you say, Tess? Will you give us another chance? Will you marry me?"

"I say try and stop me!" As soon as he slid the ring into place, she threw her arms around his neck and kissed him.

When she lifted her head, he grinned and got to his feet. "We've got a lot to do before we can get married. Clear out your house in Georgia—"

"I'd like to explain things to Lisa and my other friends and say goodbye. Lily will want to attend story hour one last time."

"Of course. There's also the small matter of rebuilding the house."

That would take months, she realized with dismay. Possibly a year or more.

"I've waited this long to be with you," she finally said. "I can be patient."

"I'm not sure I can," he announced, trailing his fingers along her cheek. "I'm ready for the three of us to be a family."

Anticipation danced along her skin. "I don't care where we live, as long as we're together."

He laughed. "Even a tent?"

"Even a tent."

She kissed him again, thanking God for His mercy and grace. With Him as their foundation, they could look forward to a union built on faith and love.

EPILOGUE

"You may kiss the bride."

Mason brushed a lingering kiss on Tessa's smiling mouth. He'd been waiting a lifetime for this moment. The small assembly of guests clapped and cheered, and he could hear Silver whistling nearby.

He lifted his head, caressed her cheek and smiled into her shining, gold-and-green eyes. "Have I told you how stunning you are, Mrs. Reed?"

Pink tinged her cheeks. The top section of her hair had been twisted into place, paper-thin white and pink flowers tucked among the shiny strands, and the remaining curls cascaded past her shoulders. The simple, elegant cut of her dress showed off her smooth shoulders, toned arms and slender waist. Round diamond studs winked at her ears.

She ran her hand down his tuxedo lapel. "Have I told you this tuxedo isn't going back to the rental store, Mr. Reed?"

"What would I need a tuxedo for?"

Tessa adopted an innocent expression. "To wear to Silver's wedding, of course."

His best man's face flushed red, and he appeared to choke. A laughing Cruz pounded him on the back.

Behind Tessa, Candace signaled him. "Are you two going to stand here all day chatting, or are you going to cut the cake?"

"Cut the cake!" Lily bounced on her toes, her beribboned dress flouncing around her ankles.

His mom, Raven and the other guests laughed as the remaining flower petals in her basket wound up on the floor.

Mason held out his arm, and Tessa slid her hand in the crook of his elbow. Together, they walked through the wedding chapel and into the May sunshine. He stopped on the porch and turned to his bride.

"I'm the most fortunate man in the world," he told her, cupping her cheek.

The danger had passed. Dante had been killed by a rival family while in police custody. Bruno, James and others in the Vitale employ were still awaiting trial. Tessa's father was too frail to continue the family business, and rumor was that the Vitale empire was quickly crumbling without anyone to take charge. Mason had asked if Tessa wanted to speak to her sister and mother, to try and reestablish a relationship without Dante around to poison it. She'd said she wasn't ready, and he hadn't pressed the issue.

Tessa leaned into him, her love for him written on her face. "I'll be forever grateful for second chances and new beginnings."

Mason had thought they couldn't re-create what they'd had in the past. He'd been right. They had to let go of the past in order to start anew. Together, he, Tessa and Lily would build a different life—a better, brighter life—as a family who loved and trusted God, above all else.

"Me, too, sweetheart. Me, too." He pulled her into his arms and kissed her again.

* * * * *

Get 4 FREE REWARDS!

We'll send you 2 FREE Books plus 2 FREE Mystery Gifts.

FREE Value Over $20

Both the **Love Inspired®** and **Love Inspired® Suspense** series feature compelling novels filled with inspirational romance, faith, forgiveness and hope.

YES! Please send me 2 FREE novels from the Love Inspired or Love Inspired Suspense series and my 2 FREE gifts (gifts are worth about $10 retail). After receiving them, if I don't wish to receive any more books, I can return the shipping statement marked "cancel." If I don't cancel, I will receive 6 brand-new Love Inspired Larger-Print books or Love Inspired Suspense Larger-Print books every month and be billed just $6.49 each in the U.S. or $6.74 each in Canada. That is a savings of at least 16% off the cover price. It's quite a bargain! Shipping and handling is just 50¢ per book in the U.S. and $1.25 per book in Canada.* I understand that accepting the 2 free books and gifts places me under no obligation to buy anything. I can always return a shipment and cancel at any time by calling the number below. The free books and gifts are mine to keep no matter what I decide.

Choose one: ☐ **Love Inspired**
Larger-Print
(122/322 IDN GRHK)

☐ **Love Inspired Suspense**
Larger-Print
(107/307 IDN GRHK)

Name (please print)

Address   Apt. #

City   State/Province   Zip/Postal Code

Email: Please check this box ☐ if you would like to receive newsletters and promotional emails from Harlequin Enterprises ULC and its affiliates. You can unsubscribe anytime.

Mail to the Harlequin Reader Service:
IN U.S.A.: P.O. Box 1341, Buffalo, NY 14240-8531
IN CANADA: P.O. Box 603, Fort Erie, Ontario L2A 5X3

Want to try 2 free books from another series? Call 1-800-873-8635 or visit www.ReaderService.com.

*Terms and prices subject to change without notice. Prices do not include sales taxes, which will be charged (if applicable) based on your state or country of residence. Canadian residents will be charged applicable taxes. Offer not valid in Quebec. This offer is limited to one order per household. Books received may not be as shown. Not valid for current subscribers to the Love Inspired or Love Inspired Suspense series. All orders subject to approval. Credit or debit balances in a customer's account(s) may be offset by any other outstanding balance owed by or to the customer. Please allow 4 to 6 weeks for delivery. Offer available while quantities last.

Your Privacy—Your information is being collected by Harlequin Enterprises ULC, operating as Harlequin Reader Service. For a complete summary of the information we collect, how we use this information and to whom it is disclosed, please visit our privacy notice located at corporate.harlequin.com/privacy-notice. From time to time we may also exchange your personal information with reputable third parties. If you wish to opt out of this sharing of your personal information, please visit readerservice.com/consumerschoice or call 1-800-873-8635. **Notice to California Residents**—Under California law, you have specific rights to control and access your data. For more information on these rights and how to exercise them, visit corporate.harlequin.com/california-privacy.

LIRLIS22R3

Get 4 FREE REWARDS!

We'll send you 2 FREE Books plus 2 FREE Mystery Gifts.

FREE Value Over $20

Both the **Worldwide Library** and **Essential Suspense** series feature compelling novels filled with gripping mysteries, edge of your seat thrillers and heart-stopping romantic suspense stories.

YES! Please send me 2 FREE novels from the Worldwide Library or Essential Suspense Collection and my 2 FREE gifts (gifts are worth about $10 retail). After receiving them, if I don't wish to receive any more books, I can return the shipping statement marked "cancel." If I don't cancel, I will receive 4 brand-new Worldwide Library books every month and be billed just $6.49 each in the U.S. or $6.99 each in Canada, a savings of at least 30% off the cover price or 4 brand-new Essential Suspense books every month and be billed just $7.24 each in the U.S. or $7.49 each in Canada, a savings of at least 38% off the cover price. It's quite a bargain! Shipping and handling is just 50¢ per book in the U.S. and $1.25 per book in Canada.* I understand that accepting the 2 free books and gifts places me under no obligation to buy anything. I can always return a shipment and cancel at any time by calling the number below. The free books and gifts are mine to keep no matter what I decide.

Choose one: ☐ **Worldwide Library**
(414/424 WDN GRFF)

☐ **Essential Suspense**
(191/391 MDN GRFF)

Name (please print)

Address   Apt. #

City   State/Province   Zip/Postal Code

Email: Please check this box ☐ if you would like to receive newsletters and promotional emails from Harlequin Enterprises ULC and its affiliates. You can unsubscribe anytime.

Mail to the **Harlequin Reader Service:**
IN U.S.A.: P.O. Box 1341, Buffalo, NY 14240-8531
IN CANADA: P.O. Box 603, Fort Erie, Ontario L2A 5X3

Want to try 2 books from another series? Call 1-800-873-8635 or visit www.ReaderService.com.

*Terms and prices subject to change without notice. Prices do not include sales taxes, which will be charged (if applicable) based on your state or country of residence. Canadian residents will be charged applicable taxes. Offer not valid in Quebec. This offer is limited to one order per household. Books received may not be as shown. Not valid for current subscribers to the Worldwide Library or Essential Suspense Collection. All orders subject to approval. Credit or debit balances in a customer's account(s) may be offset by any other outstanding balance owed by or to the customer. Please allow 4 to 6 weeks for delivery. Offer available while quantities last.

Your Privacy—Your information is being collected by Harlequin Enterprises ULC, operating as Harlequin Reader Service. For a complete summary of the information we collect, how we use this information and to whom it is disclosed, please visit our privacy notice located at corporate.harlequin.com/privacy-notice. From time to time we may also exchange your personal information with reputable third parties. If you wish to opt out of this sharing of your personal information, please visit readerservice.com/consumerschoice or call 1-800-873-8635. **Notice to California Residents**—Under California law, you have specific rights to control and access your data. For more information on these rights and how to exercise them, visit corporate.harlequin.com/california-privacy.

WWLSTSUS22R2

HARLEQUIN
PLUS

Try the best multimedia subscription service for romance readers like you!

Read, Watch and Play.

Experience the easiest way to get the romance content you crave.

Start your **FREE TRIAL** at
<u>www.harlequinplus.com/freetrial</u>.